SIMON & SCHUSTER

New York London Toronto Sydney Tokyo Singapore

GOD'S OTHER SON

◆

A Novel

DON IMUS

This book is a work of fiction. Names, characters, places, and incidents either are products of the author's imagination or are used fictitiously. Any resemblance to actual events or locales or persons, living or dead, is entirely coincidental.

SIMON & SCHUSTER
Rockefeller Center
1230 Avenue of the Americas
New York, NY 10020

Manufactured in the United States of America

10

Library of Congress Cataloging-in-Publication Data
Imus, Don.
God's other son: the life and times of the Reverend Billy Sol
Hargus: a novel/Don Imus.
p. cm.

1. Evangelists—United States—Fiction. I. Title.
PS3559.M9G6 1994 94-35001
8.'.54—dc20 CIP
ISBN 0-684-80166-3

Foreword

◆

The Greatest Story Ever Told—the life, death, and resurrection of Jesus Christ—is contained in the Holy Bible, which is available for purchasing in virtually every bookstore in the world and for pilfering in most of the motels in America. It is everywhere! Why, I'll bet you even have one.

Now the *Second* Greatest Story Ever Told was the life and times of the evangelist Billy Sol Hargus, who claimed direct membership in the Holy Family as nothing less than the *blood brother* of Christ Himself! Unhappily, the Second Greatest Story could *not* be told. It wasn't available in any bookstore on this planet, and forget about motel rooms. In fact, there are three known copies of the original in existence—I have one, my brother Fred Imus has one, and my longtime friend Kinky Friedman has the third.

How could such a thing happen? Who is responsible for such a shameful, vulgar, and, may I submit, sacrilegious act? From whose twisted hand drips this blood of despicable outrage?

Simon & Schuster. That's who! The New York publishing company that screwed me in the early 1980s. They published the original manuscript, *God's Other Son: The Life and Times of Billy Sol Hargus* through the single most transparent, duplicitous, phony scam ever committed by a publishing house. They are criminals, with a credo and behavior synonymous with the activities of organized crime.

Why did they bother publishing *God's Other Son* at all,

you ask? The chiseling bastards simply wanted to placate its author, at the time the "locally noted" New York radio figure Don Imus. Me.

The facts are these: Imus—once again, that's me—was perceived even back then as an influential figure who commanded an audience of well-educated, well-to-do potential book buyers. If he could be seduced somehow, then the conniving executives of Simon & Schuster might be able to use him as a convenient publicity outlet for the authors they *truly* cared about. So, these panty-sniffing reprobates printed just enough copies to suggest that an effort had been made on Imus's behalf, and thus sucked him in.

There was just one thing they hadn't counted on: rave reviews for *God's Other Son.* Now, when *that* happened, and with the public screaming for books, those very same executives were caught with their pants down around their ankles, not an unfamiliar condition for them, by the way, though it seldom had anything to do with the business of publishing. The results were that you had a better chance of obtaining the original Dead Sea Scrolls than a copy of this "insanely funny" book, as Dan Jenkins, the author of *Semi-Tough,* described it. The ability to buy *God's Other Son* was tantamount to having that fat goof Ed McMahon show up at your front door with a check for ten million dollars.

So here we are now—1994, soon to be 1995. And that very same Imus is today "The I-Man," a *nationally noted* figure of near-heroic proportions who emanates power and influence over the award-gobbling, now syndicated *Imus in the Morning* program, an individual followed reverentially on radio stations all across America. He is a friend of the President's. He is a confidant of senators, media giants, superstar authors, pundits, journalists, and the high and mighty of every stripe and every station—all of whom vie viciously for the few guest shots available on his enormously successful program.

Now what do you suppose all of this means today to these

very same—well, mostly the same (sorry, Dick)—Simon & Schuster charlatans? It means that all of a sudden they cannot cut down trees fast enough to get this thing printed and boxed and shipped to every shelf of every bookstore in the galaxy. It means they are saying things like "If only there were a 'hay baler' for trees." Their philosophy: Fuck the rain forests. Fuck Sting. Fuck Don Henley and every other bush-hugging, lizard-licking, spotted-owl-tongue-kissing crybaby snipping the rings out of a six-pack holder—crank out the books! No, suddenly nothing will do but that all of God's children buy their very own copy of *God's Other Son*—or at least as many as own one of my brother Fred's very fine Auto Body Express denim work shirts, T-shirts, mugs, jackets, and baseball caps with the red '57 Chevy logo on the El Paso, Texas, version and the *turquoise* Chevy on the Santa Fe edition. Call 1-800-272-1957 to order Fred's stuff, by the way.

I mean, have these Simon & Schuster bastards *no* shame? Is this the single most avaricious act ever? Jesus, what a bunch of thieves. Well, at least the astonishing story of Billy Sol Hargus is now actually in bookstores (and maybe a few motel rooms as well). And look for the movie or musical soon (details in the acknowledgments page at the end of the book) at a theater near you.

DON IMUS
New York

For Michael Lynne

THE NATIONAL ENQUIRER

HARGUS, FIFTEEN YEARS LATER: A TRAIL GROWN COLD

But Psychic Says, "His Words Survive"

LOS ANGELES—Famed psychic Marylayna Urini says she is certain some sort of record was left by the Right Reverend Dr. Billy Sol Hargus before the renowned evangelist vanished, fifteen years ago this week.

Ms. Urini, whose insights broke the Barker kidnap case in February, says she has received "powerful vibrations," suggesting that . . .

REEL 1

◆

God had *two* sons.

Jesus was His first, and I, Billy Sol Hargus, am His second.

God our Father is my Father and Jesus is my Brother, and that's the truth.

Father took Jesus and now He's takin' me. As I speak these words I'm prepared to meet Him. The Lord's comin' and He's comin' soon.

In my final days on Earth, there were many who sought me. There were those who laughed at me, taunted and humiliated me. Many doubted my words.

You are all forgiven!

Though there are heathen sons-a-bitches and atheist Communist bastards among you, I understand and it's okay.

The Lord, my Father, has directed me to leave all of you a complete record of my life, my words and deeds. Now I may be the *second* Son, but I'm gonna be the *first* to do what I'm doing—something no member of The Family ever did. Not Jesus, or Joseph, or Mary, or any of the Apostles. Not *one* of 'em ever saw fit to keep any kind of day-to-day diary.

God knows why, but they didn't.

What I am about to do here is deliver unto the world a first-person account of my life. For the first time ever, a Son of God is gonna tell His own story in His own words!

First of all, for the record, I'm white. I'm an American and I'm a Baptist. That's what I am and that's all I *need* to be.

Figure it out. If I, a Son of God, am white, an American and a Baptist, what's that make God? See?

And so, if ever again you hear some atheistic, egghead anthropologist sayin' God is something else, you got my personal, holy permission to wrap a tire iron around his head! God's what I am—period.

Yet, there are many who choose to believe that God *is* somethin' else; what *they* are, like an Indian or an A-rab or somethin'. Or a *woman,* for God's sake! A *woman!* Jesus Christ! There ain't never been or ever gonna be no *woman* that was *father* of anything, let alone *everything!* And God ain't a talkin' rock or a burnin' bush or a bird or a bolt of lightning or some peculiar feelin' down deep inside an overeducated heathen moron who's only got a cramp. Nor is God black. If you could be anything you wanted to be, would you choose to be colored? Hey, I'm sorry about all this, but I didn't make the rules.

Like Father, like Son. That also happens to mean that my brother, Jesus, does *not* look at all like them pictures you see of 'im hangin' on motel-room walls. You know, the one with the eyes that follow you all around the room, painted by some Eye-talian who's got Him lookin' like a halfbreed Mexican checkin' over His shoulder for the border patrol!

Now, pardon me, but that's a load of shit! Jesus, of course, looks like me and we *both* favor Dad.

I oughta also point out here that simply because your lot in life is something less than you might-a hoped for, circumstances got you born in a time or place you didn't like, well, that don't mean God wanted or ever intended for you to go figurin' that He's what you are. No sir. If you're of some racial persuasion other than white, well, you're just shit outta luck.

And another thing. While there sure as hell been lotsa folks who've gotten the physical image of Jesus all cockeyed, there's been a whole bunch more who have cast doubt and derision upon His Word over the years an' that really pisses me off! By God, the bastards ain't ever gonna get a chance to do that to me. No, sir! I'm takin' care of that right now with this here microphone and tape recorder! They'll never be able to go twistin' things around and castin' doubt on *my* words when all they have to do is punch a button an' play 'em back as spoken!

Poor ol' Jesus, though. I tell you, I just get to feelin' so bad when I think of how it all worked out for Him. Jesus, He devoted His whole life to doin' good things for others; savin' folks, knockin' Hisself out workin' miracles; drivin' out the most godawful diseases; cookin' for the multitudes. You ever cook for a multitude? Hell, no. You think you've worked a miracle feedin' half a dozen folks on the Fourth of July? Someday try feedin' fifty thousand with a dead fish and a hunk of stale bread. I'm here to tell you, you had to be God to pull off that kind of thing and keep all your teeth! But Jesus managed it, time and again. I'll swear, there just ain't *never* been nobody had a nicer older brother. An' what'd He get for it? Two thousand years of no 'count Communist ingrates puttin' doubt on what He did and on what He said.

You see, Jesus never got to tell His own story. Ain't that ridiculous? Here you had the Son of God, the *oh-riginal,* for Chrissakes, right here on Earth spreadin' the Word. Hell, He *was* the Word. Yet no one ever took down one single, solitary syllable straight from His mouth, a direct quote, and put it in Jesus' own book! Does that make *any* sense? Nothin' Jesus ever wrote, if He wrote anything at all, nothin' ever got into *any* book, let alone the *one* book it oughta got in, the Bible. And don't you know that a preacher like Jesus was just dyin' to tell His own story? Particularly when He was the preacher He was preachin' about! God! What a shame.

'Course, if you think about it just a minute, how *could* He? There was hardly time to write anything down, considerin' how they had to do it back then; carve it out on a boulder or stand around waitin' for a tub of marsh weeds to dry out so's they could weave it up and write something on it. I mean, Jesus was a minister for only three years. By the time He'd a-gotten around to writin' everything down He'd a-been dead a hundred.

And besides, our Father never gave Him much of a chance to take notes, even. My God, He nearly worked the Boy to death! Why, I just know that as soon as my Brother woulda got set down ready to whack out somethin' on a rock, Dad woulda run another leper in on Him. And so, today, we don't even have so much as a "Jesus Slept Here" in His own, personal handwritin'.

Nope, we don't.

What we *do* know about Jesus, His birth, His ministry, His death and resurrection, we got from the Gospels of Matthew, Mark, Luke, and John. And if Paul hadn't wandered off to Damascus, seen the light, and started spreadin' the Word, we might not even have *that.* Still, it ain't much.

What we *don't* know about Jesus also comes from the Gospels. *When* He was born. *When* He died. How *old* He was. What the hell He did for those thirty-odd years *before* He started preachin' and whatever *happened* to Him. Hell, you could write four *more* Gospels just on things we *don't know!*

If you came up with those kinds of blanks on a job application you couldn't get a day's work hosin' turds out of a manger. They have to know more about you than what we know about Jesus just to throw your ass in *jail.*

And yet, I know that God, for some *adequate reason,* did not direct that a complete biography be written about my Brother's life. He could have and, personally, I think He should have. It sure would've made it a hell of a lot easier tellin' folks about Him if He had.

Instead, God directed that the story of Jesus be written by Matthew, who was a tax collector; Mark, who we're only told was the son of Peter; Luke, who was a doctor; and John, who was a fisherman.

Now, isn't that a fine bunch to pick to write the life story of the most important figure in the history of the world?

Not exactly your basic Book-of-the-Month Club candidates, that's for *damn* sure!

But we'll just have to live with it. Their works were divinely inspired and they *are* the Word of God. I guess what we know about Jesus from the Gospels is all we're *supposed* to know. We accept that and the Word of God on faith.

Now, right there's a big problem.

We accept it, but is that good enough for a world full of heathens runnin' around huntin' facts? Nooooo! Christ! These bastards wanna know *everything!* They have no faith. If Brother Jesus just coulda done what I'm doin', told His whole life Hisself, we could have avoided two thousand years of unChristian, unholy infidels askin' questions about things that are, frankly, none of their goddamn business.

I've had to preach to these dumbbells and I know what the hell I'm talkin' about. I spent a lifetime tellin' 'em about faith. Jesus, they thought I was crazy. I explained to 'em over and over again that God had an *adequate reason* for havin' the Gospels turn out like they did.

"Okay, Hargus," they'd ask, "what was the adequate reason?"

"Goddamnit!" I'd scream at 'em. "How am I supposed to know? It was adequate! What th' hell difference does it make?"

The bastards laughed at me.

Throughout my ministry I was constantly faced by heathen skeptics who would insist, *"Facts* before faith!" Well, it nearly drove me nuts. I've spent years talkin' about Jesus an' I can tell you that after you've quoted Him a few times, there just ain't a hell of a lot more to talk about. And heathens just *love* findin' loopholes! Let them run across one thing that don't quite jibe with somethin' else and they'll jump on you like dirty on a duck! I was continually having to make excuses and fill in the blanks.

F'r instance, I don't know how many times I run up against this one They'd sneer at me, "How come the Gospels can't even agree on what the names of the Twelve Apostles were?"

Now, if they'd a-just thought a minute before they went shootin' off their mouths, they'd realize Jesus *had* to know who His men were. You can bet He just didn't up and say, "Hey, you, what's-your-face, bring me another gimpy A-rab to fix up." The Gospels tell us that Jesus even *changed* the names of His Apostles to suit Him better. So it's pretty obvious He had to know their names to start with. But a heathen won't let up.

"Okay," they snicker, "what were they?"

"I don't know."

"When was Jesus born?"

"I don't know."

"When did He die?"

"Long time ago."

"Where is He?"

"Don't know."

"When's He comin' back?"

"When it's time."

"Come on, Hargus, give us some goddamn dates!"

Honest to God, I wished I could've told 'em just to have shut 'em up! And as much as I hate to have to admit it, it's true: The Gospels got Matthew, Mark, Luke and John soundin' like a bunch of welfare loafers tryin' to explain where their new Cadillac came from! Listen, the next time you've got nothin' to do, just sit down and try to figure out, and then explain it to a heathen, how it is we're told that Jesus was born in the year 4 B.C. Does that make any sense? How in God's name can they tell us that Jesus Christ was born four years before Jesus Christ was born?!? Even with the way those stooges jacked around with the calendar you would've thought they could've pinned down a fairly important birth date, wouldn't you? But no, "Christ was born four years before Christ was born." Jesus! You begin to get an idea what I been up against? And *then,* as though just to make damned sure nobody would ever be able to figure out nothin' for certain, the Gospels were written in the city of Rome, in the Greek language, thirty, forty, and fifty years *after* Brother Jesus was gone!

See? If only we could have heard the words of Jesus Himself, we'd know. Imagine that! Jesus actually speakin' to us as I'm speakin' to you. We'd have the answers. But He didn't, and so, we don't.

Now, our pseudo-intellectual smartbutts allege that after the death of Jesus, His followers, who were Jews, *remained* Jews and drove the Romans out of Israel in the Holy Wars simply because they hated garlic. Jews, they say, became Christians when the authors of the New Testament rewrote history in an effort to brownnose the Romans. And Christianity was born, some of these imbeciles say, when they had to come up with a name for all the folks they were feedin' to the lions. I even had one of 'em point out to me that Jesus said He was a Jew *hisself!*

Well, of course He *said* He was Jewish! What the hell was He supposed to say? "Hi, there, all you fine folks of Israel. I'm the Messiah you been waitin' for, the True Light of the World, the Son of God, and, oh yeah, by the way, *I'm a Jehovah's Witness!"*

Let's get serious here. They'd a-grabbed the hammer and nails right then and there. You see, what Jesus understood is that in order to *get* along, you have to *go* along, even when you're operatin' at *that* level. Look, this Messiah business is no bed of roses.

And His followers understood, too. They weren't so damned dumb. But Jesus a *Jew?* What th' hell do you think John the Baptist was doin' to Him there in the River Jordan? Teachin' Him to dog-paddle? Givin' Him a shampoo? He was *baptizing* Him! And *that,* Mr. Heathen, is *also* in the Book! And we believe the Book, the words of Matthew, Mark, Luke, and John, on faith. Faith in the Word of God and faith in God's adequate reason for leavin' a lot of blank spots. But, you know, faith just ain't somethin' you can talk to a heathen about.

There were even times when I was literally *forced* to fabricate things to answer the crude, tasteless questions of the faithless.

"Why," they'd ask, "was Luke the only one to report what Jesus said up there on the cross?"

Well, how the hell would *I* know? So I just made up somethin': "Well, you see, Jesus never talked too loud. He kinda just muttered stuff under His breath. And the reason Luke knew what He said was because Luke could read lips."

Actually, I don't know if Luke could even read his own *prescriptions!* But what was I supposed to do? Heathens have nothin' but doubt, because there is no faith where there are few facts, which unfortunately, for them and us, is the case.

Now, I've never said that the Gospelers didn't know what they were talkin' about or were tryin' to cover up anything. I mean, God knows Jesus didn't have nothin' to hide. Not the world's only ever-Perfect Man, outside of myself, of course. It was more like a bunch of fools was always tryin' to hide *Him,* stuffin' Him in caves and what not, before finally losin' track of Him altogether.

No, all I've ever done was to fill in the spaces, and kinda in my own way. Hell, if a little white lie was all it took to convert a sinner to the righteous path, I'd have told him that Jesus fed Pittsburgh with a goddamn moonpie! If it woulda helped get a heathen to come to Jesus I'd a-sworn He turned a pint of well-water into a sea of Chivas Regal. And as I think back on it, I probably did. And I'm sure as hell not sorry because *it worked!* I could pull more people into a five-pole tent in a week than nine Negroes hittin' home runs could put in Yankee Stadium in an entire season!

Was it a miracle? Well, it certainly *could* have been. Because there were miracles worked by the hand of Billy Sol. And yes, they were questioned. Even though my Father created the Heavens and the Earth in six days flat, and Jesus walked on water, they *questioned* the miracles of Billy Sol!

The idiots! My God, if Dad could and my Brother could, don't it stand to reason that I could, too! It's just a matter of genes, for Chrissake—figure it out!

And then there were the nastiest, vilest people of the whole bunch. People who'd come crawlin' out to ask the most snotnosed, tawdry questions of all. They'd sidle up to you and ask, drawin' it out real slowlike, "Where's all the *money* goin', Billy?" As if you could carry the Word across the length and breadth of this great land on fifteen cents. They even caused those faithless, four-eyed meddlers from the Internal Revenue Service to pry, actually pry into the Divine Ledgers of the Son of God! Why, those Communist, homosexual, shitbrained, lizard pukes.

Now, what I'm gonna say next may startle you. But I told you this record was going to be complete, and I meant it. Two thousand years from now, when this Gospel testament is bein' gone over with a fine-tooth comb by all those fault-finders and finger-pointers, *every word of mine* will be there.

In that regard, you're going to be hearing things which may cause you to say, "Hold on here, Hargus, this here's the Gospel!" Well, this here's the truth, too, warts and all. This is my life and I intend to tell *everything.* Truth is beauty, and beauty is always better-lookin' if you sprinkle some natural ugly around it. So I'm not goin' to leave somethin' out just because it might prove to be embarrassin' to me or somebody else.

Why, even with Jesus, the Gospels got Him sayin', "I have come not to bring peace but a sword." Sounds like the Boy was ready to cold-cock somebody, don't it? And in another place He says, "A disciple must hate his own father and mother and wife and children." That's warts!

You may find this tough to swallow, but there were times in my life when even *my* mortal flesh was subjected to the temptations of sin and common lust. I think it's necessary to talk about 'em here, just as they happened.

Some of you may snicker, and say that these recollections

are nothin' more than cheap, sleazy thrills, but others will understand them for what they are: lessons in learnin' the will of the Lord.

Now, just as an example of the kind of thing I'm goin' to be telling that unfortunately might have to embarrass somebody, you take ol' Tyrone Jefferson.

While Tyrone was a fine disciple, he suffered some moral weaknesses that I, naturally, did not. One of 'em was watermelons. Tyrone, you see, did not eat watermelons. That don't mean he didn't like 'em. In fact, he literally loved 'em. In such an unnatural and lustful way as to sorely test Billy Sol's mighty patience.

You see, when Tyrone could find a melon just to his likin', he'd sleep with it. Sometimes we'd all wake up in the middle of the night to fearful groans and writhin' and find him wrapped around one of his beloved gourds like a monkey fuckin' a football. When he was through with it, wouldn't be no human on Earth who would eat it! I doubt Tyrone would want that story told about the peculiar weakness of his flesh, but that's the kinda thing that's *gotta* be told in this here new, New Testament; nothin' left out now, so there can't be no questions later.

I should caution you at this point: Don't throw your Holy Bible away simply because there are those who make an issue of the missin' facts in the stories on the life of Brother Jesus. Sketchy as they are, they're all we have. And it is the Word of God. Though some of them "Modern English" versions don't help things much. Lord, if it ain't confusin' enough without havin' some weird monk changin' all the los and verilys, makin' Jesus sound like a goddamn disc jockey!

If *I* had any shortcomin' at all, it was bein' far too tolerant of the weaknesses and afflictions of the yet-to-be-converted who gathered around me. But it was my divine duty to suffer through the trials brought on by their ignorance and misunderstandin', no matter *how* embarrassin'.

One time some years back, f'r instance, I, Billy Sol Hargus, a missionary, a minister of the Gospel, was actually asked to return funds that had been pledged to Jesus for work to be done in His name. God, the shame of it!

The misunderstanding that led to that sorrow came about when I had deposited in the Lord's account the life savings of a wonderful and trusting family who had turned over all their money to Jesus after I had, through a miracle, "brought Grandma back to life." It was several services later when a little boy, possessed of the Devil, came tearin' up the aisle in the House of the Lord screamin' at me and cryin', "GRANNIE'S STILL DEAD!" Was that the fault of Dr. Hargus? No. The poor woman's faith wasn't strong enough. She'd tensed up where I'd propped her there in her rocker, finally fallin' over stiff as a brick and doornail dead.

These matters, however, shall all pass, for it is God's will.

Now, then, we come to my story, my testament. This is the authorized transcription of my words recorded at the Lord's direction, by my hand. It is the Word of God. Trust me on this one, friends.

Still, there will be unbelievers among you. A book filled with facts will still find those who will call it fiction—*wish* it was fiction. For all through my account you will discover truly startlin' events surroundin' my life. Events that may leave you sayin', "Why, that's impossible," or "Hey, Hargus, who the hell you tryin' to shit?"

However, as you study my life—whether believers or doubters at the start—know in your heart that these are the facts and this is the truth.

As I am, at this very moment, speakin' these words, I feel the presence of the Lord all about me. There are dark clouds gatherin' and the wind is beginnin' to howl. The sky rumbles with His voice. There may just be enough time for me to record my entire life. The Lord's comin', and He's comin' soon.

Jesus, I hope *somebody* finds these goddamn tapes.

The New York Times

SECRET HARGUS RECORDINGS DISCOVERED

MAY REVEAL MISSING PASTOR'S LIFE

Special to The New York Times

WASHINGTON, January 25—The answer to the baffling disappearance of the powerful evangelist Dr. Billy Sol Hargus may lie in the discovery of a cache of tape recordings, purportedly made by Dr. Hargus himself sometime *after* he vanished nearly 15 years ago.

The heavily guarded stack of 14 tape reels was displayed in the Library of Congress's Hall of Records today during a stormy press conference whose subject had been kept in strictest secrecy.

Shouting to make himself heard, Dr. Charles Pedersen, the Hall of Records' Chief Archivist, resisted persistent questioning about how and where the recordings had been found, and said under no circumstances would their contents be released until the material's authenticity had been proven "beyond any doubt."

However, Dr. Pedersen did say that after personally listening to the tapes he had been strongly persuaded that they were in fact recorded by Dr. Hargus. "There seems to be no mistaking the colloquial characterizations and the syntactical individuality we all remember so well," Dr. Pedersen said. "From the first words uttered, 'God had *two* Sons,' I was satisfied it was the Reverend Hargus who spoke. Dr. Pedersen added that the recordings appear to contain a remarkably complete and candid chronology of Dr. Hargus's life, including a detailed account of his sudden disappearance.

"If these tapes can survive rigid scientific scrutiny," Dr. Pedersen concluded, "then we may have before us a chronicle of theological importance even greater than the discovery of the Dead Sea Scrolls, an account that could give the pillars supporting our Judeo-Christian beliefs more than just a gentle shake."

TIME

What About Those Tapes?

Last week's revelation that the Federal Government had discovered a first-person, tape-recorded narrative of Dr. Billy Sol Hargus's life touched a deep, national nerve. As each day passed without further elaboration from the Library of Congress, custodian of the Hargus Tapes, an already anxious public grew increasingly impatient. And not without cause.

For nearly 15 years the world has been mystified by the abrupt disappearance of the man who called himself "just a country circuit preacher," but who rose to a position of such enormous influence that many who saw him believed him to be the Son of God; a judgment Dr. Hargus ultimately accepted as true.

Tantalized by hints that the Hargus Tapes may be of profound significance, comparable to the Dead Sea Scrolls, the public outcry for access to them has become an avalanche's roar.

Reverend Hargus was this hemisphere's best known, most widely acclaimed evangelist. His daily ministry was broadcast by nearly 5,000 radio stations.

A weekly television program reached viewers in 750 American markets and 123 countries abroad. His sermons were mainstays of in-flight stereo programs offered by the major U.S. air carriers and were the *only* program heard aboard Dr. Hargus's own commercial airline, the familiar fleet of Jesus Jets. *The Watch It,* the Hargus church newsletter, was eagerly awaited each week by 56 million subscribers. And each of them, it seems safe to say, had at some time borne witness to Dr. Hargus's now-legendary live appearances: from the early haphazard tent revivals that drew the faithful from the plains towns of Enid, Perris, Kingman, and Three Rivers, to the precisely orchestrated "Walk For Jesus" crusades attended by tens of thousands in the later years—great, grandiose extravaganzas that filled San Francisco's Cow Palace, Soldier Field in Chicago, and Shea Stadium in New York.

The breadth of Dr. Hargus's reach twice brought him to the cover of this magazine as *Time*'s "Man of the Year." On both occasions, in 1964 and again in 1966, his influence was compared favorably to that of the late Mahatma Gandhi. Just this past week, while reporting the discovery of the Hargus Tapes, CBS commentator Walter Cronkite noted warmly that Dr. Hargus was "a man, or perhaps more than that, whose single word or gesture just might have altered the course of history."

But the Reverend was also controversial. His critics believed he had a darker side. While he claimed to have healed thousands of the afflicted, he also swayed followers with what he warned was a swift and terrible ability to heap misfortune upon those who failed to heed the Word of God issuing from his lips. Often he would tell them, in the straightforward but "hip" style that rankled his detractors, "Those who don't think I got it are gonna get it!" And for those who scoffed at such threats? There was the story of the Iowa farmer who mocked the Reverend and returned home to find his crops stripped to the stalk by locusts, and the inexplicable series of launch failures at Cape Canaveral after NASA accused the Hargus Crusade of staging miracles with "enough electronic gadgetry to have beaten us to the moon."

Dr. Hargus had occasional brushes with the law, though never more than that. In 1962 there was the widely publicized lawsuit brought by a blind, black blues singer who alleged that Dr. Hargus had caused him "humiliation, mental anguish and extreme suffering" by failing to restore his eyesight at a packed revival in the Los Angeles Memorial Coliseum.

Guiding him by the elbow, Dr. Hargus's attendants had helped the man mount the stage where the Reverend knelt beside him and commanded the "devils masking this man's eyes to come out! Come out in the name of Jesus and be ye gone now and forever more!" Seized by the passion of the moment, the blind man leaped to his feet, tottered uncertainly in the direction of the audience, and shouted, "I can see! I can see!" But then he stepped off the stage and fell into the orchestra pit. The case was settled out of court. The terms were never disclosed.

From time to time, Dr. Hargus's health became an issue. There were frequent and apparently sudden hospitalizations. On each occasion his aides carefully shielded the specific nature of the Doctor's distress, their reluctance to discuss his physical state only serving to deepen its mystery.

After investigating the Hargus financial empire, *Business Week* concluded that it rivaled any of the giants listed among the Dow Jones Industrials, and grossed more than most of them. When the *Business Week* cover story on the Hargus holdings appeared on June 12, 1966, Dr. Hargus was at the zenith of his ascendancy from his backwoods, country-preacher roots. Courted by presidents, a counsel to kings, he had but to speak and half a world hushed to hear.

And then, it happened.

On worldwide television, at the summit of his celebrity, Dr. Hargus suffered the now-famous humiliation that devastated him and left his vast audience dumbstricken. After what came to be known simply as "that day," the Right Reverend Dr. Billy Sol Hargus took his place alongside such other figures of legend as aviatrix Amelia Earhart and labor chieftain James Hoffa. He vanished as though struck from the face of the earth; persona and power withdrawn as swiftly as a lightning bolt's flash, leaving the air charged with only our recollections of him.

But now we have the Hargus Tapes. The experts studying them say if they do prove to be authentic, they will be of "unprecedented importance to all of mankind"; a provocative statement, to say the least.

The world—and this magazine—urgently appeal for that determination to be made as rapidly as possible.

Hopefully, we won't have much longer to wait.

The Chicago Tribune

HARGUS TAPE PANEL CHOSEN

Zeitvogel Will Lead Verification Task

WASHINGTON, February 14—The Nobel Prize-winning physicist, Dr. Enod Zeitvogel, Director of the Bell Telephone Laboratories, has been named to head a panel of internationally acclaimed academicians who will determine whether the tape-recorded narrative of the life of Dr. Billy Sol Hargus is authentic.

Making the announcement, Dr. Charles Pedersen, Chief Archivist at the Library of Congress, in whose custody the Hargus Tapes have been placed, said, "We are most fortunate to have been able to secure the services of Dr. Zeitvogel, who will have the entire support structure of the Bell System at his disposal. When his analysis of the Hargus Tapes is complete, not a fragment of doubt will remain regarding whether they are genuine or counterfeit."

Contacted at his offices at the Bell System Laboratories in Holbrook, New Jersey, Dr. Zeitvogel said he was humbled to have been entrusted with the task of studying the Hargus narrative, which he characterized as "obviously the most important undertaking of my life, and a distinct honor for America."

Discussing the manner in which he would approach the problem of verification, Dr. Zeitvogel stressed that the panel's work would go well beyond mere voice identification, explaining that "even if the voice *is* that of Reverend Hargus, it would have been possible for someone, possibly through sinister motivation, to have altered the tapes and changed Dr. Hargus's message." Noting that such a deception could become a nightmare, Dr. Zeitvogel said, "We absolutely will resolve all of this. Nothing will be left to chance."

NEW YORK POST

HOLY HOWL: HARGUS HASSLE HAS HICKS HUFFY

WASHINGTON, February 25—It is one month to the day since the discovery of the now-celebrated Hargus Tapes, and Senator Ralph Hicks (R-Ohio), Chairman of the Senate Select Subcommittee on the Hargus Tapes (SSSHT), used the occasion to challenge the Library of Congress and the Zeitvogel investigatory panel to "stop the foot-dragging and get on with telling us what the devil happened to Billy Sol."

Senator Hicks said he had informed the Library's Chief Archivist that "neither I nor my constituents have unlimited patience in this matter, and before the public literally storms the Library's hallowed halls, they'd better get this investigation off dead-center."

Sources who wish to remain anonymous informed the *Post* that a rancorous squabble has broken out over certain conditions that will govern how the tapes will be released, in the event their authenticity is certified. The sources said publishing houses, movie studios, and a half-dozen recording companies are pulling every string within reach trying to secure rights to the tapes.

None of that will assuage a restive public whose mood is turning increasingly sour. Senator Hicks's warning about a "storming" of the Library of Congress may have been neither facetious nor frivolous.

CBS NEWS BROADCAST TRANSCRIPT

Friday, March 28, 2:51 P.M.

(BULLETIN FROM CBS NEWS, NEW YORK, REGULAR PROGRAMMING PREEMPTED T. F. N. KILL BULLETIN-SLIDE CAMERA-1, STAND BY CRONKITE CAMERA-2, TAKE IN FIVE, FOUR, THREE, TWO, READY—TAKE!)

"Good afternoon.

"We have just received word that, after 42 grueling days, the Zeitvogel Panel studying the Hargus Tapes has completed its work . . ."

(STAND BY HARGUS SLIDE!)

". . . and has reached the conclusion that the tapes are authentic, the voice is indeed that of Dr. Billy Sol Hargus . . ."

(TAKE HARGUS SLIDE!)

". . . and there is *no* evidence whatsoever to suggest that the recorded material has been tampered with in any way."

(STAND BY ZEITVOGEL DOCUMENT!)

"The stunning results of one of the most comprehensive scientific investigations in modern memory were issued just a few minutes ago . . ."

(TAKE ZEITVOGEL DOCUMENT!)

". . . in an exhaustively detailed 931-page report compiled by Dr. Enod Zeitvogel, the Nobel laureate who chaired a committee of eminent scientists and academicians who conducted the Hargus Tapes study."

(OKAY, WASH IT OUT, CRONKITE UP . . . TAKE 'IM!)

"At this point the implications of the panel's findings can only be guessed at, but it seems safe to say they border on the infinite and will provide an inexhaustible feast for theologians and philosophers. For the Hargus Tapes have been judged genuine and the unavoidable conclusion is that the message we're told they carry is genuine as well.

"Meanwhile, the Library of Congress, which has had the tapes for safekeeping since their discovery, has simultaneously announced that the conditions governing their release have been agreed upon. While still declining to go into specifics, officials say the conditions include precise instructions for transcribing the recorded material and putting it into final published form.

"Perhaps the only surprise during the Zeitvogel investigation was the discovery of a second voice heard in brief conversation with Dr. Hargus at four distinct junctures in the narrative. The second speaker, according to Dr. Zeitvogel, is Tyrone G. Jefferson, a man who was one of Dr. Hargus's closest aides. The fourth and final exchange between the two occurs on the concluding tape—reel number 14."

"Coming up right now, two reports: first to Robert Pierpoint, standing by at the State Department in Washington; then to Winston Burdette at Westminster Abbey in London."

(SWITCH PIERPOINT, READY . . . TAKE 'IM!)

Los Angeles Times

WORLD TO GET HARGUS TALE TODAY

Church Leaders Deeply Moved During Private Preview of Text

WASHINGTON, April 16—One day, will a radically changed Bible begin: "And on the sixteenth day of the fourth month, from a place called the Federal District of Columbia in the country of America, gathered they there to carry forth the New Word"?

Perhaps.

The moment is upon us. The secretly recorded and long-awaited life chronicle of the Right Reverend Dr. Billy Sol Hargus, described as the most important religious discovery in the history of the world, will be formally released to the public this afternoon at two o'clock, Eastern Standard Time, in a nationally telecast ceremony to be conducted at the White House.

A carefully selected group of theologians representing all of the world's major faiths was given a preview of the

Hargus transcript last evening at the Library of Congress. When they emerged from the session the expressions on the clerics' faces were as if they had just stepped from a private audience with the Messiah Himself. Some wept. Others had to be supported by their colleagues.

At a press conference conducted later at the National Press Club, Rabbi Felix Steinberg, one of the world's foremost Old Testament biblicists, observed drily, "It appears we've overlooked a tablet or two."

On the eve of the release of the transcripts, the Library of Congress's Dr. Charles Pedersen released a statement detailing the editorial procedures that were followed in the transcription process.

The statement emphasized that *no* words heard in the tapes had been deleted from the transcribed material. Dr. Pedersen said that from a pure, literary standpoint there were numerous changes that could have been made, including correcting grammar and straightening Dr. Hargus's at times uniquely constructed syntax. However to have done so, Dr. Pedersen explained, would have risked losing the essential Dr. Hargus.

But even as the nation and the world approached the moment when the tapes would reach the hands of individual citizens, there was yet another disclosure that raised further questions while answering none. Though the public is about to receive the information contained in the Hargus Tapes themselves, it will receive *no* information regarding their mysterious discovery. The conditions set forth governing the tapes' release forbid disclosure of where they were found and by whom until fifteen years after the death of the last person involved in their discovery.

Finally, it has been learned that all parties who had a role in bringing the tapes to the public agreed under oath to rigid instructions pertaining to their transcription and publication, including a clause that forbids them to say anything to anybody about any matter involved in this, or anything else—ever.

VARIETY

SOL HARGUS TO NIX SIX MIL PIX

Shea Gross May Best Beatles

NEW YORK—He's coming.

And it seems New York City itself is "born again."

The banners shout the message from balcony, balustrade and bridge: JESUS LIVES! BILLY SOL HARGUS IN NEW YORK! The long-awaited Hargus Crusade-Shea Stadium date is at hand. The Reverend's point men, who've been in the New York area for a month now, predict his appearance there will draw upwards of a million people.

Meanwhile, Dr. Boone Moses, the famed, retired evangelist who is the brain behind the Hargus empire, has nixed an offer of six million dollars from MGM to cast Reverend Hargus as the lead in the new biblical epic, *God's Story.*

MGM execs say Moses told them, "Six million might get you a snapshot of my boy, but movies? I'll thank you to know that we will handle . . ."

REEL 2

◆

August 28th, 1966.

A Sunday afternoon.

From the helicopter it looked like lambs goin' to slaughter. And it damned near turned out to be! There must a-been a jillion of 'em. Cars and trucks and buses and campers and cabs backed up for miles along any highway that looked like it would get you anywhere *close* to Shea Stadium. Four hundred degrees out there and they stretched for miles; north all the way to the Whitestone Bridge into the Bronx; back east into Nassau County; west through the Holland Tunnel into Jersey. Bumper to bumper. And it'd been like that for hours. There was half a million people down there, maybe more. Many of 'em had forsaken their machines and were pilin' outta buses, draggin' kids and luggin' babies, wavin' banners, singin', hollerin', occasionally lookin' up, pointin' as they spotted the famous prayin'-hands logo on the chopper's sides. They had to know they didn't stand a chance of gettin' in to see the show, but still they came!

With the stadium coming into sight, our pilot turned around in his seat to look at me sittin' there with Boone, Olgemyier, and none other than the Governor of New York hisself. "Damn," he said, like he could hardly believe it, "you're bigger than the Beatles!"

"Oh, how outrageous," chirped Olgemyier. "A fan!"

Suddenly the Governor was sputtering, pointing furiously

over the pilot's shoulder. "Jesus Christ," he screamed, "the blimp! You're gonna hit the goddamn blimp!"

We all looked out, including the guy who was supposed to be driving, just in time to see the words GOOD LUCK BILLY flashin' by us on the blimp's belly close enough we coulda changed the damned light bulbs.

"You idiot!" shouted Olgemyier. "Jesus, pay attention!"

After he'd settled down a bit, the Governor put his hand on my arm as we hovered over the packed humanity on the playing field below, cops tryin' to push people back from the huge pool where I'd be doing "the Water Walk" in just a matter of minutes now.

"Tell me, Billy," the Governor whispered, "how *do* you do it?"

Boone overheard and spun around. "Just what the hell are you askin' the boy?"

"Christ, relax," said Olgemyier.

"Well, you know," the Governor went on, startled and a little sheepishly, "walk on water? I mean, do you *really* do it?"

Goddamn 'em. They all wanted to know that, everywhere we went. Doubtin', cynical heathens, questioning the miracles of God's own Son.

As often as not, Boone would put 'em straight by telling them that it was "none of their goddamn business." Mostly, I just smiled sweetly—much as I imagine Brother Jesus had done.

At last, we were able to set down without lopping off any heads. The police had cleared about a thirty-yard circle near the Crusade trucks our advance folks had brought in three days before.

As the rotors settled down, Otis jerked the door open and I stuck my head out. Well, the whole damned stadium went nuts. You couldn't hear yourself think.

Otis looked up at me. "Billy," he said, "this place is a pure-ass zoo!"

Lord, 150,000 people had shoehorned into a place not fit

for half of that. And they were screaming! Good and bad. "God bless you, Billy!" "You're a saint, precious Reverend!" "Go get 'em Rev," and, "Hey, Hahgus, ya fuckin' phony!" New York assholes.

Olgemyier had stepped out and he was standing there, wringin' his hands and moanin', "My God, this just isn't safe! This just isn't safe at all!" He was right about that.

People were oozin' outta every seat. They perched on, hung from, or clung to anything they could get hold of. Hundreds had shinnied up the light banks that soared above the stadium. About seventy-five of 'em had crawled out onto the fragile framework from which a huge banner fluttered, announcing, JESUS LIVES! BILLY SOL HARGUS IN NEW YORK CITY.

On the field they were standing, wedged against the huge fiberglass pool. They pushed against its sides causin' tons of water to heave and splash, sloppin' over to drench hundreds of people. My God, their faces beamed as if they were bein' washed in the fluids of the Lord Himself.

But Boone looked at the pool and shuddered. Then he shouted at Olgemyier, "Well, asshole? You better think of something fast. Our boy can't walk on a goddamn tidal wave!"

"How about if the genius *parts* it?" snapped Olgemyier.

"Look, you little runt," said Boone, "I'll wring your goddamn . . ."

Otis put his arm around my shoulder. "Come on, son," he smiled, "time to get your ol' sacred ass in gear."

"Yeah," I said, winking at him, "and kill a couple million mosquitoes for Jesus." Otis laughed.

We wormed our way to the Crusade trucks through a double line of police and security men. Once inside, Otis laughed again and said, "Ah damned near didn't recognize ol' Habluetzel in that silly fuckin' wig he's wearin'. Jesus, is he nervous! I told the sumbitch ten times, we's ready if they can just get that water to lay down a bit."

Otis always supervised settin' up, here at Shea in New

York and everywhere else we'd been—Dallas, L.A., Chicago—all across this great land spreadin' the righteous Word of God and leadin' the multitudes into His house as we performed the miracles of Jesus.

"Okay," shouted Boone, opening the door of the truck, "let's hit it!"

I stepped outside, hidden by the crowd pressing in on all sides. Then I walked up the little stairway to the velvet-draped platform on the side of the pool, just a step from the water. At the sight of me as I mounted the platform and stood before the waters, a cry went up from the multitude that sounded like you'd stuck your head inside a jet engine. It shook the ground and sent ripples dancin' back and forth across the pool. Later, we all agreed that at that moment we thought the stadium itself would collapse. Nearly stunned for a moment, I raised my hands and the huge throng hushed as the choir began to sing "Shall We Gather at the River."

It was magnificent.

The choir was the 350-member, all-Negro gospel ensemble from Harlem. World famous. Boone had said years before, and he was right, that "Church ain't church without Negroes and midgets." Today, just like Boone wanted, "the bastards were singin' loud an' lookin' pretty."

They were ranged along tiered platforms set up the length of one side of the pool, toward center field, and they clapped, stomped, and shook as they sang, "Ohhh, Billy Sollll, won't you pleeease heal us all!" Their robes were of all the colors in the rainbow and they were reflected in the now-calm water.

Outside the stadium, thousands were waiting for the second, third and fourth services, but here, inside, we were "havin' church." One hundred and fifty thousand people now fell silent, their hush broken only by an occasional cough or a baby's cry. The choir began to hum softly, reverently.

I stood, my face turned toward the sky. I glanced at Tyrone. He winked, nudging Boone and Olgemyier. The moment had arrived. I raised my hands and the choir fell silent. I looked at Otis. He smiled and I stepped to the water's edge, my foot poised inches above the surface. I paused, waiting for the signal from Otis to take "the step."

It never came.

Rifle shots. They cracked and echoed hollowly in that instant of silence.

"Oh, my fuckin' gaawwd! I been hit! I been hit!" It was Otis, slammed up against the truck, most of his face splattered right across the prayin'-hands logo.

Then they were screaming. More shots, and suddenly 350 screechin' Negroes, robes and all, jumped as one smack into the middle of my pool.

CRACK!

KA-POW!

I remember thinkin' to myself, Now, why would anybody want to shoot Otis, or this nice buncha colored people? Then it hit me. They wasn't shootin' to kill Otis or the choir thrashin' in the water, they were trying to kill *me!*

Well, as any living soul who was there can testify, I leaped for that pool. I hit it hard. I jumped up and down *on* the water. With bullets zinging all around me, I got on my hands and knees and tried to dig a *hole* in the goddamn stuff. I kicked it, beat on it, clawed at it, but I couldn't force so much as one damned finger *beneath* the water's surface.

More shots.

By now, maybe five or six hundred people were in the pool up to their fannies and I couldn't get my goddamn *shoelaces* wet! And suddenly, in the awful terror of that instant as it seemed I was surely about to die, I was flushed with the Glory of God; the warmth of His Power.

A revelation:

Otis was *dead!* There had been no signal. Everything had gone haywire and yet *I had walked upon the water! Myself! I did it!*

Unafraid, I threw back my head, tears running down my

cheeks as I thrust my arms to the heavens, laughing and crying all at once. It had happened! I was truly possessed of the power of my Father. Like Jesus at Galilee, I had done it!

"SHOOT ME?" I screamed at the throng, shaking my fist at 'em. "SHOOT ME?!?! YOU *CAN'T* SHOOT ME, YOU PATHETIC SONS-A-BITCHES, FOR I AM *THE SON OF GOD!"*

EDITOR'S NOTE—*At this point in his narrative, Dr. Hargus was heard in the first of four conversations with a man authorities concluded was Tyrone G. Jefferson, a trusted aide who assisted the Doctor during the recording of the Hargus Tapes. Mr. Jefferson's voice was the only other heard in any of the authorized taped material. In our effort to faithfully preserve the accuracy of the narrative and the sense of urgency that attended its communication, as well as to adhere to the conditions set forth for the tape's transcription, each of the four exchanges has been included in its entirety.* (ED.)

Jesus Christ, Tyrone, I still shudder when I think of them crazy bastards in New York. Tyrone? What the hell's the matter now?

I'm scared, Rev. Lord *Gawd,* I'm scared!

Goddamnit, will you stop that miserable whinin' an' . . .

Rev, this just ain't gonna work. I swear to God, they gotta find us.

What in the hell are you talkin' about, Tyrone? The Lord *wants* me here. I'm His *son,* you moron! There ain't nothin' gonna happen except what's *supposed* to happen!

Oh, Jesus, Rev. You need *help.* This shit's *crazy!* They almost killed your ass once. Ain't *nothin'* you can say to that.

No, you're right, Tyrone. Ain't nothin' I can say to that except "You goddamn dumb porch monkey! They *killed* Jesus!" An' I'm telling you, the sons-a-bitches ain't gonna do to me what they did to Him! I'm gettin' it all out! Whole story. Everything. Just like it happened.

Lord, Rev, you *are* nuts! They'll damn sure get you then!

Well, pardon-fucking-me, Tyrone. Some de-goddamn-sciple *you* turned out to be! I asked you for a simple favor; just help me. Now, if you're *not* goin' to help me, for cryin' out on a cross, let me go about my Father's work!

Look, Rev, listen to me, *please.* The Lord don't want you to make no goddamn tapes. What's wrong with you? You just tryin' to kill yourself?

God-all-mighty, Tyrone. Will you please have some respect for the Word of God? Look at that sky, you idiot! Look at them clouds! The Lord's comin'—any minute!

Rev, you poor, crazy bastard. It ain't gonna do nothin' but rain and there ain't nobody comin' here but the state police! Rev, let's go. Please—I'm scared!

TYRONE, GODDAMNIT! LET ME *DO* THIS! An' keep a lookout down there, if you're so all-fired worried! Let's see, now, Tyrone, when the hell was I born?

THE DEL RIO NEWS ★ HERALD ★

BIRTHS

Mr. & Mrs. Harry Tucker are the proud parents of a new son. Born at Del Rio Hospital, the baby weighed 6 lbs. 7 ozs.

Sandra Sue Cummings gave birth to a baby girl. She weighed 7 lbs. 5 ozs. Mr. Cummings is employed by the Del Rio Light Co. This is their first child.

Wilma (no last name) bore a son in the front seat of a pickup. The baby weighed 5 lbs. 3 ozs. The father is unknown.

Mr. & Mrs. Charles Rye welcomed their fourth child on Tuesday. A boy. The baby weighed 8 lbs. 9 ozs.

Bob and Elenore Wiggins have a new edition in their home, little Joe Willie Wiggins. The child weighed 12 lbs. 9 ozs. and has signed with the Chicago Bears.

REEL 3

◆

July 23,1935.

A Tuesday.

On this day, I, Billy Sol Hargus, was born in the city of Del Rio, county of Val Verde, state of Texas; conceived of the Holy Spirit in my unwed mother's virgin womb.

Now, then, some facts about my birth. I might point out, by the way, that describin' the details of one's own birth is a truth revealed only to actual Sons of God, after they've had the time to sort it all out.

Anyway, I was spanked to life squallin' there on the front seat of Elroy Hargus's old red pickup, doin' sixty-five miles an hour, runnin' stop signs and grade-crossin's, hell-bent for the Del Rio Hospital. Though we didn't quite make it in time, mother and baby were just fine, no thanks to ol' Elroy, who'd actually cried and then threw up.

Oh. My mother's name was Wilma.

My father's, as you already know, was God.

My mama knew no mortal man, as the seed of the Lord's own doin' blossomed in her Holy Body. Even though I never really knew her either, I'm sure I woulda been as proud of her as she must be of me. You see, Mama's gone. She's in Heaven—with Dad.

Before Mama left, Elroy and Edna Hargus took me to raise as their only child. They owned and operated the E & E Cafe off Route 90, out north of town. My mama had waited tables for them, even swollen with God's Son.

And that's where I grew up, listenin' to the trucks out on the highway and the trains over on the tracks that ran along Route 90 toward San Antonio. The cafe, an old, abandoned Pullman coach, sat on an unused sidin' between the main line and the highway. It might-a been pretty damned fancy one time. There were still red velvet curtains hangin' over the windows. How it got where it was, nobody knew. Which just goes to show you that there's a bunch of people runnin' around with more money than sense, leavin' trains and planes and boats and cars and three-hundred-dollar-a-week liquor bills behind 'em while they just flat out ignore the needs of the Lord. But don't you think for a minute that the Lord doesn't know that. He also knows what He needs, and sometimes He just takes it. In this case, the Lord needed a home for His second Son.

He gave Jesus a manger.

He gave me a diner.

Elroy had knocked out the backside of the coach, addin' on livin' quarters for us and a kitchen for the cafe. He started puttin' up a second story when I was old enough to have my own bedroom, and when he finished that, he added another one for him and Edna.

As I grew up in our little home, I realized just what a good job Elroy had done. Windows facin' east gave us sunlight in the mornin' and shade in the afternoon. Plus, Edna's sewin' curtains, paintin' and paperin' made the place good enough for somebody important; even the Son of God Hisself!

The RC Cola Company had donated the sign Elroy nailed up on a post out near the highway. Kids had shot it full of holes and it was rustin' around the edges. Most folks either drove on by it, or ran over it when they turned in. Those of 'em who did stop came for what they said might not've been Texas's best food but sure as hell was Del Rio's best show.

Edna, my stepmother, was the star. Every time she leaned over to wipe off the counter, the show started. Her blouse would fall open enough so's someone was sure to ask, "Hey, Edna, are them cantaloupes on the special?" Then the crude heathens, nearly all of 'em truck drivers, would start into snickerin' and elbowin' one another.

Edna'd always just smile, as she raked their change off into a dish. "I guess this oughta pay for a look," she'd say, winkin' at 'em.

Now, while I was not yet old enough to know the name of what it was we were all seein', I did know there was a whole lot of it! And it was certainly easier to see on Edna (actually I called her "Step-Edna") than it was on most other ladies. I never even knew if the ones that wore baggy gingham dresses, cinched up around their necks on one end and draggin' the floor on the other, had 'em or not. The reason you could be sure about Step-Edna, though, was because she dressed like them pictures hangin' on the wall in fillin' stations; knee-high white cowboy boots, tight leather skirts that wouldn't hide a wallet, and blouses that she'd tie in a knot right above her belly button. A lotta folks said she was pretty enough to make a hundred dollars a night in a place like Dallas. In fact, the snippy women over to church said she looked like she was "one hymn away from bein' a hooker."

Elroy swore up and down that she was the prettiest woman he'd ever seen. The way he went on about her always made me wonder why she thought he had any sinful desires for anybody else. But she did.

Fact was, Step-Edna suspected that Elroy had even had a hand in creatin' *me,* a true Son of God. Can you imagine? Of course, she couldn't have known about that part of me then, as she had no way of even guessin' that I was anything more than what folks said I was. Nearly all of 'em wrote off the virgin birth of a Son of God as just another case of a lonesome little waitress, makin' some extra tips after closin' time. Step-Edna thought it just might've been ol' Elroy who'd laid some extra change on my mama's bedroom dresser.

Well, the facts of the matter I'm a-tellin' now are going

to do for my mama what facts would've done for the Mother of Jesus. They're gonna keep a world full of doubtin' heathens from snickerin' and gigglin' in their pews on Sunday!

The facts are these: One mornin', a couple of weeks after my miraculous birth, Elroy came out to find me right where I'd been born, sprawled on the front seat of his pickup. There was a note pinned to the little blanket I was wrapped up in. My mama hadn't been to work at the cafe in nearly a week the mornin' Elroy just missed ploppin' down on top of me, snuggled there beneath the steerin' wheel. Years later, when I was first learnin' how to read, Elroy gave me the note Mama had written, and I've kept it folded and tucked away in my wallet to this day. It read:

> Dear Son,
> I've gone to try to find your father.
> Love,
> Mother

Well! Is there a single, solitary soul on Earth, heathen doubter or otherwise, who needs any more proof than that? There it was in her own writin'. She was goin' to find my Father.

Mama had gone to heaven.

Why, the way she just up an' disappeared was evidence enough. The people over to the motel where she and some of the other waitresses lived said all of a sudden my mama was "just gone—left all her clothes, everything!" Lord, it turned out she was called so quick she didn't even have time to pay the three months' rent she owed. And that's the truth!

And yet, in spite of that kind of positive proof, there were doubters. Goddamn, there were *always* doubters. For people had no more faith when I was born than they did when my Brother Jesus was born.

"Gone to heaven!" they'd laugh. "Boy, she's gone to hell!"

Then they'd tell me how she was hookin' for drinks over in San Antone an' how the truckers over there called her "Willin' Wilma," and even "Ol' Mattress-Back." The Mother of the Son of God! Jesus Christ, can you believe that?

I figured that people sayin' those things probably meant well, and were just supposin' that I couldn't bear hearin' that she'd died.

Yes, the birth of Billy Sol Hargus was indeed a miraculous event. Difficult for mere mortals to comprehend.

And therein lies a lesson.

Simply because mortals may not always understand the wondrous workings of the Lord, it's not necessary for 'em to go off half-cocked tryin' to come up with an earthly answer for what's got 'em puzzled. Nor does God want 'em to. Just because some event's beyond the bounds of logic and reason doesn't mean it didn't happen. After all, it's God who created science. It's God who allows man to think and reason. Hell, it's God who decides what we know, how much, when, and even *if* we need to know it. Anything beyond that is none of anybody's goddamn business.

But Step-Edna, as righteous and good a person as she was, just couldn't accept the miracle of my birth bein' the Sacred Event it was. You see, she made that fundamental mistake. She sought an earthly answer. And for that answer, she looked to poor ol' Elroy. God, what that man went through!

The first time I remember it comin' up we were all in the cafe one evenin' near closin'. A customer was bouncin' me on his knee. "Boy, I'll tell ya," he said, lookin' at me and grinnin', "this kid is flat out gettin to favor you, Hargus, you know that?" He was talkin' to Elroy.

Step-Edna stiffened up like she'd sat on the griddle, and she just stared at Elroy.

Well, the fellow dropped me and clapped his hand over his mouth like he'd just said "shit" in church. Elroy hunched up his shoulders, grinned real weak-like and started shufflin' backward toward the kitchen to put some distance between him and Step-Edna.

Truth of the matter was, *nobody* looked like Elroy. It appeared as though God had cranked his head down too tight in a vise and then somebody else had come along and jerked on his ears hopin' to fatten it up again.

None of it had worked.

Elroy had a head shaped like a beet with hat-hooks, what you could see of it, because he always had his dirty ol' brown Stetson pulled down as far as those right-angle ears would allow.

Well, after our customer friend had stuck *his* foot in *Elroy's* mouth, Step-Edna had stomped over to a window and just stood, arms folded, lookin' out through them velvet curtains at the parkin' lot where the truckers wheeled in, lettin' their rigs choke in the dust outside while they shoved their rent in the jukebox inside.

All of a sudden, I heard her begin to mutter to herself real low, "Son of a bitch. Son-of-a-bitch bastard sinnin' fool."

Then louder: "Son-of-a-bitch bastard fool makin' a horse's ass outta me!"

Then louder still: "I shoulda knowed it couldn't take no three hours to go no two goddamn miles!" Several people gulped down their coffee at that point and started headin' for the door, grinnin' over their shoulders as the screen slammed behind them. Some hung around outside, peerin' in through the windows as Step-Edna now began to scream, "TWO MILES! THREE HOURS! WHY, YOU ROTTEN SONOFABITCH!"

You see, it was a couple of miles down the highway toward town, to the motel where my mama and the other ladies who worked at the E & E lived. There were times, I remember, when they'd be so busy in the cafe that some of the ladies would serve the customers out in the parkin' lot in their trucks. Sometimes, they'd be out there a half-hour or so. On weekends, that parkin' lot would be so jammed that they'd take customers over to the motel so that they could eat there. And after the cafe closed at night, Elroy and a bunch of stragglers would run the ladies home, back to the motel. Some of 'em explained that that's where they had dessert. I learned Elroy had been drivin' my mama home for nearly a year. "She wasn't like them others," he'd said.

Well, I hope the hell not! The Mother of a Son of God!

By now, Step-Edna was workin' herself into a lather. She'd got herself into a state I've since witnessed only in those possessed of Satan himself: terrified, squirmin', screechin' heathens beggin' Billy at prayer meetin's to snatch the demons from their souls!

But that wasn't the case here with Step-Edna. Why, there wasn't an evil bone in her body, and yet, now she appeared to be taken with the Devil. Her hands fluttered and clutched and veins stood out like wires in her neck. I walked over to her, scared, and reached up, tuggin' at her skirt. She whirled around and stared down at me. I could see little white bubbles sneakin' out the corners of her mouth. Then, shovin' me aside, she started for Elroy. It seemed like the whole damned cafe was holdin' its breath. Her boot heels began clickin'—easy at first, then harder and louder—as she headed toward the other end of the coach, where Elroy was backed up against the jukebox. In a dozen strides she was on him like the glory on God Hisself. She started in to kickin' on him, as she swore at 'im under her breath. First, she went for the shins. Then, when that bent 'im over, she moved up and sunk her boot tips into his stomach. Folks watchin' from outside were whistlin' and hollerin'. Some started honkin' their horns.

When Elroy crumpled to the floor, they cheered, as Step-Edna went to work on his face, gougin' and a-grindin'. She was attackin' with such a fury that her hair whipped the air like the fan that hung above the stove and slung grease all over the kitchen. My God, she looked like an animal. Her lips were stretched back tight against her gritted teeth and you could see her tongue coilin' and strikin' the insides of her mouth as she mumbled prayers and chants, eyes bulgin' like a lizard's! Then she started screamin' again as she punched and kicked: "LORD" (POW!), "YOU MADE ADAM" (WHAM!) "AN' YOU MADE THIS SON-OF-A-BITCH BASTARD" (CRUNCH!) "ELROY" (SMACK!), "AN' I AIN'T NEVER" (OOF!) "GONNA FORGET" (BLAM!) "WHAT ELROY MADE!" (ARGH!) "LORD, HERE'S ONE FOR JEEEEEEEZZZUS!" (BIFF!) "AN' HERE'S ONE FOR YOU!" (UNGH!) "AND HERE'S ONE FOR TH' HOLY GHOST!!!" (CRASH!)

Now th' folks outside were beatin' on the windows, stompin' their feet, and jerkin' open the door to throw money on the floor.

But then, at the height of th' insanity, just when it seemed that Step-Edna was gonna kill 'im sure, suddenly her whole body kinda snapped up straight and froze as she cried out, "OOOOOOOOHHHHHHH, GAAAAAWWWD!!" I remember thinkin' that it sounded like she was actually grateful, relieved. Then she collapsed square on top of Elroy, her body twitchin' and her breath comin' and goin' in great gobs of air as she continued mumbling, "Oh, Gawd! So *good!*" And I'll be damned if she didn't fall asleep, right there on the floor on top of Elroy in the middle of the cafe.

It wasn't till Elroy was stretched out like that, that you realized how long he was, two or three inches over six feet. But he wasn't any bigger around than a prayer tower. He lay there underneath Step-Edna, moanin' and bleedin' as he tried to pull hisself together. Meantime, I was runnin' around, scoopin' up nickels, dimes, an' quarters off the floor.

What Step-Edna had just done to Elroy went a long way toward explainin' why he looked like he did. And why he *sounded* like he did. Because, from the time I could remember, I couldn't ever recall 'im ever havin' had a mouth or nose that wasn't either swollen out or cut up. And it just goddamn near ruined Elroy's life. The poor bastard not only looked funny, he talked funny. He couldn't pronounce words that required 'im to close his lips. They *wouldn't* close. So "bacon and eggs" came out, "*d*acon and eggs," "hamburger" came out "han*d*urger," and "hot roast beef" sounded like "hot roast *d*eef, ho *d*a *d*ashed *t*otatoes," when he'd repeat an order, hollerin' back out to Step-Edna from the kitchen.

As I was growin' up, I guess I might-a liked talkin' to him, but because of the way he sounded, he never said much more than he had to. He called me "son" once, and Step-Edna nearly killed 'im again. After that, he mostly just nodded to me, sometimes sayin' "Doy" or "Dilly." Jesus, he sounded stupid.

If I had not known about my real mother, and even if Step-Edna had let me call *her* "Mama," I still would've known that Edna wasn't my flesh and blood. I would've known because of the things I thought about her, things you just don't think about your own mother.

I suppose it was the *way* she looked, some. But mainly it was *how* she looked, especially workin' around the diner. When she wasn't leanin' over the counter showin' her produce, she was movin' around so's whoever was in the place just couldn't help watchin' her. She had a way of standin', with one hand perched on her hip and the corner of her mouth tilted up so's her teeth glistened, that had the truckers nudgin' one another whenever they thought she wasn't lookin'. But that was just the thing. She was *always* lookin'. And so was I! Lookin' at the way she tossed her head, making her hair fall back on her shoulders and her melons push out tight against her blouse. That was a picture that kept me awake *many* a frightful night. No—not thinkin' heathen thoughts, mind you, but just thinkin' about how pretty she was and how holy I felt lookin' at her.

I wasn't quite six years old when she first took full notice of my watchin' her. "Do you like what you see, boy?" She'd kinda purr it out.

"Yes, ma'am," I'd answer, "I sure think you're pretty. I really do, Step-Edna."

"I'll bet you do at that, little boy," she'd smile. Then she'd go on, "What are you thinkin' when you look at me, boy? You ain't thinkin' no bad thoughts now, are you?"

And though I was picturin' her wipin' down the counter, I'd answer, "Oh, no, ma'am!"

Often as not, that made her angry and she'd send me to my room.

There were people who said that Step-Edna *wanted* folks thinkin' awful things about her body. Little did they know. But I came to find Step-Edna as pure and holy as my thoughts of her were. Her actions to me were simply the wondrous workings of the Lord.

In fact, throughout my life and my ministry, I often rejoiced in the teachings of Step-Edna. For I learned a lesson from her that I've passed on hundreds of times during my crusades to thousands of the righteous.

The lesson is just this: that our mortal bodies are tools for God to work through, not ends in themselves for childish enjoyment. Any pleasure our sinful flesh may seek sure as hell is gonna have a pain to match it. Or should have. You must keep your body free from the temptations of sin and lust, and you can't trust your flesh when you are seekin' a good time.

Step-Edna began her teachings with me soon after my sixth birthday. I learned that nothing in this world is all pleasure or all pain. I learned to be strong. Step-Edna would tell me, "Boy, I'm gonna see to it that you're gonna be under control. You ain't gonna be no sinful, lustful heathen with a rovin' eye and a foul mind. You're gonna control your mind and body, boy. That you are!"

The night she began her instruction, I'd been layin' awake in my bed, tossin' and turnin' as I thought about how funny I felt havin' seen Step-Edna get undressed earlier in the evenin'. She and Elroy just never left their bedroom door open, but it had been standin' ajar a little bit that night and

I'd peeked inside. What I saw I didn't understand, because it appeared that Step-Edna was inflictin' pain upon herself. In fact, when I first heard the groanin', I figured she must be kickin' the shit outta Elroy again. But that evenin' he wasn't even home. I wasn't sure right then, but it seemed to me there was some kinda pleasure in the pain Step-Edna was sufferin' while doin' the Lord's will. She looked like she was enjoyin' instructin' herself!

The thoughts were racin' through my head so fast I was actually dizzy later when Step-Edna came tiptoein' into my room. She'd slipped on one of Elroy's shirts. When she sat down on the edge of my little bed, silhouetted by the light from the hall, I could see she didn't have nothin' else on. I felt my pulse start hammerin' through my body.

She reached for my hand. "Do you know why I'm here, child?" she whispered.

I told her I'd already said my prayers.

She giggled. "That's a good boy," she said, "but I'm here for another reason. I'm here because it's lesson time." Then, Step-Edna told me how she knew I'd been watchin' her earlier. "Did you learn anything, boy?" she asked. "What did you think about what your Step-Edna was doin'?"

I said it appeared she was instructin' herself. God, I couldn't think.

She laughed. "Yes," she said, and her voice sounded kinda funny, a little hoarse. "And now, we're gonna teach *you!*"

Then, Step-Edna got up and smoothed Elroy's shirt down real tight, moldin' it to her melons as she arched her back, all the time lookin' straight at me. She held that pose for a moment, then started moving around the room, twistin' and bendin' like she did down at the diner.

"Keep your eyes on me, boy," she said. "Don't look away."

Lord, I kept 'em on her. Mercy! I couldn't take 'em off! I just knew it was happenin'! I was learnin' the ways of the will of the Lord! And yet, my damned double-crossin' flesh seemed to be thinkin' on its own. My blood nearly boiled as it raced up and down my little body. Step-Edna wouldn't let me calm down! Praise the Lord, I was *learnin'!* She turned her back to me and then bent over and looked at me from between her legs! *Ohmigod!*

"Gettin' an eyeful, are you, boy? Like what you see?"

"Yes, *ma'am!*"

Then, she came back to the bed and stood right over me as she slowly unbuttoned Elroy's shirt, startin' at the top and workin' her way to the bottom. She slid one half back an' off one shoulder, exposin' her left melon, runnin' a finger over the tip. Then she let the whole shirt drop to her wrists, then fall to the floor. She sat down again, never takin' her eyes off mine, and began pullin' the covers back off me slowly till they slid off the end of the bed. Pretty soon, my pajama bottoms followed as Step-Edna's fingers found the waistband and began slidin' them down till they were around my ankles! She started workin' her hands on me, rubbin' my neck, my shoulders, my belly, and then—*Lord, have mercy*—she put her hands down into my *heathen area,* makin' me as hard as Peter's Rock!

I felt myself suddenly fill to near overflowin' with all sorts of fluids coursin' through my veins. Praise Jesus! She was teachin' me "The Pleasure," an' Lord, didn't it feel fine!

Hell, it wasn't nothin'.

For all of a sudden, Step-Edna leaned over. I felt her warm breath and then—LORD, HAVE MERCY UPON THE LITTLE CHILD—SHE TOOK MY PRIVATES IN HER MOUTH!

OHMIGAWWD!!

I was sure I was goin' to *die* with this message she was a-givin' me! But I quickly found out that it was only *half* of her message—the top half, the pleasure part that goes into doin' God's will.

I was nearly set to explode when suddenly, without any warnin', Step-Edna leaped straight up off the bed, lurched back, and stared down at me.

"My, ain't you just lookin' ridiculous," she snarled. "Look

at yourself, boy!" She pointed between my legs, shakin' her finger furiously. *"Just look at that!* Do you think the Lord would be proud of you that way? Could you go to church lookin' like that? Or walk down the street? Huh? Could ya, Goddamnit?" She'd started to scream at me.

"I SAID, LOOK AT YOURSELF, BOY! YOU CAN'T GO AROUND WORSHIPPIN' NO FALSE IDOL LIKE THAT LITTLE THING YOU GOT STICKIN' UP THERE! LORD JESUS GOD, BOY, AIN'T YOU GOT NO *CONTROL* OF YOURSELF? THAT THING MAKES ME SICK, BOY! D'YA HEAR ME?!? SICK! GODDAMNIT, *SICK!* AND . . . I . . . WON'T . . . STAND . . . FOR . . . IT!!"

And with that, she curled a finger, reached down, and gave it a snap that would've splattered a cat against the wall.

My false idol, my sinful rod of lust, just disappeared, leavin' behind only a shriveled noodle, and a painin' one, I might add.

Step-Edna smiled, though. "There, now," she said, "that's a good little boy. You're gonna do just fine. You remember what I'm tellin' you, boy, the Lord don't want you abusin' your body. He wants you *strong.* And you're gonna *be* strong! You ain't gonna be struttin' that thing and makin' yourself and everybody else miserable, right?"

"Yes, ma'am."

She reached for my hand again.

"Now, now," she whispered, "everything okay?"

"Yes, ma'am."

"You love your Step-Edna?"

"Yes, ma'am."

"Okay, then," she said huskily, "let's go over it again."

It took a long time and lots of lesson sessions before I was really doin' the will of the Lord. But finally, it got to where Step-Edna could work on me most of a night before the milk of Satan felt like it was ready to spill from my false idol. But then, *whack!* And I'd be okay, ready for the lesson to start again.

Yes, Step-Edna taught me well, and one day I was *ready!* For I was under *control* and I looked no more to my heathen flesh for joy in followin' God's path. Step-Edna told me it was His will that I had learned well.

Ours was a Christian home.

THE DEL RIO NEWS
★ HERALD ★

FAMILY OF FOUR SURVIVES DEL RIO INFERNO

Japanese Bomb Pearl Harbor

Otis Blackwood Bombs "Japanese"

DEL RIO—Otis Blackwood's familiar Shell Service Station, located on Route 90 north of town, was the scene of what may have been the first American mainland reaction to the Japanese attack against Pearl Harbor. . . .

REEL 4

◆

December 7, 1941.

A Sunday morning.

We got the news from Otis Blackwood. He'd come over from the fillin' station on a dead run, damned near tearin' the door off the diner as he screamed inside, "They done it! Them goddamned slant-eyed bastards has *bombed* us!" He tore his cap off and slammed it to the floor. "Them pissant little pricks! God *damn!*"

Dear ol' Otis. What a sweetheart. God bless him. He's safe now. He's with the Lord.

Otis's Shell Station was situated directly across the highway from Elroy and Edna's E & E. It was a gas station but it could've been just about anything. He'd nailed the place together usin' hunks of wood, scraps of tin, old tires, hubcaps, transmission housin's, weeds, and wire. When he'd run across somethin' layin' around, he'd expand. That's how he got his front porch. From the bus wreck out front.

It had happened late one evenin'; the driver turned her over in a heavy rainstorm, and by the next mornin' Otis had the thing peeled right down to the seats and floorboards and bolted across the front of the station. He had the only porch in Texas that would seat forty-two.

"Comfy, ain't it?" he'd say, grinnin'. "All aboard," he'd holler, laughin'.

Otis sold gas when he had it and groceries when he could

find somebody desperate enough to buy 'em; assorted packs of cheese, canned stuff, meat, hot soda pop, bread. A lot of it was flecked with mold—"special seasonin'," he'd tell folks—and all of it was caked with the fine red dust that smothered and choked Del Rio.

That is, of course, 'cept when it rained. Then the place turned into a mud farm. A shower always made Otis's driveway look, as he described it, like "somethin' you could drown alligators in."

I liked Otis. You would've liked 'im, too, if you'd taken the time to get to know him. Big, round, freckled, pink face. Friendly, funny. His eyes were set maybe a pinch too close together, makin' him look like his parents might've been related through more than marriage, and Otis *was* greasy; greasy, but easy to like.

Right now, though, his good humor had left 'im. He was standin' in the middle of the diner ragin' about Japs, so mad he could hardly put one sentence together before startin' in on the next one.

"For Chrissake, Otis," said Step-Edna, turnin' on the radio, "shut up, an' pick up your goddamn hat. People have to walk in here!"

Otis, still plenty upset, said, "What the hell are you talkin' about, Edna? This is th' only cafe in the world that's so scummy you can come in for a bowl of soup and catch the clap!"

"You crazy bastard!" said Step-Edna, smilin' in spite of herself.

The same kind of folks who cast doubt on my virgin birth and made heathen remarks about Step-Edna also thought Otis was a trifle strange, if not downright warped. Even Elroy said, as best he could, "That doy's a duckin' nut!"

Step-Edna was always tryin' to caution me about him. "Now don't go gettin' no heathen ideas in your head, boy, hangin' around with that damn cesspool."

I don't think anybody ever really understood Otis. Still, I'll bet you would've liked him. I sure know I did.

One of my favorite things to do was to go over and visit Otis at his station. Sometimes he'd let me help out. "Here, son," he'd say, handin' me a pack of Trojans, "go fill the balloon machine in the turdhouse!" Boy, was he funny! "The balloon machine in the turdhouse!" Otis was always sayin' great stuff like that. Step-Edna caught me tryin' to blow one up once and nearly had a heart attack.

And Otis let me feed his dog. "Ol' Green," he'd named him. Otis explained that every asshole in Texas had a dog named "Ol' Blue." But then, Ol' Green *was* green. Otis painted him. He was also sick a lot. From the fumes, I guess.

By now, there was a good-sized crowd in the diner, all gathered around the radio.

"Can you believe that?" said Otis, retrievin' his cap, "bombin' the U-S-of-A! Them bastards! God *damn!*"

"Shhhhhh!"

"Hush up!"

"Can it, ya idiot! Let's hear what th' hell's goin' on!"

"Fuck 'em," said Otis. "Ah'm proud of this country an' you can bet your ass we'll get even." Otis might've been too old to enlist, but he did what he could to help out.

Scarcely a week had gone by when Elroy came roarin' across the cafe parkin' lot in his pickup one afternoon, dust flyin', horn blowin', an' him leanin' out the window hollerin', "DIRE! DIRE!" He was pointin' back across the road toward Otis's station. Everybody in the diner ran to the windows to have a look. Sure enough, there was a sedan ablaze over in Otis's driveway, not a dozen feet from the pumps. We all poured outside. Cars and trucks were backed up on the highway in both directions. People were hollerin' an' runnin' ever' which-a-way, generally doin' absolutely nothin'.

"Grab th' hose!" somebody yelled.

"No! Get back! Get back!"

"Jesus H. Christ! They's *people* in there!"

The strangest thing to me was how Otis was reactin' to all of the commotion. He was standin' out on the front porch with his arms folded, just watchin' as this here car turned into a cinder smack in the middle of his driveway.

Somebody yelled to 'im, "Goddamnit, Otis, *do* something!"

"Fuck 'em," he said. "Let 'em burn."

Sheriff Buff Wallace's old patrol car came screechin' sideways into the drive in a swirl of dust. The door swung open even before the car'd stopped and out rolled ol' Buff hisself, three hundred pounds of self-importance.

"What th' hell's goin' on here?" he bellowed.

"Get back, Buff, ya moron! She's gonna blow any second!"

Otis still hadn't budged offa the porch. They started hollerin' at 'im again.

"Otis, God *damn!*"

"Goddamn my ass," he said, an' then he spilled it. "These fuckin' gooks come in here actin' all hot-shit, wantin' this an' askin' how do you get here an' there, an' then their crummy yeller Jap kids start yappin' about my soda pop bein' hot—well, I guess I said to em, 'Here, I'll give you little pricks somethin' hot!' "

Somebody shouted, "Give me a hand, f'r God's sake!"

Otis didn't notice. "Then they make a run for their car here just like I knowed they would, but before they could start 'er up, I by God sloshed 'em down with ethyl an' lit their ass on fire!"

As Otis continued his harangue, somehow Elroy managed to get the driver's door open, and was gropin' inside the car with one hand while he raised the other 'cross his face tryin' to shield it from the heat. And Otis? No help. He just kept on screamin,' "THEY'S FOUR FUCKIN'A JAPS THAT AIN'T EVER GONNA BOMB SHIT!"

Finally, an Oriental man and woman, singed and chokin', tumbled out and collapsed in the dirt. Elroy just was able to yank their two kids free seconds before the car exploded like somebody had tossed a stick of dynamite inside. It burned for three hours.

"Well," Otis was to say later, "how th' hell was *I* supposed to know they was Filipinos?"

The family recovered, though it took months. They were detained in Del Rio then, until after the war.

Those were boom years for Elroy, Step-Edna, and the E & E. In 1942, Laughlin Air Force Base opened just a few miles away and the E & E became one of the regular stops for military personnel. Elroy was tickled. "All them Air Dorce doys," he'd say, "sure eats a lot!" He and Step-Edna finally were gettin' so backed up with business that they built a small motel right next to the diner to soak up the overflow.

If they were salad years for Elroy and Step-Edna, they were lean years for ol' Otis. The government's rationing gasoline had hit him pretty hard. About once a week, Otis would get a letter from Washington marked, "Urgent." And about once a week, he'd tear 'em up. Rationing also riled his customers, some of whom started gettin' a little on the pushy side.

"When ah had all the goddamn fuel in the world," Otis'd say, "nobody'd come in here for a week. Now, every idiot in the world all of a sudden's got some real important trip to make." Then, throwin' up his arms in disgust, he'd say, "Well, they can all just go straight to hell! Fuck 'em again!"

When customers'd come in and start wavin' a ration book under his nose, he'd tell 'em, "Well now, folks, why don't you take your coupons there and shove 'em up your ass. And have a good day!"

Lots of times he'd run after somebody all the way out to the highway, hollerin', "How the hell you expect us to kick them Japs' ass with you out toolin' around all over kingdom come in this goddamn car?"

Then he'd come bouncin' back, grinnin', and the truth would come out. "Ah'll tell you what it is, son," he'd say to me. "Ah holler at 'em but ah just really don't give a shit." Then he'd wink and add, " 'Cept, o'course, for my barrel."

Now then, I hope you haven't just had breakfast, 'cause I gotta tell you somethin' right here concerning Otis that tested even our long friendship.

Otis, you see—God, this is awful—Otis, uh, liked to save his own, uh, body waste. I know, I know. It's hard to believe, but believe it, because I saw it. Otis saved his own waste! Honest! Reason he got to doin' it was because he refused to go in the station's bathroom. "Shit, son," he'd say, motionin' toward the restroom, "that's a goddamned health hazard!" And he was right. You couldn't have rented that place to a maggot.

So Otis relieved himself in a fifty-gallon oil drum that he kept over by the soda machine, just inside the repair bay and left of the lift. Every few days, he'd haul it out behind the station and set it on fire. "Takes away the chill, don't it, son?" he'd kid. Maybe, but it laid down a smell that covered Del Rio like a Bible salesman.

I was helpin' Otis every day now, after school and on weekends, too. There really wasn't very much to do. Mostly we'd sit out on the porch, wavin' at folks drivin' by, talkin', laughin', givin' directions to Eagle Pass when somebody asked how to get to Comstock. God, I just loved it! Summers, mostly, customers'd wheel in, hollerin' out, "How far's Mexico?"

Every time Otis would yell back, "Not fuckin' far enough!" and then he'd let loose with a long, loud laugh.

Mexico *was* just a taco toss away. Del Rio lies along the banks of the Rio Grande River, just across from Ciudad Acuna, Mexico. Ol' Otis hadn't had much learnin', which suited the local school system just fine, but he could've written th' textbook on Del Rio history.

"Buncha goddamned wetbacks settled here back in the 1600s," he'd told me, shakin' his head disgustedly. "Back then, they called th' place San Felipe del Rio. Ignert bastards. It wasn't till near 1900 before they got a white person to make any sense outta all that tamale talk."

That's how we spent many a long, drowsy afternoon; Otis talkin', Billy listenin'. It was quite an education.

. . .

As I look back on it now, I might've learned more about life from Otis than anyone else. In one of our talks, sittin' out there on the porch, rockin' in the mid-afternoon sun, he asked me, "Boy, what're you goin' to do with yourself anyway?"

I looked up at 'im from where I was sittin' on the step, an' saw that ol' Otis was just kinda gazin' way off, lookin' down the road there toward not much of nothin'.

"Well," I answered, "my Step-Edna says that the Lord wants me to do His will. She says the Lord has a plan for everybody's life, so I guess I'm just kinda waitin' on mine to come along."

Otis gave me a little chuckle. "Nah, son. Ain't sayin' nothin' bad about Edna, now, but Jesus was the last person on Earth th' Lord had anything planned out for. All the Lord wants anybody to do these days is to stand up for what they believe in and do with their lives whatever they want. So if you're just gonna sit an' wait for somebody to come along and draw you out a picture of what you oughta do, you're gonna be waitin' a hell of a long time. And then you're gonna be just like everybody else around here, livin' out a miserable, crummy life." He chuckled again and said, "Shit, son. Ain't no use in waitin' for somethin' you already got."

"You mean," I asked, "that the Lord leaves it up to everybody to decide for themselves?"

"Ain't it the goddamned truth," said Otis. "Except nobody ever understands that. They all start out thinkin' the Lord's got a hot deal for 'em, and that He's gonna send somebody into their lives to show 'em what it is. They think that all they've gotta do is to sit on their ass and wait for it to land in their lap."

"You're talkin' about Jesus, right?" I asked.

Well, you could see Otis was thinkin', 'cause the words came slow and careful. "There ain't too many people that believe Jesus is gonna do anything but keep 'em from burnin' in hell. Mostly they believe in Jesus because that's easier than believin' in themselves. And besides, they know the Lord wants 'em to believe in Him, so a lot of 'em just do."

"No," he went on, shakin' his head, "what they're really doin' is lookin' around for somebody to pop up somewhere with the 'good news.' "

"And?" I asked.

"And," said Otis, "they spend their lives goin' from disappointment to disappointment because nobody ever pops up with nothin'. But still they wish, and hope, and pray, and get older and more miserable, sayin', 'Tomorrow, maybe tomorrow.' But tomorrow never comes and finally they just throw in the goddamned towel and give up."

"Not on Jesus, I hope."

"Shit, no," said Otis. "They give up on there ever bein' a plan. You see, they all been doin' things they hate. Their jobs, mostly. But they figure, 'Oh, what th' hell, it ain't so bad.' But it is, 'cause they're miserable. But you better believe that they still love the Lord and Jesus, in fact, more than ever."

It didn't seem to me much like they would.

Otis got up, pulled a screwdriver out of his pocket, and went over to the pop machine to jimmy out a Grapette. "Well, ah'll tell ya," he said, gruntin' as he pried at the machine. "The reason the poor bastards hang onto that faith is because they think somehow, some way, sometime they's gonna be rewarded for puttin' up with a lousy life."

"The Lord does reward us," I agreed. "Step-Edna said that."

Otis laughed as he sighed back down into his chair. "He sure does, now, don't He! The only problem with that kind of reward is that in order to collect it you gotta die! Folks is lookin' for somebody to bail 'em outta the hole they done dug for themselves *now, here,* while they're still alive."

"Yeah, but Jesus does that, don't He?"

"Son, let me tell you somethin'. If Jesus Hisself walked

up to most anybody here in Del Rio, or anywhere else, an' told 'em there wasn't no reason for them to be so goddamned unhappy, and even if He showed 'em that they already *had* the plan if they'd just wake up to it, they'd have His ass locked up and nailed up quicker than they did before."

I laughed.

"It ain't funny, son," said Otis. "Every poor, unhappy bastard you'll ever meet is waitin' for a check to come in the mail." He drained the Grapette and winged the bottle at Ol' Green, snoozin' on his side out by the pumps. Didn't faze 'im. "Did you ever notice how folks acts when the phone rings or they get a letter? They're afraid to *not* answer the phone an' they can't wait to tear open that damned envelope. They just know there's somebody on the other end of the line, or out there somewhere with a stamp, who's got good news. Goddamnit, son, the telephone company and the U.S. Mail has disappointed more people in this world than all the weddin' nights and funeral services there've ever been, all rolled into one."

Otis could see I was a little confused, so he went on.

"You see, it's because of what folks expects. Nobody ever figures that they're gonna meet anyone face to face who's gonna be important enough to change their life. But the phone and mail—now, they're a different story. Ever'body understands that they got no control over whoever calls 'em or writes 'em a letter. So they just figger that since it could be anybody, just maybe it's somebody with something *good!*"

"Well," I asked, "'couldn't it be?"

"Sure as shit could," said Otis. "But it ain't! *Never!* The asshole that calls you up with bad news is the same prick who writes you a letter two days later, confirmin' it! Every telephone conversation th' poor slob ever has starts out with, 'What's wrong?' and every time he opens a letter you hear 'im say, 'Oh, shit!' "

We both laughed at that. "I guess you're right," I said,

"but there wasn't anyone ever who was gonna call me, and I can't remember ever gettin' no letter from nobody, so I guess none of it means anything f'r me."

"You wait till you get a little older," Otis corrected. "All them dope-dicks with their bad news and their petty-ass problems will be on you like stink on a stool. And if you're like most folks, every time you get a call or a letter, you'll not only be disappointed, you'll also start thinkin' that there ain't no sumbitch nowhere who's gettin' a fair shake. Why, Christ, even if you're halfway happy, you'll get to feelin' guilty, wonderin', If every other poor bastard is as miserable as I suspect he is, there ain't any reason I shouldn't be. And you *will* be!"

"Well, what do I do then, Otis?"

"You can start," he said, "by not answerin' the goddamned telephone or openin' any goddamned mail. Then, understand that there ain't never gonna be no sumbitch who can make you believe somethin' you know down deep just can't be true. And there ain't nobody, nowhere, who can force you to be somethin' you don't want to be. Shit, son, you're free, white and one day soon you'll be twenty-one. There's no reason on God's Earth why you can't be whatever th' hell you want. *You* decide!"

Otis looked down at me a moment, smilin'. "You follow what I'm sayin', son?"

"Yes," I said, "I think I do."

He looked off in the distance again, ponderin'. Finally he said, "Son, ah'm sittin' right here on this chicken-shit porch 'cause nobody ever had the smarts to tell me that ah didn't *have* to sit here. But now, ah'm tellin' you! You get out there an' do whatever th' hell crosses your mind."

Otis then said somethin' I truly did *not* understand. He looked down at me an' said, kinda quiet, "Son, ah want better for you. You're all ah got."

There were tears in his eyes.

Yes, you'd a-sure liked him.

THE DEL RIO NEWS
★ HERALD ★

PEACE TAKES HOLD

Laughlin Air Force Base to Close

Del Rio Business Already Suffers Slump

DEL RIO—To the dismay of local merchants, Laughlin Air Force Base is among military installations around the country whose operations are being phased out, now that the war is over.

Elroy Hargus, proprietor of a cafe north of town which became a popular spot with Laughlin personnel, said he was deeply concerned about the certain loss of business. "Ah dus don dow dot 'e donna do," Mr. Hargus explained. "Dit donna dit real dad! I dud dow dit dis. . . ."

REEL 5

◆

"You the boss man here, boy?"

"No, sir!"

He was the single biggest, meanest-lookin' man I'd ever seen. Instantly, I found myself reminded of the souvenir sign that hung inside Otis's little office, right over his old hand-crank cash register: YEA, THOUGH I WALK THROUGH THE VALLEY OF THE SHADOW OF DEATH I SHALL FEAR NO EVIL, FOR I AM THE MEANEST SON OF A BITCH IN THE VALLEY!

This here *had* to be the man they wrote that sign about.

"Well, get the boss man out here, boy! Move your ass!" He was a colored man. Otis called 'em "nignogs." I doubted he'd call this one anything other than "sir." The sumbitch blotted out the sun.

"Mister," I ventured, "th' boss is sleepin', an' he gets awful cranky if I wake 'im up."

His next words rattled the tin coverin' the bottom half of the screen door. "HE'S GONNA BE DEAD AN' YOU GONNA BE CRIPPLED IF YOU DON'T WAKE 'IM UP! NOW, *GIT!*"

My God, he was pointin' a *gun* at me! In my lifetime I was never so scared before and I swear I hardly ever been so scared since.

"Yessir!"

I jumped off the porch and made the ground smoke gettin' back to the pickup where Otis was sprawled out snorin'. I shook him, hard.

He raised one eye a bit and mumbled at me, "Son, don't be wakin' me up with no bullshit about no nignog in here with a gun." But then he saw that I was shakin' and white as a sheet. He snapped awake and looked out front.

"God *damn!"* he said, openin' the door and clamberin' out of the truck.

"Be careful!" I called after him, but he was headed straight for that overgrown gorilla in the driveway. "Tyrone!" he shouted. "Tyrone! You nappy-headed sonofabitch!" Next thing I knew he was leapin' clear off the porch and throwin' his arms around this man who I'd been sure was gonna kill us, an' the both of 'em fell into the dirt, rollin' and laughin' and poundin' each other on the back.

I'd never seen Otis so happy.

"Hot shit, boy!" he said to the colored feller. "Lemme look at you! My God, the damned war done you good! You is one pretty colored boy, you know that?"

They were standin' now, brushin' the dirt off themselves.

"I'm a *what?"* sputtered Tyrone.

"Pretty boy," said Otis, walkin' around him, grinnin'. "Sure as shit, that's what you are, 'Rone. Th' army done you good."

"Damn," said Tyrone, shakin' his huge head, "you still the craziest white man I ever saw. Lord, you silly!"

Otis clapped his hands together. "Wait a minute, 'Rone," he said. "What's this? Look at you, boy! What've you done to that nappy head o' yours?"

"Got me a process, O'," he said, runnin' his fingers over what looked like buckled asphalt. Tyrone called Otis "O'."

"And look at them hot-shit shoes," shouted Otis. "Them's alligator, ain't they?"

Tyrone didn't seem so mean now. Oh, he was still big enough. But he was Otis's friend, so he became mine. Otis described a friend as somebody you could like longer than it took to screw 'em outta something they had that you wanted.

We all climbed back up onto the porch, and sat down to

talk. Both of 'em was tickled about the way I'd reacted when I first looked up and saw Tyrone—and looked up, and up, and up.

" 'Rone," Otis giggled, "when you first showed up out there this afternoon you just damn near had little Billy here wettin' his pants. He come runnin' back to the truck hollerin', 'Oh, Otis! Oh, Otis! Saaaaave me! They's a giant colored man out there, an', an', an' . . . he's *got a gun!'* "

God, they both howled 'till they got tears in their eyes. After a spell, when they got themselves settled down, Tyrone looked down at me on the step and said, sorta sadlike, "You done forgot me, didn't you, boy?"

Well, it was true, but as the Lord is my witness I was beginnin' to feel real sorry that I had. Then Tyrone started rememberin':

"Lessee," he said, as he started to count on the fingers of one of them big hands of his, "you couldn't a-been more'n six years old when I recollect seein' you come runnin' outta your daddy and stepmama's cafe holdin' onto your little business there." He pointed below my belt. "And I remember how you would be a-cryin', tears just a-streamin' down your face. Lord, Lord."

Neither he nor Otis was smilin' now.

"What was that all about, boy?" Tyrone asked. "Was you sick or somethin' a lot?"

I explained to 'im that I had been learnin' the pleasure and the pain of doin' the will of the Lord, gettin' personal instruction from Step-Edna in how to keep my false idol in check.

"Good Gawd, son!" said Tyrone, shakin' his head. "That ain't got nuthin' to do with havin' yo' privates snapped. Why, that shit's just crazy!"

Just then, Otis caught Tyrone's eye and said to him, sharp, "I don't think it's somethin' we ought to be talkin' about."

Tyrone, th' poor dumb bastard, never did understand nothin'. God bless him.

A cloud had come up and big ol' Texas-sized raindrops began to splatter out in the dust. "If you'll wait a few minutes, 'Rone," said Otis, "you can throw them slick-ass alligator shoes out there in th' mud and we'll sit here an' watch 'em grow up an' eat Mexicans!"

We all laughed, as we just sat, passin' the afternoon, rockin' and watchin' the rain. By and by, Otis recalled how he'd first met Tyrone.

"Aw, shit, O'," Tyrone interrupted, "ain't nobody wanna hear about that."

I did. So Otis started in:

"This little poor ass," he said, jerkin' a thumb toward Tyrone, "shows up here one day; couldn't a-been a minute over twelve years old an' hungry—looked near starvin', in fact. Well, ah'm workin' on a truck over there by the pump when ah catches the little rat outta the corner of my eye, tryin' to prise open my pop box."

" 'Course," Tyrone jumped in, laughin', "what he didn't know was I'd done stuffed three loaves of bread in my face before he ever seen me gettin' a pop."

"Th' shit ah didn't," argued Otis, continuin' the story. "Anyway, ah runs up here on the porch and as loud as ah could ah hollared, 'GET TH' THIEVIN' LITTLE BASTARD!' "

Otis was on his feet now, wavin' his arms, startin' to roll with the story. "Well, this little bugger's eyes got big around as dinner plates an' he starts backin' up, then makes a run for it off the corner of the porch right over there. Sure 'nuff, he's fast, but he oughta been faster 'cause ah nailed 'im right over there by the water barrel."

Otis had run out into the rain now, to show us exactly where this importan' piece of hist'ry had taken place. He hollared back at us on the porch, "God, you oughta heard 'im! That little monkey was screechin' and scratchin'—why, Christ, ah thought he'd break a leg or a vocal cord, sure!"

"Let me tell this part, O'." Now Tyrone was gettin' into it. "Lord, Billy, it's true. I was one scared little runt. See, everybody 'round here knew Otis was just as liable as not to act crazy jus' anytime! Shit, I figured this insane white man was gonna kill me!" Tyrone paused, relishin' the recollection as Otis clambered back up onto the porch.

"Well, go on, go on," said Otis, "tell 'im the rest of it."

Tyrone grinned again. "Well," he said, layin' a big hand on Otis's knee and leanin' over toward me, "you know what this crazy sumbitch did? He lifted me up, carried me right back here to this porch where we're sittin' right now, and he said, 'You know what, boy?' Lord, I was so scared I couldn't even scream no more. All I could do was jus' feel that rope goin' 'round my neck! But—I'll be goddamned—this ol' Otis stooped down, took me by the shoulders, looked me straight in th' eye, an' said, 'Lessee now, boy, three loaves of bread and a broke RC machine. That sounds like ah jus' bought myself a young'un!' "

"Ain't it the goddamned truth," said Otis, laughin'. "An' ah put the little bastard to workin' that very minute, too, an' kept 'im, an' raised 'im up. Sent his ass to school, taught him some sense, an' made a man outta this here nignog."

Now right there was the deal. Just the clearest insight into ol' Otis anybody'd ever need. Otis called colored people "nignogs," largely because the other term of the day, "niggers," made him feel just awful 'cause he knew how people used it. Otis was way ahead of his time, as it turned out. Th' way he had it figured, a black-skinned man was ever' bit the equal of a man whose skin was white, ever' bit. Th' thing he always told me he couldn't get straight in his mind, though, was how come th' Lord had to ever go an' make 'em black, or make the other 'uns white in the first place. " 'Cause just look at the shit it's caused," he'd say. "Why couldn't God a-just made one damned color? What th' hell was the need for all this variety? Every damned one of us is ab-so-fuckin'-lute-ly equal underneath the skin, so how come He had to make His children paisley?" Otis loved that. It was one of his big words; "college words," he called 'em. Paisley.

It had stopped raining.

Now, wouldn't you just know it that the same kinda folks who doubted my virgin birth, Step-Edna's morals, and Otis's stability also took to callin' Tyrone "that thievin' nigger boy."

Otis told me that Tyrone used to come home cryin' about it, till he growed up enough to kick the livin' shit outta an entire visitin' football team that got to hasslin' him down to the school one day.

Some people still called Tyrone a thief, but you better believe it was never so's he could hear 'em.

Now, another thing that bothered me and Otis was the fact that Tyrone wasn't welcome most places. Elroy and Step-Edna tolerated him, but just barely, because he was my friend. Generally, though, they wouldn't have let nobody near the cafe who wasn't white, unless they was comin' to carry off the trash. Then Elroy called 'em "th' garbage, comin' to pick up the junk." Or actually, "th' gardage, conin' to tick ut th' dunk." What a dumb bastard.

Tyrone, though, was a far cry from the lowlife most people considered his sort to be. "Sure he's a big ol' boy," said Otis, "but he ain't no oh-rang-you-tang." He drew the word out real long. "He don't play with his member out in public an' he don't eat no goddamn watermelon!"

No, he didn't. But he did *sleep* with one.

"Just look at 'im," Otis'd say, studyin' Tyrone. "Why, he ain't a whole lot darker than *I* am. An' he's got a tattoo. How many of his kind you ever seen with a tattoo? Show 'im, 'Rone."

Tyrone pushed up the sleeve of his shirt.

Sure enough. There it was on his arm, just below his shoulder. A heart with an arrow through it, an' th' name, "Wilma."

It was 1946.

The war had been over a year now.

As Otis was fond of sayin', "We finally got around to bombin' them little pricks back!"

The world and Del Rio were pretty much back to normal, although Otis said, and accurately, as it turned out, that it wouldn't be five years before we'd have to be barbecuin' some more of 'em somewhere."

With Laughlin now completely deactivated, Elroy and Step-Edna were forced to board up the motel they'd built when the base had brought 'em all that business. But Step-Edna took it okay. She said, "It'll give us all a chance to get back on our feet around here and start talkin' to one another again."

Oh, she was talkin' to me plenty, and had been all during the war years. I was still learnin' the will of the Lord from her. I also continued helping out Otis and Tyrone over to the station, a fact that rankled Step-Edna to no end. "Do you have to hang around with them goddamn outcasts?" she'd ask me.

And I was now learnin' the *Word* of the Lord, too.

The Reverend Gleason Beamer presented me with that opportunity when he gave me his very own Bible.

"Well, *he* sure as shit don't need it," said Otis.

Reverend Beamer was something of a theological pioneer. He'd struck out on his own, abandoning a strict interpretation of the Gospel. He'd often tell our small congregation, "If at first you don't receive, ask for somethin' else."

The day he brought my Bible by the station, he'd turned to Otis, who was the original backslider, and said, "We sure hope to see you in church on Sunday, Otis. The Lord's got a plan for your life."

Normally, when Reverend Beamer said something like that Otis would tell 'im to blow it out his ass, or some such. But this day he said, "Beamer, why don't you see if the Lord's got a plan for you to pay your goddamned gas bill!"

"Well!" huffed the Reverend, drawin' hisself up to his full five-feet-five. "You can just deduct the boy's Book here from my bill."

Otis had chased him all the way out to the highway, then hollered after him that Jesus would have turned over in His grave, or cave, or wherever th' hell they left Him, if He had known an asshole like Beamer was gonna be goin' around quotin' 'im!

Next day I was sittin' out on Otis's porch steps, thumbin' through my new Bible, shadin' my eyes from the glare bouncin' off th' crisp, white pages. Tyrone saw me and walked over, wipin' his hands on a filthy rag he'd pulled out of his overalls. "Watcha got there, Billy?"

"Bible."

"Well, ain't that jus' fine, jus' fine, now. Yessir, little Billy, you ain't never gonna go wrong studyin' that Book."

Otis had been inside, hunkered down on top of his barrel, "meditatin'," as he called it, and he had overheard us. Pretty soon, he came lumberin' out, drawin' up his drawers, and you could see he was gettin' set to put his two cents in. He shoved his cap back a bit and scratched his head, thinkin'. Finally, he said, " 'Rone, ah just don't see why your people are always goin' on about God and Jesus. Pardon me, but it just seems downright stupid."

Tyrone frowned, lookin' at Otis like he just couldn't believe how thick he was. "Lord, O'," he said, "my people ain't got nothin' *else* to talk about!"

Otis laughed at that. "Tell me, 'Rone," he said, still chucklin' at the irony of what he'd said, "what kinda God would do what He's done to your people?"

"What d'ya mean?" asked Tyrone, surprised. "What's He done to us?"

"Well, Jesus Christ, Tyrone," Otis exploded, "just look th' hell around you, ya dumb bastard. Your coloreds can't eat where they want. Your coloreds can't go where they want. They can't get nothin' but shit jobs, no learnin' worth a damn, nothin'! What's He done? Hell, what *hasn't* He done? Nothin' but to keep you people knocked down an' beat an' whipped! An' all just because your skin happens to be black! Now, ah suppose you think that's real fair, huh?" Otis stood there, squintin' at Tyrone and lookin' real superior.

Tyrone was quiet for a moment, then he said, softly,

"They's better days a-comin', O'. Remember, they's better days a-comin'."

"Well, where the hell'd you get that information?"

Tyrone grinned. "Jesus said so."

Otis thought a moment. "Okay, then," he said, "explain this to me, 'Rone. How is it that colored people is the only folks on the face of this Earth who believe in a God and a Jesus what don't look like they do?"

"What you talkin' about?"

"Them Japs, f'r instance," explained Otis, "they got that there Booga or whatever that looks like them. Indians and Eskimos and A-rabs and Lord knows what-all, got a God that looks like them, and they all got their own feller like Jesus."

Tyrone just let 'im dig it deeper.

"It just don't make no goddamn sense," Otis went on, "that coloreds think a white God and a white Jesus is gonna do anymore for 'em, *ever,* than they's doin' right now. So how do you figger you got a better day comin'?"

Ol' Tyrone got out the skewer. "An' what," he smiled, "makes you so sure God ain't black?"

Wham!

Well, Otis was squirmin', but he tried to salvage what he could. "Ah guess ah don't really know. But they's some smarter people around than me *or* you, 'Rone. Like the people that make pitchers of Jesus, boy. You want me to prove what Jesus looked like?"

"That I do."

"Okay, Mr. Tyrone Jefferson, they got a *pitcher* of Jesus hangin' over there in Elroy's motel, an' you can just trot your ass right over there an' see for yourself that Jesus ain't like you! And if, *Jesus* ain't . . . like . . . you, you can bet your butt that *God* ain't . . . like . . . you, so there!" Otis looked like a Peacock in heat. But Tyrone wasn't gonna let 'im off *that* easy.

"That ain't no pitcher of Jesus, fool."

Otis snickered. "Oh, yeah? Then just what the hell is it?"

"That's a *paintin'* of Jesus," said Tyrone. "How were they gonna take a *pitcher* of Jesus two thousan' years ago? Shit, O', they ain't nobody knows what Jesus looked like, or God either. Christ, you don't know nothin'."

Otis leaned back in his chair, lookin' at me and Tyrone. He gazed around the station, across the highway, and off toward town, then beyond the Rio Grande over into Mexico.

Finally, not lookin' back at either of us, he said quietly, "You know, you just might be right, Tyrone. The Lord could be anything. Christ, he could be a wetback! Who else would come up with a godforsaken place like this?"

EDITOR'S NOTE—*At this point in his narrative, Dr. Hargus was heard in the second of four conversations with a man authorities concluded was Tyrone G. Jefferson, a trusted aide who assisted the Doctor during the recording of the Hargus Tapes. Mr. Jefferson's voice was the only other heard in any of the authorized taped material. In our effort to faithfully preserve the accuracy of the narrative and the sense of urgency that attended its communication, as well as to adhere to the conditions set forth for the tapes' transcription, each of the four exchanges has been included in its entirety.* (ED.)

Rev! Rev! Get your ass offa there! Quick! Hurry! God *damn!*

Jesus H. Christ, Tyrone, what th' hell is it *this* time?

Down there. The highway! They's people comin' up here, Rev!

Aw, Tyrone. Goddamnit, you *know* we gotta finish this. . . .

Rev, don't you argue with me now, baby! This is it! Come on! Let's get the fuck gone!

Christ! Will you please get yourself under control? Goddamnit, *goddamnit,* GODDAMNIT!

Shhhh, Rev. Jesus! Shut up! Aw, shit! *Now* you've done it. They've heard us. Oh, Gawwd. We're dead men. That does it. I'm goin'. We gonna get our ass locked up.

Tyrone, *stop!* You hear me? You just *stop!* Don't you move another inch!

Okay, Rev, okay. But we're dead.

Tyrone, just quit jumpin' up and down like you're about to wet your pants, and listen for a minute! Look. Just go on down there and see what the hell they want.

Oh, Jesus, Rev. It's the po-lice. I just know it!

Christ, Tyrone. I can see from here it ain't nothin' but a bunch of goddamn kids. Now go ahead on down there an' run their ass off.

> EDITOR'S NOTE—*At this point, a 3-minute-56-second interval occurs in the recording during which no words were spoken, but what were assumed to be footfalls could be heard retreating, then approaching, followed by laughter.* (ED.)

Well! What happened? An' what's so goddamned funny?

They wanna take your pitcher.

They wanna *what?*

They wanna take your pitcher an' they wanna know what the hell you're doin' up here.

Jesus Christ! What'd you tell 'em?

What th' fuck was I supposed to tell 'em? I told 'em you'd lost your goddamn mind.

Son of a bitch! You didn't tell 'em who I was, did you?

And get our ass locked up sure? Shit, Rev, give me credit f'r havin' a thimbleful of sense, will you?

No.

Aw, Rev.

Now get back down there and tell 'em they ain't gonna be no goddamn pictures and to get the hell outta here.

Okay, okay. But Rev, *please* listen to me. For the last time, let's go, son. Lord, it's gonna rain and, honest to God, I'm scared.

Tyrone, do what th' hell I told you, goddamnit!!

Don't have no fit now, son. I'll do it. I'll do it. Lord, Lord.

THE DEL RIO NEWS
★ HERALD ★

RIDDLE OF MINISTER'S DEATH STILL PUZZLES POLICE

DEL RIO—A mystery continues to cloak the death of the Reverend Gleason Beamer, the prominent local minister found dead last Sunday at the First Baptist Church of Del Rio.

Val Verde County Sheriff Buff Wallace, speaking with reporters yesterday, once again said he was certain foul play was involved in Beamer's death. "People just don't up and fall over dead," Sheriff Wallace said. "At least, not in my town they don't. We'll pin this thing. . . ."

REEL 6

◆

July 23,1950

A Sunday.

I lay awake, watchin' the little specks of dust float through a pillar of early mornin' sunlight, anglin' in through my bedroom window.

With my right hand, I reached over and swirled the dust into little patterns and circles, and watched it slowly settle back down again.

My left hand was holdin' onto my false idol. It felt like a tent stake. It had been that way ever since I woke up an' started thinkin' about last night. I tried, but I just couldn't get it off my mind, not with my idol down there just beggin' for some worship. Lordy, I thought, I sure do need a snappin'!

Step-Edna had come to my room about eight o'clock the night before, as I lay in bed readin' my new Bible.

"Billy?" she'd called from the doorway.

I looked up to see that she had on one of Elroy's shirts again and I knew another lesson was comin'.

"Yes, ma'am?"

She strolled over to my bedside then, her fingers twined behind her back and her hips thrust forward, sassy. A circle of light from my little lamp shone across her bare legs.

"My goodness," she said, talkin' sweeter than I think I'd ever heard her before, "you're just about to wear that ol' Book out, aren't you?"

Uh-oh. I felt somethin' kind of wakin' up down there in my heathen area.

Then, sitting down beside me on the bed, she said, "I'll bet you've read everything in there—probably twice." She looked down at me softly, and her eyes drifted toward my heathen region, which was beginnin' to betray me.

Step-Edna saw it, too. She smiled, and, bringin' her hands to her throat, she began unbuttonin' her shirt.

It was time for some learnin'.

I watched, fascinated as always by this part of the lesson plan, and I said, "Yes, ma'am. I sure do like to read the stories in my Bible, even if they kinda confuse me sometimes. That's why I read it so much, I guess, tryin' to straighten everything out." My eyes were followin' the progress of her hands, watchin' as the shirt fell open in an ever-widening V.

"Well, gracious me, boy," she said, as she reached the bottom button, "what's not to understand?"

The shirt slipped down about her waist. She leaned back across the foot of my bed, slow, proppin' herself on her elbows an' raisin' one knee. I remember thinkin' about the way a cat'll stretch real big when it first wakes up.

Her eyes locked on mine as one hand began tracin' lightly over her breasts, back and forth like a feather duster. I sure wished the breeze floatin' in through my window had been a little stronger.

"Well, ma'am," I stammered, closin' my Bible, "you know how Reverend Beamer's always tellin' us how th' Lord has a plan for everybody's life. . . ."

"Well, *I* told you that, too, silly," she interrupted gently.

"Yes, ma'am, I know, but . . ."

She reached for my hand and placed it on one of her breasts.

". . . in the Bible Jesus says that we all gotta . . ."

"Do you like the way Step-Edna's breasts feel, boy?" she whispered.

"Yes, ma'am." My wicked wand jumped. It was now

makin' the covers look like a circus tent. I sure hoped she would hurry an' give me a snappin', so I could get it under control and we could talk about th' Bible an' life."

"Reverend Beamer says that Jesus . . ."

"Take hold of the tips, honey. Easy—here, let me show you."

Oh, Lordy. This was gettin' a little tough. "Reverend Beamer . . ."

"Fuck Reverend Beamer," said Step-Edna. "Tell me how th' tips feel."

"They sure are hard, Step-Edna. I like the way they feel—a lot."

All of a sudden she sucked in her breath. She pulled my face to her and roughly guided one of her nipples right into my mouth. She moaned low in her throat and arched her back. "That's it, Billy boy," she said hoarsely. "Honor thy stepmother. That's the way. Mmmmmm. God! You're really learnin'!"

I mumbled against her, "But ma'am, I can't find nothin' in my Bible where th' Lord says what Reverend Beamer does, about havin' a plan, or tellin' somebody what he oughta be."

Step-Edna didn't answer. She released me, stood up quickly, and let her shirt fall to the floor. Her breasts glistened where she'd had 'em in my mouth. She started swayin', one hand massagin' her melons and the other rubbin' herself between her legs. She was moanin' again, a little louder. Finally, she said, "Okay. Tell Step-Edna what you mean, boy, an' hurry! Get it out! Come on!"

"Well," I began, "you know, what kind of job is everybody supposed to have? I mean, Jesus says in the Bible how we're supposed to act, but He doesn't say anything about what we should do, you know, with our lives. And that's not the way Reverend Beamer tells it."

She reached down and pulled the covers back on my bed, smilin' again, eyes heavy and her head movin' side to side. She murmured, "Oh, you silly. Look. I told you the Lord had a plan for your life. Reverend Beamer told you He has a plan. Now, that's all. Don't worry about it."

"Well, it don't say that in this Book," I said.

"Shhhh."

Step-Edna had layed down on the bed beside me now, tuckin' a pillow under her head and another, which I found strange, right beneath th' small of her back. She took my hand and placed it between her thighs, movin' it up and down through th' thick mat of hair there. "How does that feel now, Billy?" Her chest was risin' and fallin'. "Tell me. Tell your Step-Edna what it feels like. Come on, baby. Talk to me."

"Well . . . it feels kinda, I don't know, real warm an' all creamy."

"I want you to say it feels like a hot, steamin' cunt. Lemme hear you say it—come on—'a hot, steamin' cunt.' " She had pressed herself tight up against me an' her hand had stolen over to stroke my false idol. "My God. You're gettin' *big,* boy," she whispered, her lips brushin' my ear. Then she darted her tongue right inside and swished it around while she gripped my false idol, hard.

She lifted her head to look down toward my middle. "Lord, Billy, look at you! Feel it! I wanna see you feel yourself! Go on!"

I reached down an' covered her hand with my own as she nipped at my neck, her breath ragged, quick an' short.

"Tomorrow you're gonna be fifteen years old, darlin', an' Step-Edna's got a little surprise present for you."

Now she was strokin' my sinful rod of lust up an' down fast with her left hand, an' fingerin' herself between her legs with her right hand, both of 'em in rhythm.

My God! I was needin' a lesson *bad!* My idol had begun to throb like it never had before! My heathen flesh was burnin'. When was she gonna give me my snappin'? Then, all of a sudden, Step-Edna's arms went around me an' she pulled me over right square on top of her! Lord Jesus! "Snap it, Step-Edna," I pleaded. "Snap it now because the Devil's gettin' in it! Hurry! Oh, please!"

"No," she said. "Not tonight, boy. Not tonight. What we're goin' to do tonight," she said, thrustin' her hips up against mine, "is *hide* your false idol from the eyes of the Lord." Now she was grindin' back an' forth, heavin' herself against me and draggin' her fingernails up and down my back.

I found it hard to speak. "What are we . . . gonna . . . do with it?" I was near tears. "We . . . gonna put it . . . in a shoe . . . box? Can . . . we stick it . . . in a . . . jar?" I gasped.

"No, shhh . . . now just relax, relax. Leave everything to Step-Edna."

She reached down between her body and mine, grasped my member, and panted, "We've got a real special hidin' place for it." She grunted. "It goes . . . it goes right in . . . *there!*"

OHMIGOD! OHMIGOD! I had never felt anything like it!

Suddenly, warm, slipp'ry fingers, a thousand of 'em, gently wrapped 'round my idol an' squeezed, squeezed so nice. Step-Edna raised her hips an' the fingers pushed all th' way down to the base of my idol. She lowered her hips and they pulled all th' way back out to the tip. Oh, no! This was like no lesson ever before! "When's th' snappin', Step-Edna?" I begged. "When's th' snappin'? Please!"

Suddenly her legs wrapped around me. "No snappin' tonight, boy," she breathed. "No snappin' this time."

"But, but, my idol's gonna *spill!*" I cried. "I'm not strong enough yet to stop it."

"Shut up, boy, an' fuck me," she choked. "FUCK ME! DEEPER! DEEPER! COME ON, YOU LITTLE SHIT! FUCK ME! OH, GOD! HARDER! OH, JESUS! FUCK ME! FASTER!" She was whimperin' and a-groanin', her breath comin' in huge gulps. I thought I was killin' her. I told her between my own gasps that I didn't see how this was hidin' my heathen tool, if we were gonna keep takin' it out and puttin' it back . . . takin' it out an' puttin' it back.

But I don't think Step-Edna heard. She sounded like she'd lost her mind. She was screamin' about "The Comin'." At least, that's what I think she was sayin'. I truly did not understand. I *did* understand that somethin' was for sure about to happen down in my idol area. But I couldn't help it anymore. Every other time, way before my lesson had even come close to this point, Step-Edna would already have given me a snap.

But, "Not tonight, boy."

She was pumpin' her hips up and down now like the pillow under her back had electricity in it and was shockin' her. Our stomachs slid against each other an' made squishin' sounds.

And then, it happened.

I lost all control and surrendered to the terrible tension buildin' up somewhere inside of me like a volcano. There was no snappin'! There was no snappin'! There wasn't gonna *be* no snappin'!

Our bellies started slappin' against each other like they were applaudin'.

"That's it!" Step-Edna squealed. "That's it! Ohhhh, Jesus!"

It was awful. Our bodies blurred into one another. And then, all of a sudden, her hands clutched my shoulders like claws. Her eyes went big, then clamped shut, then started flutterin'. Her body arched off of the bed like a rainbow an' she screamed, shook, and screamed again. At the same instant, somethin' happened down deep inside of me that I was sure was the Devil's doin', even though it felt like heaven. My false idol exploded. It just exploded. I couldn't help it. I had failed . . . totally.

Step-Edna and I were fused together in that moment like somebody had welded us at the hips. We locked, held, and then fell back. She lay with one arm across her forehead, her breath hitchin' in her chest. I lay with my head off her shoulder a little bit, raggedly vacuumin' in air as I tried to get my breath. The covers were a hopeless tangle, soaked with sweat.

It took a good ten minutes, but at last, Step-Edna lay quiet. Then she turned her head to me an' smiled. "Happy birthday, boy."

My God. I'd forgotten. I was so ashamed.

. . .

Lookin' back on it, it hadn't seemed like much of a present at th' time. I had spilled the sinful milk of Satan from my godless flesh. I had been weak, despite all of Step-Edna's careful and loyal instruction. I know I resolved right then and there never to let it happen again. If ever I found myself in that shape at some other time, maybe in some other place, and there was nobody around to administer to me a snappin', then, by God, I'd snap it myself. That's what I'd do.

You see, I'd nearly been able to stop it. Almost. Step-Edna, after all, had taught me well over the years with what she called her "oral instruction." Gettin' me time and again right to the point of no return an' then, POW! Limp noodle time. Well, as I lay there that mornin', watchin' th' dust float in the sunshine, I just figured that if she could do it, then so could I. I felt myself again. Still like a tent stake. "Okay," I muttered under my breath as I pulled the covers and my pajama bottoms down. "Okay. *Satan, get thee out!!*"

POW!! ARRGGHH!! JESUS!! SHIT!!

AHHHH . . .

MMMMMM . . .

I peeked down. By God, I'd done it. There was a nice reddened area right on the tip an' it looked to me like it was huntin' for a place to hide, it had gotten so tiny. Perfect, I thought to myself. Just perfect.

And then it struck me: the real meanin' of what I'd just done. It was a staggerin' realization. All at once th' pieces snapped together and locked. Because, you see, I had done it. Not Step-Edna.

I had the control and I had made the choice!

Suddenly, the reason for Step-Edna's years of patient instructions became crystal clear, and Otis's often-repeated message about th' Bible allowin' us to take control of our own lives made perfect sense. For my false idol had challenged me on that Sunday morning, and I had won!

I HAD SNAPPED MY OWN DICK! ISN'T THAT WONDERFUL?!?

I felt prouder at that moment than I'd ever felt before.

"Come on, boy, it's time for church." It was Step-Edna. She'd stuck her head in my room. "Sleep tight, did you, birthday boy?" She winked at me slyly.

We attended Reverend Gleason Beamer's First Baptist Church; a white, Baptist church. There were others, of course: Congregational, Pentecostal, Methodist, Assembly of God, Catholic, Mormon, and th' black Mt. Zion Fire-Baptized Baptist Church. All of them others, Elroy said, was attended by people who fucked geese.

"White Baptists," he'd say, "are th' chosen people. Th' *only* chosen people." Actually, he'd say . . . well, you can imagine.

Even though ours was a rock-bound, fundamentalist Baptist church, nobody ever thumped th' Bible there. There was never any shouts of "Hallelujah," or, "Take me, Jesus," or talkin' in tongues. None of that stuff. About th' only thing you ever would hear sittin' out there in the congregation was "Pssssst. What time is it now?"

"Two minutes later than when you asked me the last time."

Th' reason for that was because Reverend Beamer never changed his sermon. Not once. Not a word. We'd been goin' there ever since I could remember and we'd heard the same sermon ten hundred times. Every single person in the congregation knew it by heart. As I look back, Otis was right—he was the most boring son of a bitch on the face of the Earth.

Elroy'd come upstairs and stuck his head in the door. "Haddy dirthday, doy." Jesus Christ. Here was the dumbest bastard alive.

I got up an' got dressed for church.

"Let's do, Dilly." It was Elroy—who else?—hollerin' up at me from down in the diner. "Ty-doan's dere."

"I'm comin'," I called back.

Each Sunday we'd load up Elroy's pickup truck—me, Step-Edna, Elroy, and Tyrone, who'd either stroll over from across the highway at Otis's station, or we'd wheel in over there to pick 'im up. Either way, Elroy'd always announce, just like it was a news bulletin, "All lowlifes in the dack of the truck." He was talkin', of course, about Tyrone. But I'd hop in the back, too, and ride with him.

Tyrone went *to* church with us, but he didn't go *in* with us. "We gots our own church, chile," he'd say, "but trubble is, I can'ts makes me no money ovuh there. Our people too po'." He'd wink and grin at me.

So, on th' way to church, Tyrone would set to work gettin' ready for what he called his "Flock Fleece." First, he dressed hisself in some raggedy, greasy ol' clothes he'd borrowed offa Otis. Ever' time, they'd argue over what *was* raggedy and what was, as Otis saw it, his Sunday go-to-meetin' best. Th' thing about it was, though, that Otis hadn't ever gone-to-meetin' in his life. "Tell Beamer," he'd holler at us as we drove away toward town, "that Otis Blackwood says t'blow it out his ass!"

He was one funny man.

After Tyrone had got his raggedy clothes on, next thing he'd do would be to strap up his legs with a pair of belts he'd cut down just for the purpose, pullin' his heels up tight against his rear end so's it looked like all he had was a pair of stumps. When we'd get to church, we'd lift 'im out of the pickup and set 'im down on a little wooden dolly he'd made that was mounted on roller-skate wheels. Usin' his hands to propel himself, ol' Tyrone would scoot over to the church steps, turn around, and plant hisself right square in the middle of 'em; right where you either had to go around 'im, left or right, or fall over 'im.

An' there he'd sit, wearin' a pair of sunglasses an' holdin' out an old, rusty, gallon paint can, greetin' the people.

"Yessir, boss, welcome to the House of th' Lord. My, my, ain't it a fine Sunday mo'nin'! Sho wish I could walk like norm'l folks can, but ah ain't complainin' none, nossiree. Good mo'nin', Missus Landry! Maybe you might have a nickel or a dime to he'p out a dumb ol' cripple boy here what ain't got nothin'?" He'd smile, noddin' first to this one, then to that one, just as happy, he'd say, "as any po' boy gots any rights to be!" And the coins would dribble into his bucket. Folks would always get kinda backed up at the steps, tryin' to get around Tyrone. When they tried to get by without puttin' anything in his bucket he had a way of sneakin' his knee out to the left or right an' trippin' 'em. Then he'd howl he was hurt. "Ohhh, Lord, Lord," he'd say. "You got me right there where I got hit goin' asho' on Iwo! No, I beez okay. It'll quit in jes' a minute. Could you spare somethin' for this po' veteran of the armed fo'ces? Yes, yes. Fought fo' my country an' give up my limbs. But 's all right. 'S all right. Jesus loves you fo' heppin' such a lowlife unfortunate as me."

"I wouldn't mind him comin' round the cafe," remarked Step-Edna, "if he always acted as nice there as he does here on Sunday mornings. But all he ever does is drag one of the girls off and fix her so she can't work or walk for a week."

And ever' time somebody would just brush on by 'im, or worse, slipped 'im a paper plate with a slice of watermelon on it instead of some change, you could hear Tyrone mutter under his breath, "Ignert muthafucka." But he'd still be smilin', sayin', "Thank you, Jesus. Thank you, Lord . . . I's jes' so damn happy."

Most everybody thought Tyrone was truly crippled, and really, they paid 'im pretty well. In fact, Tyrone claimed he was makin' more workin' the folks outside than Reverend Beamer was workin' 'em inside.

Small wonder, since the congregation kept slowly shrinkin' as folks finally would get a bellyful of hearing that same awful sermon time after time after time. Title? "The Lord Has A Plan For Your Life." The main reason people would put up with it was because we couldn't get no other preacher to come to Del Rio. Otis figured that the other reason people kept on goin' to Beamer's church, aside from the fact that it was th' town's one-an'-only all-white Baptist congregation, was because they were afraid not to, and because there wasn't any mail delivery on Sunday so there was nothin' else to do. Unless you made your own excitement, you see, Del Rio was about as stimulatin' as enema duty in an old-folks' home.

We'd all filed inside, leavin' Tyrone out there with his change dumped out in front of him, countin' the take. Reverend Beamer began the sermon. "Welcome, my friends." Here we go again, I thought. "Welcome to the House of th' Lord. We are gathered together," he said, spreadin' his arms wide, "to receive the Lord's blessin', the plan He has made for our lives, and to worship Him and feel His wondrous power. Let His spirit wash over you now and cleanse you and restore you, and give you peace."

"Give me a break," someone muttered.

"For His love passeth *all* understanding."

"An' you make me wanna passeth out."

Damn heathens. Most of 'em said there was but one good thing about Beamer's sermons. You couldn't understand much of 'em because he couldn't talk for very long without runnin' out of breath. We were about at that point. Reverend Beamer was very short and very fat. In order to be seen, he stood on a metal folding chair behind a pulpit from which a half-moon had been cut out so it would accommodate his stomach. When he spoke, after about three or four minutes had gone by, he'd start losing his breath toward the end of his sentences. The last few words would come out in little puffs, soundin' for all the world like the whoosh of a busted balloon. You got about the first six words—"And the Lord said to Adam"—and then you'd see his eyes start bulgin' and the veins in his neck'd tighten up, and everything else would be a wheeze until the next sentence. Though I thought he was wonderful at the time, I now realize that his runnin' outta breath was the only thing that made him barely tolerable.

When he'd spread those short, stubby little arms, he'd jerk 'em up and down, emphasizin' who knew what, an' with 'em flappin' like that it made 'im look like he was tryin' to fly. He had no neck you could see and beads of sweat would form on his forehead, run down his nose, an' drip onto the same old gray suit and vest he wore buttoned between his rolls of flab.

And where did we sit? Right up front. You couldn't have missed any of this if you'd a-wanted to. There we sat, front row, with Step-Edna between me and Elroy. "So I can keep Elroy's heathen carcass awake," she'd say, turnin' toward me so that her breast would press against my arm.

Reverend Beamer preached on. "Th' Lord has invited us into His splendid home . . . (gasp, gasp, wheeze, whoosh)."

The sweat was beginnin' to shine up there on his forehead an' he swiped at it with the back of his sleeve.

Did he say "splendid"?

Jesus. The inside of Beamer's church looked like the outside of Otis's fillin' station, with its patched-together pews, cracked windows, burned-out lightbulbs, and two big ol' wooden ceiling fans, both of which had a blade missin' so that they wobbled off balance when they turned.

Reverend Beamer pulled a huge handkerchief out of his hip pocket and mopped his brow an' the back of his head. He paused, and took a big drink of water from the pitcher and glass on the card table to his left. It helped. He kinda got a second wind.

"Many of you," he said, "are lost in the eyes of God. Many of you are miserable and unhappy. Your lives are an endless series of disappointments and frustrations. There are many here today . . ." His voice died away in a raspy wheeze.

"Oh, shit," someone muttered.

"Speak up, Beamer," somebody shouted.

Then someone else: "I can't hear."

Suddenly, Elroy, who had been noddin', let out a loud snore. Step-Edna dug her elbow into his ribs an' said, "Wake up, goddamnit. He's talkin' about you."

Elroy's head jerked up. "Huh?"

Somebody behind us said, "Shhhhh."

". . . who are lookin' beyond the Lord for an answer to their lives. But," said Reverend Beamer, pausin' for another drink of water, "th' Lord has The Plan. And to find out what it is, you must come to the Lord. And how do you get there?"

No one answered.

"You get to the Lord," the Reverend puffed, "through His Son Jesus Christ."

"Who'd he say?"

"Huh?"

"What's he talkin' about now?"

"Shhhhhh."

"I can't understand 'im."

". . . you must accept Jesus Christ as your personal savior. Turn your life over to Him. Ask forgiveness of your sins. Give Him your life . . . (snuff, snort, gasp, wheeze, *whoosh*)."

"My *wife?"*

"Whose wife?"

"Wait just a goddamn minute here!"

"Hey, Beamer, shut up an' let's sing a song, or somethin'."

It was the same every Sunday. We all reached for the hymnals in their racks on the backs of the pews, automatically turned to page fifteen, and started in:

"Whaaaaat a friend we have in Jeeeeesus. Alllll our sins and griefs to bearrr. Whaaaaat a priv'lege tooo caaaaary, eeevrything to God in praaaayer."

This was my favorite part. Th' singing. And I hated th' kids at the back of the church who, every time we sang the Amen, would add, "Wop-bop-a-loo-bop, a-wop-bam-boom."

They thought they was cute.

I thought they were heathens.

Finally, Reverend Beamer, wheezin', fished his old pocket watch out of his vest and, lookin' at it, said, "Well, we'll finish up next Sunday."

Now it was time for the offering. Reverend Beamer didn't have any bona fide collection plates. He'd borrowed some dishes from Step-Edna. In the middle of each one of 'em was written, THE E & E CAFE, and around the rim was the message, ASK ABOUT TODAY'S SPECIAL.

The plates whizzed up and down the pews, most of the people havin' already given their change to ol' Tyrone out there, at his one-man toll gate.

Reverend Beamer was flappin' his arms for attention. "It's time for the closin' prayer," he said.

"Lord," he began, "we thank You for this opportunity You have given us to come into Your house, and we thank You for washin' us in the glory of Your love. . . ."

Folks looked up, stretched, yawned, rubbin' sleep from their eyes, and strained to hear the final words . . . and it was over. Reverend Beamer, worn out, slumped into his metal foldin' chair for a moment. Then Elroy and a couple of the others went forward and helped him up, walkin' him back to the front door so he could bid farewell to th' faithful.

We all began filin' out.

"Wonderful message, Reverend."

". . . Thank you, child."

"Very inspirational, Reverend Beamer."

". . . Bless you."

"It sucked."

It was the same snotnosed kids who thought they was Buddy Holly.

It had dawned on me when we were singin' "What A Friend We Have In Jesus"; you know, the part about the burdens we bear 'cause we don't take 'em to the Lord in prayer. Well, here I was, burdened; tryin' to straighten out just what th' hell I was supposed to do with my life. Now, why hadn't I thought of this before?

Reverend Beamer. A man of God. I'd just take my burden to him.

I scrambled down the steps of the church and made a dash to the parkin' lot, hollerin' at Step-Edna just as she was puttin' a foot up on the runnin' board of Elroy's truck.

I put on my most pleadin' look an' asked her if I could stay and talk with Reverend Beamer.

"Why, what for, child?" She looked puzzled and a little suspicious.

"You know, ma'am," I said, "about last night's special lesson."

She nearly swallowed her cigarette and her hands flew to her throat. "You wanna *what?"*

I explained that I wanted to talk with Reverend Beamer about th' Lord's plan for my life.

Th' color that had drained away started creepin' back into Step-Edna's cheeks.

"Oh, *that,"* she said. "Jesus Christ, child, you gave me a start. Okay, you catch a ride home with Missus Hooper, all right?"

"Yes, ma'am!"

I trotted back to the church's dilapidated front porch where Reverend Beamer was tryin' to duck the last hangers-on, and not havin' much success. I stood at the bottom of the steps, off to one side, waitin', watchin', as he mopped his face with his handkerchief and tried to excuse himself so he could get in out of the sun. It really was fierce.

Finally, he was alone, wavin' a last goodbye to some folks still strollin' out to their cars. He turned to go inside and that's when he spotted me.

"Why, Billy," he said. He was still havin' some trouble catchin' his breath, it seemed. "Where's Edna and Elroy?"

"They went ahead on back to the café."

"They forget you?"

"No, sir."

"Well," he said, "how d'you propose to get home, Billy?"

"I'm s'posed to catch a ride with Missus Hooper."

"Oh . . . oh. Well, what're you doin' here, anyway?"

"Reverend Beamer," I started. "Can I talk to you about somethin'? It's real important."

He kinda sighed, heavy, but he said, "Sure, son, sure. What's on your mind?" He walked over and joined me where I'd sat down on the steps. "You got trouble?"

He was breathin' easier somewhat, but the sun caused 'im to squint through his glasses and his handkerchief just wasn't a match for his perspirin'.

"No, not real trouble, exactly, Reverend Beamer. It's just that . . . well, you know the Bible you gave me?"

He nodded, smilin', as he blotted his forehead with his sleeve.

"I can't find anything in there about the Lord havin' this here plan for my life, what I oughta be or what kind of job I oughta try to go out an' get."

I could see Reverend Beamer was sweatin' heavier now, though I hardly would have thought it possible. He loosened his tie, unbuttoned his vest, and popped open the first couple of buttons on his shirt, wipin' his throat with his handkerchief an' squintin' up at the sun.

"Well, boy," he began, and I noticed the wheezin' comin' back. "You see, there's nothin' real specific about all that in th' Bible. No, it's gotta be right in here." He pointed to his heart. "Th' Lord's plan for your life is just that you accept His Son Jesus as your personal savior, ask forgiveness of your sins, and . . ."

"I know, sir, I know all that stuff."

"Oh, you do, do you?" He sounded just a tiny bit annoyed.

"Please, sir, let me tell you what I mean."

He nodded, moppin' his face again. My Lord! He was sweatin' still worse now, an' he'd started feelin' his left shoulder, rotatin' the joint there like it was stiff or somethin'.

"Hurry up, Billy, I want to get in out of this sun."

His face was gettin' kinda red and it seemed I could see more little blood vessels than usual, fannin' out across his nose. I peered at him real close.

"You all right, sir?"

"Yes. Fine, fine. It's just the heat, an' my arm here's been painin' me off an' on the last couple of days. But it's okay. It'll quit directly. Why don t we go into my office, though, to continue this. It'll still be close, but at least we'll be out of this sun."

Grunting, I helped him to his feet. I needed, I realized, a tow truck. But I got 'im up and we walked inside, back up the aisle to the rear of the church, with the Reverend still a-wheezin' an' rubbin' on his left shoulder.

Reverend Beamer's office was a mop closet that'd had the slop sink tore out so's he could move in a card table an' some stuff. It was such tight quarters, though, that he had to back in. There wasn't room in there for him to have turned around. I nearly laughed out loud watchin' him. You know how a crawdad scoots backward into a hole in a rock or somethin'? The Reverend reminded me of a 250-pound crawdad. He finally got himself seated behind the table, I pulled up a foldin' chair on the other side, and he immediately commenced into fannin' himself with the New Testament.

"Okay, Billy." I noticed his breathin' now seemed real labored. "Where'd we leave off out there?"

"Well," I said, "what I don't understand is, once I do all that acceptin' Jesus and gettin' forgiven stuff, how come I just can't decide for myself what I want to do?"

Reverend Beamer's face looked to be losin' its redness, but a purplish tinge was creepin' up from his collar to replace it.

And he was gettin' short with me again.

"Well, boy, wouldn't it just be a fine how-do-you-do if everybody in this world jus' ran around doin' whatever they felt like, satisfyin' their own selfish little desires and ignorin' the wishes of the Lord? Wouldn't that just be a fine how-do-you-do?"

Now he was pissed.

"Damnit, boy," he snapped, "the Lord will reveal the plan for your life when He's goddamn good 'n' ready!"

He was coughin' now, huffin', puffin'. His eyes were popped out and the purple color was now all over his face. He was rubbin' his left shoulder hard, rockin' back an' forth a little in his chair, and I noticed his hand was purplish, too.

All of a sudden, I just wanted out of there. But he went

on. "Son, it sounds to me like you've got somethin' more on your mind."

"Yessir," I said. "I guess I do. You see, I've been learnin' the pleasure an' th' pain of doin' th' Lord's will from Step-Edna. . . ."

"Wonderful woman," he said, tryin' to smile. "Course, then, so was your mama. She wasn't like them others." He was coughin' again. No, this was more like chokin'.

"Yes, sir," I said, watchin' him real close, "but what I was gettin' at is, you know, what with learnin' the Lord's Will and studyin' His Word, I figgered maybe . . ."

Now, he *was* chokin' and I wasn't sure he could still hear me. But then he held up his hand to cut me off and sputtered, "You thought maybe *you* could run around now and tell everybody else what it is you've been learnin'?" He shook a finger at me as he clutched his chest with his left hand. "Well, see here, boy. You just let the Lord decide if that's what He wants you to do. Th' Lord . . ."

He gasped, his face now a beet purple.

"Th' Lord don't just pick every sucker that comes along to go around spreadin' His Word, you know." His hands were shakin' like leaves. "And . . . an' . . . He . . . certainly didn't intend for you or anyone else . . . to decide for themselves . . . what they oughta . . . do!"

I jumped up from my chair.

"Reverend Beamer!" His whole body was shakin'.

"Th' Lord," he choked, "will let you know!"

And with that, his body convulsed. His chair tilted backward as his hands shot forward, openin', closin', graspin' for balance.

Then, with a tremendous clatter, sweeping everything from the top of the table, the Reverend Gleason Beamer slumped sideways against the wall, slid slowly down to the floor, and died.

I just stood there, unable to move, staring down at that huge form. His tongue was violet and pushed out of his face, and his eyes were rolled back in his head. I was more scared than I thought it was possible for a human being to be. I started slowly edgin' back toward th' door, not even darin' to breathe.

That's when it caught my eye. The picture. It was on the floor, spilled from the cigar box of stuff that the Reverend's arm had swept off the table.

With a quakin' hand, I bent over, reached down, and picked it up. And as I looked, all of a sudden, standin' there in a mop closet with this dead fat man gapin' at me, I was struck by the glory of the Lord as surely as if somebody had walked up and hit me with a hammer.

It was the picture! Don't you see? My God, I was not alone!

There it was, clear as day. A snapshot of the Reverend Beamer, this dear man of the cloth, naked, lying atop one of his disciples. You couldn't see her face but I know it must've been filled with joy, for they were engaged in a sacred rite. Just *exactly* like my Step-Edna had taught me, they, too, were "Hidin' the Idol!"

I rejoiced. For I knew at that moment, at that crossroads, that I was truly on the Righteous Path.

There was an inscription on that wonderful photograph. It read simply:

To Reverend Beamer,
Y'all come by anytime.
Love,
Wilma.

THE DEL RIO NEWS ★ HERALD ★

DEATH OF LOCAL MINISTER SADDENS BOONE MOSES CRUSADE

Del Rio Youth Detained in Beamer Case

DEL RIO—The famed Boone Moses Crusade of Miracles is embarking upon its fall campaign, and Dr. Moses's schedule this year includes a stop in Del Rio.

Dr. Moses says the purpose of his trip here is twofold: to spread the Miracle of the Message in Del Rio, and to honor the memory of the late Reverend Gleason Beamer, pastor of the First Baptist Church.

Meantime, a local youngster, 15-year-old Billy Sol Hargus, has been remanded to the custody of Juvenile Authorities to await possible action against him in Reverend Beamer's death. . . .

REEL 7

◆

"All rise."

Step-Edna squeezed my arm. "Don't worry, boy." She managed a weak smile. "Just tell 'em the truth."

"The Juvenile Court, county of Val Verde, state of Texas, Judge Selmon Higgins presidin', will now come to order."

A door off to the left of the bench swung open, and Judge Higgins swept through, his black robes flowing, a fistful of manila folders tucked under his arm. He walked purposefully to the back of the bench, raised his right foot to mount the short stairway, snagged his shoe in the hem of his robe, and fell flat on his face.

Horrified, a bailiff and a sheriff's deputy rushed over to help him to his feet, grabbin' him beneath the arms, but he yanked loose. "Get your goddamned hands off'n me!" he hissed.

When he finally got seated in his high-backed chair and his face poked up above the bench, I could see an ugly welt right across the bridge of his nose, and the wire rims of his glasses were out of whack so that the right side dropped half an inch lower than the left. The razor-straight part in his white hair was still in place though, neatly dividing his head into equal halves. Still, he looked disheveled. That'd been a hard fall. He'd really cracked his nose a good 'un.

And that's just all I needed. He looked like he was ready to string somebody up and he didn't care who or what for.

"I'm scared, Step-Edna."

"Shhhh. It's gonna be all right."

"Please be seated," said Judge Higgins, as he forced a tight little smile onto his face. Maybe it would be all right, like Step-Edna said. There was a shuffle as the seventy or so people wedged into the little courtroom sat down and adjusted themselves, tryin' to get comfortable on the hard benches.

Then I heard it.

Somebody snufflin' and a-whimperin'. I looked around behind me. A row back and across the center aisle there was a lady with a tissue pressed to her nose, leaning on another lady who was pattin' her shoulder. They both had boxes of Kleenex in their laps.

I turned around again as Judge Higgins cleared his throat and began to speak:

"Ladies and gentlemen, we are convened here this morning in the matter of the death of the Reverend Gleason Beamer." The cryin' lady let out a sob. "I should like to make it clear," Judge Higgins cautioned, "that despite a lot of rumor and speculation, and especially some editorial assertions made by Frank Crowley in *The Del Rio News Herald,* that no one has been or is being charged with any crime."

Well. I was certainly relieved to hear *that!*

"Even though," Judge Higgins went on, fixin' me with a stare, "I think probably that a certain somebody *oughta* be charged with one!"

As he spoke, he half-rose out of his chair and leaned way out over the bench, his eyes lookin' darts at mine. All of a sudden I saw the back bottom edges of the bench begin to lift. It was Judge Higgins's weight! He was overbalancin' the thing. It wavered for just a moment and then, just like it was on hinges, the whole bench pivoted right on over and toppled into the front of the courtroom with a tremendous crash. Judge Higgins, looking around desperately, rode it down like a waterbug on a toilet lid.

Wood splintered, a pitcher of water that had been atop the lectern catapulted off and smashed, and the front row of spectators scattered like leaves in a gust of wind.

Stunned, everybody just sat, not quite believin' what they'd just seen. Then, a voice came thinly out of the wreckage:

"There'll be a ten-minute recess. . . ."

When we reassembled inside the courtroom the bailiffs and sheriff's deputies had dragged the smashed lectern off to one side, set up a long folding table in its place, and Judge Higgins was now seated behind that.

His glasses were gone and he had a Band-Aid coverin' what I presumed was a pretty nasty gash over one eye. A bailiff was bendin' over the table, quietly tellin' him about how they hadn't been able to get all his papers sorted out again in his case file.

The Judge told him, in a harsh whisper that carried five rows toward the rear of the room, "Fuck 'em. Stick 'em in any damned way you can!"

"But Judge . . ."

"Fuck 'em, I said! Call th' first case. . . ."

"Uh, Judge, 'member? It's the Hargus boy. The Beamer thing?"

"I know, I know, goddamnit! Where th' hell was I?"

"You'd just stated before the court, sir, the purpose of th' hearin'. You know, sayin' how nobody's been charged or nothin', but somebody, you figgered, sure as hell *oughta* . . ."

"I know what I'm doin', you goddamn baboon! Now get outta my face before I find you in contempt of this court!" Glowerin' at the man, he raised his gavel and brought it down with a crack, square on the fingers of his left hand.

I believe you coulda heard the Judge all the way back to the E & E.

Ol' Otis was sittin' in the bench right behind us. He'd kept hisself under control through th' Judge fallin' up the stairs and turnin' over his lectern, but this was too much. He exploded laughin'. He howled. He cried. He stomped his feet. 'Course, he was far from alone. The whole damned place was in an uproar. People were jabbin' their fingers toward th' Judge and absolutely *roarin',* tears in their eyes. Judge Higgins, his face goin' red, started yellin' for order.

"Order! Order in this court!" He was on his feet, gingerly holdin' the hand he'd whacked, which was swollen and startin' to turn purple, and he was hollerin'.

"I SAID ORDER, GOD-DAMNIT! ORDERRRR!"

But the place was just gone.

Judge Higgins whirled around and stabbed at a button located on the back wall. All of a sudden, the doors at the top of the aisle crashed open and a swarm of sheriff's deputies rushed in, led by ol' Mr. Order hisself, Buff Wallace. He had a revolver in each hand.

"TH' JUDGE SAID ORDER!" he screamed. "ORDER!" and he started firin' into the air.

Suddenly, screams replaced the laughing as everybody started diving under benches and behind tables. The rest of the deputies unlimbered their guns and started backin' up Buff. It sounded like the goddamned Alamo. Plaster was flyin', windows were shatterin', and there were groans and shouts.

"Get down!"

"Watch your head!"

"Jesus Christ!"

"OH, MY GAWD! WE'RE GONNA BE KILLED!"

"Somebody call the goddamned Sheriff!"

"Son of a bitch, it *is* th' Sheriff!"

"Goddamnit, Buff!"

I'd curled up on the front bench, tryin' to roll myself into a ball. Step-Edna and Elroy had dived forward under Judge Higgins's table, then they'd all three flipped it up so that it made a shield between them and the action.

The Judge was now peekin' over the tabletop, shoutin' at the top of his lungs at Sheriff Wallace. "CEASE FIRE! CEASE FIRE, YOU GODDAMNED IDIOT! DO YOU HEAR ME? CEASE FIRE!"

Sheriff Wallace swung around, smoke curling from his pistols. He saw Judge Higgins peeping over the table and nodded.

"Okay, men," he said. "That's it. We got 'er under control. Right, Judge?"

Judge Higgins's voice sounded like he'd been sick a long time or somethin'.

"Right, Buff. Right. You've got 'er under control."

The Judge got shakily to his feet. Elroy helped him set the table up straight as Buff and his boys filed out. Slowly, people started peerin' out from beneath benches. Heads poked out here and there, then they cautiously stood up, dustin' plaster off themselves and countin' fingers and toes.

Elroy and Step-Edna came back over and sat down beside me. Otis got up off the floor and eased down again on the bench behind us. Judge Higgins righted his chair and sat down behind the table. Then, with a little shudder, he said weakly, "First witness."

It was the cryin' fat lady. A court officer led her to the witness stand, seated her, and swore her in. She was dabbin' at her eyes with a wad of tissue. The woman was easily as fat as Reverend Beamer had been. She had huge red cheeks, flushed even more by all the excitement, crushin' a tiny little pink mouth. Big green curlers clung to her head like fat caterpillars. Judge Higgins spoke to her.

"Now, Missus Beamer," he said, "would you kindly tell us when and how you discovered your husband this past July twenty-third?"

She began to cry again, and she glared at me. "I found my poor Gleason," she said, "right where that little murderer left him!" She was pointing at me like I was a virus. "He was in the office at the church," she sobbed, "layin' up agin' the wall!" There were gasps around the courtroom and the place broke out in mutterin'. Judge Higgins called for quiet, as my mind jumped back to that Sunday.

Right after Reverend Beamer had keeled over and I'd found the holy picture, I'd stuffed it in my pocket and had run, terrified, all the way back to the cafe. Step-Edna had seen me tearin' across the parkin' lot and had run around from behind the counter to throw open the screen door for me.

"My God, boy," she'd said, "what's wrong? What is it?"

I was breathin' so hard, tryin' to talk through my gasps, that she couldn't understand a thing.

"Whoa, child," she said, takin' me by the shoulders, "whoa. Lord, you're white as a ghost!"

Finally, I had choked it out. "He's dead, Step-Edna! Reverend Beamer. He . . . he's dead!"

Then I'd gotten downright hysterical, bawlin', sobbin', and Step-Edna shook me. "What? What is it you're sayin', boy? Jesus Christ! Elroy!" she'd screamed. "ELROY!"

Sittin' there in the courtroom now, I would've given a hundred million dollars if it'd never happened . . . if I'd *had* a hundred million. 'Course, all things in due time.

Otis, sittin' there behind us, had listened to Missus Beamer on the witness stand and had got about all he intended to take. Before anybody could stop him he'd jumped to his feet and hollered at her, "Why, you fat sow! You don't know what th' hell you're talkin' about!"

Judge Higgins pounded his gavel on the table, takin' care to put his left hand in his lap first. "Mr. Blackwood!" he shouted. "That'll be just about enough!"

Otis sat down, but grumbled, "Aw, shit, Selmon. You an' me both know that this boy ain't done one goddamned thing."

"Mr. Blackwood!"

"All right, all right."

"You may step down, Missus Beamer."

Mrs. Beamer squeezed out of the witness chair like a cork out of a bottle and waddled back to her friend.

Then, gesturin' to me, Judge Higgins said, "Son, step up here and let's see if we can't get to the bottom of this."

Step-Edna put her hand on my thigh, squeezed, and smiled at me. "Go ahead, son," she said quietly, "it's goin' to be fine."

"Yes, ma'am," I said, and went with the bailiff to the witness stand. I sat down and looked at Judge Higgins.

"Now, son," he began, "is this your full name—Billy Hargus?"

"Billy *Sol* Hargus, sir," I corrected.

"Ummm-huh." He erased somethin' on a piece of paper and then jotted in the new information.

"Are you in school, son?"

Step-Edna raised her hand. The Judge nodded to her and said, "Yes, Missus Hargus?"

"Your honor, if I can I'd like to say that the boy's scheduled to be goin' back to school in th' fall, but some of the kids here in town have been makin' it a little rough on him. They're callin' him 'killer,' an' the like."

Judge Higgins looked concerned. "I see. Yes. Thank you. The clerk'll make a note of that, please. They're callin' the murderer here 'killer.' Thank you, Missus Hargus. And may the court just state for the record, ma'am, that you are a fine, upstandin' woman." He smiled. " 'Course, so was the boy's mother." Then, lookin' down at his papers, he added, almost so's you couldn't hear him, "She wasn't like the others."

Turnin' back to me, the Judge asked, "Is it true that the other children are callin' you 'killer,' boy?"

"Yes, sir."

"Well, *did* you kill Reverend Beamer?"

"No, sir. I most surely didn't. I didn't do nothin' to him. He just fell over, sir, honest. That's all he did. He just fell over right out of his chair onto the floor."

"All right, son. Take it easy. You did leave him there,

though, didn't you? Sprawled out against the wall while you ran all the way home. Now, that's true, isn't it?"

"Yes, sir, I did. I was terrible scared, sir. I didn't know what to do, so I just ran."

Judge Higgins was frowning. "Didn't you think that just maybe gettin' some grownup help from nearby would've been a good idea? Couldn't you have run out to the road an' stopped a car goin' by an' told somebody that somethin' was wrong with Reverend Beamer?"

"I . . . I don't know, sir. I guess so."

"You *guess* so." Judge Higgins said the words slowly, emphasizin' each one. He reached up with a finger to push his glasses back up on his nose, but quickly brought it down again, rememberin' his glasses were broke.

"Well," he went on, "before Reverend Beamer fell over, you *did* help him to get a glass of water, didn't you? You did do that, right?"

"Yes, sir."

"Why?"

"Because he got to coughin' real bad."

"So you thought the water would help him?"

"Yes, sir, an' he asked me to pour it for him."

"And yet," Judge Higgins went on, his voice risin' as he looked around the room, "and yet, when the Reverend fell, chokin' his life out, gaspin', wheezin', slobber runnin' out of the corners of his mouth, eyes bugged out like a frog's, you *ran?"*

(A cry and a sob from Missus Beamer on the other side of the courtroom.)

"Yes, sir," I answered. "But I didn't just run away, sir, I really didn't. I went to get help at home. Honest. I was just so scared."

"You were scared? And what did you think Reverend Beamer was?"

"Well, I guessed he was dead."

"Oh! You 'guessed' he was dead. Tell me, boy, are you a doctor?"

"No, sir."

"How many dead men you seen in your lifetime, boy?"

"Just Reverend Beamer, sir."

"So," his voice risin' again, "in other words, you had never seen anybody dead before in your life, but suddenly, there in Reverend Beamer's office, you became an authority?"

"I've seen lots of cats an' things, sir, mashed out on the highway."

"Don't you get flip with me, boy."

"I didn't mean to, sir."

"Isn't it a fact that you didn't really *know* Reverend Beamer was dead?"

"Well, no . . . I mean, he sure didn't look alive or anything."

"Hmph! Well," the Judge said, riffling through a file of papers, "would it interest you to know that we've got eyewitness reports here from a number of people who say they saw you and th' Reverend, shortly before he suffered his fatal attack, out on the front steps of the church?"

"Yes, sir."

"And these same people tell us that the Reverend looked to be waggin' a finger at you. The next thing they know is that you're pullin' him to his feet and walkin' him back into the church. That a fact, boy?"

"Yes, sir, but it wasn't the way you're makin' it sou'—"

"You'd threatened him there, hadn't you, boy?"

"No, sir! I most surely had not! I was just a-talkin' to him. That's all. Honest!"

"Talkin' to him? About what, boy? *Killin'* him?"

"Oh, no, Judge Higgins, no, no! I was just asking him about the Lord's plan for my life. You c'n ask Step-Edna, honest."

I turned toward Step-Edna and Elroy.

"Hadn't I, Step-Edna? Hadn't I just run out to th' truck an' asked you if I could stay an' talk to Reverend Beamer about plannin' my life? Tell 'em, Step-Edna, please!"

Judge Higgins turned to Step-Edna and looked at her questioningly. "Well?"

She shrugged.

Judge Higgins looked back at me, th' suspicion deepening in his face.

"Now, son," he warned, "it'll go better on you if you're honest with me here. Talkin' to a minister of the Gospel about the Lord doesn't hardly appear to be somethin' that would cause him to get angry . . . so angry that he'd blow a gasket!"

(Another sob from Missus Beamer.)

"No, sir. I . . . I guess it wouldn't. But Reverend Beamer wasn't mad about that, about me talkin' to him."

"So, you're admittin' there was something else, then?"

"Well, no, sir, I mean, I . . ."

"You *did* threaten to kill him, didn't you, and scared him so bad that he died?"

"No, Judge Higgins . . . I . . ."

"Then why . . . just *why* didn't you go get help?"

"I did, sir . . . I . . ."

"You'll do well not to interrupt me again!"

One of the bailiffs jumped to his feet.

But Judge Higgins motioned him back down. He wiped his forehead with a tissue and took a drink of water from a thermos one of the deputies had brought in to replace his shattered water pitcher. He looked down at my case file spread out in front of him, shook his head, sighed, and said to himself, "I just don't know here. I just don't know."

"Sir?" I asked cautiously.

"Yes, boy?"

"You know what made Reverend Beamer get mad?"

"Well, of course not. That's what we're tryin' to get to here."

"Well, what it was, sir, honest now, was that I had told him how I couldn't find in my Bible where it says God has a plan for your life, leastways nothin' like the way Reverend

Beamer was always sayin', so I asked him how come it was, then, that a person couldn't just decide for himself what he wanted to be, and that's when he started gettin' real mad."

Judge Higgins looked squarely at me. "Well, of course he did, boy. God *will* reveal a plan for your life just like Reverend Beamer always taught! You'll do well to stop wonderin' so much and meddlin' in th' Lord's affairs." Then, gesturin' toward Otis, he said, "Now, just look there. There's a prime example of what happens to a person what runs off doin' anything he wants to do. Just look at that!" He slapped his hand on th' table and knocked over his thermos bottle. Otis turned around and looked behind him like he was tryin' to find who the Judge was talkin' about.

"And," the Judge went on, "you'll do yourself a big favor, young man, if you stop hangin' around with the likes of that Tyrone Jefferson, too."

"Yes, sir," I said.

Judge Higgins paused, thinkin', and he drummed his fingers on th' tabletop. After a minute or so he said, "I'm afraid that we're going to have to have you bound over for Grand Jury action, boy. It looks like I have no choice except to hold you on suspicion of murder in the death of the Reverend Gleason Beamer!"

He brought his gavel down with a crack. The head flew off and hit him in the mouth. It sounded like a gunshot in the hushed room. I just sat, real quiet for a moment, but then I decided that I had to tell 'im.

"Sir?"

"What is it?" He was feelin' a front tooth to see if it was loose.

"There was one other thing."

"What was that?"

"Well, it was a picture I found on the floor after Reverend Beamer fell down. It was a holy picture, sir, and because I found it, I now know that anything you decide to do with me will be the will of the Lord, sir, and the right thing, and just what I deserve."

"Huh? What are you talkin' about? Where's this picture, boy?"

"I got it right here in my pocket."

The whole courtroom kinda leaned forward, hopin' to catch a glimpse of whatever it was I had.

"Here, sir, see? It's a holy picture of Reverend Beamer with one of his disciples." I had leaned over to the Judge, pointin' out the details in the snapshot. "See? That's him right there conductin' a holy rite. And see, right back there, kinda in that corner? The fella takin' the picture reflected in the mirror there? That's you."

I was back at Otis's garage.

A couple of weeks had passed since Judge Higgins had recommended that I be placed on probation and no further charges against me be considered.

I was sittin' on the steps out front, watchin' Ol' Green ignore th' cars goin' by. Otis was up on the porch, sittin' readin' the paper. He tossed it to me.

"Would you just look at what that bastard newspaper id-jut wrote in there," he said.

The headline read: RENOWNED MAN OF GOD LAID TO REST.

Otis reached over and grabbed the paper back from me. " 'Renowned,' my achin' butt!" he said. "Where's he come off sayin' that? That fat fart Beamer wouldn't have made a pimple on a real preacher's ass. Not like Billy Sunday, God bless 'im. Now *there* was a preacher!"

"Billy Sunday? Who's he?"

"You mean, who *was* he," Otis corrected. "Died the year you was born, son. But ah'm here to tell you, th' man could flat lay on a sermon! Jesus Christ! An' they knowed him from here to there, just like Boone Moses. But *this* tub o' turds?" Otis rattled the paper at me for emphasis. "Good Gawd almighty!"

"Is he dead, too?" I asked.

"Who?"

"The other one you said."

"Who? Boone Moses? Lord, God, I hope to shout he ain't dead. And is *he* somethin' else. I'll tell you somethin', boy. You see right over there by th' tire rack?" Otis pointed off to his left, out in the driveway. "Well, ah'll have you know Boone Moses hisself stood right in that very spot, back there . . . lessee, back about '34 it was, while ah fixed his big ol' Crusade bus. The whole damned mess of 'em was in here; th' bus, th' truck that hauls the tents an' stuff, buncha cars, all of 'em, right here! Can you imagine that? Bus broke down right in front of ol' Otis Blackwood's fillin' station and out stepped Boone-by-God-Moses!" Shakin' his head at the wonderment of the recollection, he got up to go inside, still mutterin' to himself. "Boone Moses. Right here. I still can't believe it happened."

I sat there on the steps, quiet for a moment; then, just as Otis's hand was pullin' open the screen door, I asked him, "Otis, who's Boone Moses?"

Otis froze in the doorway, half in, half out. He turned around real slow and looked at me utterly thunderstruck.

"What'd you ask me?"

"Who . . . who's Boone Moses?" I thought he was gonna backhand me or somethin'.

"You asked me, 'Who's Boone Moses?' "

"Yes, sir. I'm . . . I'm sorry, Otis, I didn't . . ."

Otis's mouth flopped open an' he just stared at me. Then he threw th' paper down on the porch and stalked into the station, slammin' the screen door behind him so hard it caused Ol' Green to raise his head. Understand, a stick of dynamite set off under his nose wouldn't have made Ol' Green raise his head once he was asleep.

I picked up the paper, sat back down on the steps, and started readin' the article about poor old Reverend Beamer. It didn't say a whole lot. Mostly stuff I already knew.

I flipped open the next page, though, and learned somethin' I *didn't* know. The whole lower half of page two shouted the identity of . . . Boone Moses!

REVIVAL

THE MAN WITH THE MIRACLE ARM, BOONE MOSES, ONE NIGHT ONLY, OCTOBER 15TH. COME TO THE "MIRACLE TENT," TWO MILES NORTH ON ROUTE 90 AT THE JUNCTION OF HIGHWAY 277. SEE, HEAR, AND YES, PERHAPS TOUCH THE LEGENDARY BOONE MOSES.

IS THEE AFFLICTED? THOU SHALL BE HEALED.

IS THEE TROUBLED? THY BURDEN SHALL BE LIFTED.

IS THEE CONFUSED? THOU SHALL BE ENLIGHTENED.

IS THEE WEAK OF SPIRIT, FAINT OF FLESH? A TOUCH FROM DR. MOSES'S MIRACLE ARM SHALL SUSTAIN THEE AND LIFT THEE UP!

YEA, VERILY, IT IS THE BOONE MOSES CRUSADE OF MIRACLES, IN TEXAS! BRING YOUR FAMILY AND TELL YOUR FRIENDS.

"Otis!" I shouted. "Otis! Just wait till you see here!" I scrambled up off the steps and ran inside. "Otis! Where are you?"

Tyrone shuffled out from his little quarters over behind the compressor. "He's out back, boy, burning th' barrel. What you want?"

"Lookit, Tyrone. Right here in the paper. It's the man Otis was talkin' about!"

"What man? Lemme see."

I held the paper so's we could both look at it.

"Well, I'll be a son of a bitch. I thought he was a-bullshittin' us, like usual."

"No, Ty', this here's Boone Moses. Lookit. There's his picture."

In the upper corners of the ad there were photographs of a man with long, knotted, gray hair, kneeling before a wheelchair. He had one arm restin' on his knee and the other was extended, palm out, to the bowed head of a person in the chair. The expression on his face was like he was in pain, and on the floor around him was a shower of dollar bills.

In the lower right-hand corner of the ad was an accompanying "news" story. It said that Dr. J. P. Boone Moses had announced from his headquarters in Tulsa, Oklahoma, that his Texas crusade would be includin' a stop in Del Rio. There was a quote from Dr. Moses sayin' how he would be goin' down there to honor the memory of his dear old friend, the Reverend Gleason Beamer, whose untimely passin', according to Dr. Moses, "had left a huge void in the ranks of God's messengers on Earth."

The item concluded with a word of advice to the faithful, that if they intended to witness one of Dr. Moses's Miracle Meetings live, they'd better seize this opportunity. Though in apparent good health, the Doctor, the story said, was nevertheless gettin' on in years and the current crusade might be his last.

Tyrone took it all in again. "Well, ah'll be goddamned!"

He jumped up and headed 'round back to tell Otis the news, his voice trailin' off as he shouted, "Hey, Otis! Burn that shit some other time. Guess what Billy found in th' paper. You ain't gonna believe it!"

I turned back to my readin' and flipped another page. There was a legitimate news item headlined on page four that made me think that, just maybe, ol' Del Rio might be a-gettin' on th' map.

It read:

Only God Can Make a Tree But Washington Tries Its Hand at Forests

WASHINGTON—The Del Rio, Texas, Armistad Lake Basin has been chosen for a federally funded demonstration project in forestry science. A spokesman for the Department of the Interior says a three-thousand-acre site twelve miles north of Del Rio on Armistad Lake's Pecos River arm is being designated as a sheltered

> preserve, under the auspices of the National Park Service.
>
> The site will be used for forestry experimentation to determine which species of coniferous trees might be adaptable to southwestern Texas's harsh climate.
>
> The project is expected to create some 100 jobs in the local area. Construction work at the site has already begun and the first shipment of 10,000 seedlings has been delivered and awaits planting.
>
> The goal of the project is to determine whether a complete coniferous forest can be established in this latitude, including animal life such a forested area would normally be expected to sustain.

"Billy! Billllly!" I looked up from the paper and saw Step-Edna, hollerin' at me from across the highway. She was standin' just outside the door of the diner, and there was a stranger beside her lookin' over this way. He had on a suit an' was carryin' a briefcase.

"There's a man from the Juvenile Authority here wants to talk to you."

Oh, shit.

"Yes, ma'am."

Tyrone and Otis were comin' around the corner of the station, talkin' excitedly, Otis goin' on and on about this visit of Boone Moses. I could tell from the sound that he was just about beside hisself.

I stood up and hollered at 'em, "You think *that's* something, look at this! We're about to get us a forest!"

"What the hell are you talkin' about?" asked Otis.

"Lookit here. You think this Del Rio ain't becomin' just somethin'? Lookit. We're gettin' us a national park."

"A what?" said Otis, grinnin'. "Gimme that paper."

"BILLLLY! DID YOU HEAR ME TALKIN' TO YOU?"

"Yes, MA'AM! I'm comin'!"

. . .

I wandered back over to Otis's about three quarters of an hour later. He was just finishin' up lubricatin' some ol' boy's pickup. He saw me comin' across the drive, ducked his head out from under the chassis, and wiped his hands on a rag that was dirtier than his hands had been in the first place.

"Well?" he asked.

"Well what?"

"Damn it, now, Billy, don't go pullin' that shit with me."

"Ohhhh. You mean the Juvenile Authority guy?"

"Yes, I mean the 'Juvenile Authority guy.' Now, what the hell did they want with you?"

"Work."

"Work?"

"Yep."

"What d'ya mean, 'work'?"

"They want me to go to work."

"Well, So do I. Now get your bucket and scrub down th' pop machine. Damn thing's gettin' greasier than the bottom of this here truck." Otis thumped his fist on an axle.

"No, Otis, you don't understand. They want me to *go* to work, for them."

"How's that?"

"They got me a job."

"Just what the hell's wrong with the one you got right here?"

"Ain't nothin' wrong with th' one I got here except it ain't th' one they want me to have."

"And just what is?"

"You ain't gonna believe it. . . ."

"Try me."

"You know the article we was readin' in th' *Herald?* About that new forest they're fixin' up out by the lake?"

"Yeah."

" 'Member how it said it was gonna make jobs for some people around here?"

"Yeah." Otis paused. Then he said, "Wait just a minute. . . . You?"

"Yep. Me."

"Jesus Christ, Billy. You gonna go plant itty bitty twees? Is that what bigums Billwy's gonna do? Grow wittle pwants? Myyyyy, my!"

"Aww, shit, Otis. I don't wanna go do it, but I got to."

Otis shook his head, not wantin' to believe what I was tellin' him. "And you're gonna plant *trees?* Jesus!"

"Well, not exactly. I'm gonna be a forest ranger."

Otis laughed. Then he looked off up the road in the direction of Lake Armistad. "How in the hell," he asked, "do they think they're gonna build a goddamned forest in this kinda crap?" He bent down and picked up a handful of clay dust. "And you're gonna be a forest ranger?" He looked back up the road again as he sifted dirt out through his fingers. "Well, boy, let's go up on the porch and talk this through. Tyrone? 'Rone? Where are ya, boy? Get off your dead ass an' on your dyin' feet, 'cause you and me and Billy here's gonna talk."

Tyrone shuffled out onto the porch. Otis looked at 'im.

"Park it," he ordered.

I'd already taken my customary position on the steps. Otis leaned back up against the buildin' in his frayed ol' wicker chair, and Tyrone lowered himself into his beat-up rocker. It was worn more on one side than the other, so that it made a little "clip clop" noise as it wobbled back and forth.

We were all just gettin' set down comfortable when suddenly, like a razor slashing through the heavy afternoon, there was a horrible scream of tires on asphalt. It was followed by the goddamndest string of swearin' you ever heard. We looked up. Yep. Ol' Green had gone to sleep again out on the yellow dividing line in the middle of the highway, lyin' on it crosswise.

Stopped not a quarter of an inch from his hind legs was a Packard, tires smokin'. Green was lyin' facing the other way and he hadn't even flinched.

"GET THE HELL OUTTA TH' ROAD!" Otis hollered, getting to his feet. "JESUS CHRIST, WHAT A STUPID ANIMAL. COME ON, YA IDIOT, OUTTA THERE! Sorry, mister. Next time, do me a favor an' run over the sumbitch, will ya?"

The guy in the Packard backed up and then pulled way to the right to get around Green, who opened one eye, yawned, smacked his lips a few times, and then went right back to sleep, his muzzle twitchin' away a fly. What a fuckin' dog.

"Here, Billy," Otis said, flippin' me a big screwdriver after things settled down again, "beat the bottlin' company out of a couple of Grapettes over there, will ya?"

I got up, went over to the pop machine, and levered out three of 'em, handed one to Tyrone and one to Otis, then we sat down to do some serious talkin' about forest rangerin'.

It quickly became apparent that everything we knew about forestry and growin' shit woulda rattled if you dropped it in a thimble.

Finally, Otis asked me, "Now, son, is this forest-growin' really what you want?"

"Well, it don't seem like it matters none what I want."

"Now, don't you go knucklin' under to that crap, boy," said Otis. And then Tyrone chimed in, "Lord, nice-lookin' white boy like you? Shoot, son, you be just what th' hell you want, hear?"

"Well," I said, "I really think that what I want to do with my life, that is, if I really could, would be to just keep learnin' about th' Lord an' doin' His will, you know? Just like Step-Edna says. And . . . I don't know, maybe someday I could tell people about th' Lord."

Tyrone looked at me for a moment, confused, then he said, "You talkin' about preachin', boy?"

I just stared down at my feet and kinda shrugged.

Otis thought a moment. "Well, you better oughta think on it some, Billy. You gotta keep in mind that you'd be a-preachin' to some awful iggurmint people out there. No, sir, they ain't all gonna be like me and Tyrone here. Most of 'em are goin' to be dope-dick dumbbutts. And then there's another thing. They're all sure as shootin' gonna be lookin' to the Lord to straighten out their lives for 'em, and they'll be pissed sure ever' time they figger you or the Lord's lettin' 'em down. No, sir, they want quick answers and easy fixes and they'll be houndin' you for both."

Nobody said anything further for a spell. Tyrone just rocked an' took an occasional pull at his Grapette. I rested mine in my lap, twirlin' the bottle back an' forth, squintin' down the neck and watchin' th' liquid inside rotate first this way, then the other. Directly, though, I asked, "Well, what'd be wrong with just tellin' people the truth?"

Otis's chair tilted forward off the wall. "The truth?" he grinned.

"Yeah. The truth. You know, that the Lord only asks people to believe in Him and in Jesus, and . . ."

"And," interrupted Otis, "that they solve their own problems and do with their lives whatever the hell they want, right?"

"Yeah," I said, "that is right, isn't it?"

"Damn sure is," answered Otis.

"Well, then?" My question just hung there between us.

Otis looked at me and then at Tyrone. Then, leanin' his chair back up against the wall again, he smiled and said, "Yeah! I s'pose so. Yeah. Just why the fuck not?" He laughed.

Tyrone picked up the thought. "Right, by God. Reverend Billy! Reverend Billy Sol Hargus! Shit, what d'ya think, O'? Sounds pretty good, don't it?" He tried it out a little more. "Th' *Rev!* Yes-*suh!*"

Otis gazed out toward Ol' Green. "The Right Reverend Billy Sol Hargus. Hmmm. 'Tain't bad. No, sir. 'Tain't bad at all." Green finally stirred. He got up, turned around three times, and flopped back down, still dead in the center of the highway, but facin' th' other direction, back toward town.

Otis pulled off his hat and fiddled with it a moment. Then,

without liftin' his eyes, he said to himself, "Reverend Billy Sol Hargus." He chewed on it for another minute or so, and then said, "Son, if that's truly what you want. But do think on it some."

"And pray on it, too, boy," added Tyrone.

Otis chuckled at 'im. "Your God, 'Rone, or his?"

Tyrone laughed with 'im. "Go for what you know."

THE DEL RIO NEWS

★ HERALD ★

BIZARRE TRAGEDY MARS OPENING OF LAKE ARMISTAD NATIONAL PARK

DEL RIO—Seven Del Rio citizens died Monday in what officials are describing as the single worst disaster in this city's history.

A spokesman for the National Park Service expressed official government condolences, saying, "Those who gave their lives did so in the service of their country."

Local fatalities included . . .

REEL 8

Otis and Tyrone rode out with Elroy and me on my first day on my new job. I remember I felt real important. They'd given me a pair of heavy green, twill pants and a matching shirt to wear, along with a pair of heavy-duty, lug-soled work boots. A round, green and white patch was sewn on the shirt's left shoulder, identifyin' me as an employee of the United States Department of the Interior, Forestry Division. I figgered I looked pretty damned official.

We headed north, on up the road out of Del Rio, me and Tyrone jouncin' around in the back of Elroy's pickup, Elroy and Otis in the cab. Several miles of thorny southwestern Texas scrubland rolled by. I found myself thinkin' as I watched it, They *are* crazy. This kind of ground won't even grow old.

Maybe because the forest site was to be situated close to th' lake they figured the trees would soak up some water or somethin'. Who the hell knew. It just didn't make good sense.

"We've come eight mile'," Otis hollered out the window at me. "Where th' hell is this place?"

I was wonderin', too. No matter what direction you looked, the same old nearly barren, monotonous land stretched to the horizon. I knew Armistad Lake was just another three, maybe four, miles north and west of where we were, though, so we'd have to be comin' up to the government reservation just any time.

Sure enough, I thought, there, down the road about a mile and a half, was somethin' glintin' in the sun.

"Hey, Tyrone, what's that runnin' off to the left down there?" He looked, squinted, and shaded his eyes with his hand.

"See it?" I asked.

As we got closer it looked like a thin, gray line stretchin' off over the low hills till it, too, vanished at the horizon. Finally, we could make it out. A fence. A big, expensive fence, I could tell. Chain link. Six foot tall. It bordered the highway on our left as far as I could see. And it just sat there. For no goddamn reason any of us could figure out. There was absolutely nothin' that distinguished the scrub inside from the scrub outside. Nothin' except a sign, four foot by four foot, about, fixed to an enormous, sixteen-foot-wide double gate.

WARNING! KEEP OUT!
UNITED STATES GOVERNMENT PROPERTY
DEPARTMENT OF THE INTERIOR
AUTHORIZED PERSONNEL ONLY

Elroy eased th' pickup into the turnoff that led up to the gate. We sat, peerin' down the road that wound away inside.

Leanin' forward, hunched over the wheel, Elroy said, "Don't look like no dorest to me."

"Shit," Otis agreed, "don't look to me like they done nuthin' but throw a damned fence up around ten mile o' dirt!"

"Wait a minute," I hollered at 'em. "There's some trees right there. Look."

Tyrone followed where I was pointin'. "Nah, Billy. Them's weeds." He shook his head, disgusted.

Otis swung open his door and stood with one leg out on the running board. "Well, where is everybody?"

He hadn't gotten the words out before we heard the

cough of a motor startin' up somewhere beyond the fence. Pretty soon, we saw a plume of dust crawlin' along the road, half-mile or so away, and in just a minute a green Forestry Division jeep came snortin' up to the other side of the gate. A fella with one of them big, round, flat hats on his head bounced out, and he looked all business.

"Uh-oh," said Otis, "highway dick."

"You mean, 'dolice dosser,' " Elroy corrected.

"Yeah, sure, Elroy," Otis groaned, "you're right. 'Dolice dosser.' How could ah have forgot?"

The man walked up to the gate, and I saw he had on the same kind of outfit I did. He worked a key in the padlock on the hasp, unfastened it, and pulled the gate back toward him.

"Howdy," he said. "You boys part of our planters?"

"Uh, no," said Otis. "We're—"

"We're dingin' dis here doy to dork dor doo, dee?" interrupted Elroy.

"Huh?"

"Di daid, we're dinging dis dere—"

Otis mercifully stepped in front of Elroy. "You'll have to excuse him, sir. He's an idiot." He winked at the ranger, and made a twirling motion at his forehead with his finger.

"What we're here for," he went on, "is to deliver this boy to you an' get 'im squared away. He's got some papers on 'im." Otis reached in my shirt pocket. "Here you go," he said, handing the papers over.

The ranger scanned them quickly, finally smiled, and said, "Okay, Billy." He extended his hand. "My name is Ross, Ranger Glenn Ross. We're glad to have you with us. Which one of you is the boy's father?"

Tyrone started to step forward till Otis frowned at 'im, then he jerked a thumb behind him at Elroy.

I was afraid of that. "Well, anyway," said Ranger Ross, "if you want to get back in your truck and follow me in, I'll show you where Billy's gonna be spendin' his time."

Tyrone and I leapfrogged over the tailgate as Elroy and

Otis climbed back in the cab. Ranger Ross waved us through the gate and relocked it, fired up his jeep, and started jouncin' off down the road with Elroy close behind.

After we'd gone I figured, oh . . . maybe a mile, mile and a half, we veered right and suddenly, spread out in front of us, blue as the sky overhead, was Lake Armistad, and relieving the barrenness was a band of green growth for thirty yards or so down to the water's edge. It was still scrub, nothin' over a couple of feet tall, but at least it was green instead of the same ol' yellow splashed here and there with browns and grays. Just this side of the natural growth I could see where about an acre of little fir seedlings had been poked in the ground. They were laid out as regular as a checkerboard and each row was marked by a small white sign that told what kind of tree they were a-tryin' to keep from dyin' there. I knew that damned land an' I wished 'em luck.

We drove for another quarter of a mile, skirtin' the edge of the lake, then bending around a curve to the right. All of us saw "it" at the same time.

"What the hell is *that?*" Otis.

"A grain elevator, in the middle of this nuthin'?" Tyrone.

"Dot dat ding, dinnyday?" Guess.

I had seen th' thing in the literature they gave me over at the Juvenile Office when they told me about the job they had located for me.

Elroy stopped the truck. "It's a fire tower," I said, jumpin' out the back.

Otis opened the door and slumped to his knees right down in the dirt, slappin' his thigh, just about to kill hisself laughin'.

"A fire tower? A *fire* tower? Like in *forest-fire* tower?? Jesus Christ! You wanna know where our *taxes* go?? Into a fuckin' *fire* tower in the middle of the goddamned Texas desert! Jesus!" He was howlin' and he'd infected Tyrone and Elroy, too.

Ranger Ross had stepped from his jeep and walked back

to see what we were up to. Even he saw some humor in it. This big ol' fire tower pokin' up in the middle of ten square miles you couldn't have gotten to burn if you had soaked it in kerosene.

He chuckled. "You think *that's* somethin', wait'll the bears get here." He turned back toward his jeep.

"Huh?"

"What'd he say?"

I pulled a pamphlet outta my hip pocket and unfolded it. "Right here," I said, pointin'. "Look, see? They're transferrin' some honest-to-goodness bears down here from someplace up north. Lessee. Yeah, right here. Grizzilies, see? From Yellowstone Park."

"Bears!" hollered Tyrone. "BEARS! They don't eat colored folks, does they?"

"Not if you'll wear a hat like this," said the ranger, grinnin', "but they might kiss ya."

"DEARS! DO, DESUS, DINNY DING!"

Maybe they ate idiots.

I lived atop the fire tower during the week, and was off duty from noon Saturday till six, Monday mornin'. Step-Edna packed me a lunch and drove out with it every day, regular as clockwork. She'd either make sure she brought enough so's that I'd have something left over for my supper, or, more often than not, she'd drive back out with supper, too.

Those were the nights we'd continue my religious training. As she put it, "Here's some food for th' body before we have some food for th' soul."

I had been doin' my homework, too; don't you think I hadn't. Ever since that first night, months ago, when I snapped my own dick, knockin' the sass out of it when it got to pokin' up all Mr. Smarty, I had been strivin' to perfect my snappin' technique. And I had many an opportunity. Every time Step-Edna brought me my lunch, for instance, and there wasn't enough in there for me to have any supper, my heathen rod would go to throbbin', gettin' filled with th' Devil. I got to where I could hardly wait, just so's I'd have a chance to knock some respect in 'im. I'd go lay down on my cot or my sleepin' bag, lower my pants, prop my head up so I could see real good. Then I'd curl up my finger, take real careful aim . . . and KER-THWACK! God! Shit! It hurt like fury. But, strangely, only for a minute or so. Because, as I drove the Devil out an' my tool shrank, it got to feelin' real good. And I knew that the Lord was pleased.

But lately there had been a problem. It had first cropped up about a week before. Step-Edna had "short-lunched" me and I knew body food and soul food would be a-comin' that evenin'. Well, just as soon as Step-Edna had climbed down from the fire tower in the early afternoon, sayin', "See you tonight, sugar," my heathen region had got to stirrin'. Pretty soon, goddamnit, I had what I called "tent-stake-condition-1" down there. I crawled over to my sleeping bag, laid down, opened up my pants, and got ready to apply the remedy. It looked like my member was tryin' to grab for the ceilin' or something, as I kept thinking about Step-Edna servin' me her dinner. So I carefully curled up my finger, drew a bead on the most sensitive part of my Satan shaft, and let 'er rip. WHHHAP! Oww! Hmmmm. Ahhhhh.

"There, you traitor," I said, lookin' down at mysel'. Huh?

What?

My God, nothing had happened! It was still stickin' up like a dagger!

Take two. I curled up my finger again and zeroed in, as little beads of sweat popped out on my forehead. POWWW! Argh! Oh, damn! Ohhhhh.

I was almost afraid to look, but I peeked at it just out of the corner of my eye.

Shit! Nothin'! Not a goddamn thing! It was hard as a length of cold-rolled steel an' I could've sworn it was grinnin' at me, smirkin', mockin' me.

WHAM! OWWWWWW! Jesus Christ! Shit!

I looked again. NOTHIN'! OHMIGOD! STEP-EDNA! OHMIGOD! All I could think of was Step-Edna's years of faithful instruction just goin' to waste. I felt dirty, soiled. God, what was I goin' to do? I stared at it. Goddamn! It was smirkin' at me, I was sure! I peered at it real close and thought I saw grinnin' there the red-eyed demon himself.

"YOU SERPENT!" I screamed. "OH, THOU FOUL FIEND, UNLOOSE MY DICK!"

Nearly sick with panic, I reached up and swept everything on top of the table onto the floor. A twelve-inch metal ruler fell with a clatter near my feet. I snatched it in my right hand, grabbed my rod in my left like I was chokin' a chicken, and let it have it!

KERRR-THWAAANG! JEEEE-ZUSSS KEEERRIIIHH-SSTTTT!

Flashes of neon-red and purple splattered before my eyes. My head swam and I toppled over on my side, bent double, clutchin' my member in both hands, groanin' and moanin'.

I lay there, chest heavin' for a good five minutes, cradlin' my damned Devil-pole. And then, the single most peculiar thing happened. It started feelin' warm and . . . cozy. And once again, I was seized by that same feelin' I had the night I first snapped my false idol and again when I found the holy picture in Reverend Gleason Beamer's office. It was a mellow warmth starting right in my belly and rapidly radiating out to every part of my body. I felt complete and, somehow, secure. Yes, it was happenin' again. The Lord had seen and the Lord had approved and He was washin' me in His glory. There was no denying it.

Once again, I had found "The Path."

Say hallelujah.

One evenin', late, as Step-Edna lay spread out on my sleepin' bag in the top of the tower, catchin' her breath, I told her about something that had been goin' through my mind for the past month. She sat up, reached for her blouse, and started to slip it on, her graceful arms bathed by the moonlight comin' in through the tower windows. I found myself just wantin' to watch, she looked so pretty, an' not talk, but I did anyway because it was time to tell her about th' decision which had become clear to me, after I'd knocked some sense into my heathen rod of lust with the ruler.

"Step-Edna," I began, a little uncertainly, "I been doin' a whole lot of thinkin', ma'am, about what I wanna be."

"Oh, have you now," she said, and her fingers paused with their buttonin'. She looked at me kind of dreamily, cockin' her head a bit in a way that made her look prettier still. "You can tell me what you wanna be," she said, "but I'll tell you what you are." She whispered the words out. "You're somethin' *else!"* She reached over and ran her fingers through my hair.

"Yes, ma'am," I said, "but what I been thinkin', ma'am, is that I really do *want* to be 'somethin' else,' somethin' other than a forest ranger, ma'am."

"Well, what is it, son? Don't you like Step-Edna's suppers no more?" She stuck her lower lip out and pouted at me, then ran her tongue over her lips like a kitten.

I tried not to notice too much. "Step-Edna, I know you're gonna be proud of what I've got to tell you because of all the years of wonderful instructin' you've done for me."

She had stood up, tuckin' her blouse down inside her white shorts, but now she stopped, one hand at her waistband, the other pushed down inside at her hip as she looked at me.

"Ma'am, I . . . I want to be . . . a preacher."

She froze, stunned. Then a smile started to creep across her face, but got swept away as her chin began quivering. She zipped up the back of her shorts and turned away. Then she reached down, picked up a corner of my sleepin' bag, and held it to her nose as she looked off into the dark. She stayed like that for some time, not sayin' anything.

I was thinkin', Uh-oh, now you've done it, as I sat cross-legged on the floor, just starin' down at my hands in my lap.

Finally, I heard her take a deep breath. I looked up, saw her straighten her back and turn, arms folded across her chest. She looked straight at me, and I could see in the moonlight that her eyes were damp.

"Jesus Christ," she said as she bent to kiss the top of my head. Then, sitting on her knees in front of me, she touched her hand lightly to my cheek, fixed her eyes on mine, and said, "Jesus made His decision in the wilderness, and to think, here you are, too."

She took her hand from my face, began to unbutton her blouse, and whispered, "Thy will be done."

Frank Crowley, the editor of *The Del Rio News Herald,* had taken to makin' regular visits to the forest, "keeping tabs on tax dollars," as he put it. He'd drop by in his aging delivery truck once, maybe twice a week, and I'd walk him over to what I'd started callin' my own E & E—my Evergreen Experiment. The trees were comin' along pretty good, actually, given the painful growin' conditions they were subjected to. And crews from town were gettin' day pay to put in more and more of them.

I kind of liked ol' Crowley; leastways, I didn't mind him near as much as most folks did. Nearly everybody found him disagreeable. God, Otis flat couldn't stand him.

"That skinny little inked-up prick," he called him. "Have you ever seen a neck like that on a human being before? Bug-eyed little bastard, too. You watch 'im. Everytime he talks, his Adam's apple goes to bouncin' up an' down like a mouse trying to fuck its way out of a sock! It's repulsive, I'll tell you. And so's he."

The feeling, Crowley'd be quick to point out, was mutual.

It had been that way between the two of 'em ever since they'd had a run-in over some damned barfly on the other side of town. I guess ol' Frank had really had somethin' serious for her. I'd been down to his newspaper office one time, when me and Tyrone had to return one of their delivr'y trucks Otis had ground the valves on.

There was a picture of a lady on Frank's desk, in a little frame. Tyrone had said it was the woman Frank and Otis was wranglin' over. A folder was open against it so's I couldn't see the face, but I could tell she was naked, and I could read the inscription in the upper lefthand corner. It seemed a little peculiar to me, but then Frank was a little peculiar hisself, so, I figured, what the hell?

It read:

For Frankie,
Anytime, sugar, anytime.
Love,
Wilma.

As I said, Frank was kind of odd, and in ways which most people found obnoxious, but the peculiarity that got the blue ribbon was th' way the man talked. Printer's ink really had seeped into his veins.

He talked in headlines!

He'd been through the reservation one week, drivin' slowly by the pines, lookin' 'em over real close and scratchin' down notes on a pad at his side. I waved to him from the tower and he'd hollered up at me, grinnin', "HARGUS BOY ON JOB! FOREST PROGRESSING!"

"Thanks, Frank," I'd yelled back at 'im, "but really, them trees ain't up hardly half a foot yet."

"TREE GROWTH IMPAIRED!" he'd shouted back. "SOIL BLAMED! YOUNG RANGER UNBLEMISHED!"

He really was a good ol' boy.

Early one morning, I was just gettin' ready to go down the tower ladder to begin inspectin' my trees, when I saw Frank's delivery truck burnin' up the road toward the forest with a long plume of dust chasin' its wheels. I watched him roar in down below. The door of the truck popped open and Frank jumped out, a-hollerin:

"ANIMALS ARRIVE! BUS BRINGS BEARS!" He raced halfway up the tower ladder, missed a rung and toppled backward, landing in a heap.

"Frank! Frank! Jesus, are you all right?"

"LOCAL JOURNALIST SURVIVES FALL! TOUCHED BY YOUTHFUL ARBOR-MANAGER'S CONCERN!"

I grinned as he started back up again, and this time he made it. I lost sight of him for just a minute, but pretty soon I heard him hammerin' on the trap door in the floor of the tower.

"Keep your pants on, Frank. I gotta unlatch it."

I pulled the door up and Frank clambered through. "ANIMALS DUE MOMENTARILY! DEL RIO PRESERVE TO BE NEW HOME!" He was pointin' back down the road he'd just come over.

I picked up my binoculars and had a look. Yep, sure enough, just comin' in through the gate there was a Greyhound bus, and I saw Ranger Ross shutting the gate behind it. Wait a minute, I thought. Bears? Greyhound *bus?* What the hell?

Then I noticed that the bus was racing over the road, pitching and yawing like the driver thought he was about to die. Little did I know. I kept my glasses on 'im as he got closer. What th' fuck's this? Wisps of smoke comin' out the windows? Then I saw an enormous bear hangin' his head out in the breeze. Another one was apparently in the seat in front of him, ridin' along with an elbow nonchalantly restin' on the windowsill—just like he was commutin' to Dallas.

Then the bus was at the foot of the tower, shudderin' to a stop, rockin' up and down on its springs as it settled in right next to Frank Crowley's delivery truck.

Nothing moved on board for a moment. The bears I had seen had been on the other side, the side away from me.

Everything looked okay—except quite a bit of smoke was coming out of the windows which were . . . smashed out! Jesus! The smashed windows hadn't even been opened!

Frank and I looked at each other, then back at the bus down below. Somewhere, a long way off, a mockingbird was trilling. The morning was hot, ponderous, and still. Suddenly, the door of the bus crashed open, giving both of us a start. It slammed back on its hinges against the bus's body and the driver bolted outside. It seemed as though his feet never even hit the ground as he made a mad, pell-mell dash for the fire tower. A massive bear was galumphin' along right behind him, inches from his heels.

"LOOK OUT!" the driver screamed. "I'M THE LAST MAN ALIVE!"

He made a desperate lunge for the ladder, caught a rung, and hauled himself up as the bear's jaws clamped onto his shoe. He yanked his foot free and allowed the bear to have himself filet of Florsheim.

From halfway up the ladder the driver yelled to us, "Those goddamn assholes at Yellowstone put them bears on the bus as *passengers.*"

He climbed a few more rungs, then paused again. "They had chains on 'em and were locked in the seats when we started out. . . ." A few more rungs. "But they gnawed their way loose, and ate their handlers. Goddamn! Please, you gotta help me—I'm hurt!"

"Come on," I yelled, "you can make it. Just a few more feet. There's a trap door. We'll help you through, just don't give up!"

Frank and I hauled open the door, got the driver under each arm, and lifted him inside. He slumped down in the corner, head back against the wall.

"They . . . they . . . *ate* everybody." He turned his head away and sobbed. "Oh, God."

"Take it easy, take it easy. It's gonna be all right. Frank! Hand me my canteen over there."

I held it up to the driver's lips and he drank a little. His uniform was ripped and his hair was singed, but it looked to me as though he'd be okay if we could just keep him from goin' into shock. He had a wild look in his eyes as he told us more of his ordeal. "They been throwin' suitcases and mail sacks and seats out the windows ever since they busted through their chains over aroun' San Antonio. God! Cars were careening all over the highway, and I couldn't do anything! One of 'em got between me and the door. I couldn't even *stop!* The only thing that saved me was my driver's cage. They couldn't quite get to me. Jesus, oh, Jesus." He turned his head and started to sob again. "Finally, the sons of bitches somehow started a fire back there and settled down a bit. I think the smoke confused 'em."

I gave the man some more water and then looked outside. The bears weren't confused now. They had started rockin' the bus, six on a side, sure as shit tryin' to turn it over. I couldn't believe it! "Frank, Frank, look at this. Look at what these goddamn bears are doin'!" Frank pulled himself up to the window and peeked over. "BEARS BERSERK! EMERGENCY AID URGENTLY SOUGHT!"

Just then, we heard sirens risin' and fallin' off in the distance. I grabbed my glasses and looked out toward the highway. Nothing. No, wait . . . yeah, there! By God, it was the Val Verde County Fire Department. Their old pumper was hurtling down the highway, hell-bent for leather, and trailin' 'em . . . my God, it was Sheriff Buff Wallace! No mistakin' that car. It was the only police cruiser I'd ever seen with two racks of lights and four sirens, one on each fender.

Both vehicles careened through the gate on two wheels, raisin' a veritable storm of dust, and sped toward the tower. Frank Crowley was now nearly beside himself, never having had a story to cover like this one in his whole life. He was scramblin' down the fire ladder to get a better look. The bears had all gathered on the far side of the bus when they heard the sirens approaching. They just stood, lookin' around at each other as the pumper bounced to a stop, and Buff made his customary slide-for-life entrance.

Five men rolled off the fire truck and, with remarkable efficiency, started strippin' off hose and hittin' the pumps in one smooth simultaneous operation.

All they had been able to see was the burning bus, situated between them and the bears. The bears, however, had seen them, and with equally remarkable efficiency, ate them.

"OHMIGOD!" screamed Frank, tryin' to keep from throwin' up as the bears nosed around in the bloodied bodies. "OHMIGOD!" It was the first time I'd ever heard him unable to come up with a headline. Suddenly, his grip on the ladder slipped and he fell. A huge bear looked up, saw him, and fielded him as neatly as a shortstop. Inspired, Frank came up with a headline. "BELOVED REPORTER," he screamed, "INTO JAWS OF DEATH!"

His *last* headline.

Buff had been radioing back to the county courthouse when he and the men on the pumper rolled up. He had been callin' for a backup when he'd spotted the bears and he had stayed in his car. Until, that is, the bears started attacking the volunteer firefighters. I'd never before nor have I since witnessed anything like what Buff did.

Suddenly, he literally erupted from his car, a bloodcurdling snarl on his lips and a loud, guttural scream in his throat. He opened the door of his car so hard the hinges bent back, and he exploded into a fury of movement. Bellowing like a bull, he charged twelve grizzly bears. "YOU ROTTEN, GODDAMNED SONS OF BITCHES. YOU GODDAMNED KILLLERRRS! I'LL KILL YOU!" The bears regarded him with mild interest, and when he got close enough, the first one, a tremendous brute, took his head off. Just like a scythe cuttin' wheat. Swish! The Sheriff's head flew through a broken window on the bus. His body continued forward five or six steps before it crumpled.

The Greyhound driver an' I sat up there in the tower and witnessed the whole thing. He was now a raving lunatic. I tried my best to calm him, pointing out that the bears seemed to be settling down, largely, I thought, because they were full. "See?" I said. "Look, sir, they're peeing on the trees, see? And some of 'em are laying down."

"DON'T LET THAT SHIT FOOL YOU!" he raved. "THEY PULLED THAT CRAP ON ME WHEN THEY FIRST GOT ON MY BUS. NO, SIR!" He was grittin' and grindin' his teeth and he'd curled up in a little ball over in the corner, arms clasped around his knees, huggin' himself and rockin' back and forth on his feet.

"THEY'RE NOTHING," he screamed, "BUT A BUNCH OF *ANIMALS!!!*"

Thank God, poor ol' Buff's radio call had gotten through. I'd been watching the bears lollin' around down below for twenty minutes or so when three more cruisers pulled in. I saw some shocked faces peerin' out through windshields as they took in the carnage. Then all three had backed up, turned around, and sped away.

A couple of hours later, the squad cars returned, leadin' a small caravan of trucks and ambulances. I watched as men shoveled drugged meat out the back of the trucks, then slammed the doors shut. The bears investigated the stuff, took a few bites, and that was it.

The worst tragedy in Del Rio's history was at an end. They built a terrifically strong pen for the bears over the next week. The job would've gone even quicker if the installation crew hadn'ta kept having to interrupt their work to go to funerals.

The dust and the dirt and the blisterin' southwest Texas sun took their toll on the animals. It had been a stupid idea in the first place, dreamed up by some heathen moron in Washington. One by one the bears got sick, and then sicker, and eventually they all died.

It had been my job to feed and water them. And after awhile, I truly got to like them. Even after what they'd done, because I knew it wasn't their fault. They were just doin' with their lives what the good Lord intended them to do.

You see? That's the way it's supposed to be. Of course, they became easier and easier to deal with as the poor bastards got sick and weak. Sometimes, I'd even let them out of their enclosure so they could crawl over to the fire tower to get a little spot of shade. If Ranger Ross had found out, he would've killed me. And you know what I did? I talked to 'em.

Well, actually, I practiced preachin' to 'em, pretendin' that they were my congregation. I'd let 'em out, then stand atop the fire tower and look down on them. "We are gathered here today," I'd say, spreadin' my arms wide, "in this splendid patch of God-given wilderness to worship Him from whom all blessings flow, and to feel His wondrous power." The bears would look up at me with a "why don't he can it" kind of look on their faces, but I didn't care. I was perfectin' my technique. "Let His spirit wash over you and cleanse and restore you and give you peace. For His love surpasseth all understanding."

I can't truthfully say they understood me. Or found peace. Or got clean, even. It appeared, in fact, that much like human-being heathens, the bears blamed their misfortunes on someone else. They'd growl and become irritable when I'd say to them, "The Lord asks only that you believe in His Word and accept His Son Jesus into your life. For you are responsible," I'd shout, "for your *own* happiness. You, yes, *you,* have the God-given power to take control of your lives, to rise above the squalor of your present circumstances, and do for yourselves as you wish."

But, just like many of us, they threw in the towel, gave up, and starved to death.

Pusillanimous bastards.

After the bears were gone—and Jesus, don't you know they gave me the job of buryin' the goddamned things; took two weeks and 150 blisters—the government decided that the entire forestry project was a bust and recommended that it be abandoned. I was anxious to get on with my decision to dedicate my life to the Lord, so it suited the hell outta me. God, the way them people made decisions, Elroy coulda been President. Jesus, he *shoulda* been President. "Dood evenin, my dello Anerikans."

Never mind.

The following month, Elroy, Otis, and Tyrone rattled into the parking space below the tower in the old pickup, and I climbed down the ladder for the last time. I had lowered a duffle bag full of my stuff down to 'em on a rope and now I hefted it up on my shoulder, flipped it into the back of the truck, and climbed in after it. I was leavin' the same way I first came out. Tyrone joined me in the back and Elroy and Otis swung into the cab. Then Tyrone looked around at the tiny trees, all of which had gone brown and yellow. They'd struggled, but in the end . . . the Texas scrub had won.

We watched the plot of trees dwindlin' behind us as Elroy followed the road out toward the highway.

"Told ya," said Tyrone, squintin' back into the sun.

"Well," Otis was sayin', his chair leaned back up against the station wall, Tyrone to his left, rockin', "what the hell you gonna do now, son?"

"First thing," I said, "is to get me a Grapette."

Otis flipped me the screwdriver. "You want one, too, 'Rone?" Tyrone nodded and I went over to the machine, stuck the blade in the mechanism that released the bottle, and pushed down. Three bottles of Grapette went noddin' their way down the track and I lifted 'em out past the guard that was supposed to keep me from doin' what I'd just done. I handed one to Otis and tossed one over to Tyrone along with the opener.

"You thought about doin' anything else, boy?" asked Tyrone.

"Just what I was tellin' you about, before all of this government business came up."

"You mean about bein' a preacher?"

"Uh-huh."

Otis took a swig of his Grapette and said, "Well, you're gonna have a chance Sunday a week to see just what you might be able to become one day."

"How's that?" I asked.

"Because Dr. J. P. Boone Moses is comin' to town, that's 'how's that,' " Otis answered.

"No shit? It's that soon?"

"No shit, son."

By God, I sure felt like I was ready. Thanks to them bears. And you know, as I think back, if the poor bastards had a-listened to me they'd be fat and sassy and in a zoo somewhere. Jesus, what a shame.

"Boy, that's great," I said. "And I'm going?"

Otis let his chair fall forward onto all four legs and he leaned down and patted me on the shoulder. "Wouldn't let you miss it for the world, son. It's somethin' you won't soon forget."

Well, now, maybe my life was about to straighten out after all. Was it because I was takin' control of it? Back then, I didn't know. Now, of course, I understand that it was God's will.

I wonder what Brother Jesus thought when Dad put Him on the Path?

Just one thing was hangin' in the back of my mind, naggin' there like a persistent dull ache. The religious trainin' I'd been gettin' from Step-Edna.

The last time the Devil'd invaded my heathen region I had been forced to use my shoe.

WHAAMMM!

It had felt good.

Me, Otis, and Tyrone just sat there on the porch, relaxed, watchin' some big thunderheads liftin' up in the sky to the southwest. "I'll bet we catch us a shower directly," said

Otis. "Maybe that'll get that iggurmint goddamned dog to move." Ol' Green was layin' out in the dust midway between the porch and the pumps.

The idea hit all of us at the same time. We looked at each other and grinned. Otis kicked it off. "Ready," he giggled, "aim . . . *fire!*"

Three empty Grapette bottles zinged over the driveway like tiny glass torpedoes and converged on Ol' Green.

Bullseye!

Well, Green came off the ground like he'd been jabbed with a cattle prod. Yelpin', tail tucked between his legs, he streaked onto the highway and was mashed flat by a tractor-trailer truck.

It was the first time I'd ever seen Otis cry.

THE DEL RIO NEWS
★ HERALD ★

BORN-AGAIN CHAOS!

Dozens Hurt at Turbulent Tent Revival

DEL RIO—Forty-eight people remain hospitalized this morning following last night's opening of the Boone Moses Cavalcade-of-Miracles Revival.

A Sheriff's Department spokesman said while most of the victims in the crowd of 3,000 had simply become overwrought and had fainted, at least 10 persons suffered serious burn injuries. . . .

REEL 9

◆

Otis nudged me. "That's him," he whispered. "That's Boone Moses. . . ."

He was tall, rangy, solidly built, though ever-so-slightly bent. It gave him a look of constantly bucking a headwind. Now, he prowled the length of the platform, a closed Bible in one hand, an eighteen-inch sterling silver rod grasped in the other. Long, silver-gray hair hung in clumps and ringlets about his neck, and his eyes blazed as he stared at his audience, riveting first this person, then that one.

"IS JESUS CHRIST HERE TONIGHT?" His voice exploded from within him and thundered off through the night air. An organist situated off stage to his left stung the keys with a staccato burst of sound after each sentence, underscoring Moses's words.

"IS JESUS CHRIST HERE TONIGHT? LOOK AROUND YOU, HEATHEN!"

People nervously stirred in their seats, their eyed darting from side to side.

"WELL?" He paused.

"IS HE HERE? IS JEEZUS IN THIS TENT TONIGHT?"

He thrust his Bible aloft and threw back his head.

"YES!!" he shrieked. "YES!" (Organ!) "YES!" (Organ!) "YES!" (Organ!) "JEEZUS CHRIST *IS* HERE TONIGHT! COME ON, NOW, SAY IT!" he commanded.

Most people continued to fidget self-consciously in their chairs, glancin' around the huge tent, but a few muttered mechanically, "Yes, He's here."

Dr. Moses recoiled like he'd been slapped. He clutched his chest and staggered backward a couple of steps, his mouth agape in mock surprise.

"Did someone say Jesus was here? DID I HEAR THAT?"

"Ye . . . yes," said a hesitant voice.

"JESUS CHRIST IS HERE? IS THAT RIGHT?" asked Dr. Moses, his eyes peerin' hard into their stunned faces. Tucking his Bible underneath his arm, he sidestepped along the platform, lookin' at 'em, crackin' his rod into the palm of his hand like a drill instructor reviewin' his recruits.

He stopped, hands clutchin' the rod behind his back.

"WELL???"

"Yes."

"YES, *WHAT?*"

"Yes, Jesus is here," came the reply, thin and weak.

"I CAN'T HEARRR YOU!" Moses shouted back.

Louder now, "Yes, Jesus is here!"

"Yes, He is! He's here tonight!" shouted several more.

Moses walked briskly back across the stage, then reversed direction and stalked back, black boots glistening, Bible held high, thumpin' th' Book with his rod. Many of 'em were shoutin' now, and Dr. Moses built 'em up, urging on each voice.

"You say He's here tonight—could it be? Could it really be?"

"YES, YES!" they screamed back at him. "HE'S HERE TONIGHT!"

The all-Negro Del Rio Mt. Zion Fire-Baptized Baptist Church Choir, forty voices strong, were into it now, clappin' their hands.

Two extremely short men suddenly materialized at Dr. Moses's side, shakin' tambourines nearly as large as they were. They took up the chant in strange little squeaky voices that reminded me of drawin' a file across a taut wire: "HE'S HERE TONIGHT! YES, LORD, HE'S HERE TONIGHT!"

Dr. Moses was leadin' everybody, roamin' the stage now,

shoutin', urgin' them on. "HE'S HERE TONIGHT! COM'ON, EVERYBODY, HE'S HERE TONIGHT!"

And they screamed back at 'im rhythmically, "YOU'RE SO RIGHT, HE'S HERE TONIGHT!" They became delirious, standin', clappin', tears in their eyes. The organist was playin' ol'-time blues gospel with a hypnotizin' beat that had row after row of 'em holdin' hands, noddin' to one another, smilin' as they swayed with the cadence and the chant.

"SAY IT AGAIN!"

". . . HE'S HERE TONIGHT!"

"JESUS CHRIST?"

". . . HE'S HERE TONIGHT!"

"ONE MO' TIME!"

". . . HE'S HERE TONIGHT!"

"JESUS CHRIST!"

". . . HE'S HERE TONIGHT!"

"I SAID JESUS CHRIST!"

". . . HE'S HERE TONIGHT!"

"TH' LORD MY SAVIOR!"

". . . HE'S HERE TONIGHT!"

"WHAT THE HELL Y'ALL SAYIN'?"

". . . HE'S HERE TONIGHT!"

"HAVE Y'ALL LOST YOUR MINDS?"

". . . HE'S HERE TONIGHT!"

All of a sudden, Dr. Moses fell flat on his back in the center of the stage.

". . . HE'S HERE TONI—"

They stopped, stunned. A few shouts could still be heard toward the rear of the tent. "Yes, He IS!" And, "Say it on, now!" But in just a moment, they stopped, too, as a hush dropped like a thick blanket over the entire audience.

"What happened?" somebody whispered.

"Is he dead?"

"Heart attack, I'll bet."

Somebody stood up about five rows back. "Is there a doctor in the house?"

But just then, Dr. Moses stirred. He slowly raised up on one elbow and looked out at the crowd. "Don't need no doctor," he whispered, "because . . ." He paused, peerin' into their bewildered faces, "WE GOT A SAVIOR IN THIS HOUSE TONIGHT!"

Pandemonium.

Dr. Moses leaped to his feet and, thrustin' first his Bible, then his silver rod, into the air, he marched toward the front of the stage like a drum major, liftin' his knees high as the chant of "HE'S HERE TONIGHT!" rolled off the sides of the tent and met itself comin' back across.

Then, the damndest thing happened.

Dr. Moses didn't stop. As the organist pumped out a furious version of "Onward, Christian Soldiers," the Doctor marched right off the front of the stage and pitched forward face down. What only a few people could see was that two burly assistants caught him. The rest of the audience stood, shocked. But then, to their astonishment, they saw Dr. Moses, appearing to ascend miraculously. His assistants were slowly lifting him on their shoulders. A spotlight followed his ascent as he raised his arms high, Bible in one hand, silver rod in the other. A slow cheer started building in the crowd. In a moment it had swelled to a roar. Dr. Moses put his hands on his hips and stared at 'em haughtily, almost menacingly. He stood that way until he had glowered them into silence—it might a-been five full minutes.

Then, ever so softly, the organ began sneaking back in. "The Old Rugged Cross" seeped into the still as seductively as guilt after a sinful night of lust, and Dr. Moses, his voice a whisper, asked:

"Where . . . is He?"

By that point, people were so dumbfounded by all that had happened that nobody spoke. Nobody stirred, except to lean forward, strainin' to hear.

Dr. Moses asked again, louder, "Where . . . is He?" His eyes appeared to search every face.

Then, his voice risin' to a shout, he said, "SOMEBODY *TELLLLL* ME—WHERE . . . IS *JESUS?"*

His voice rang unnaturally through the tent, his question trailin' off as the audience sat, frozen.

"YOU SAID HE'S HERE," Dr. Moses shrieked. "WELL, WHERE? WHERE IS JEEEE-ZUS? YOU! YOU, THERE, IS HE NEXT TO YOU? YOU, SISTER, YOU GOT 'IM IN THAT PURSE? HEY, YOU! YOU STANDIN' ON HIM, BROTHER? HUH? ARE YOU? I WANNA KNOW, DAMNIT! YOU TOLD ME HE'S HERE . . . WELL . . .

"POINNNNT TOOOO HIMMMMMM!"

His voice was a wolf's howl. Dr. Moses's head was thrown back and his arms were outstretched as though he was bein' crucified.

People looked around at one another furtively, embarrassed, not knowin' what to do or what to expect. The Doctor let the moment stretch to its maximum, but not a moment longer. Slowly, he lowered his arms to his sides and then raised just his Bible in front of him. He smiled at them and, tappin' the Bible with his silver rod, he said, "Jesus . . . is in here."

"Huh?"

"Wha'?"

"Jesus Christ, my savior who left His blood on Calvary for you and me, is right here. In The Book."

Well, the relief washin' over them could almost be followed, as though it was a wave breakin' toward the rear of the tent.

Dr. Moses smiled. "How many of you here tonight brought Jesus, brought your Bibles? Hold 'em up, let me see em!"

Several, scattered through the hundreds, held up their Bibles.

Dr. Moses pointed out each one with his silver rod, noddin', then shakin' his head. "That it? *Is that it?* Well, all right," he said sadly. "Lemme ask you, how many here tonight *own* a Bible? Raise your hands, let me see 'em."

Most everyone stuck a hand in the air.

"Well, *all right!"* Dr. Moses exclaimed, smilin' again. He began pacin' the stage once more, his eyes seekin' out each face. "Jesus Christ," he began, rappin' his Bible with his rod, "is in this Book, my Book, an' He's in *your* Book! Jesus Christ, is in *everybody's* Book. So," he said, his smile becomin' a broad grin, "you didn't need to come here tonight to *find* Jesus, did you? No! You didn't! Anytime you want to find Jesus, all you've got to do is to open your Book. *He's there! Jesus Christ! In th' Book anytime you want 'im!"*

Several people nodded.

"No," Dr. Moses went on, "you didn't come here tonight to *find* Jesus, you came here, whether you knew it or not, because you want to get Him in your *heart!"*

More people nodded and there was a scatterin' of amens.

"BUT WHAT HAPPENS," Dr. Moses shouted, "IF YOU LOSE YOUR BIBLE? DOES POOR OL' JESUS WIND UP IN THE LOST AND FOUND?"

There was some muffled laughter.

"If you lose your Bible, do you lose JEE-zus? Will you have to go down to the Missing Persons Bureau an' say, 'Excuse me, I'm lookin' for a fella, 'bout five-ten, blue eyes, got a halo, an' goes around savin' mankind'?"

More titters rippled across the room.

"NOOOO!" he screamed. "NO! NO! NO! YOU DON'T LOSE JESUS IF YOU LOSE YOUR BIBLE, *IF* YOU GOT 'IM IN YOUR HEART, AND . . . *THAT'S* WHY YOU'RE HERE TONIGHT, TO GET 'IM IN YOUR HEART! EVERYBODY, NOW: I WON'T LOSE JESUS . . ."

". . . I WON'T LOSE JESUS!"

"IF HE'S IN MY HEART!"

". . . IF HE'S IN MY HEART!"

"I WON'T LOSE JESUS!"

". . . I WON'T LOSE JESUS!"

"IF HE'S IN MY HEART!"

". . . IF HE'S IN MY HEART!"

They were on their feet again, clappin', singin', screamin'. And then once more they hushed, as Dr. Moses played 'em like th' strings of a violin. Now he stood, his chin in his hand, as though he was puzzled.

"WELL, NOW, WAIT A MINUTE HERE," he shouted, abruptly. "HOW ARE YOU GONNA GET JESUS IN YOUR HEART?"

Before anybody could say anything, he whispered, "Ask Him."

They leaned forward, strainin' to hear.

"Ask Him," said the Doctor, louder. "That's all. *Ask* Jesus to come into your heart. Say it now. Say, 'Jesus'. . ."

". . . Jesus."

"Come into my heart."

". . . Come into my heart!"

"Say, 'JEEEEEEEE-ZUS!' "

They were screamin' again, "JEEEEEEEE-ZUS!"

"COME INTO MY HEART!"

". . . COME INTO MY HEART!"

"THAT'S RIGHT!" Dr. Moses yelled, "ASK! ASK JESUS TO COME INTO YOUR HEART, AND HE WILL! SAY, 'HELP ME, JESUS,' AND HE WILL. LET'S DO IT. SAY, 'HELP ME, JESUS!' "

". . . HELP ME, JESUS!"

"MY LIFE AIN'T WORKIN' OUTTTTT, JEEZUS!"

". . . MY LIFE AIN'T WORKIN' OUTTTTT, JEEZUS!"

"I DON'T FEEL GOOD, JESUS! I NEED YOUR HELP, SWEET SAVIOR!"

He was slashin' the air with his silver rod, wavin' it over their uplifted and outstretched hands, struttin' back and forth across the stage as he spoke, his voice once again a rhythm against the background of their cries and shouts.

And then once again he stopped dead and peered intently into their faces. "How many here tonight want Jesus to come into their hearts?"

Hundreds of hands shot into the air.

"All right," he said gently, "all right. How many here

tonight are in need of Jesus' help? In neeeeed of the Savior's tender touch?"

A sea of hands waved in the air.

"ALL RIGHT, THEN," shouted Dr. Moses, puffin' out his chest and thumpin' his Bible again with his rod. "HOW MANY HERE TONIGHT WANT TO HELP JESUS IN RETURN???"

A few hands lifted, tentatively, here and there, the people appearin' confused.

Dr. Moses hit 'em again.

"I SAID, HOW MANY HERE WANNA HELP JESUS? YOU ALL WANT JESUS TO HELP YOU. NOW, HOW MANY HERE ARE WILLIN' TO GIVE HIM A HAND? COME ON! HOW MANY? I WANT A SHOW OF HANDS . . . *NOW!!*"

It was a direct order. The hands wavin' in the air looked like a field of grain.

Dr. Moses's smile woulda lit up Los Angeles.

"ALL RIGHT!" he said. "ALL RIGHT, now! Praise Jesus!"

Suddenly, there were a dozen or so of the Doctor's aides, "Mosettes," he called 'em, fannin' out into the aisles, each carrying several bright, shiny, chrome buckets nested inside one another. They began peelin' 'em apart and passin' them up and down the rows.

"I want each of you, now," said Dr. Moses, "to reach into your hearts to help Jesus. Say, 'Jesus, I want to help You.' Say, 'Jesus, what can I do for You?' Say, 'Jesus, look what You done for me.' Say, 'I wanna *thank* You, Jesus.' Say, 'Jesus, I can't do for You all You've done for me, but I'm gonna try!' "

As Dr. Moses wheedled and cajoled, th' money poured into the buckets. People just couldn't dig deep enough.

"Nobody's too poor to give to Jesus," Dr. Moses cried, his eyes goin' misty. "He helps all of us, so all of us got to help Him. It's only fair!" Tears of sincerity were now trickling down his cheeks.

At that point, when the buckets had been out about seven

or eight minutes, one of the Doctor's aides came to him and drew him aside, tenderly takin' him by the elbow. The two spoke in whispers, th' Doctor noddin' now and again, and claspin' his hands together in front of him as though in prayer.

Directly, he nodded his head vigorously, and you could see him sayin', "Yes! Yes, bring her on. Bring her unto me!"

A woman, crippled, wheelchair-bound, was pushed across the stage as the organist softly played "Jesus Loves Me." Her limbs and head looked as though they didn't have any bones inside of 'em, and she flopped about like a puppet on a bad set of strings.

Her hair was gray and her skin was sallow. Her cheeks were drawn, eyes vacant. Her feet kept slippin' off the chair's footrests and the Doctor's aides would gently put them back. They rolled the woman—she could've been forty-five or eighty-five—to Dr. Moses in the center of the stage. He gazed down at her, hands holding his silver rod in front of him, prayerfully. Somewhere from the back of the tent a single pencil spotlight threw a narrow beam just on the two of 'em as the rest of the lights dimmed. Slowly, Dr. Moses extended his rod toward the woman, and lightly touched her hair with it.

"Sister," he said softly, "do you believe in Jesus?"

The woman nodded, her head flopping loosely from side to side.

"Is Jesus in your heart?" asked Dr. Moses.

She tried to nod but her head flopped straight back so that she looked at the top of the tent.

"Look at me!" ordered Dr. Moses.

Two aides lifted the woman's head so it pointed at the Doctor. They let it go and it flopped back up at th' ceiling again.

Doctor Moses took hold of the arms of her wheelchair and leaned down close to her.

"SAY, 'JEEEEE-ZUS, I WANNA BE WHOLE!' " he screamed.

The woman's lips quivered as she struggled to comply.

Dr. Moses knelt down beside her and pressed her mouth against his ear.

He rose, turned to face the audience, and smiled.

"She says," he announced grandly, "that she believes in Jesus! She says that Jesus is in her heart! She is askin' Jesus to make her whole!"

All eyes were on Dr. Moses. Cries and sobs arose from the darkened tent.

"Jesus did it," he shouted. "Jesus made her speak! Now, let's do somethin' for Jesus!"

Flashlights flipped on out in the aisles and moments later the buckets were weaving up and down the rows again.

Dr. Moses raised his rod high above him.

It flashed in the spotlight. Then he shouted to the heavens, "NOW, HEAL HER, JESUS! HEAL THY SERVANT! EVERYBODY, I WANT YOU TO JOIN HANDS WITH YOUR NEIGHBOR AND HELP ME. HELP ME SAY IT. HEAL HER, JESUS!"

". . . HEAL HER, JESUS!" they screamed back.

"MAKE HER WHOLE!"

". . . MAKE HER WHOLE!

Then, seizing the woman's head in his hands, he pressed his nose into her face and shrieked at 'er, "HEAL ME, THY JEEEE-ZUS! HEAL ME, THY JEEEEEE-ZUS!" He repeated it, over and over, the organist hitting a jazz-lick after each phrase and the spotlight now switchin' from white to reds and blues.

Suddenly, abruptly, Dr. Moses released her and stepped back.

"It is done!" he gasped, and collapsed to the floor. Instantly, two assistants rushed out with fans and began coolin' him. In a minute, he appeared to regain his composure, and he stood, calm and at peace. He gently shooed his aides away and turned back to the woman, who was smiling at him, eyes bright, alert, head erect.

"Sister," he said to her softly, "arise. Get up and walk now. Get up and walk for Jesus."

Dr. Moses stepped back from her several feet. He said it

again, pointing his rod at her, louder now. "Get up! Walk! Jesus says, *'Walk!'* "

Shouts came from the audience.

"YES, YES! WALK!"

"PRAISE TH' LORD!"

"GET UP!"

"WALK FOR JESUS!"

They were sobbing again, and starting to chant, "GET UP! GET UP AND WALK FOR JESUS!"

The Mosettes hit 'em with the buckets.

The woman gripped the arms of her chair. Her knuckles turned white. Her feet slid off the footrests. She struggled, pushed, then stiffly rose and wobbled for a second, and then, weeping, she rushed across the stage to the outstretched arms of Dr. Moses, who embraced her and once again lifted his head to the heavens.

"THANK YOU, JESUS!" he cried, tears cascading down his cheeks. The spotlight narrowed till it just picked out their faces. "THANK YOU, JESUS!" The spotlight opened then as the Doctor fell to his knees, hands clasped together in front of him as the organist swung into an up-tempo "Just a Closer Walk With Thee."

People were sobbin', huggin' one another. Some tore at their clothes or the clothes of their neighbors. A few began making the strange utterances called "talking in tongues." Some writhed in the dirt. Several set themselves on fire. Fifty or so rushed the stage, hoping to be healed. They crawled, hobbled, staggered, limped, and lurched. And for each one of 'em, Doctor Moses appealed to the heavens, layin' his hands on 'em and screaming, "PRECIOUS JESUS! HEAR ME! HEAL THIS WRETCH! MAKE HIM WHOLE!"

As each turned away, to lurch, stagger, limp, and weave back to their seats, one of th' Mosettes would push a chrome bucket in front of him, blockin' his retreat until he paid the toll.

And then, it was over.

Bathed in perspiration, holdin' his Bible and rod aloft in

victory, Boone Moses strode from the tent right up the center aisle, running a gauntlet of hands grasping, clutching, reaching out in hopes of touching his garments. One long, sustained, tremendous cheer accompanied his exit.

Praise Jesus!

I sat soaked in the excitement of my own sweat, drained, just as though I were at the mercy of the teachin's of Step-Edna. I looked around me as the house lights came up. I was reminded of the big circus tent I'd seen in San Antonio. Outside, flags snapped from every pole and a banner stretched across the entrance, proclaiming, BOONE MOSES HERE TONIGHT!

Over to the left and a ways behind the tent glistened the Cavalcade of Miracles' fleet. I had watched the trucks rollin' in the night before. They were two gleaming gigantic chrome-and-white Peterbilt semis. Eight-foot-high letters announced BOONE MOSES! along their sides. They'd been followed in by a schoolbus stuffed full of Mexicans, and followin' that had come a double-decker Greyhound bus, in brilliant matchin' chrome and white, with BOONE MOSES! runnin' its entire length.

Its destination window read HEAVEN.

They had set up near the highway about a half-mile west of Elroy and Step-Edna's cafe. One of the trucks housed a diesel generator and lights burned through the night as the crew of Mexicans pulled, tugged, pounded, and cursed the tent to its full glory.

I was sittin', still dazed by Doctor Moses's service, when I felt Otis's hand shakin' my shoulder. "Snap out of it, son, come on, now." He grinned at me slyly. "Ah got somebody back here ah want you to meet."

We made our way through the crowd. Many people were weeping. Several still writhed in the dirt. Others just stood, starin' at the stage an' the spot Dr. Moses had occupied just minutes before.

"Here, comb your hair," said Otis, as we walked toward the rear of the encampment.

I saw we were not too far from Dr. Moses's bus. It looked to me to be longer than the E & E and the lights strung up around the tent rippled and shimmered on its highly polished sides. I tugged at Otis's arm. "Hey, can we get up close to it, Otis, please? I won't touch it or nothin' . . . honest."

Otis chuckled. "We can do better than that, son. Why don't we just go ahead on in?"

"Oh, Jesus! Otis, I just wanna look at it!"

He gently took me by the shoulders. "I said, boy, 'Why don't we go *in* th' bus?' "

"Otis, we can't break in this bus. God, I can't get in no more trouble."

"Ah told you, son, ah had somebody back here for you to meet."

"An'," I gulped, pointin', "you mean they're in *there?*"

"Yes, he is."

"He is?" I just couldn't figure it out. Who in the world could be inside Boone Moses's private tour bus who'd want to see me or Otis?

"Who is it, Otis?"

"Boone Moses."

Oh, Lord.

The inside of the bus was fancier than any picture you'd ever seen of somebody's livin' room. Soft plush sofas; real wood tables, waxed and shinin'; glass and marble lamps hung from the ceilin'; genuine-leather chairs; an' chrome and brass sparklin' everywhere. And sitting on one end of one of those plush sofas was Doctor J. P. Boone Moses hisself. And sittin' on the *other* end of that very same sofa was Billy Sol Hargus, utterly flabbergasted.

"Back there," Doctor Moses was sayin', gesturin' toward the rear of the bus, "is where I rest these ragged ol' weary bones."

I looked back up a central hallway and into the rear area, where a steel door stood ajar. I could see the two tiny people who'd been shakin' the tambourines during the show. Dr. Moses called 'em Nubby and Stubby. They were emptying chrome bucket after chrome bucket brimmin' with money into large canvas sacks. Their strange little voices carried to the front: ". . . 751, 752, 753, 754," they counted, gigglin' and squealin' with delight.

"Love those little bastards," said Dr. Moses, frownin' as he lit up a cigar.

Strange, I could hardly ever remember havin' heard a minister swear before—'cept for poor ol' Reverend Beamer—and I embarrassed Otis by askin' about it. He started to scold me but Dr. Moses shushed him and said it was okay.

"It beats th' shit out of a week's worth of los and verilys," he explained. "In fact, the only people who don't cuss are east-coast morons with a mouth full of teeth and these poor bastards around here with a head full of mumbo jumbo. Besides," he said, grinnin', "I'm not interested in knowin' people who can't express themselves with a little color, and," he spread his arms grandly, "I'm interested in knowin' everybody!"

"Fuckin' A," said Otis, "fuckin' A."

"Ya see there?" said th' Doctor. His voice rumbled up from deep inside him like it was coming out of a rocky well. "Hoarse, too," he observed, clearin' his throat, "from screamin' at them poor souls for thirty years." He looked over at Otis and smiled. "That's why I liked ol' Otis here ever since I first run into 'im at that broke-down fillin' station of his. He interested me when he come flyin' outta there swearin' at me to move our truck outta his driveway. Why, my God, th' man used some stuff I'd never heard before nor since. 'Get that toad-rapin' pile of swamp-suck offa my property, ya mammy-jammin' chicken-fucker!' "

Boone threw his head back and let out a laugh, long and loud.

Just then a woman walked forward from the rear of the bus. She looked remarkably like the woman Dr. Moses had healed during the services, except she had dark hair, her complexion was rosy, and she looked as fit as could be. Wait a minute! My *God!* It was her! I fell to my knees and looked up at her. "PRAISE JESUS!" I shouted. "SHE'S WHOLE! SHE'S WHOLE!" I bowed my head.

Otis kicked me in the rump. "Get up, ya id-jit. This here's Mrs. Moses."

The Doctor then formally introduced her around, and she sat down beside him. He put his arm around her and looked at her fondly. "Been right where she is now," he said, "for over thirty years. I love her like she was my wife."

The woman smiled and put her hand on his arm. "I *am* your wife," she reminded him gently.

Dr. Moses laughed and blew a mushroom of smoke that hung over us in a cloud for most of the next two hours, as he periodically added to it.

Mrs. Moses got up and excused herself as a series of noises came out of the back room that sounded like a couple of alley cats fightin'. It was Nubby and Stubby. She said she'd rejoin us after she'd "straightened out those two."

"Now, don't you go layin' a hand on them, woman," warned Dr. Moses as his wife entered the hallway. "Let the little bastards have some fun." He wiped his face with a large red handkerchief pulled from his hip pocket. He seemed tired. The lines in his face deepened as we sat and talked.

"Y'all right, kid?" he asked.

"Yes, sir."

He laughed and stuffed his handkerchief back in his pocket. "Don't ever say 'sir' to anybody, son, unless they're handin' you money. Now, since I don't feel no sudden surge of generosity sweepin' over me, why don't you just call me Boone."

"Yes, sir."

He laughed again and said, "Goddamn, Otis, where'd you come up with th' boy here?"

"Damned near raised 'im from a pup on my front porch," Otis replied. "Plus," he added, "you may not remember it, but you met his mama when you was through here back in '34."

Boone appeared puzzled. "I did?" He shot a nervous glance back over his shoulder toward the rear of the bus, where Mrs. Moses had gone. Then, lookin' at Otis, he whispered, "Wilma?"

Otis nodded.

Boone stared at me hard. "Yep. Yep, I can see it." Then he smiled. "Fine woman your mama was, boy. Sure as hell wasn't a hysterical hollerin' spoilsport like them others was."

He settled back, puffin' on his cigar. "Otis tells me you want to preach. That right, son?"

"Yes," I answered. "I have thought on it some."

"What you gonna preach?" he asked.

"Why, I guess, the Word of God," I said, startled, wonderin' what in the world he could mean by such a question.

He chuckled. "You gonna read the Bible to 'em, are you?"

Before I could answer, Mrs. Moses came marchin' out with a screamin', squirmin' Nubby and Stubby. She had each of 'em by the collar and she thrust them in front of Boone. "All right," she said, angrily, "tell Boone what you been a-doin'."

Nubby, wigglin' free from her grasp, screamed in a shrill, irritating little voice, "I'M FORTY-SEVEN GODDAMNED YEARS OLD! I DON'T GOTTA TELL NOBODY NOTHIN'!"

Stubby took a swing at Nubby with a short, fat, tiny arm. His fist missed its target by a good foot and crashed into Mrs. Moses's knee. She screamed, and he screeched, "NUBBY CALLED ME A FUCKIN' FREAK!"

Boone leaned forward and grabbed them both by the scruff of the neck, then banged their heads together. Their eyes crossed as he picked 'em up and propped them on the sofa. Four knotty little feet dangled in the air over the edge. Boone shoved a cigar in each of their mouths and, laughin', he said, "Here, now stop your goddamned bickerin'."

They puffed away, nudgin' each other and gigglin'. Nubby peered at me an' Otis. "Who's the hayseeds?" he squeaked.

Boone, laughin' again, reached over and slapped Nubby into the opposite wall. Then, wagging a finger at 'im as he introduced us, he said, "Now, you two mind your manners. The little bastards work for me," he explained, noddin' at the dwarfs. "They came with the tent." He chuckled and blew a big cloud of smoke at 'em.

They screwed up their noses and fanned at the smoke with their little arms. Nubby continued to stare at me an' Otis. "Do you think we look funny?" he asked.

"Well . . ." drawled Otis.

"Well," said Nubby, grinnin', "we think *you* do!" And they both collapsed in gales of laughter.

Boone joined in the hilarity, and with tears in his eyes, reached out, picked 'em both up, and goodnaturedly hurled them *through* the door. They landed with a thud in the dirt outside.

Boone smiled after 'em, lookin' at the door hangin' askew on one hinge. He shook his head and said, "Lord, I truly love those little fucks. I sure do."

Rubbin' his eyes, he sighed and looked back at me. "So you wanna preach the Word of God." Then he stared at me intently for a moment before askin', "How old are you, son?"

"Fifteen," I said.

He turned toward the back of the bus as Nubby and Stubby struggled back on board and headed to the rear.

"Honey," he shouted.

"What is it?" came the reply.

"Th' boy here's the same age as Ameline." Gesturin' toward the wall, he said, "That there's Ameline's picture."

She was the most beautiful girl I'd ever seen.

"Only one I ever had," said Boone, winkin' at Otis. They laughed at the private joke.

"Looks a little like your stepmama, don't she?" asked Otis.

My God! She truly did. The same long hair; full, pouty mouth; long legs; the way she stood. Her boots!

"That's a picture of her in her cheerleadin' outfit," said Boone, proudly.

"Right now, she's back home in Tulsa with her grandmother," added Mrs. Moses, excusin' herself once more to go tackle Nubby and Stubby, who had resumed pullin' teeth and gougin' eyeballs in the back.

Boone leaned forward, knockin' the ash off his cigar into a glass of scotch he'd just drained. He spoke to me without lookin' up. "You study your Bible much, boy?"

"Nearly every word in it," I assured him.

"Think you know it pretty well, do you?"

"Yes, I think so," I answered.

Boone looked up and smiled at me. "Matthew: twenty-two, fourteen."

I caught on at once an' started to open my Bible.

"No, no," Boone said, "don't look it up. Just tell me what's there, boy . . . if y'can." His eyes narrowed.

"It says," my mind was racin', " 'For many are called but few are chosen.' "

Boone was impressed. "Goddamn sure does at that! You *have* read the son of a bitch."

"Told you," I said, smugly.

"Well, sayin' it's one thing; now, what do you think it *means?*" he asked.

"Well," I said, "I think—"

Boone held up his hand to stop me. "Son," he said, "before you try to answer that, let me tell you that it don't make any goddamned difference what it means."

"But—"

"No difference," Boone went on. "*None!* Son, it just ain't important. Nothin' in that whole Book means a damned thing when you're talkin' about preachin' the Word of God." He leaned back against the sofa again and tucked a foot underneath him. Smilin', he asked, "What happened in that tent tonight, boy? D'ya know?" He picked up his silver rod from the table and slapped it in his hand, waitin' for my answer.

I looked out the window at the tent. Mexicans were swarming over it like a buncha fleas.

"Well," I said, "everybody got awfully excited."

"They damned sure did at that!" agreed Boone. Then, pickin' his Bible off of the table, he said, "And it wasn't over anything I read 'em outta this here Book, was it?" He tossed it back down. "I haven't opened a Bible to preach from in twenty-five years," he said, relaxin' like he was enjoyin' his philosophizin'.

"You see, son, every bastard in the world's got his own Bible. Some of 'em study it. Some of 'em leave it out on the coffee table for show. Most of 'em flatten out leaves 'n' stuff with it. So they ain't gonna come out and get excited if I stand up there and read stuff out of it that either they already know, or really don't care a whole lot about, are they? Hell, they can go to their own church and get a big dose of that."

I nodded, but Boone could see that this was troublin' me.

"Somethin' wrong with the way I got it figgered, son?"

"No, I guess not," I said, "but you talked a whole lot tonight *about* the Bible. . . ."

"Not true, son. I talked about JESUS. JESUS CHRIST! I talked about Him bein' *in* the Bible, but I didn't open it up, not once. I didn't read one word outta there." All of a sudden he began to sound like he had earlier, preachin'.

"I TALKED about," he continued, his voice risin', "FINDIN' Jesus Christ! I TALKED about ASKIN' Jesus to come into your heart and into your LIFE, boy!"

"Boone, you're gettin' to goin' again. . . ." It was Mrs. Moses, and it was a warnin'.

Boone caught himself, stopped, and smiled. "Jesus," he

said, "I really am gettin' too old to carry on like this." Relightin' his cigar, he continued, "These nights are startin' to take too much outta the ol' preacher boy here." He flipped his match into his empty scotch glass. "Son," he asked, "why do you figger people go to church?"

"I guess," I said, glancin' over at Otis, "it's because most of 'em's afraid not to. And . . . and they think the Lord's got a plan for their life an' if they go to church He'll reveal it to 'em."

Boone chuckled. "That's pretty goddamned true, son."

"But," I added, "the Lord don't ever have no plan, does He?"

"Right again," Boone said, impressed. He puffed and thought a moment, settlin' back just studyin' me. It made me feel a little uncomfortable. Next time he spoke it was like he was thinkin' out loud. He said, "Now, who th' hell is ever gonna tell 'em that?"

"Somebody should," I ventured.

"Oh? Oh, they should, should they?" asked Boone.

"Well, it is the 'truth,' isn't it?"

Boone held up both hands. "Whoa, there. Wait just a minute now, boy. Don't you *ever* make the mistake of thinkin' that the 'truth' has got one single solitary thing to do with what we're a-talkin' about here! We're talkin' about people goin' to church. An' that's it! Not another damned thing!" He said it firmly, though not angrily. Just like he wanted to make absolutely sure he got his point across.

"Son, you're not the first person to figure out that the Lord ain't got no plan for anybody's life. And you're not the first who ever wanted to go around explaining that to folks. But what we're talking about is people going to church, and we're talking about preachin'. We are *not* talking about runnin' willy-nilly all across the country spoutin' some damned drugstore philosophy. Y'follow what I'm sayin'?"

"I . . . I guess so."

"Look. It's like this," said Boone. "Every unfortunate son

of a bitch you'll ever meet is livin' life thinkin' somehow things'll get better."

"I know. That's exactly what Otis told me," I said.

Boone looked at 'im. "Otis," he said, "I knew there's a reason I liked you right off. You got natural smarts, boy, natural smarts."

Then he turned back to me. "Most every ignoramus out there's got nothin' in this world to look forward to. So the *real* 'truth' we're talkin' about here is 'hope.' Because, what with all these people *don't* have, 'hope' is all they *can* have. They ain't got what they need to change their lives. They can't make themselves happy. They can't even admit that what happens to them is their own damned fault, result of somethin' they themselves did. And they are surrounded by people who're in exactly th' same shape. So here's the fix they're in: They can't look to themselves for help, because they refuse to recognize *that* fundamental truth, and they sure as hell can't look to each other because they're all in the same sinkin' boat."

"But," he went on grandly, "but," he tapped a finger on his Bible and said, "a-*ha!* They *can* look to Jesus, can't they?"

I nodded.

Otis was wringin' his hands in delight. "Shit," he said. "Ah'm learnin' a whole hell of a lot just a-sittin' here listenin'!" He pulled his shirt down over his puffy, freckled belly and fired up the cigar Boone had shoved at 'im, drawin' on it till his big ol' pink face turned red.

"Why do you think there were so many damned people here tonight?" asked Boone.

" 'Cause you're so famous?" I speculated.

"Nahh," replied Boone, "I ain't *that* famous."

"Well, then," I tried again, "it was because you healed 'em."

Boone laughed so loud he caused Mrs. Moses to holler from the rear, "What's wrong?"

"Nothin', honey," Boone answered, "nothin'." Then, still chucklin' to himself, he said, "Son, I didn't heal anybody!"

Well, of course, I thought to myself, of course! Jesus had healed them. "I know you didn't heal 'em yourself, Boone. You got Jesus to heal 'em, didn't you?"

"Nope, wrong again," Boone said, smilin'. "They healed *themselves!"*

"I don't understand. . . ."

You damn sure lost me, too, on that one," said Otis, from somewhere behind a wall of smoke.

"Okay," said Boone, "let me explain somethin' to you. Now, here's the deal. You see, *anybody* who goes to church knows that the Lord wants 'em to believe in His Word and in His Son, Jesus. They *know* that! That's a 'given.' Now, once they go along with that, once they say, 'Yes, I believe in Jesus and I want Him to come into my heart,' well, instantly they start lookin' around for something good to happen to them. They expect th' doorbell to ring and standin' there'll be a guy who'll say, 'Here's a check for a million dollars an' there's a gallon of hooch and a naked blonde waitin' out in the car.' "

He lit up another cigar. Puffin' and then brushin' at the air, he put his hands on his chest and said, " 'Course there ain't no messenger from heaven, but what there *is,"* he thumped his chest, "there is *me!* Ol' Boone Moses! *Hope,* in the flesh! Somebody who can *do* somethin' for 'em, they figger. Oh sure, they *ask* Jesus to help 'em, and they *thank* Jesus, but they expect *me* to do the work."

"But you really *do* help them, don't you?"

His eyes sparkled. "Sure, after they help Jesus!" He grinned. "But you're right, Billy," he went on, "I do help them, because I help them help themselves. I don't say to 'em, 'All right, now, you people got no right to be unhappy because you can take control of your own lives. God's given you th' power. Help thyself! Heal thyself! You can do it! In fact, *only* you can do it!' No." He smiled. "They'd think I'd lost my goddamned head and sold 'em out. What *I* do is show them the joy of havin' Jesus in their heart. I show them the power of askin' Jesus for His help. All I really do, son, is get 'em into a positive frame of mind, without them even knowin' it. An' you know, thinkin' positive can work wonders. 'S true, y'know."

"But," I said, "they *think* it's you, they *think* it's Boone Moses helpin'."

"Sure they do, son. They'll never, ever think somethin's gone right because of somethin' they did themselves. And they don't *really* expect Jesus to show up at their front door with a hot deal for 'em. So who's left?" He slowly turned his silver rod around until it was pointin' right at the middle of his chest. "See, boy? They got no choice *but* to think it's me."

"Yeah, and it's *really* themselves, right?"

"Right as rain, boy, it's them. And don't you ever, ever forget that." He paused to let it sink in. "All in the world I do is get 'em started, an' then fan the spark a little bit. I don't read to 'em, I don't promise 'em anything. I simply say to them, 'Believe in Jesus! Ask Him to help you!' And of course," he said, smiling, " 'Help Jesus in return.' " His eyes searched mine. "That's reasonable, ain't it, son?"

"Yes," I said, "I think so."

"Sure, boy," he said, reachin' across to slap me on the back. "Man's gotta eat!" He grinned, puffin' away at his smoke.

"Now, then," he said, startin' to gesture with his cigar, stabbin' it back toward the rear of the bus, "once they all see Mama there gettin' up out of her wheelchair and *walkin'!* Well, PRAISE JEEEE-ZUS!"

"Boone!"

He ignored her. "Hell, they'll line up for miles, crippled, broken, bleedin', sick, and dyin'. They let me squeeze 'em and shake 'em, scream at 'em, an' . . ."

"And," I blurted out, "they go an' heal themselves!"

"That's it, boy! By God, you got it!" He fell silent for a moment. Then, slowly shakin' his head, he said, "Yes, son, they heal themselves. Y'know, the human mind is a mysterious and potent thing. If it gets convinced strongly enough that it can do something, or convinced that some certain thing's gonna happen, well . . . it just up an' happens as often as not, whether it's mendin' a broken back or walkin' across a lake! For one moment in their miserable, hopeless lives these folks up an' do somethin' for themselves. But the poor sons of bitches never realize it. They give the credit to th' Lord and ol' Boone Moses."

"See there? Then you can't argue with th' fact that you *do* give them help."

"Yes," said Boone, sighin', "I guess I do at that." A smile lightened the lines in his face as his eyes again probed deep into mine. "An' you're sayin' to me that that's what you want to do?"

I nodded.

Boone waited a moment, expectin' me to say something at that point, but I was thinkin', so he continued. "Son, I asked you a while back why you thought people came out to see me. Let me tell you why they do, and why they go to see any preacher. Let's just take you, for example. Here we got a boy talkin' about Jesus, not readin' th' Bible, now, but *talkin'* about Jesus. Now, the first thing most everybody knows about Jesus is that He was a preacher Hisself. All right, you're a preacher, or you want to be, and Jesus was a preacher. Did Jesus go around reading from some book? Hell, no! There wasn't no book to read *from!* So what'd He do? He talked about Himself! Who He was, who His Father was, what folks oughta believe in and how they oughta treat each other. Why do you suppose people listened to Him? Here you had an average boy: never went to college; never traveled nowhere; had a dead-end, common kinda god-damned job hardly no different than any buncha others back then, so why would they listen to Him? Well, aside from the fact that Jesus thankfully wasn't boring everybody to death by readin' to 'em, they listened to Him because He was *special.* Now, how'd they know that about Him?"

Boone answered his own question. "They knew it because He healed people. He performed miracles. He walked upon the water; fed the five thousand; brought people back from the dead! Now, who th' hell would risk not lissenin' to somebody like that?"

"But Jesus really did do those things," I said.

Boone smiled. "Well," he allowed, "they sure as hell do swear He did, no arguin' that. But think about it just a second, son. You've read your Book. Jesus walked upon the waters. Okay. Fine. But wait a minute. Now we're told Peter pulled the same stunt, too. Right out there on the water with Jesus, right?"

"Matthew: fourteen, twenty-nine," I boasted to him.

"Okay, son," Boone went on, "so Peter walked upon the water, but do you know what happened to him when he did? He got to thinkin' about what he was doin' and got scared and began to sink. He began to sink because . . . he started losin' his confidence!"

"Matthew: fourteen, thirty." It rolled off my tongue like silk.

"Goddamn!" laughed Boone, "I know what it is, boy!" Still chucklin', he continued, "So Jesus says to Peter—Matthew: fourteen, thirty-one" (he fired it out before I could)—" 'O thou of little faith, why didst thou doubt?' "

Boone paused, his fingers pressin' against his temples. "So the difference between Peter and Jesus was simply a matter of believin' you could do somethin' . . . faith, boy, that's what it was, faith."

"I see," I said.

"Well now, son, all that's only important when you understand that every preacher in the world is measured against Jesus. To tell the truth," said Boone, "I don't think Jesus ever really healed a soul."

"What? You really don't? Nahh, you're funnin' me."

"No, I'm not," said Boone. "Y'see, I think that all Jesus did was to give people enough faith to heal themselves! Remember? It's all right here," he said, tappin' his temple. "Jesus gave Peter the faith, the confidence, and, sure as shootin', th' boy took off and walked across the water. So why couldn't Jesus just as well give somebody else the faith to heal themselves, or feed themselves, or whatever th' hell they wanted or needed? Why, sure! He could, and He did!"

"But Jesus," I reminded him, "also raised the dead . . . the *dead.*"

Boone smiled once more. "Son, do you know if a dead person can hear or not? Or feel or not? Or see? No, you don't know that because *nobody* knows that. Oh, sure, these doctors'll tell you that *they* know. But you pin 'em down about it and you'll find that they can't tell you nothin', nothin' at all except in terms of some fuzzy, hazy, high-falutin' theory they learned in school. Well, pardon me, but horseshit! All that anybody knows for sure is that dead people don't *react* the same as live people. Beyond that, it's anybody's guess, Billy."

"Well," I asked, "who gave Jesus the faith to know that He could walk on water?"

"Or," added Otis, sittin' on the edge of his chair now, "who give Him the faith or whatever to do all that other shit He done with water, all them tricks an' stuff; turnin' it into wine an' gettin' it outta a pile o' goddamned dirt?"

"Well, now, I'll tell you something, boys," said Boone. "You ain't never heard me say that Jesus *wasn't* special, have you? Shit, no, simply because He was! Special something fierce!" He fixed his eyes on mine once more. "And, son, people expect a preacher to be somethin' pretty special, too. Unfortunately, most all the time they're awful disappointed. Every town I've appeared in, they's been some ol' boy like Reverend Beamer, for example, God bless 'im, standin' up each Sunday, readin' th' Bible and hopin' his people'll love Jesus enough so that he'll be able to pay th' goddamned rent! But, *you* know, and *I* know, an' you better believe that *they* know, anybody can read the Bible. Yes, *anybody* can read the Bible, but . . ." He poked a finger right in my chest. "But 'many are called; few, though, are *chosen,'* chosen to give them *faith;* the *faith,* boy, to help themselves! Son, once they find Jesus, they shouldn't have to look one inch farther than where you're standin' for the answer to their horrible, hopeless lives.

He stared down at his cigar, which had long since gone cold, rollin' it between his fingers.

I looked down at my lap, where my fingers were playin' with themselves.

Finally, it was Otis who broke the heaviness of the moment, as he laughed and slapped hisself. "Goddamn!" he said, "ah never heard nothin' this good, never!"

Boone smiled at 'im. You could sure tell he liked ol' Otis. But then, damn near everybody did.

"Yes, son," said Boone, "they come see me and they'll go to see you if they even get the slightest glimmer that you might be able to pull off some of the stuff that Jesus did."

"You mean, give them faith?" I asked.

"Understand me now, boy," Boone cautioned, "if they believe Jesus healed people, they're gonna believe you c'n heal people. I told you the poor sons of bitches will never see it any other way. And," he added, grinnin', "the more stuff you can pull that Jesus did the more people are goin' to come see you do it."

"You mean," I asked, "I gotta actually do it? Pull off the same stuff? Heal people? Raise the dead? Walk on water?"

"Whoa, now, young'un." Boone threw a rein on me. "You don't have to *do* anything, you just gotta make them *think* you can. Once they *think* you can, they'll do the rest themselves. Your job is just to prime th' pump a little."

"Like with Mrs. Moses?" giggled Otis.

"Egg-fucking-zactly," laughed Boone. "Egg-fucking-zactly."

He looked out the window then, frowned, and said, "Shit!" He hollered at Nubby an' Stubby. They bounced into the room, bobbin' and jerkin' like they were on springs. "Get over there," Boone said, pointin' out the window, "and straighten out them assholes before they wreck the goddamned tent."

Nubby and Stubby skipped an' ran out the door, their

little arms pinwheelin' as they hollered at what appeared to be about a hundred fairly-well-confused "wetback bean-bandits," as Otis described 'em.

Boone liked that. "Goddamnit, Otis, you know, I sure as hell could use somebody like you to handle that bunch of whatever you called 'em . . . y'know that?"

"Ah'd shoot the sumbitches," said Otis, lookin' at the mild chaos outside."

"And then, I suppose," laughed Boone, "*you'd* put up the tent?"

"Well," figured Otis, "ah'd wait till they got it up, an' then ah'd shoot 'em."

Boone slapped his thigh. "An' then who'd take the tent down?"

"Aw, shit," grinned Otis, cornered.

We all laughed.

"How much money you makin' with that junkyard of yours you call a service station, anyway?" Boone had turned serious.

Otis shrugged his shoulders. "Ah eat. Ah do what the hell ah want when ah want to do it, so ah'm' gettin' by."

"Don't sound like much," said Boone. "Why don't you sell th' son of a bitch an' throw in with me?"

"Aw, shit, Boone." Otis frowned. "Ah couldn't do that. Ah couldn't come out on it."

"Leave it, then. Burn the goddamned thing down!"

Otis chuckled. "Ah guess ah *could* do that, now." Then, lookin' over at me, he said, "But ah couldn't do that to th' boy; nope, ah sure couldn't. He's all ah got."

"Otis," Boone said quietly, "th' boy's goin' with me."

Otis stared.

"I'm gonna take him, O', if he'll go. And you'll let him go if you really want what's best for him. I been around this racket an awful long time, Otis, and I can smell a natural, and Otis, this boy stinks."

"I *do?* D'ya really mean it, Boone?"

"I really mean it, boy."

Otis looked first at Boone, then at me. "God, Billy," he said, "are you absolutely sure this preachin' thing is what you wanna do? I mean, if it is, you'd be luckier than you could ever realize havin' Boone Moses take you under his wing. But are you certain, son?"

"It's really not me who's sure, Otis," I said. "It's Jesus."

Boone rolled his eyes, and then he said, "See what I mean, Otis? . . . Stinks."

Otis fell quiet for a full minute. He started to speak, and then stopped. He tapped his cigar with his forefinger, studyin' it. Finally, he said, "You'll have to talk with th' boy's stepmother." Then he added, almost to himself as he continued studyin' his cigar, "You sure as hell can't talk with his 'fodder.' "

Boone, all business at the moment, missed th' joke."

"Okay," he said, "I'll take care of it. We'll see to it first thing in the mornin', me and the Missus. Done."

Otis had turned to the side, awkwardly lookin' out one of the bus's windows, away from us. I reached over an' tugged at his arm. He waved me away, still lookin' out the window at nothin'.

"Otis?" I said. "What do you think?"

"Sounds like a damned fine deal to me, son," he said to the window. "A damned fine deal."

I took hold of his shoulder and pulled him around. It was the second time I'd seen Otis Blackwood cry.

Boone saw, too, an' thoughtfully excused himself so we could be by ourselves for a moment. "Gotta go water my snake," he said.

When he came back, me and Otis was sittin', quiet. Boone settled hisself back down on the couch. He looked at us, raisin' his bushy eyebrows as if to say, "Well?"

Otis spoke first. "Boone," he began, "you really weren't talkin' serious, were you, when you was sayin' 'bout needin' somebody to ride herd on that buncha wetbacks?"

"Is two hundred and fifty dollars a week serious? And," he laughed, "all the ammunition y'can burn?"

Otis's eyes were lookin' a little misty again. He laughed, and his words caught for just a second in his throat. "Aw, Boone, ah just can't believe it! That'd be well, it'd just be the best, that's what. Just th' best!" Then he turned to me, his eyes urgent. "But, Billy," he slapped his hand on his forehead, "I forgot. Tyrone! Jesus Christ. Tyrone! We can't go anywhere. What would we do about that nappy-headed ol' son of a bitch, just throw his ass out? Leave 'im? Boone, ah'm sorry, but ah just couldn't—"

"You mean," Boone interrupted, "that goddamned colored feller who was on his knees out there in front of the tent tonight? That th' one?"

"That's him," Otis answered. "You see, Boone, I damn near raised him from a pup, too. I wound up with a black 'un and a white 'un here. And they's a set, Boone. God, me an' Billy'd just love to go with you. You're more than generous, but—"

"YOU MEAN THAT GUY SITTIN' ON THAT LITTLE THING WITH THE SKATE WHEELS OR WHATEVER ON IT?" Boone bellowed.

Otis, taken aback, nodded.

"Why, shit, O', that's the slickest act I ever saw, or at least one of 'em," he said, winkin' at us. "LEAVE him?!? God-DAMN! We'll make him the chairman of the board!" He threw back his head and laughed till he was cryin', too.

He got up, as Mrs. Moses came rushin' from the rear of the bus. Otis and I stood up and Boone put his arms around us both. "I love you boys," he said, "I love that colored boy, and I truly love them goddamn little midgets." And then he shouted, "AND JESUS LOVES US ALL!"

It was October 15, 1950.

A Sunday.

EDITOR'S NOTE—*At this point in his narrative, Dr. Hargus was heard in the third of four conversations with a man authorities concluded was Tyrone G. Jefferson, a trusted aide who assisted the Doctor during the recording of the*

Hargus Tapes. Mr. Jefferson's voice was the only other heard in any of the authorized taped material. In our effort to faithfully preserve the accuracy of the narrative and the sense of urgency that attended its communication, as well as to adhere to the conditions set forth for the tapes' transcription, each of the four exchanges has been included in its entirety. (ED.)

Hey, Rev!

Yes, Tyrone, what th' hell is it now, Tyrone?

Lissen, Rev, I hate to do this to you, but there's somebody down there on th' highway wants to come up here an' talk to you.

Tyrone! Goddamnit! I told you to run those kids' asses outta here. Now do it!

I did, Rev, damnit! This ain't them. Will you jus' lissen to me a minute? It's . . . it's your mama, Rev.

Step-Edna? Here? Oh, shit!

No, no, Rev. Your mama! Your real, true mama!

. . . Wilma?!?

Yes, goddamnit, an' she's an old woman, Rev. I can't be goin' down there and tellin' her to get the hell outta here.

You sure as shit can too! You know goddamned good and well my mama's been dead for years 'n' years. Now, whoever the hell it is, get rid of 'em, fast!

Rev, so help me, I know it sounds crazy, but it is her, an' she ain't no ghost neither.

. . . Holy Ghost?

Fuck that, Rev, it's Wilma. It ain't gonna help nobody in the world for you to do this. I just can't tell that ol' woman that you don't wanna see 'er.

Goddamn! Let me explain somethin' to you, Tyrone. Every son of a bitch I ever met claims he knew my mama, you an' Otis an' Boone—everybody; even a crippled-up ol' bastard I tried to heal in Houston. 'Member that one? The one that died on me in front of eighty thousand people?

Well, the last thing th' son of a bitch says to me, he says, in his dyin' goddamn breath, "Your mama, Reverend, she wasn't like them others."

Yeah, Rev, I know all about that.

Well, I don't believe all that shit. Never did. So now I'm supposed to believe some crazy woman out here in the middle of nowhere is my long dead mama? That's shit, Tyrone, an' so are you if you don't get down there an' run her ass off.

Rev, it's her. I swear to God.

You poor dumb bastard. You never did know nothin'! Get your sorry butt down there before this goddamned rain drowns us and GIT RID OF HER! JESUS! IS THAT SO DIFFICULT TO UNDERSTAND?!?

. . . I can't do it, Rev.

GODDAMNIT, TYRONE! WE'VE COME THIS FAR AND YOU'VE HELPED ME; ARE YOU GONNA SELL ME OUT NOW? YOU GONNA TURN OUT TO BE MY FUCKING JUDAS?

'Course not, Rev. You know I ain't got no choice, what with everybody in the whole damned world huntin' us. But it ain't gonna work. They gonna get us. I know it! So it just ain't gonna help you or nobody else to break that old woman's heart!

FUCK HER HEART! D'YA HEAR ME, YA BASTARD? FUCK HER HEART! MY MAMA'S DEAD! DEAD! DEAD MAMA, MAMA DEAD! UNDERSTAND, YOU THICK-SKULLED MORON?

Shhhh! Jesus, Rev, you gonna *raise* th' dead, you don't lower your voice!

THE LORD IS COMIN', YA SON OF A BITCH! HE'S COMIN' T'GET ME ANY GODDAMNED SECOND NOW AN' YOU'RE ABOUT TO RUIN THE WHOLE DEAL!

. . . My God, Rev. I'm honestly afraid you really do believe all this shit. I swear to Christ I think you do.

Okay. Look, Tyrone, if it'll make you happy, how 'bout if I wave to her?

Wave? You're gonna wave to your own flesh-and-blood mama?

Yeah. Go on down there, tell 'er to look up here. I'll wave, and then tell 'er to get the fuck outta here.

Lord, Lord.

. . . And Tyrone . . .

What?

Hand me a stick before you go down there.

What for?

Never mind.

. . . This 'un?

Nah, bigger, that one over there. Yeah, right there. Is that one heavy?

Yeah.

Give it to me.

LIFE

YOUTHFUL TEXAS MINISTER DOMINATES RENEWED REVIVAL SCENE

New York Ad Agency says, "You Ain't Seen Nothing Yet."

NEW YORK—He may be, as his Texas mentor says, "hardly dry behind the ears," but 21-year-old Billy Sol Hargus has burst upon the American scene as the predominant force in a dramatic revival of old-fashioned evangelism. And, with the retention of the New York City advertising firm of Godfrey, Olgemyier and Dunleavy, Billy Sol Hargus appears to be headed for the rarefied atmosphere of true superstardom.

Already, the Hargus Crusade has attained miniconglomerate status with holdings that range from cattle to motels, and now Godfrey, Olgemyier and Dunleavy are launching the Reverend into a huge new mail-order business whose potential seems limitless. Radio and a nationwide television show . . .

REEL 10

◆

September 1, 1957.

A Sunday.

"Billy!" hollered Tyrone, "Bossman's lookin' for your ass!"

"Boone?"

Tyrone looked exasperated. "Your name might be on the trucks, Billy, but Boone's still th' boss."

The door of the bus flew open and Boone stormed through. If it was physically possible, smoke woulda been venting out his ears. He slammed his rod down on a crystal lamp and expensive glass exploded in every direction. He glared at me. The muscles in his face twitched. His nostrils flared. He looked like he was ready to kill. Towerin' over me, tremblin' with fury, he started in:

"WOULD YOU MIND TELLIN' ME, YOUR WORSHIP, WHAT THE HELL IS GOIN' ON HERE? WOULD YOU JUST GODDAMNIT TELL ME WHAT THE VERY FUCK IT IS YOU'RE DOIN'?"

I didn't dare try to answer him.

"WOULD YOU BE SO GODDAMNED KIND AS TO TELL ME WHAT TH' SHIT THAT WAS IN THERE TONIGHT?" He was bendin' over me with one arm gesturin' wildly behind him in the general direction of the Flagstaff, Arizona, Civic Center where we'd just appeared. Our bus and the support trucks were drawn up in a tight circle at the rear of the buildin'.

"WELL?" Boone screamed, his voice crackin' with emotion.

"Wha' . . . wh'-what d'ya mean, Boone? I . . ."

"YOU, GODDAMN YOU! YOU KNOW EXACTLY WHAT I MEAN!"

"But, Boone . . ."

"BUT BOONE MY GODDAMN ASS! What th' HELL could have POSSESSED you?"

I don't think I had ever seen anyone so furious. Finally, he slumped into a chair across from me. He didn't look at me nor speak to me for several minutes. When he did, he was calmer, though only by degrees. His voice still trembled.

"Son," he began sternly, evenly, one fist clenching and unclenching on the arm of the chair, "don't you ever, *ever* in your life stand up again in front of ten thousand people and *tell them to go home!* Jesus H. Christ, I can't believe it!" He shook his head and laughed scornfully. "You actually stood up there and told all of those people to go home and solve their own fuckin' problems! Honest to God, you've just lost your mind! Tellin' them to stop comin' to see you if they were thinkin' you were gonna do somethin' for 'em. I'll be dipped in shit if you didn't tell ten thousand people that they were *assholes* for believin' you could help 'em. *Assholes!* My God, my God," he said, still shakin' his head.

"Yes, Boone, but . . ."

"YES BOONE! YES BOONE! YES BOONE BULL!" he hollered.

"Boone," I said quietly, "I been preachin' like you taught me now for—"

"For six goddamn years, son. *Six!* I know how long it's been. A sixteen-year-old boy wonder, they called you. I know the whole goddamn story because, to straighten out your obviously short memory, I *wrote it!* I *made you everything you are right now, boy!* An' lemme tell you somethin' else, genius. We're gonna do five million this year. *Five million dollars,* barrin' any more stunts like you pulled in there tonight!"

"Yes, Boone, I know. . . ."

" 'Yes, Boone, I know,' " he mocked. "Do you, now? Do you? Do you know what we should've done here tonight? Seventeen grand! In this pisshole Flagstaff, we should've pulled seventeen thousand dollars! All you had to do was bring Tyrone back from the goddamned dead and we would've done seventeen! But, nnnOOOOooooo! You couldn't do that. Huh-uh. You had to go tellin' them the one thing they can *not* handle, that they can fix up themselves without Jesus' or your help. Then we capped it, didn't we," he said derisively, "by callin' them a bunch of stupid assholes. Jesus H. Christ!" He paused, unsure of just where to go next. But he found it. "Well," he said, "just you lemme tell you who the stupid asshole is."

"Who?" I asked weakly.

"Got a mirror?" he sneered.

Boone was on his feet again, pacin'. "Eight hundred seventy-four dollars! We did eight hundred seventy-four fuckin' dollars." He stopped and leveled his rod at me. "You know how much that is outta ten thousand people?"

"Uh, lemme see . . . it's about . . ."

"Moron! It ain't quite nine-cents-per! NINE CENTS! Jesus Christ, that don't pay th' goddamned Mexicans!" He sat down and buried his head in his hands, still mutterin', "Seventeen thousand right out th' ol poop chute. Sweet Jesus!"

"Boone," I said softly, hopin' he'd let me finish, "what's wrong is, I ain't really been preachin' the Word of God. You know, like . . ."

He looked up at me. "Billy," he asked plaintively, "how many times we been through this?"

I nodded. "Yeah, Boone, I know, I know. But goddamnit, it just ain't right no more. It's like I'm lyin' to 'em—and doin' it in the name of God. I'm just helpin' twist their thinkin'. Maybe if I was up front with 'em, we could straighten out in their minds how it really is. We both know that Jesus ain't really gonna personally do nothin' for 'em, and I can't personally do nothin' for 'em either. It don't seem right anymore for me to stand up there and *not* tell 'em the truth; that it's *them,* and *only them,* who can make a difference in their lives. Goddamnit! I just can't go on preachin' a lie!"

Boone leaned forward, elbows restin' on his knees and his head hangin', a perfect portrait in frustration. "Well, fine, son," he said. "Fine. Just fine." He sat back, looked at the ceiling, and pressed his fingers against his forehead. Then, sighin', he started in:

"You know, Billy, because we've plowed this same goddamn row enough times, they ain't never, ever gonna believe it's them that can change things because they don't *want* to believe it. Shit! They want, Billy, somebody to hand 'em stuff. *Hand* it to 'em, Billy. They don't want to know it's them that can change things because that would make them responsible, Billy, and they don't want th' responsibility, Billy. They want to be *led,* Billy. We are dealing with sheep, Billy! Do you get the picture, Billy???"

I sat quietly for a moment with him glowerin' at me, and then I decided to make a stand. It was a mistake. "Well," I began, "the reason they want to be led and don't want the responsibility is because nobody ever told 'em otherwise."

"IDIOT!" Boone shrieked. "IDIOT! YOU SURE AS HELL TRIED TO TELL 'EM TONIGHT, DIDN'T YOU? AND WHAT TH' HELL HAPPENED WHEN YOU DID? EIGHT HUNDRED SEVENTY-FOUR LOUSY GODDAMNED DOLLARS IS WHAT HAPPENED!" He rolled his eyes at the ceiling. "Eight hundred seventy-four dollars. And most of that they threw at you. Plus, they liked to tore the goddamned building down, and Nubby layin' back there damn near dead 'cause somebody tried to stuff him in a bucket. But you told 'em. Yep. You damn sure straightened their ass out! Boy, you were just terrific!"

"I didn't think . . ."

"Now that's the first intelligent thing you've said all night. You 'didn't think.' I sure as shit *hope* that wasn't any demonstration of thinkin'. Just what the hell did you figure they'd do when you called 'em assholes? Thank you? Jesus!" He stared at the opposite wall for a full minute before continuing. "Boy, you think about this: You got a chance here to become the greatest there's ever been. An' I know because I've seen 'em all. There ain't never been none better. You've watched 'em react to you for a long time now. The ignorant sons of bitches actually worship the ground you walk on."

"Yeah, Boone, but they don't really know why, and that's all the more reason we oughta tell 'em th' truth. . . ."

Boone let out a little whimper, an' got up and started pacin' again. "Goddamnit!" he shouted. "They understand a hell of a lot more than you'll ever have the sense to realize! I've told you ten thousand times if I've told you once that all they've got is hope. *Hope!* And you represent it for 'em." He stopped and looked at me in disbelief. Well, son, they ain't ridin' all over the country in a fine, big, fancy-ass bus, are they? They ain't wearin' hand-tooled boots an' three-hundred-dollar custom suits, are they? They ain't big-shot big-shits, so it's easy for you to call them assholes, isn't it? Well, get this through your thick head: These . . . 'assholes,' as you call 'em, are responsible for everything you've got, all of this!" His arm swept around th' room. "Every goddamned thing you got, boy, they put here. And you know the pathetic thing about it? They don't mind. They're *glad* you got it. They know who you are and they know how you came to be who you are, and they're happy for you. *Happy!* Why? Because you're able to give them something that nobody can buy at any price. *Hope,* you fucking idiot! An' you're gonna call 'em 'assholes,' huh? Okay. Fine. But you think about this:

"They will take this bus, and those trucks, and th' ranch, and the high-rise in Dallas, and them two hotels in Austin, your club in Reno, the Hargusday Inn Motels an' . . . and every other damn thing down to and including the chrome buckets and that zoot-suit diamond ring about to break your pinky there. You take their hope, boy, and they'll see to it that your ass burns. And you can take that to the bank because that's a Boone Moses guaran-goddamn-tee!"

Boone got up and stepped to the door. "You sleep on that, son. Tomorrow night they'll be twenty-five thousand waitin' for you in Phoenix. So you just think it over, and we'll talk in the mornin'. I gotta go see Otis."

Instinctively I flinched, waiting for the door to slam, but it closed silently. I sat there starin' at it for a full five minutes doin' just what Boone had said to do, thinkin'. I hadn't even seen Ameline come wanderin' out from the back of the bus.

"Turn around here, Billy," she said, startlin' me.

"What for?" I asked, seein' that she only had on her bra and panties.

" 'Cause I want to see your ass," she said.

"Now, damnit, Ameline, don't go startin' this again. What're you talkin' about?"

"I just want to see if anything's left of it now that Daddy's through chewin' on it," she giggled.

"You heard?"

"Most of Arizona heard."

"Don't you think you ought to go put some clothes on 'fore he comes back?" She'd curled up a little ways down the couch from me. When I looked at her, she put one foot up on the back of the couch and the other one on the floor, her legs formin' a huge V.

"What's th' difference what I wear or don't wear, Billy, sugar? You ain't never gonna do nothin' about it, are you?" she teased. She extended the leg that had been restin' on the floor and began gently rubbin' her foot in my heathen crotch area.

Uh-oh.

I pushed it away, but it came right back. "My, my," said Ameline, feelin' my Satan shaft startin' to rear up. "What's that there, Billy?"

"Ameline, don't, now."

But she kept it up, purrin', "Why not, Billy? Hmmmm?"

Damn! I turned away from her. I'd show her a thing or two about good Christian will!

Suddenly, though, she sat up and scooted over next to me. She put both hands on my shoulder and rested her chin atop them, her lips just inches from my ear. "Billy," she said softly, serious, "what's wrong? What is it, honey?"

"Well," I told her, "it's just that me an' your daddy don't quite see eye to eye on just what we oughta be tellin . . ."

She put her finger to my lips. "No, Billy, I don't mean that ol' stuff." She snuggled up against me, tight. She dropped a hand down on my thigh and began gently squeezin'. "I mean, you know, how come you never—well, you know."

"I told you before, Ameline," I said, "it don't seem like somethin' we ought to be talkin' about." Jesus! My rascal rod felt like it was trying to tear its way outta my pants. Ameline saw and smiled. She laid her head on my shoulder, moved her hand up into my lap and began drawing lazy little circles around my member which looked as though it might just chew its way outside my zipper. She was hummin' softly.

"Ameline," I said, halfheartedly.

"Hmmmm?"

"Come on now, stop it."

"Hunnnh-uhmmm."

Goddamn 'er! Now she took hold of th' shaft right through my pants and began squeezin' it, tenderly, rhythmically.

Shit!

"I'll be right back!" she whispered hoarsely, pushin' her tongue into my ear. Then she jumped up and skipped off to the back of the bus, rear end bouncing fetchingly in her white silk panties, long blond hair switchin' back and forth across her creamy shoulders.

Damn!

When the door at the end of the hallway shut, I grabbed my heathen tool and began desperately lookin' around the room. There was Boone's silver rod lyin' on the table, but I thought that it just wouldn't seem right usin' that. There was a copy of *Life* Magazine. I could roll it up. That was a possibility. . . .

Wait! The heavy brass candlesticks on the shelves on the opposite wall. Perfect! I jumped up, ran over and grabbed one, and unzipped my pants. I pulled out my member with my left hand, hefted the candlestick in my right . . . WHAM!

ARRRGH! *God*-DAMN! *Oh,* SHIT! *Owww! Ohhh!* JESUS!

A little hesitantly, I looked down. Oh, NO! Not this again! Nothing had happened. It was standin' up at a sixty-degree angle like a rocket launcher! I put the candlestick back and now began frantically searching the room. There! There, by God. Boone's oak desk. I'd slam the sonofabitch in the drawer, that's what I'd do! I ran over to the desk, my foul tool swingin' side to side like a cobra on the prowl. I yanked open the big center drawer, stuck the insolent bastard inside, closed my eyes and . . .

SLAM!

Ameline's door shut loudly behind her as she padded back into the living room. I turned, startled, and what she saw was ol' Billy, holdin' his ramrod-stiff dick in his hand, lookin' for all th' world like he was about to pee in her daddy's desk!

She stopped short, cocked her head, and put her hands on her hips. A smile crept across her face as she patted her foot on the floor and said, sarcastically, "Bathroom's that way." But then her eyes went smoky and, gliding toward me, she said, low, "Well, all right, Billy. All right!" She'd taken off her bra and panties and had slipped on one of my shirts. Her own heathen region peeked in and out through the tails as she walked. When she reached me, one hand went straight to my sin shaft and gripped it hard. The other went around my neck as she sucked my tongue outta my mouth with her lips. She pressed herself to me, pushin' one of her thighs between mine, and her hips gently rocked against me. Locked together like that, she began pullin' me back toward the couch until we both toppled down on it. I was near hysteria. Trapped!

"God, I love it!" she whispered against my mouth. She broke away long enough to look down to see what she was holdin' there in her hands. She gave a little cry and said, "Oh, Billy, it's beautiful! . . ."

Then, with a shake of her head to flip her hair up out of the way, she buried her face in my lap.

"OHHH, LORD . . . !"

"LADIES AND GENTLEMEN . . . THE RIGHT REVEREND DOCTOR BILLY SOL HARGUSSSS!"

"Okay, son," said Otis, "go out there and tear 'em a new one!"

Everything hit at once. We had it down so perfect it was like simply flippin' a switch. At my first step from the wings and onto the stage, smilin', wavin' my Bible, the organist struck the opening chord and the choir, still hidden by the curtain, swung into our theme song, "Billy and Jesus Would've Been Best Friends."

One spotlight followed me out while three others danced and crisscrossed over the stage and the audience. As I neared the podium, the curtain began liftin' dramatically to reveal the choir, shimmerin' in their white, sequins-and-rhinestones robes.

And tonight, all of this was occurring against a backdrop of twenty-five thousand wildly cheering people. Twenty-five thousand! Boone had predicted it on the nose. "And, son," he'd added later, "after they hear about you and know you're comin', you won't have to do a thing but walk out there and flash that pretty smile before we can start hittin' 'em with the buckets!"

They had already begun to form lines leadin' back from th' stage and into the aisles; the sick, diseased, broken, limp, lame, halt, an' deaf. I hated to admit it to myself and wouldn't have told another soul, but every single time, lookin' at 'em made me wonder whether there really was a God.

Now, I looked down at 'em again and that same feelin' crept over me. They were thrustin' their arms up toward me, wigglin' their fingers, tryin' to touch me, graspin', tears in their eyes as they pleaded: "Oh, heal me, Thy Jesus. Touch me, Billy!" Or, "Dear Revern', take my baby! Please! Jus' touch th' child!"

My God! I thought. Boone's right. These poor, ignorant, trustin' souls have only Jesus and hope, an' hope means me, Billy Sol Hargus.

That night, I laid it on thick for 'em for two solid hours. I laughed with 'em and I cried with 'em. And, glancin' at my watch, every fifteen minutes I'd hit 'em with "LET'S HELP JESUS, NOW. JUST ONE MORE TIME! PRAISE HIM! SHOW HIM YOU CARE! LOOK INTO YOUR SOUL AS YOU REACH INTO YOUR POCKETBOOKS! SHOW JESUS JUST HOW MUCH YOU LOVE HIM!"

And, of course, the biggest pitch would be saved for the moments right after "The Resurrection," as we billed it: bringing ol' Tyrone back from the dead. Now, th' way that worked was like this:

As always, our advance people would go into a town ahead of us to set things up and to locate and hire an entire colored family—"to help with the service," we'd tell 'em.

Then, along about an hour and three quarters into the show, two aides would enter the back of the arena and slowly bear Tyrone down the aisles and to the stage on a stretcher. He would be lyin' beneath a sheet on which was embroidered **ETERNAL REST FUNERAL HOME.** The colored family we'd hired would trail along behind, weepin' and moanin', the man always supportin' his woman. They'd all climb slowly onto the stage and the stretcher would be tenderly placed atop a six-foot-long foldin' table that we'd draped all in white. A "doctor" would come forward with a stethoscope, peel the sheet back from Tyrone's face and chest, and solemnly kneel, listenin' for a heartbeat. Then, with the organ softly playin' "Swing Low, Sweet Chariot," and me standin' a little ways back, hands folded in front of me, watchin', our "doctor" would rise, slowly shake his head, and say, "I'm sorry. He's gone. There's nothin' more I can do."

That was my cue.

I'd step through the "family," look down at the still figure of Tyrone, then, lookin' out over the audience and holdin' my Bible high, I'd shout, "Nothing more YOU can do, sir, but . . . JESUS may not be through with this boy yet!"

Often as not, some heathen smartass would holler out just then, "Leave th' nigger lie, Billy!"

First time that had happened Tyrone had got to gigglin' and I'd had to ad lib, way ahead of when it was scripted, "PRAISE JESUS! TH' BOY'S ALIVE! WHY, LOOK, HE'S LAUGHIN'! OHHH, IT'S TH' MERRIMENT AND JOY OF TH' LORD AT WORK! THANK YOU, JEEEEE-ZUS, THANK YOU, JEEEE-ZUS!"

Tonight, though, everything went without interruption or foul-up. I invoked the name of th' Lord over Tyrone. His eyes blinked open. The "family" gasped. Tyrone slowly sat up and the house went wild. We had actually had to run for the rear exits because they were comin' over the stage, bustin' right through the line of highway patrolmen we always arranged to have set up to cover our retreat.

Later, back in the bus after things had calmed down, Boone was all smiles. Boots propped up on a table, a cloud of cigar smoke encirclin' his head, he said, "Goddamn, son, now *that's* what th' hell I'm talkin' about. Son of a bitch, I ain't never seen anything to match it."

"Yeah, you're right, Boone," I grinned, "an' I'm sorry about the other night."

He waved his hand in the air. "Don't mean a goddamn thing now, son, not a goddamn thing." His smile slowly turned into a frown, though, as he leaned forward to stub out his cigar, sayin' soberly, "I think, however, that we got us a problem here with Tyrone."

He completely took me by surprise. "Tyrone?" I asked. "Why, Boone, I think he's doin'just great."

"No, son," Boone went on, "it ain't nothin' that Tyrone's doin'. I just think we're gonna have to give some thought to that whole affair."

"The Resurrection, you mean?" I was thoroughly puzzled. "But that works. It helps 'em, I know it does!"

"Sure as hell does, don't it? No, son, the problem we have here is we've wore out its welcome. It ain't gonna be no time before somebody figgers it out. We're gettin' too big now, too much publicity. They could catch on tomorrow and blow our ass right out of the water. Nope, it's comin' out," he said flatly.

"Why, shit," he added, after pausin' for a moment, "did you know there were three families there tonight who'd packed in dead relatives? Jesus Christ! You think the word ain't gettin' out? Thank God they never made it through that damned madhouse to th' stage. What in the hell would we have done?"

I had no answer, but I had a thought and I let it out.

"Well, Boone," I ventured, "you know I'm gettin' so good that maybe, just maybe, I really could fix up one of 'em, you know? I mean, if I really concentrated an' thought on it hard enough while I was up there . . . maybe . . ."

"Watch it, boy," he warned. "That's another thing we need to talk about. I know you got all wound up in there tonight, an' there's nothin' really wrong with that. But I think it's a little strong to say stuff like, 'Well, friends, even if Jesus ain't here tonight, I am!' " He gave a little laugh, but he was serious. "Don't you think that might be stretchin' things just a little too far?"

I smiled.

"Son?" he prodded.

"Yeah," I chuckled. "I expect you're right, Boone."

But I wasn't really all that sure. No, sir, not sure at all!

Boone settled back, puffin' on a fresh cigar after pourin' hisself a little taste of Chivas. He was still chucklin' to hisself, " 'Even if Jesus ain't here, *I* am!' " He shook his head. Then, yawnin', stretchin', he said, "Well, long day tomorrow. Tucson. I'm thinkin' about turnin' in."

"Wait a minute, though, Boone," I said, stoppin' him as he started to stand. "If we can't use Tyrone, what are we gonna do?"

"Back to basics," he replied, sittin' down. "Heal people! Preach to 'em! That's always worked fine and it'll continue to work fine."

"Yes," I said, "but—"

"I know, I know," said Boone, "not like that colored boy, but we just can't risk it anymore."

He leaned back again an' freshened his drink, ponderin'. In a minute he shouted back toward the rear of the bus. "Ameline!"

"Comin', Daddy!"

She'd been back with Nubby and Stubby helpin' to count the take. It looked like it would keep 'em up most of the night. Mrs. Moses stayed home in Tulsa most of the time now. The pace of the travelin'—the one-night stands, knockin' down here an' settin' up there—had been a real strain on her.

Ameline came into the room. "My, don't you look pretty!" grinned Boone.

Lord! She did at that! She had on a shirt I'd given her and a full frilly skirt.

"That's a mighty fancy shirt you're wearin' there, honey!"

"Billy gave it to me," she said, twirlin' around, posin'. "He said it cost a hunnert an' fifty dollars!"

She wore the shirt knotted at her waist, in the manner favored by Step-Edna, and it emphasized the slimness of her waist. When her back was to her daddy she winked at me an' ran her tongue real slow over her lips, temptin' my tool as she pushed her breasts out against pure silk.

"Honey?" said Boone, gettin' her attention back. "Has that goddamn ad agency of ours come up with anything yet? We're going to have to do a little revampin' here."

"Some new stuff came in the mail today," Ameline replied.

Couple of months earlier, Boone had signed a contract with the New York advertising firm of Godfrey, Olgemyier and Dunleavy to take over our promotional matters when it became clear that we'd gone "national" and had just become too big to keep all the complicated logistics straight. Boone called the firm the "best bunch of Jews this side of Jesus. Plus," he'd laugh, "who's gonna argue with a set of initials like that—G.O.D.?"

Ameline had flopped down on the couch by Boone, reportin' to him that the agency had put together some radio and television proposals for us.

"Fine, honey," he said. Then she was up again, posin' this way an' that in front of a mirror. Boone watched her for a moment, then said, frownin', "But remember, they ain't been hired to make you no goddamned movie star."

"They should," Ameline pouted, stickin' out her tongue at us.

"Git!" Boone barked at her. "And look up that stuff they've sent us."

Ameline trotted off toward the rear. When she returned, she handed Boone a lavender notebook trimmed in gold. Raised gold script on the front announced: **GODFREY, OLGEMYIER & DUNLEAVY RADIO & TELEVISION MARKET GUIDE—BILLY SOL HARGUS.**

Boone surveyed its gaudiness and laughed. "Ain't that just like a bunch of goddamned New York phonies. Jesus, they ain't got a sincere bone in their bodies."

Ameline snuggled up next to me on the couch, nudgin' her breast against my arm. "When can I have another lesson?" she whispered. Lord! The other night I had taught her somethin' Christian!

"Now, honey," said Boone, lookin' up, "leave him be. We got work."

Otis lumbered in and sat down. "Coffee on?" he asked.

"Nubby!" hollered Boone. "Get Otis a cup, will ya?"

The rear door slammed back and Nubby barreled through, headin' for the dinin' area. He threw Otis th' finger as he trundled past, but in a minute he did return with a cup of coffee for 'im. "Here, Otis," he squeaked, an' then he flipped 'im th' finger again as he waddled back to his room.

Boone grinned at us, held his finger to his lips, gestured down the hall at the departing Nubby, and quickly overtook him on tiptoe. Just as Nubby reached up to pull open th' door, Boone turned and, givin' us a wink, he good-humoredly kicked th' little varmint against the ceiling. We all doubled over, howlin', as Boone came back in and sat down, tears in his eyes. Nubby just lay back there in the hallway, not movin'.

Boone grinned at Otis. "That'll teach the little son of a bitch, won't it, O'?"

"Sure will, Boone," Otis nodded.

Otis glanced out the window as he took a slurp of his coffee. "Damn, am ah ever glad we don't have to tote that tent around no more." He shook his head.

"Oh?" asked Boone. "And ain't you got enough to do to keep you busy anymore, boy?"

"Aw, sure ah do, Boone, you know how much ah . . ." But then he looked an' could see Boone was teasin'. He grinned down at his coffee. "Tell you what, though, ah'd sure like to shoot me a buncha goddamned Mexicans now." Otis could say anything to Boone. "We don't need near as many of 'em now that we're shed of that damned overgrown tarpaulin."

"Well," Boone said, layin' a hand on Otis's arm and lookin' real serious, "all right, O', but just one, now, hear?"

We all laughed.

Turning back to the media presentation, Boone came to a stop about a quarter of the way through the book and his eyebrows shot up. "Would you look at this," he exclaimed, runnin' his finger along the page as he read. "This here is a proposal, honest to God, for a line of . . . now get this: 'Billy Sol Hargus's Personal Products and Religious Items for a Closer Walk with Jesus'!" He looked up at us incredulously.

"What're they talkin' about, Boone?" I asked.

"Products! Services! Stuff people'd write in for and buy that's been personally endorsed by you, get it? Why . . . my God! How'd I ever miss out on this deal? Jesus Christ, this is a goddamned *gold* mine! D'you realize what we're talkin' about here?" He sat there, starin' down at the book and shakin' his head. "These people are *geniuses!* Understand this, Billy, your own line of religious stuff—think of the market! All those people, tens of thousands of 'em who hang on your every word, could get sort of a little piece of you that they could have with 'em always. Get it? *Mail order hope! Jesus! A goldmine! A goddamn goldmine!"*

"By God, Boone," I said, "I think you're right. We done just got handed us a whole new branch of our church and the wonderful services we can provide."

"Aw, shaddap," said Ameline. "You're makin' me wanna gag. You just got handed a check for ten million dollars, ya dope. That's what you just got handed."

Rare, I thought, such insight in one so young.

"What th' hell they got him sellin'?" asked Otis. "Goddamn sandals?"

"Close," laughed Boone. "Listen to this memo to us . . . says:

> The following suggestions from our creative department and market research experts represent, we believe, a vast, untapped lode of potential new revenue. Each product and/or service has been carefully designed to establish in the customer's mind a direct link between Mr. Hargus and God. In certain instances, we have created accompanying jingles to enhance the advertising of a Hargus product."

"Blue suede sandals," Otis interjected. "Bet your ass!"

"Well, I think you're close." Boone grinned. "Lemme go on here." He read once more. "As an illustration, we have included a jingle we propose to accompany a Hargus Fast Food Item, *Billy Sol's Sacred Fried Chicken.* I ain't gonna try to sing the son of a bitch, but this here's the words . . . goes like this:

One sacred chicken to go,
One with a heavenly glow,
One that's religious, nutritious, delicious,
An' so sacred it won't dirty your dishes!"

"Daddy," cried Ameline, "they're gonna die! They're just gonna die!"

"Wait." Boone held up his hand. "There's more.

Ohhh, th' kids'll be tickled to dickens,
When Mom serves one of Billy's fried chickens,
No, don't cook tonight, call Hebrew Delight,
An' for folks in th' South, the meat is all white!"

"Jesus," Boone exclaimed, "brilliant! Just all you can say—brilliant!"

"Don't it sound, maybe, just a little crazy, though?" I asked.

"Crazy like a fox, boy!" hollered Boone. "They even got a script here to go along with the thing." He unsnapped a page from the binder. "Here, 'Reverend,' read it!"

"Me?" I asked. "Out loud?"

"Come on, boy . . . you're the star!"

"Yeah," I said, "I guess you're right. Gimme it."

"Hi, friends!" the script began. "It's the Right Reverend Doctor Billy Sol Hargus comin' to you live and direct from the Discount House of Worship, right here in Del Rio, Texas, for the salvation of your soul." . . . "But, Boone," I frowned, "I ain't really no doctor of nothin'; that's just somethin' we say, you know, in our show. I can't say that on radio an'—"

"Prove it," said Boone. "Show me where it says you ain't no goddamn doctor. Play back the tape where it says you ain't one. If I was a doctor when it was me out there preachin', then *you're* a doctor, too. You name me one big-time preacher who *ain't* claimed to be a doctor of this or that. Okay? Now, no arguments."

"Okay, Boone. You're th' boss. You want me to read anymore?"

"Of course, numb-nuts, read!"

"Yessir . . . uh, Boone?"

"What now, Billy? Jesus!"

"Well," I said, "they got me talkin' here from Del Rio, Texas."

"So? That's a nice touch. They got you back in your hometown. What about it everybody? Ain't that sweet?" Boone raised his hands like he was gettin' ready to lead a choir, and everybody went, "Ahhhhhhhhh."

"Yeah," I said, "but we're buildin' our studios in Tulsa."

"Jesus," said Boone, growin' impatient, "just read the goddamn thing, would ya? An' besides, that's gonna be our mailing address: Billy Sol Hargus . . . *Doctor* Billy Sol Hargus, Del Rio, Texas. See how it works? Now read, please."

"Friends," I continued, pickin' up my place in the script, "have you sat down to Sunday dinner lately and wondered if the chicken you're eatin' is kosher? Have you wondered, friends, was the chicken you're eatin' raised by someone who perhaps does not love Jesus as much as you do? ARE YOU EATIN', FRIENDS . . ." I stopped. "Boone, what's this mean where it's wrote in big letters?"

"Raise your goddamned voice, son," laughed Boone. "Let's hear it now!"

"All right!" chorused Ameline an' Otis.

I yelled, "ARE YOU EATIN', FRIENDS, A HEATHEN CHICKEN? DID JESUS CHRIST BLESS THE FOWLS GOIN' IN YOUR JOWLS? HUH? DID HE? Friends . . . why take the chance? Just write to me here in Del Rio, Texas, an' say: 'Billy, I'd rather be safe than sorry. Send me one of your sacred friers! Same chicken sold in Billy Sol's Sacred Fried-Chicken Kitchens everywhere.' "

"Well," Boone smiled, "I just love it, that's all. It may need a little work, but I goddamn love it!"

"That's the craziest shit I ever heard in my en-tar life," muttered Otis.

"What else they got, Daddy?" giggled Ameline.

"Look here!" said Boone, thumbin' deeper into the book. "A line of dairy products an' the first one on the list here —you ain't gonna believe it—the first one is *Cheeses of Nazareth!"* He slapped his thigh and let out a howl. Ameline used the moment to ease herself over onto my lap. She started into wigglin' her behind just a tiny bit so's no one could see it, but I could sure feel it.

"Wha-what else th'-they got, Bbb . . . Boone?" I stammered.

Boone shot Ameline a sharp glance. "You botherin' him, honey?"

"No, Daddy," she replied innocently.

"Well, if ya are, stop."

"I'm not, promise," she said, wigglin' a little bit harder as she felt my heathen sword startin' to unsheathe itself and climb up against her bottom.

Boone returned to the G.O.D. proposal. "Jesus," he said, "this stuff just goes on and on. 'Billy Sol Hargus's gas-fired burning bush—cook your hamburgers on it, then worship it.' 'Billy Sol's inflatable Jesus doll, so He can always be at your side.'

" 'Billy Sol's fully illuminated portrait of Jesus with eyes that cry real tears.'

" 'Billy Sol's Automotive Jesus—put Him on your dash and you won't crash.'

. . . "Lessee. 'Billy Sol's trick Bible. The pages are blank so you can swear on it at no risk."

" 'Prayer cloths.'

" 'Towels.'

" 'Bed Sheets.'

" 'Garden hoses from Moses.'

" 'Slip covers for recovering backsliders' furniture.'

"God! Just look at this," Boone said, holdin' the book so we could see. He flipped through a list of shit that ran for fifteen pages. "Can you believe it?" he asked, chucklin'.

"No," I allowed, "I honestly can't."

Uh-oh! Jesus! Ameline was now kind of rockin' her pelvis back and forth softly, and flexing her muscles in her rear so that they nearly grabbed my now ironhard rod right through my pants. I reached up under her skirt just a bit to try to scoot her down in my lap a few inches and get her away from my member and . . . OHMIGOD! My hand hit bare flesh! She wasn't wearing any panties underneath there! Oh, SHIT! My rod convulsed upward and Ameline giggled. Swearin' at her under my breath I excused myself from the group. "Gotta go to the bathroom," I grinned through clenched teeth. "It's th' damn coffee. Runs through me like shit through a goose." Now she had to move off me, though she made a face at me as I stood up. Bein' careful to keep my back to Otis and Boone, I slipped down the hall toward the lavatory, walkin' fast. God-*damn* that girl, anyway! When I got inside, I shut and locked the door, then started lookin' around for somethin' I could use. There it was. The long-handled brush the Mexican woman used to swab out the toilet. It wasn't very heavy but it would have to do. I unfastened my pants. My Satanic shaft fired through the opening like a torpedo. And, by God, it was grinnin' at me again, so help me! I thought to myself, I'll wipe that grin off your heathen face, you cyclops-lookin' demon! Holding my dick with my left hand, I reached down, grabbed the brush with my right, raised it high and . . . POW!

GODDAMNSONOFABITCH! SHIT! OWWW! DAMN! OHHHH, Ch-RIST! Ohhh!

. . . Whew! I looked down. Oh, NO! Not again! It had done exactly nothing! No effect!

"What happened, Billy?" It was Ameline, hollerin' at me from the livin' room. "You fall in?"

Goddamn her!

"Yeah, son," yelled Boone, "come on. We got some more to go over here!"

And there I stood with my dick doin' its tent-pole act. Desperately, I looked around once more. I opened up the medicine cabinet. Nothing at all. And then I got a brainstorm. No, not the toilet brush, but the *toilet!* Quickly, I knelt down, lifted the lid and the seat, and hung my traitorous tool over the porcelain bowl so that the whole arrangement was like a mouse stickin' its head in th' trap just before she goes KA-THWANG!

I grabbed the seat and lid in my right hand, closed my eyes, gritted my teeth . . . and stopped. I couldn't do it. Shit! Weak flesh, I thought. Weak flesh! Step-Edna, I need you now!

"Billy, damnit! Hurry up in there! Now *I* gotta go." It was Otis.

"Okay, okay. Hold your horses. I'm almost done," I called back, lookin' down at my heathen dick. It was still grinnin' at me, even though it was stretched out across the bowl like it was layin' in a guillotine. Bastard, I thought. Goddamnit, this'll serve you right, once and for all!

Again, I closed my eyes and set my jaw. Then, I counted to myself. One, two, and . . . TIMBERRR!

I slammed the lid shut

. . . and fainted.

I awoke a few minutes later to the sound of somebody outside the lavatory hammerin' on the door. "BILLY! BILLY! GODDAMNIT, ARE YOU ALL RIGHT IN THERE?!? DAMNIT! ANSWER ME!" It was Boone. I could hear Ameline right behind him, snickerin'. "Maybe he's upset about somethin', Daddy. He was gettin' kinda squirmy on the couch, ya know." Rotten bitch, I thought.

As I came around I became aware of a sharp throbbin' down in my "sin-bin." I looked. My member, quite understandably, was more shriveled up than I'd ever seen it, and I'll swear, it looked panicked. Just like whatever possessed th' damned thing was in there beggin', Hey . . . Jesus Christ, take it easy! Please, not again, okay?

No, I thought, *not* okay.

Gently, I tucked it back inside my pants, zipped, stood, a little wobbly, splashed some cold water on my face, and then opened the door. I grinned sheepishly at Boone and said, "Sorry, took a little longer than usual."

"Well, goddamn, boy," he said, "we coulda driven halfway to Tucson."

Ameline was standin' behind him, grinnin' at me. She stuck out her tongue and made a face, then we all trooped back into the living room.

I sat way at one end of the couch, the opposite end from where Ameline had flopped, makin' sure I put plenty of distance between us.

Boone picked up the G.O.D. "idea" book again and held it in both hands, studyin' th' cover. "I just love it," he said quietly. "Just goddamn love it! Ameline, honey, you call these bastards in the mornin' and tell 'em that. Just tell 'em that I love it *and* them, okay?"

"Sure, Daddy, first thing in the mornin'."

Why that little shit, she was scoochin' down the couch toward me again!

"And tell 'em," Boone added, "that as far as we're concerned at this end, it's 'go!' all the way to goddamned New York! Right, son?" he asked, lookin' at me.

"Right, Boone," I said, "it all sounds great except for just one thing."

He frowned. "What's that?"

"Tyrone," I answered. "What are we gonna do about Tyrone if we're cuttin' the Resurrection bit?"

Boone folded his arms across his chest, holdin' the media book to him and looked at the floor, obviously tryin' to puzzle it out. In a moment he spoke. "Ameline, when you talk to them New York boys in the morning, explain the Tyrone situation to 'em and get 'em to come up with something we can use out here on the road."

"Okay, Daddy."

Boone stood up and smiled down at all of us. "Well," he said, still cradlin' the book across his chest, "there's plenty for Tyrone to do. Let's not worry about it. We got Tucson tomorrow, right?"

"Right!" we chorused.

"Okay," he said. "I'm goin' to hit the hay and I'd suggest that y'all oughta do the same right quick." He started movin' off down the hallway toward his room.

Otis stood and stretched. "Well," he said, "guess ah'll hit it, too."

"Yeah," I agreed, startin' to stand, "you an' me both."

A hand grabbed the back of my pants and yanked me back down. Ameline. "We'll be along directly," she told Otis. "Just got one or two more things I want to get straight between me an' Billy."

Oh, shit, I thought, here we go again. Otis shuffled off on down the hallway and Ameline, hangin' onto the back of my belt, leaned out and watched him till his door closed with a soft click.

Instantly, she reached up and grabbed my shoulder, spun me around toward her, and rammed her tongue into my mouth. Her other hand was clawin' open her blouse, and then pullin' her skirt up around her waist.

"Ameline . . ."

"Shut th' fuck up," she mouthed against me.

She raised up and pushed a nipple into my face, then, grabbin' me by the ears, she fell backward and pulled my head down smack between her legs.

Odd, I felt, that it should occur to me just at that moment, but nevertheless, I suddenly found myself thinking of the Parable of the Fishes.

How holy!

SATURDAY EVENING POST

LIVE*COAST TO COAST RADIO*LIVE*COAST TO

THE

JUMP FOR JESUS SHOW

Sunday, February 23, 1958*

Starring

BILLY SOL HARGUS

The Hargus Crusade Choir

The Solettes

with teenage sensation
Bobby Kirschenbaum

AND
SPECIAL GUEST STAR
J E S U S C H R I S T

*Check local listings for time and station in your area.

representation: godfrey, olgemyier & dunleavy new york
management: dr. j. p. boone moses, tulsa, oklahoma
copyright 1958 hargus crusade, inc., del rio, texas

LIVE*COAST TO COAST RADIO*LIVE*COAST TO

REEL 11

◆

"Five minutes!" shouted Boone. He was wringing his hands nervously. "Five minutes! That's it, just five!"

"All right, Boone," I answered. "Jesus. I'm ready, already. Okay? Would you relax, for Chrissakes?" He had me on edge, the way he'd been carryin' on, although really, his agitation was entirely understandable. We were gettin' ready to take an awfully big step; our first Dr. Billy Sol Hargus *Jump For Jesus* Show was, like he said, only five minutes from hittin' the air and our new Tulsa broadcast complex was in a mild state of chaos.

"You kill those pussies! Do you understand me? Kill them! Just positively level them! Take no prisoners, okay, darling?" The voice, a cross between an opera aria and a fox terrier, came from somewhere behind me. I turned and, sure enough, mincing his way toward me was Olgemyier. Murray Olgemyier of our Madison Avenue media people, Godfrey, Olgemyier and Dunleavy. ("I'm in the middle and I simply *love* it!")

He was something else. Short, five-four, pixie face, with a fringe of salt-and.pepper hair that ran around his otherwise bald head. He'd tried to let one side grow real long so that he could part it just above his ear and comb the strands over the top to cover the bald area. It looked ridiculous, and it wasn't helped by the fact that Murray had this annoying habit of standin' real close when he talked to you, holdin' you by the elbow or layin' his hand lightly on your forearm and squinchin' up his nose like somebody had just farted. He always appeared to be just on the verge of whining. He favored tight trousers and shirts unbuttoned to his waist, exposin', as Otis described it, "enough shit hangin' around his neck to open up a hock shop."

Right now, damn 'im, Olgemyier was standin' four inches from me with his right hand resting lightly on my left forearm. "Look at this, Billy," he cooed, pluckin' a diamond-inlaid cross from the tangle of chains dangling on his chest. "I bought it just for you, sweetie."

Otis, who'd been standin' in a knot of technicians outside our main studio, overheard and strolled over. "Well," he said, "if you got it for him, then give it to him, goddamnit!"

Olgemyier raised his hands in front of his face as if to fend off a blow. "Don't hit me," he cried. "Don't you hit me."

Pathetic.

Slowly, not taking his eyes off Otis, he lowered his hands and whispered to me, "Who is *this?* Jesus, he is sooo *rural!*"

"Murray Olgemyier," I said, "meet Otis Blackwood, the man who just about raised me up to be what I am today."

Olgemyier took a step back, looked Otis up and down, smiled, and placed his hand lightly on Otis's forearm. "Hi, simply hi. My, you are a tall one, aren't you?"

"No, little feller," grinned Otis, "you're just a short one."

Suddenly, Boone came rushin' down the hall. "Let's go!" he hollered. "Where in the hell is Tyrone? Has anybody seen that damned Tyrone? And where are them goddamned midgets?" He breezed on by us down the corridor, no one havin' paid one whit of attention to him, it appeared.

Olgemyier turned to me again, movin' in tight. His voice was low and confidential. "This is show biz, sweetie; you know that, don't you? We're talkin' Vegas, babe; Big Apple! Here, let me see those gorgeous baby-blues. Oooo! Love 'em, just positively love 'em. Look at those eyes, Mr. Blackwood, could you cry? I mean, could you just break down over those?" He reached up and pinched my cheeks. It made my eyes water.

Boone had done a one-eighty down at the end of the hall and was now barrelin' back. "TYRONE! YOU, GODDAMN YOU! WHERE THE HELL'D YOU GO?"

"Boone," I soothed, "just settle down." I guided him over to the settee on the opposite wall. "Just light here a minute and calm yourself. Tyrone's haulin' the choir over, that's all."

He didn't seem to hear.

"And you, goddamn you, Otis!" he fumed. "Get your ass in gear! There ain't nothin' for you to just be standin' around for. Do somethin'! Anything! Jesus! FOUR MINUTES, EVERYBODY! FOUR MINUTES! Lord, Lord." He steamed off in the direction of the main control room, muttering under his breath. Suddenly, he stopped and whirled around. "Wait a minute here," he said. "Billy, you seen all this?" He waved an arm toward the studio.

"No, Boone, I ain't. You always been so damned busy with—"

"Well, come on, goddamnit. I gotta show you where you gotta stand, for Chrissakes. Jesus! How do these things get so fucked up?!"

"Better go ahead on, son," said Otis. "I'll keep ol' Olgedick what's-his-face company here."

Olgemyier put *both* hands lightly on Otis's forearms. "God," he exclaimed. "You are big, aren't you? *Look* at you!"

I trotted off and caught up to Boone as he stepped into the broadcast control room. He walked inside past a veritable Christmas display of lights and switches, then into an airlock chamber, and finally into the studio itself. "Well," Boone said quietly, "here she be. This is where you become the object of national attention, boy. Just look at this. A million dollars worth of electronic bullshit that only that four-eyed little Jap in there can figure out how to run!"

He grinned at the Japanese technician seated at the console in the control room, and flipped him th' finger. The little fellow smiled and waved back. Boone looked all around, noddin' to himself with satisfaction and pride. "Some layout, ain't she, Billy? Why, hell, the glass in this here bastard cost more'n our whole goddamned bus. Walls are a foot thick and this whole damned thing sits on oil-filled shock absorbers to soak up any vibrations from the street outside. And look at this. Just stick your boot down in that carpet. Ain't that somethin'? That son of a bitch could sop up a lake! Yessir," he said, gazin' around him again, "you could murder somebody with a pair of knittin' needles in here and nobody out there'd ever hear a thing."

"Boy, you ain't said th' half of it, Boone," I told him. "This place is unbelievable."

"Yeah, I know," he replied, "and just listen to this. Hey! Won Hookey, 'r whatever your name is in there, turn on them speakers for a second!"

The technician smiled at us blankly, and waved again.

"Goddamn it," Boone swore. "Hey, Charlie Chan!" he tried again, "turn-ee on-ee speak-speak. Make-ee big noise, get it?"

The engineer's eyebrows arched in understanding and he nodded vigorously behind the glass separating the control room from the studio. We watched him reach forward, twist a few knobs, and suddenly sound enveloped us.

"Jesus Christ!" I winced as the decibels hit me. "It hurts your ears!"

"Yeah, it does, don't it?" Boone said proudly. Olgemyier had come into the room and Boone slapped him on the back. "Olgemyier, you boys done a hell of a job here," he congratulated him.

"Creative did it," Olgemyier corrected. "Those little bitches are really a case! Jesus, you should see them. They work their tushes off just to be in Manhattan. They all live out in Jersey, but they work for nothing and schlepp over on the bus, rain or shine, just to be a New Yorker. God! It's just the best!"

"What is?" Boone asked.

Olgemyier looked at him like he wasn't quite bright. "Why, to be a New Yorker, of course."

It was Boone's turn to wince. "Well," he asked, when he'd recovered, "what do you New York boys think of Tulsa?"

Olgemyier's eyes disappeared into the top of his head. "Oh, my God. It's really here, isn't it? I mean, there really honest-to-God is a Tulsa! Can you survive that? It really exists!"

Boone frowned at him like he was somethin' th' dog had just thrown up. "Damn!" he exclaimed, pullin' his watch from his pocket. "Three minutes! Goddamnit! Where's the kid? Where is he? Hey! Has anybody seen, uh, oh . . . you know, whozit?"

"You wouldn't be a-meanin' this brat, would ya?" It was Otis, draggin' a boy into the studio by the scruff of the neck. The kid was trailin' a black guitar case.

Olgemyier spotted him and clasped his hands to his cheeks in horror. "Bobby!" he squealed. "Oh, my God! What have they done to you? Unhand him, you perfect savage! Turn him loose! You're creasing a genius!" He rushed over and embraced the boy protectively, a little longer than was necessary, as he stared darts at Otis.

"Ah caught th' little prick wanderin' around outside," Otis explained. "Sumbitch tried to tell me how he's gonna sing on the Rev's program. Ah figgered he was a fuckin' thief or somethin' so ah told him that he'd better sing somethin' fast or ah'd have him eatin' a git-tar sandwich!"

"Hold on, Otis," said Boone, "th' boy's alright. He really is a singer, a gospel singer, and believe it or not, he's a reconstituted Jew! Ain't that right, boy?"

Averting his eyes, the kid nodded. "Yes, sir."

Boone went on grandly. "This here is Bobby Kirschenbaum, orphaned when he was five, now a ward of the state of Oklahoma, and a flat-out prodigy, I wanna tell you, when it comes to singin' praises to th' Lord!"

Boone was beamin'. He'd discovered Bobby a few months earlier on a Tulsa street corner, singin' for his supper. Passersby would flip an occasional nickel or dime into his guitar case which he had opened at his feet. Boone had stopped to listen when the kid had begun singin' "Amazing Grace." He'd spotted the name Kirschenbaum on his guitar strap and asked him why he had chosen to sing perhaps the number-one bedrock Baptist hymn of all time.

"Because," Bobby had told him, " 'Havah Nagila' just don't cut it in Oklahoma."

Boone signed him up on the spot.

"Where are the girls?" shrilled Olgemyier. "Jesus. Whatever we do, let's keep this Otis character away from 'em. Is he large? Heavens!"

So, naturally, Boone turned to Otis and told him to go get 'em.

"My pleasure," Otis replied, givin' Olgemyier an evil little grin.

"No!" cried Olgemyier, horrified. "I'll get them!"

Otis laughed and said, "Settle down, shortstuff. If it's them four spooks in the boots you're worried about, they're right out there in the hallway nailin' their hairdos on their heads."

"You're awful," Olgemyier told Otis. "Awful, awful man. Is he awful? Christ."

Boone looked at his watch again and what color had been left in his face drained out like somebody'd pulled a stopper. "TWO MINUTES!" he shrieked. "TWO FUCKIN' MINUTES UNTIL WE GO BORDER TO BORDER AND WE'RE STANDIN' HERE LIKE IT'S TH' GODDAMN COCKTAIL HOUR! WHERE'S THEM MIDGETS? JESUS CHRIST, WHERE'S TYRONE? HUH? JUST WHERE IS HE?"

"Right there, Boone," I said. "Look. Right there through the window, see? He's got the girls, just like we said. Okay?"

"All right, goddamnit," he growled. "And Nubby and Stubby? I'll kill them little bastards."

Olgemyier shook his head, mutterin' to himself. "Jesus, Nubby and Stubby! Is this a circus? Honest to God."

"You'll love 'em," said Otis. "They're puny little runts, too!"

Boone screamed at everyone. "SHUT UP, GODDAMNIT, JUST SHUT UP! Okay, now, Olgemyier, how's this thing stackin' up? Where are we? Are we gonna make it, or what?"

"Jesus," said Olgemyier, "don't press!" He frowned, flippin' the pages of a clipboard he was carryin'. "Just give me a sec' to get myself together! How's my hair, hmmm? Be honest, now. Good? Okay, let's see here. Ummm. All right, I got it now." He dropped down on a small sofa beside me, again, I thought, unnecessarily close. "Now, then," he went on, turnin' toward me and laying a hand lightly on my forearm. "You open the show, sweetie, right?" He tightened his fingers on my arm and squeezed his eyes shut. "God!" he said. "You'll kill them." He shook his head. "Sorry, uh, where was I? Oh, yes. Anyway, you open the show, see, right here in the script, just like we went over it before. We haven't made any changes. After your opening, you introduce Bobby. God! Are the nation's young people going to adore him? Then, uh, let's see. Oh, yeah. The girls. Jesus, the girls! Billy Sol's Solettes! Can you stand it? They sing all the jingles and the bridge riffs that tie everything together. I vow to you sug', you're going to love it, and America is going to positively drool over you! God, I'm getting excited! Look at me! Am I excited?"

"Where's the goddamn choir?!" Boone was hollerin' again.

"They're right here!" somebody yelled back.

"Well, goddamnit, get 'em lined up over there," he ordered.

"Ninety seconds!"

"Jesus H. Christ," Boone wailed. "We got a minute and a

half to pull this fuckin' thing together." Then, throwin' his arms up in the air, he said, *"And where the fuck are them goddamn midgets?"*

"Boone," Otis hollered from across the studio, "they's in the bus. Jesus, you locked 'em in there. Ah'll get 'em."

"No," said Boone, "hell with 'em. Leave 'em be."

"How many people you figure are going to be listenin'?" I asked.

Olgemyier had the projections on his pad. "This is America," he said. "Look, sugar buns, we're talkin' national!" He stood up, waving his arms. "We're talking fifty, maybe sixty, million! And you're gonna demolish 'em. Remember! Take no prisoners! God! Just feel me! Am I perspiring? I mean, let's talk excitement! Jesus!"

Mostly, he just felt clammy.

"Well," sighed Boone, "the Lord knows you bastards spent enough of our hard-earned money promotin' this piece of shit. They better be listenin' out there."

Olgemyier cocked his head and winked at 'im. "Trust me on this one, big guy. You're gonna adore it, right, Billy?" He looked at me but reached over to give Boone's arm a squeeze.

Boone pulled away. "Thirty seconds!" he hollered, kind of desperately. His voice cracked.

Olgemyier took my hand in both of his and pulled me to my feet. His eyes were moist as he walked me over to my announcing position. "You truly *are* a religious man, aren't you?" he whispered.

I assured him I was. His hands felt like th' belly of a dead carp.

"When were you born?" he asked.

"July 23rd, 1935."

"Ohhh!" he squealed. "A Leo! God, I just *knew* it!"

Tyrone came lumberin' into the studio with the four Solettes in tow. *"There* you are, Tyrone!" said Boone. "Where in the hell have you been?"

Olgemyier gave Tyrone a quick once-over. "Christ," he

breathed, "who is *this?* Jesus! And *indigo,* yet! God, I positively feel faint!"

"FIFTEEN SECONDS TO AIR!" Boone hollered. "LET'S GO, GODDAMNIT! EVERYBODY WHO DON'T BELONG IN THE STUDIO, SHOVE OFF! MOVE!"

Otis headed for the door. "Go get 'em, son!" he called back. "Break y'ur dick!"

"Kill those pussies," Olgemyier shouted as he retreated toward the door. "Just leave them breathless, sugar."

"CHOIR! GIRLS! BOBBY! . . ."

"FIVE SECONDS, EVERYBODY! QUIET!"

"STAND-BY THEME . . . READY . . . OKAY!"

". . . Three, two, one, and . . . GO, GODDAMNIT!"

EDITOR'S NOTE—*The following is a verbatim transcript of Dr. Billy Sol Hargus's first national radio broadcast, aired February 23, 1958, a Sunday. The program originated in the Hargus Crusade, Incorporated, studios, KSOL, Tulsa, Oklahoma. Over three thousand radio stations contracted to carry the initial program, and eighteen hundred more joined the Hargus network in the following week.* (ED.)

ANNOUNCER: Ladies and gentlemen, the *Jump for Jesus* Show is on the air! And now, here's your host, the original *Jump for Jesus* man himself . . . the RIGHT REVEREND DOCTOR BILLY SOL HARGUS!

HARGUS: Thank you! Thank you, Boone Moses! Thank you! Well, hi, friends!

CHOIR: HI, BILLY!

HARGUS: Yes, friends, it's Billy Sol Hargus here on behalf of the Discount House of Worship comin' to you live and direct from Del Rio, Texas . . . for the salvation of your soul! We're glad tonight! We're happy! We're filled with joy! We're just bubblin' over! And you know why? I just can't keep my little secret here another second. I gotta surprise guest with me here tonight for our initial show, who you are *not* going to believe. You know who's with us here in the studio tonight?

CHOIR: Who, Billy? Who you got? Tell us!

HARGUS: All right, all right. Just settle down. Are you ready? You got hold of somethin'? Friends, our special guest tonight is . . . JESUS CHRIST! THAT'S RIGHT! JESUS CHRIST IS HERE TONIGHT AND WHAT'S MORE, HE'S COMIN' TO SEE YOU! WE ARE GOING TO SEND JEEZUS INTO YOUR HOME THIS EVENING! CHOIR? SOLETTES? HELP ME HERE A MINUTE NOW! CAN I GET A WITNESS? GREAT GOD!

CHOIR/SOLETTES:

Jesus Christ is here tonight!
Ain't no reason to be uptight!
Everything's gonna be all right
'Cause Jesus Christ is here tonight!

HARGUS: PRAISE GOD AN' PASS IT AROUND AGAIN!

CHOIR/SOLETTES:

Said Mr. J. C., Th' Man Hisself, is our guest!
You know He's better than all th' rest!
Comb your hair an' shine your shoes,
Tell the old man to lock up the booze,
And maybe you should show a little remorse,
'Cause tonight we're sendin' Jesus from our house to yours.

HARGUS: Thank you, Choir! Thank you, Solettes! Yes, friends, it's true. Jesus is with us here tonight, and we're gettin' ready to send Him out to each and every one of you. We pray there is love and charity wherever you are this night . . . and we thank you for allowin' us to visit with you for awhile. And right now, are you ready? Huh? You want *Him* to come into your home? You want Him to come into your heart? Have you prepared His room? Well, okay then! I want everybody out there to put your hands on your radio! Put your hands on your radio and close your eyes! Choir, tell 'em!

CHOIR: Here comes Jesus!

HARGUS: When?

CHOIR: Here comes Jesus . . . NOW!

HARGUS: FEEEEL YOUR RADIO! AIN'T IT WARM? YES, IT IS! THAT'S HIM! THAT'S JEEZUS! THAT'S THE WARMTH OF JESUS CHRIST SEEPIN' INTO YOUR HOUSE! DON'T HE FEEL GOOOOOOOD?

CHOIR: HALLELUJAH!

HARGUS: Friend, you better go set an extra place at the table there . . . because you asked for Him an' you got Him! Jesus is right there in your house with you. Oh, I know you can't actually see Him, but, PRAISE GOD, HE'S THERE! OHMIGOD!

CHOIR: OHMIGOD!

HARGUS: Shall we pray?

CHOIR: Say it on, now!

HARGUS: Lord, we want to thank You for sendin' Your Boy out there into the homes and hearts of each and every person lissenin' to this broadcast tonight. Yessir, that was right white of You an' we 'preciate it. Amen.

CHOIR: Amen!

HARGUS: Friends, now that we've sent you Jesus I want to tell you about the rest of our show. We got a wonderful lineup for you this evening. The choir's here as you know; the Solettes are standin' right over there lookin' snappy, and right now I want to introduce 'em to you 'cause they're lookin' and soundin' so fine. Come on over here, girls. Don't be bashful, now. Just step right up an' say "hi" to all our friends. Who's gonna go first? Thelma. Come on over here, honey. Folks, this here's Thelma!

THELMA: Hi, everybody!

HARGUS: And Bethea? Say hi, sugar.

BETHEA: What it is, y'all!

HARGUS: And Tina? Tina, folks!

TINA: Uhhhh-HUH, now!

HARGUS: Ain't she jus' somethin'? Now, that's a package, ain't it? Praise the Lord! An' last, but far from least, specially if you could see 'er, folks, meet . . . Big Mama Bobbie Mae Morton!

BOBBIE MAE: Woooowee, sugar!

HARGUS: Woooowee yourself, baby doll! That's them, folks, and they're ready to sing for you and Jesus! And friends, get th' kids around the radio there, too, because we got somethin' on the agenda tonight just for them. I'm tellin' you we got a talent gem here. A youngster who's gonna take over this country, take it over in the name of you-know-who. I want you to welcome him *right* now. . . . Friends, meet little Bobby Kirschenbaum, who's about to put a giant hurt on ya, the way he's gonna sing tonight. Hiya, Bobby!

BOBBY: Hello, Doctor Hargus.

HARGUS: How about that, friends—isn't it a miracle on feet? Come on over here, Bobby. Here. Let me put this microphone down a bit so's we can talk. Folks, I'm sure little Bobby won't mind if I tell everybody something that happened to us here just before we went on the air. Okay, Bobby?

BOBBY: Wha—

HARGUS: I didn't think so. You see, little Bobby here, friends, is a Jew, God bless 'im, and this evenin', while I was back in the Hargus Crusade bus, prayin' for guidance before we went on the air, Bobby knocked on my door, didn't you, son?

BOBBY: Mrf—

HARGUS: Yes, he knocked on my door and I opened it and saw this youngster, troubled. For tears were a-streamin' down this little face! And I looked at 'im and I said, "Why, Bobby, Bobby, why is your heart heavy? What is it, son? What could it be?" And friends, I want you to know right now that he stood there, lookin' tiny and helpless, framed in my doorway, and he said to me, "Doctor Hargus?" And I said, "Yes, son?" "Doctor Hargus," he said, "I want to apologize." Well, friends, I was taken aback. I looked at him, thinkin', What could this fine boy possibly have done? And then, chokin' back his tears, little Bobby Kirschenbaum looked up and said to me, "I want to apologize for what we did to Jesus."

BOBBY: I did WHAT?

HARGUS: It's all right, son. No need to be 'shamed. Isn't that *wonderful,* folks? All over America now, isn't that *wonderful?* Choir?

CHOIR: It's wonderful, wonderful, so they say.

HARGUS: So they say! So they say, indeed. Well, Bobby, I want to tell you right now, young man, speakin' for Jesus . . . apology accepted! That is, if you'll sing somethin' for us. Will you?

BOBBY: I said WHAT?

HARGUS: Wonderful, Bobby! What's it goin' to be?! Your brand new record?

BOBBY: Album . . . bu—

HARGUS: Album! Sorry! Isn't that Jesus at work, friends? It's a whole album! And do you know what, dear people? I want you to get a hankie now or a tissue, because . . . well, because when you hear what I got to tell you next, it's gonna cause some damp eyes here and there amongst you, just as it did right here when we first heard it a little while earlier tonight. You know what little Bobby came up and whispered to me just before we went on the air? He said, "Doctor Hargus, I want to donate *all* the money I make from my new album, I want to take all of that, an' give it to Jesus!" PRAISE THE LORD! GOD'S HANDS ARE PICKIN' BOBBY'S GUITAR TONIGHT! And, this, this magnificent young man—

BOBBY: I DIDN'T DO SHI—

HARGUS: I know, Bobby, I know, son . . . and I want to thank you on behalf of th' church an' Christian fellowship everywhere. For, friends, Bobby said he would give us all that money in the hope that it would make up for what happened, lo those many years ago! Well, son, it sure can't hurt!

BOBBY: YOU MOTHERFU—

HARGUS: Thank you, son, and you're absolutely right. Your mother *would* be proud, boy . . . proud. Now, Bobby, we don't have time, of course, for your *whole* album, though

I sure wish we did, so jus' reel us off one of the best, okay? What's it gonna be?

BOBBY: YOU'RE GONNA TALK TO MY LAWYER!

HARGUS: Okay then, friends, here he is! Little Bobby Kirschenbaum, from his new album of Gospel Favorites, "You're Gonna Talk To My Lawyer"! Take it, Bobby!

BOBBY: God (unintelligible) stinkin' (unintelligible) rot' (unintelligible) hole!

HARGUS: Havin' trouble there, Bobby? Step over here just a minute, son, I'll see if I can't fix it. 'Scuse us just a second, folks.

BOBBY: OWWWWWWWWWW! JESUS!

HARGUS: There we found the Righteous Path, folks. Now, Bobby, go ahead on. Good Gawd! He's playin' that git-tar an' the harmonica at the same time! Praise Gawd! Go Bobby, for JEEE-ZUS!

BOBBY: My song's called "Jesus Knows My Name." Goes like this:

> I'm searchin' for the key
> That will unlock the door.
> Somebody tell me who I am,
> And what I was before.
> Will there be a mansion
> For me up in the sky?
> Or just twelve angry soldiers,
> And a draft card when I die?
>
> Read in a magazine
> About a man in Abilene.
> Had this machine,
> Could tell you where it's at,
> And what it means,
> By what you dream.
> Went to Abilene.
> Got plugged in and dreamed.
> Woke up in an hour or so.
> Said, "I've got to know."
> Man said, "You dirty little scummy creep,
> Seen what you did to my daughter, in your sleep."

Tryin' to understand,
Found me in a far-off land,
Rappin' with a dude,
Named Bama Lama Jude.
Thirty days and a thousand nights,
We smoked his pipe
Till we both got right.
Then he says, "The answers?"
Ah, they've all been told.
It's the questions
We don't know."

When folks heard I was lookin',
They came lookin' for me,
At the door and in the tree.
One said, "It's here, in a brand new book!"
Another says, "Come with me,
Or else you'll cook!"
Then a dark-haired beauty,
With holes for eyes,
Screamed till she died,
"SURPRISE! SURPRISE!
You're all wrong!
Ain't you heard?
World's come and gone!"
Well, I said, "You got me confused,
I hate to refuse,
But I'll land on the moon,
With the stuff y'all use!"

My travels took me back
To Ma and Pa and Arkansas.
Ma calls Pa, and Pa says, "Son,
Your grandpa knows it all;
The questions and the answers
He has found.
But you'll have to get your shovel,
And dig him out the ground!"

Parking meters, electric fans,
Peanut-butter jars, marching bands.
Wind and sleet and snow and rain,
Jesus Christ knows my name!

HARGUS: Praise God, that was just wonderful, Bobby! JESUS KNOWS MY NAME! Well, one thing's sure, Bobby, you singin' like that He's sure as hel—uh, He's sure not gonna forget *your* name. Thank you, Bobby. Little Bobby Kirschenbaum, folks. Pick up his album. Yes, sir. Now, then. Friends, from time to time here on the *Jump for Jesus* Show we're going to be suggesting to you ways for you to get closer to the Lord, ways that'll make it easier for you to maintain your relationship with Jesus Christ. Because once you got Jesus in your heart, you don't want Him sneakin' off someplace, do you? Of course not. Once you got Jesus in your heart, you wanna lock Him up in there. Well, friends, each item, each service we'll be offerin' to you will help you do just that. So get out your paper and pencil now . . . 'cause we have an item for you tonight that you're not going to want to be without if you really are a Christian and love Jesus. Solettes? What's tonight's FAITH DEAL?

BETHEA: Well, Billy, tonight we have for the folks a plastic Jesus!

HARGUS: You mean our little Jesus that goes up on the dashboard of your car?

BETHEA: That's the one, Reverend. He's cute, too!

HARGUS: OHMIGOD! FALL DOWN ON YOUR KNEES AND PRAISE JESUS WITH ME! A PLASTIC JESUS FROM OUR AUTOMOTIVE NOVELTIES DIVISION FOR YOU TO AFFIX TO THE DASHBOARD OF YOUR OWN PERSONAL AUTOMOBILE! TURN THAT THING FROM A CHRYSLER . . . INTO A *CHRIST*-LER! THAT'S RIGHT! SOLETTES? WHY DON'T YOU TELL 'EM, IN SONG?

SOLETTES:

> I don't care if it rains or freezes,
> Long as I've got my plastic Jesus,
> Ridin' on the dashboard of my car.
> I can go a hundred miles an hour,
> Long as I've got the almighty power,
> Glued up there by my pair
> Of fuzzy dice.

HARGUS: ALL RIGHT! Thank you, Solettes! Mighty fine. Yes, friends, it's absolutely true. You can actually have Jesus Christ keepin' you company on the road. He's tiny, but strictly lifelike, with little bitty eyes that light up when you hit the brakes. The eyes of Jesus, lookin' down the road for you . . . checking for that unseen hazard or lead-footed heathen. Jesus Christ will see them and say to you, "Better get on the binders, before we hit the business end of that bridge abutment, bub."

And the best part is, it's absolutely free. It doesn't cost you a penny to be able to drive around with this kind of divine intervention just waitin' there to warn you before you get turned into mucilage on the front of some semi or somethin'. Just send me a prayer pledge, anything over twenty-five dollars and ninety-five cents, and we'll get your little Jesus in the mail to you this very day.

And, friends, when you write to us here in Del Rio, Texas, I want you to tell Billy how much Jesus has done for you in your life. I want to hear your testimony so that we might be able to share it in the future with everybody over these microphones. Just take a page and make a list. Say, Billy, these are the things Jesus has done for me. Then, on the other side of that page, I want you to make another list and say, Billy, these are the things I've done for Jesus. Then, add 'em up. Are they a little outa whack? Of course they are. Jesus has done everything for us—and we can't never fill up that balance sheet under the "What-I've-Done-for-Him" headin'. I want you to ask yourself this question. Say, Billy, have I done enough for Jesus? Am I doing enough after all He's done for me? Am I fallin' down on my end of the bargain here? Well, friends, why don't you make sure you're covered in His eyes. Why don't you, when you write to me, bump that prayer pledge up to fifty, seventy-five, a hundred dollars and SHOW THE LORD JESUS CHRIST HOW GRATEFUL YOU REALLY ARE! SAY, JESUS . . . HERE'S A LITTLE SOMETHIN' TO HELP OUT. I KNOW IT AIN'T MUCH, BUT I PROMISE YOU I'LL SEND ALONG SOME MORE REAL SOON.

Then, friends, you might want to have each member of your family help you help Jesus. Why, you might want to organize your neighborhood to help th' Lord by helpin' our ministry here. This ain't no bed of roses, friends; we have missionaries in every country in the entire world that we must support with your prayer pledges and blessing vows.

Hell, you might just wanna organize your entire town or city to help in this vital work. Say, Jesus, here's two hundred and fifty thousand dollars, JUST TO SAY THANKS! Get it together, wrap it up, and send it to the Right Reverend Doctor Billy Sol Hargus, care of the Discount House of Worship, Del Rio, Texas. I'll just tell you what. You get us two hundred and fifty thousand dollars and I'll PERSONALLY see to it that you get TWO plastic Jesuses for your automobile. Choir, say thank you to Jesus!

CHOIR: THANK YOU, JESUS!

HARGUS: My Gawd, ain't it wonderful to be in th' land of opportunity. Say it, Choir!

CHOIR: IT'S TH' LAND OF OPPORTUNITY!

HARGUS: PRAISE TH' LORD! YES, SIR! All right, Choir, time now to sing one of our favorite hymns—it's an original, penned by Reverend Billy hisself and available to you for a nineteen-ninety-eight Faith Promise from the Discount House of Worship's Audio Branch—"Oh, Billy Sol, Won't You Please Heal Us All!" Let's hear it, now!

CHOIR:

Oh, Billy Sol, won't you please heal us all.
Oh, say, Billy Sol, won't you please heal us all.
Grandma's ticker's gettin' weaker,
She's got her hand up on the speaker.
Oh, say, Billy Sol, won't you please heal us all!

HARGUS: Let me jump in here, Choir!

Late last night, Mama took a fever,
Little Tommy killed the kitty with Pop's meat cleaver.

Sister came home with a social disease,
Even our dog's got terminal fleas.
Oh, Billy Sol, won't you please heal us all.

CHOIR: OH, BILLY SOL, WON'T YOU PLEASE HEAL US ALL!

HARGUS: Praise Jesus! Yes, it's true. Billy Sol does have that healin' hand, the gift of settin' right that what's wrong with you and those you love. For I can feel out there that many of you tonight, all over this great land, are burdened. You have troubled hearts and minds tormented by worry. You're sayin', "Billy, I'm powerful unhappy. I'm miserable. I don't know what to do with my life, because nothin's workin' out for me, Billy! I'M SICK, BILLY! I'M LAAAAAME, BILLY! LORD, BILLY! I NEED YOUR PRECIOUS HELP!" CHOIR? I WANT YOU TO SAY IT NOW! SAY, "BILLY?"

CHOIR: BILLY!!

HARGUS: "I need your HELP!"

CHOIR: I NEED YOUR HELP!

HARGUS: Say, "BILLY!!"

CHOIR: BILLY!!

HARGUS: "I NEED YOUR HELP!"

CHOIR: I NEED YOUR HELP!!

HARGUS: Yes, say, "Billy, I want you to help me tonight!" Say, "Reverend Hargus, I want you to come into my heart." Friends, somewhere in America right now, in some small, sleepy little town or some bustlin' big city, there is a poor, or perhaps even some wealthy, soul cryin' out in despair! Beggin' for guidance, for some one to show them the direction in which they oughta be pointin' their lives. Friends, praise Jesus, that help is available to you right now. For we have here at the Discount House of Worship a wonderful and truly holy item that can point you to that Righteous Path! Never again shall ye waver! For you can carry with you, every day, our St. Peter's Compass—yes, the very same compass the Apostle Peter used to navigate his frail craft on the storm-tossed Sea of Galilee. This is it! The same exact instrument! Isn't that wonderful? Write to me here in Del Rio, Texas. Say, Billy, send me the compass. And guess what? It'll come to you completely free of charge. All we ask is that YOU remember Jesus when you write your order . . . and include a Bible bestowal. Anything over sixteen-ninety-five will do. For you don't want to stray from the path that guarantees you your reservation in Paradise, do you? Of course not. You want to prepare yourself now, here, while you're in this mortal life, for your day of IMMORTALITY! The day when you'll be able to step right up to JESUS HISSELF and say, "Jesus, I raise my cup to You!" But, but . . . just a minute. There's nothing in your cup. It's dry! It's empty. And you, standin' before the Son of God with nothin' to give Him. Why? Why, because they told you back on Earth that "You can't take it with you"! And sure enough, you listened and you got "there," and sure enough, YOU'RE BROKE! OH, THE SHAME OF IT! Let me ask you somethin', friends. Who *knows* that you can't take it with you? Huh? WHO KNOWS THAT INDEED YOU CAN'T TAKE EVERY SINGLE LAST STINKIN' PENNY WITH YOU? HUH? WHO? WELL, DR. HARGUS IS HERE TO TELL YOU RIGHT NOW THAT YOU CAN TAKE IT WITH YOU!! ALL OF IT!! EVERYTHING!! YOU CAN OPEN A BANK ACCOUNT IN HEAVEN WHILE YOU'RE STILL RIGHT HERE ON EARTH!! SOLETTES? LET 'EM IN ON THIS ONE!!

SOLETTES:

Woooweee!
Save a nickel or a dime,
Think of all that peace of mind.
Send it now while you're alive.
It'll be in heaven when you arrive.
Don't be dead and caught out on a limb,
Deposit now in Billy's First National Bank of Him!

HARGUS: You heard it right, folks. Billy's First National Bank of Him. Send me all your money now, and I'll arrange for it to be waitin' for you in heaven after you're gone! Isn't that divine?

SOLETTES:

> Yes, a check will be okay.
> Get it in the mail today.
> Why have the folks who love you so
> Fightin' for it when you go?

HARGUS: Isn't it the truth, friends? You work your whole life and leave whatever you made for your relatives to gouge eyeballs over. All that money, suddenly in the hands of heathens. Heathens who will not help Jesus! Who won't help Billy! Here you got that nice little nest egg sittin' someplace where it's not helpin' Jesus, and it won't be helpin' Jesus then, after you're dead, unless you can get it to me RIGHT THIS INSTANT, so I can get it into the First National Bank of Him AT ONCE! You'll help Billy, you'll help Jesus, and you'll be helpin' yourself. Helpin' us while you're alive, and waitin' for you in Paradise when you arrive! OHMIGOD! Let's have an amen from the Choir on this deal!

CHOIR: AMEN!

HARGUS: Thank you, Choir. Now, before we close for tonight . . . remember, ol' Billy Sol's gonna be in your town in person, to see you in person, sometime soon . . . somewhere. Because I want to MEET YOU! Don't forget, now, send for your plastic Jesus, don't go through another day without your St. Peter's Compass, and send me those bank deposits *immediately*. You never know!

And remember: For the Lord thy God loves you, Jesus loves you, and, yes, Billy Sol Hargus loves you. Thank you, Choir! Thank you, Solettes! Little Bobby? Bobby? Where are ya? Oh, there you are, boy. Thank you! And . . . THANK YOU, JEEEEEE-ZUS! See ya next week! Write to me now, Billy Sol Hargus, Del Rio, Texas. Goodnight, y'all.

ANNOUNCER: You've been listening to the *Jump for Jesus*

Show. A weekly presentation of the Doctor Billy Sol Hargus Crusade, and this station. If you would like any or all of the holy items Doctor Hargus was privileged to offer to you during the program, call us right now at this number: 512-GO-JESUS. That's right. 512-GO-JESUS. It's the same as dialing 512-465-3787. Or write to us here at the *Jump for Jesus* Show. The address: Billy Sol Hargus, Del Rio, Texas. Write or call now. Operators are standing by to take your order. This is Boone Moses saying Billy will see you next Sunday when we all join together and *Jump for Jesus.*

> EDITOR'S NOTE—*This concludes the broadcast transcription of the first* Jump for Jesus *radio program. The following resumes the Hargus narrative as transcribed from the Hargus Tapes.*
> (ED.)

I looked up at the control room window. The whole damned bunch of 'em was there; Boone, Tyrone, Otis, Olgemyier, even Ameline had joined 'em. And they was applaudin'. I couldn't hear 'em through the soundproofed windows, but I could see 'em clappin' like crazy! And they were slappin' one another on the back, and grinnin'!

Olgemyier and Otis, of all people, linked arms and spun around dancin' a little jig. As I stepped from the studio, Tyrone was first to get to me, and he started pumpin' my hand, shakin' his head, lookin' at me, and just sayin' "damn"!

Then Olgemyier broke away from Otis, a little reluctantly, I thought, and skipped over to me. "I am positively drenched!" he said. "Feel me—am I wet? Am I? Billy, you hunka wonderful, you! I lived and died each moment you were in there! Just feel me! I am positively liquid!" I squeezed his upper arm just to shut 'im up. "See?" he bubbled, "God, Billy, you *did* kill them! They were decimated! Take no prisoners? Hell, you *buried* them! Oh, God, I think I just wet my pants!"

Although they were as different as night and day, the better I got to know Olgemyier, the more 1 found myself thinking of Elroy. Jesus!

Otis was next. He just stood there, lookin' at me for a long minute. "Th' fuckin' phone's ringin' off the wall, boy," he said. "And it's all good. 'Bout eighty percent of 'em wants plastic Jesuses and the other twenty is signin' up with the bank. Goddamn, son, we thought so before, but now—well, you're really on your way. Ah'm proud, boy, proud."

"Thank ya, O'," I said, "that's great." I started lookin' around, though, for Boone. Where the hell was Boone?

Just then, the control-room door opened and Boone stepped out into the hall, a little hesitantly, it seemed. My glance caught his and he stopped short, his hand still on the door, then he dropped his eyes and started over to me. When he reached me he done somethin' he'd never done before. He took both my hands in his, and he looked up at me. I'd shot up to where I was a good two and a half, three inches taller than Boone by now. His eyes looked into mine searchingly until I found myself becoming uneasy. Everybody had dropped back a step or two and was watchin' us. Finally, Boone spoke, his expression both soft and stern. "Don't forget where you came from, boy," he said, huskily. "Don't forget where you came from."

The radio program was an instant breakaway success. Over the next several years it became one of the underpinnings of the whole Billy Sol Hargus movement, as important to our continued prosperity as was our road show.

Those were building years, a period during which we were testing, flexing, probing what Boone and our media consultants soon understood was a nearly unlimited growth potential, if skillfully managed and given the right vehicle. Boone continually pressed Godfrey, Olgemyier and Dunleavy about that, and, just as firmly, they stood 'im off as they searched for just the exact formula.

By *Jump for Jesus*'s fourth anniversary program, the direction which that next step must take was coming into focus, and hazy outlines of a plan began taking shape during a conversation we had following the show. We needed to raise our profile further—and do it in dramatic fashion.

"Four years! Can you believe it? Show number 208!" It was Olgemyier, and he was comin' for me on a dead run, or on what for him passed as a dead run—little, mincing, stutter-steps that made him look like he had somethin' pressed between his knees and was tryin' to keep from droppin' it.

"Two-hundred-eight little nuggets of gold!" he squealed as he intercepted me stepping out of the studio. He reached up, threw his arms around my neck, and hugged, liftin' one foot off the ground. I had to practically peel him loose.

Otis, Tyrone, Boone, Ameline . . . all of 'em was there, standin' with several of the technicians, and they were singin' "For He's a Jolly Good Preacher!" I stood there a little self-consciously with Olgemyier while they finished their song. Olgemyier held me lightly by the elbow. They all whooped and hollered as the last words died away in a smattering of applause.

"Thank you," I said to 'em. "Thank everybody. Couldn'ta been nothin', nothin' at all, without all of you." Then the whole bunch of 'em was rushin' over to me, clappin' me on the back, and shakin' my hand. A bottle of champagne and a stack of paper cups were passed forward over their heads and there was a sharp report as somebody pulled the cork.

Olgemyier had now linked one arm through mine and was leadin' me around as everybody sipped the bubbly and talked warmly, reminiscing about the last four years. Now we were in front of Boone and a couple of the Solettes. "But that's background now, Boone," Olgemyier was sayin'. "You're talkin' history. I'm talkin' tomorrowland, capeesh? I mean, this thing has gotten out of hand. We're now talkin' TV. Just look at this face." He reached up and pinched my cheek. "Is this gold? I mean, we're talkin' precious metal here. This face is goin' tubesville. It's time. My God, is it time?"

"Well," Boone replied, "that's all fine and good, and you're right. You're certainly familiar with the mail. We've had people beggin' us to put him on television for two years now, beggin'! But I've told you for *four* years that we needed more . . . a new gimmick, I guess, that's really gonna blow this boy sky-high, put 'im over the top, and damnit, it's there, I know it's right there, if you people or somebody can just reach out and grab hold of it."

"Booney, sweetheart," Olgemyier soothed, "it *is* there, and we'll get it for you, but you gotta be patient. We don't have to even look for television; it's here, right now, just pantin' for 'im. Now, I know what you've been tellin' me; that you gotta have the really big 'hit' for the road show. Visual, you're talkin' visual." He turned to a couple of technicians standin' off to one side. "Is he talkin' visual?" They looked at him like he was nuts. "I mean," he babbled on, turnin' back to Boone, "we're going after . . . stop-look-and-listen time. But Boone, Jesus. I'm only one person! God, let's put one foot in front of the other. I mean, my God!" He began fannin' himself with his free hand and his eyes fluttered.

"Ah, now," chuckled Boone, "don't go gettin' your bowels in an uproar. I know you'll figure it out, especially if you want to keep this account."

Then Boone was climbin' up on the settee at the side of the hallway. "Okay, everybody," he shouted. "Party time! To the bus! Drinks, food, merriment!" He hopped down, gigglin' like a kid.

Olgemyier reached out and snagged Ameline, hookin' his free arm through hers so that now he had us both. "Amy, sugar pie," he gushed. "Celebrationsville, okay? Listen, you simply haven't *had* a daiquiri until you've had one of Murray's Maulers. Come on, you two," he said, "let's."

But Ameline resisted his tug. "You go ahead, Murray," she said. "I got somethin' I need to talk to Billy about."

Uh-oh, I thought, uh-oh. I watched the last of 'em go out the doors, and then I turned to Ameline. She had her arms folded across her chest, and she'd turned her back to me. I saw a shudder go through her and I realized her shoulders were shakin' just a bit. Why, hell! She was cryin'! I walked over, put my hands on her shoulders, and gently turned her around. She turned her face away from me. I put a finger under her chin and pulled her back toward me. "Hey, Ameline, what is it? What's gotten into you? What's th' matter?"

"Oh, Billy," she said, "I'm so sorry! I never meant for it to happen this way!" She threw her arms around my neck and buried her face in my shoulder, sobbing.

I was genuinely frightened. "What, Ameline? What's happened?" At that moment, I suddenly realized I cared for that girl a whole lot more than I'd ever let myself admit. "Ameline, honey, please tell me what's happened."

"Bil . . . Billy?" she snuffled, her breath hitchin' in her chest, "I . . . I love you. An'. . . an' I wanna *marry* you."

For a moment I was utterly speechless.

"Well, uh, . . ." I stammered, "I . . . I love you, too, Ameline."

She looked up at me, still cryin'. "Do you, Billy? Honest to God, do you?"

"Well, sure I do," I said. "And I love Boone and Otis. I love Tyrone and Nubby and Stubby. . . ."

She let out a quiet whimper and buried her head back in my shoulder.

"And don't forget," I added, "Jesus loves us all."

The Dallas Morning News

HARGUS ASSERTS HOLY "TIES"

Pastor's N.Y. Representatives Say "Proof" Exists

NEW YORK—The famed evangelist Dr. Billy Sol Hargus claims a miracle has occurred in his life that has given him the ability to walk on water.

Dr. Hargus says he was visited by the spirit of God while at his Austin, Texas, ranch two days ago, and was instructed to go out to his swimming pool where, the Lord said, he would find himself unable to jump in. "On," said Dr. Hargus, "but not in."

According to Hargus's New York media representatives, Godfrey, Olgemyier and Dunleavy, the Reverend will soon be sharing the miracle with his thousands of followers. . . .

REEL 12

◆

"Who was that?" asked Ameline, as I replaced the receiver in the telephone's special housing. I didn't answer her for a moment, fearin' another go-'round with her, but then I sighed and said, "Step-Edna."

Ameline slumped back in the seat, lookin' out the window in exasperation, and said, "What the hell did she want *this* time? Can't that woman *ever* leave us be? Goddamn!"

"Look, Ameline, now I've just about had it with this shit. Every time she calls you put us through this and I am just up to *here* with it!"

Ameline folded her arms across her chest and stared hard out the window as the plane tracked toward Kansas City.

I remember that day bein' so clear that it almost startled you . . . but then, the midwestern sky could get like that. The section lines that cut Kansas wheat fields into one-mile squares stood out like they'd been drawn by a draftsman. It made it easy to gauge our forward progress as they slipped by below.

Tyrone was in one of the big leather loungers opposite us. He'd heard me and Ameline arguin'. "Rev," he said, "you oughta be gettin' a little rest. Ain't nothin' to see down there 'cept a buncha poor white-ass farmers diggin' dirt."

Good ol' 'Rone. He broke the tension between me and Ameline, causin' us both to chuckle. Lord, though, those people 24,000 feet below us were anything but poor. All that land. And occasionally you could see dust billowin' back across a field from one of their big fancy tractors. Huge new grain silos poked up here and there, th' sun glintin' off their tops like they'd been coated with silver. Hell, to hear Boone tell it, the way the government threw taxpayer money at farmers, maybe they had!

Boone was always pushin' us to get in on the "agronomy action," as he called it, because farms were such good tax dodges, or rather, "shelters." That was a big part of the reason we'd changed our basic mode of transportation—from fancy bus to fancier airliner, because of the tax advantages. Actually, I should say, "airliners"—plural, because we had three of 'em now, twin-engine Convair 440/600-D's. The one we were aboard was the main ship, though, outfitted strictly, and, may I add, lavishly, in an executive configuration with leather this and leather that, two staterooms aft, a galley forward, and an office area in the middle that shared space with a sizable lounge. And I'll swear they musta had a sale on Honduran mahogany the week they put the interior in the thing. It was beautiful, and I liked it a lot. I was always goin' up into the cockpit and buggin' Frank McCord to let me take the controls in the copilot's seat. It drove him nuts but I thought I was gettin' pretty good. Besides, I'd tell him, just what the hell could possibly happen to us as long as I was aboard? Right. Nothin', 'cause I had Jesus in my pocket. In fact, that's what we called our little air force, th' Jesus Jets. The other two planes, though, were set up in the usual airline configuration and we leased 'em out. The whole airplane acquisition, while principally for tax purposes, would've become necessary anyway to keep our constantly expanding schedule manageable. The deal had worked out so good, though, that Godfrey, Olgemyier and Dunleavy had made a presentation to us for becomin' a commercial air carrier, somewhere down the road, with a theme based on Jesus and pitched to the public as "Flying the Wings of Him."

> No need to worry, no need to fret,
> When you're flying aboard a Jesus Jet!

Frank dipped the starboard wing gently as he corrected our course a bit. Ameline turned back toward me. "Billy?" Uh-oh, I thought, here comes some more. But she reached down and took my hand in hers. "Honey," she said, "I'm sorry; it's just that . . ."

"Really, Ameline, I don't care to hear about it anymore. You're talkin' about my Step-Edna, the woman who raised me and taught me and made me nearly everything I am today."

"God, don't I just know it," she said bitterly. "She sure as hell did teach you, didn't she? And what? What did the woman teach you?" Her voice was risin' again. "She taught you how to be an asexual freak, that's what!"

"Ameline—"

"Taught you that the most natural act in the world between a man and a woman was dirty, sinnin'. The woman's a certifiable lunatic and you're just too damn dumb to recognize it!"

"Ameline, you're about to go too far."

"Too far! *Too far!* Just how long," she hissed, "do you think it's been since I did anything other than cry myself to sleep at night? How long you suppose a woman's gonna have to live like that, huh?"

"You ought to care," I said evenly, "more about doin' the Lord's will than you do about satisfying the hot desires of your flesh! *Your body's more than a goddamn playground for th' Devil, damnit!*"

Tyrone swiveled his chair away from us, pretendin' not to hear, as Ameline began cryin' softly.

"Now what th' hell's the matter?"

"Billy," she said, "something's terribly wrong with you. You do know that, don't you? Honey, how can you possibly think *this* is normal?"

She pointed to the bulge in my pants where a sterile dressing encased my heathen member. I'd spent another week in the hospital after my last "slammin' episode," when th' rotten thing had defied me after Ameline had gotten after it one night. Finally, I'd clapped it between a couple of bricks, one in each hand. *Wham!* A week in the hospital, yes, tubes and a bunch of stuff, but you better believe that the son of a bitch hadn't even so much as dared to have a look around since I'd driven the demon out of him! No, sir!

"No, Ameline," I told her, "what's not normal is what *you're* always wantin' to do. You're weak, woman, weak! You know what th' Bible says about fornicators! And you're goin' straight to hell less you change your wicked ways! I'll swear, if I'd known you were constantly goin' to be dwellin' on wickedness I'd never have married you. James: one, fifteen: 'When lust hath conceived, it bringeth forth sin; and sin, when it is finished, bringeth forth death!' So fuck you!"

"God," Ameline moaned, "how I wish somebody would!"

Boone came in and sat down across the polished tabletop from us. "You two going at it again, aren't you?" he asked, shakin' his head. "Billy," he said, takin' in his daughter's voluptuousness, "you're a fucking idiot. You think she's the pervert. Look at you. You got your dick in a sling and you say she's the one that's not normal? I'll swear, boy, if I didn't feel so goddamn responsible for you I'd be shed of you in a minute! Won't you please talk to that doctor again?"

"You mean that shrink in Palm Springs?"

"No, I mean that *doctor* in Palm Springs!"

"Shrink! Fuckin' shrink, an' no I won't! I talk to *Jesus,* and that's it! *You understand me, goddamnit, you dumb old bastard?"*

Blinding pain arced through my jaw and temple and I went down like I'd been poleaxed. It had happened so fast I'd never seen it comin'. As I pushed myself to my hands and knees there in the aisle, shakin' the redness from my brain, I saw a pair of boots swimmin' in front of me. It was agonizin', but I raised my head. Boone stood above me, tremblin', saliva at the corners of his mouth. His right hand gripped his silver preachin' rod and an indentation that matched it perfectly ran from my jaw to my temple. As he spoke, his words had an unnatural and sinister calm:

"Don't you ever, ever talk to me like that again. Not . . . never. And from now on out, you'll be showin' my daughter some respect. I no longer care whether you're ever a real husband to her or not, but you will be showin' her some respect."

He walked back to the rear of the plane, leavin' me weaving unsteadily on my hands and knees, stunned as much by the enormity of what had just transpired as by the blow itself. I pulled myself back up into my seat, hit the recline button, and laid my head back, gently touchin' the side of my face. Ameline sat by me stiffly, lookin' out the window at nothin'. Tyrone remained with his back to us. His chair hadn't budged during the whole episode.

A hand appeared at the side of my head. I flinched instinctively and shrank away from it. It was Boone, and he was holding out an ice pack to me.

"Here," he said gruffly, avoiding my eyes.

Gingerly, I took it from him. "Th . . . thanks, Boone."

"Can we talk now, boy?" he asked.

The cold helped. "Ye . . . yes, sir."

"Fine," he said, takin' his seat again. He gazed off through the window, twiddlin' his rod with his fingers. Boone's hair had turned pure white in the past year. He wore bifocals now, and the lines in his face had deepenened into furrows.

"Somewhere," he began, "we allowed things to get off track. We didn't think things through good enough." He shook his head and went on, almost like he was talkin' to himself. "I can't figure how I couldn't see what was becomin' of you, Billy. But since you refuse any kind of outside help, then we will just have to live with it, and do the best we can to keep this business going forward. But you could try, Billy, you could try to overcome whatever the hell it is that eats at you and has got you so goddamn twisted!"

"But Boone," I said, as quiet and sober as I knew how, "I can't change what I feel and what I believe is right and wrong. I can't."

He looked at me, took a deep breath, and sighed it out, shakin' his head in surrender.

"Jesus, Billy," he said.

"Right, Boone," I agreed, but it sailed clear over him and was lost.

Five minutes passed with the three of us sitting there rigidly like department-store dummies, Boone and Ameline watchin' an occasional cloud drift by; me, leaning back, eyes closed and holding the ice pack to my face. The bag was getting kinda squirmy as the ice melted and it was makin' my hand cold, so I put it down on the table in front of us. Boone must've taken that as some sort of signal that the oppressive mood was beginning to lift. "Ameline," he said, straightening around in his chair, "would you go get us two cups of coffee, honey?"

"All right, Daddy."

"Well, son," he said (it was "son" again), "can we talk some business now, you s'pose?"

"Yeah, Boone. Sure."

"Good," he said, and he reached over and patted my hand. "Good."

Steepling his fingers in front of him and leanin' back in his chair, he said, "Let's see, now . . . " and looked up at the ceiling, thoughtfully.

"You know, Billy, I got to thinkin' last night, while I was havin' a . . . cocktail. I got to thinkin' that that goddamn Olgemyier, with all that silly horseshit of his, really ain't far from bein' right. This really *is* show business, just as much as it is religious business. Sure, we're leadin' people to Jesus and savin' souls along the way, praise the Lord, but we're also puttin' on a circus! A whole damned extravaganza! There'll be fifty thousand of them out there tonight, comin' to hear you talk about the righteous life, but also comin' to be entertained. So we gotta do both, you know."

"Sure I do, Boone. That's what we've been doin', isn't it, for twelve damn years here, ain't it?" I grinned at 'im real big just to make sure he didn't misinterpret my meanin' any. The left side of my face still felt like somebody had sicced a bear on it.

"That we have, boy," he grinned back. "That we have. But, you see, the deal's this here. You give 'em a dose of hope for a couple of hours up there, and some of them probably actually feel better about their lot in life for a week or two, but not long after we're gone they nearly all will be slidin' back into the drudgery of life, and then you become just a ticket stub in their goddamn scrapbook."

"Jesus," I said. "Why, you make it sound like I'm nothin' more 'n a damn hillbilly up there bangin' on a git-tar."

"No, boy," he said, drily, "you can't play the guitar.

"And that brings up somethin' else, son," he went on. "You're supposed to be a preacher, right?"

I nodded.

"And a preacher is a person what talks about Jesus, right?"

I nodded again as Ameline came in and set down two cups of coffee in front of us. Then she walked back toward the rear of the plane.

"Where you goin', honey?" Boone called after her.

She answered, but didn't turn around, and I could see that she had a tissue pressed to her nose. "I . . . I'm just goin' back to lie down for a while. I . . . I'm a little tired, that's all."

Boone looked at her sympathetically. "Okay, honey, you just get some rest. It'll be good for you."

He stared after her a moment. His eyes fluttered and he swallowed hard. Then, he turned back to me. "Now, where was I?"

"You were talkin' about Jesus and preachin'."

"So I was, and the reason I was, Billy, is because you wasn't!"

"What d'you mean, Boone?"

He picked up his coffee, took a slurp, and then peered intently at me across his cup. "Boy," he said, "how many times you mentioned the name of Jesus these past three months when you been up there preachin'? No, I'll tell *you,"* he said, before I could give him an answer. "Twice. Two times. That's it. I don't quite know what's goin' on here, Billy, but I think I've got a pretty good idea. I think, boy, from quite a few things I've been noticin' here lately, that you're startin' to lose some perspective. I think it's startin' to slip just a little bit, who you are, who I am, and who *they* are, and we gotta get this set right again. Now, I know where it's comin' from. 'Billy! Billy Sol Hargus,' they scream. It's 'Help me, *Billy!'* 'Heal me, *Billy!'* 'Ohhhh, *Billy!'* Hundreds and hundreds of thousands of 'em, *'Billy!'* And you're standin' up there, bathin' in it, *feastin'* on it."

"Well, I can't help it," I ventured. "They love me. Jesus, Boone, you admitted that yourself."

"Yes, I did, son. And I'm thinkin' it was a big mistake. They *do* love you, but . . ."

"But?"

"But, boy, they love you because—and this is what you're in danger of losin' sight of—they love you because *you* are their *link to Jesus!* It's not *'Billy,* save me!'; it's 'Billy, can you lead me to Jesus so *Jesus* can save me?' You are the *bridge* over which they can walk. You are *not,* though, their destination! 'Behold, I send you forth as sheep in the midst of wolves: be ye therefore wise as serpents, and harmless as doves!' "

"Matthew: ten, sixteen," I said.

"Correct," replied Boone. "And I'm afraid you're tending to forget the wisdom and the harmless angle."

"But," I reminded, "Isaiah: sixty-one, one: 'The Lord hath anointed me to preach good tidings.' "

"Sure He has, son, sure. But let's keep 'em 'good.' And that means, let's keep 'em 'Jesus.' "

He paused for a moment, gazin' out the window again. The soft whine of the engines eased down in pitch as Frank started backin' off power to start our descent into Kansas City.

Boone noticed it, too, and then muttered to himself, "Damn. Jets. Jets and jewels. Who would've ever thunk it?" He chuckled, then turned serious again.

"Son, when we was just first startin' out I sat there in the front of that old bus in Del Rio, and I warned you not to never, ever get to thinkin' that you're doin' any more with preachin' than jus' primin' the pump. Gettin' 'em to come to Jesus is just primin' the pump, gettin' 'em into a little more positive frame of mind. But this is the point: If things *should* start workin' out for 'em in their lives after they've been to see you, it's a result of somethin' they themselves have done. 'Course you and I both *know* they'll never believe that. Hell, they'd sooner take a horse-whippin' than believe that. But let me tell you somethin' right here and now, boy; you better sure as hell never, ever get it in your head that it's *you* bringin' about them changes, 'cause it ain't. You understand what I'm sayin' to you, Billy?"

I nodded my head, but it was just to appease him. I really didn't mean it. It was becomin' more and more clear all the time that somethin' really special, somethin' almost unique was goin' on with me. "For many are called but few are chosen." Few indeed, I thought. In fact, it was beginnin' to look to me like it had been only two—me and Jesus.

"I'll tell you what," said Boone. "Mention Jesus a couple of times up there tonight, okay? Why, hell," he laughed, "I don't care if you tell 'em you're God's other Son, or somethin'." He reached over and slapped me good-naturedly on the knee. "But let's just remember what we're doin' up there, right?"

"Right, Boone," I smiled back at 'im. But I was thinkin', Wrong, Boone, wrong. You're just not seein' it.

"Remember, Billy," he said, "Psalms: thirty-one, twenty-three: 'He that is greedy of gain, troubleth his own house.' "

He winked at me, and nodded his head toward the rear of the plane—Ameline's quarters. "See about her, won't you, son? We're goin' to be landin' directly."

. . .

I opened the door a crack to Ameline's cabin. She'd drawn th' curtain and it was dark.

"Ameline?" I called softly. I heard her snufflin' a little on the bed.

"What?" Her voice came back muffled and pouty. She had her face pressed into her pillow.

"Why d'you have it so dark in here?"

"Didn't want no light."

"Well, what're you doin'?"

"Nothin'. What d'you want?"

"I . . . just wanted to see if you was okay."

"Yes, I'm just fine."

"Well, okay. I guess I'll just go, then."

I heard the bed covers rustle, and then Ameline's voice, no longer muffled. "Did Daddy send you back here?"

I stepped on inside and closed the door. "Naw, he didn't send me. I came by myself because you were so upset and all."

"Really?"

"Really."

"How's your face?"

"Fine, jus' fine," I lied. I stepped to the window and pulled up the shade an inch or so. "You're too pretty," I said, lookin' down at her, "to be a-cryin' like this." I sat down beside her on the edge of the bed and gently began strokin' her hair.

"Oh, Billy," she said, turnin' over and holdin' her arms out to me. "Put your arms around me, please. Hold me. Tell me you love me, please say it, please."

"Jesus loves you," I said, brushing a tear from her cheek.

"Aw, SHIT!" Ameline exploded. "Get the fuck outta here and send in them goddamn midgets! They may look like half a person but they're more of a man than you, you goddamn freak!"

I ducked as the lamp that had been at her bedside grazed my head and shattered against the bulkhead.

"Ameline . . . I . . ."

" 'Ameline I,' SHIT!"

I was backpedalin' toward the door, fast. Her alarm clock smashed against the door behind me as I let myself out and retreated back to Boone and Tyrone.

"Still riled, son, huh?" asked Boone.

"Sure is," I said.

"Well," he sighed, lookin' older and more tired than I could remember. "At least you tried, son. Pay it no mind. Pay it no mind. We gotta look ahead here."

Frank had dropped the flaps and landing gear, and the plane was pitching and yawing slightly in a layer of ragged air that lay a couple of thousand feet off the ground. We were on final for Kansas City's Who the Hell Knows Airport.

"All right," Boone said, regaining some of his spunk, "Kansas City tonight. Omaha Friday, and Monday, would you believe, New York."

"New York?"

Now Boone grinned as the FASTEN SEAT BELT signs blinked on. "Yep," he said, "New York. Those crazy bastards have cooked up somethin' there at Godfrey and the rest of 'em." He pulled his old pocket watch out of his vest. "In fact," he said as the telephone beeped in its wall receptacle, "that'll be Olgemyier now with some details, I'd reckon."

The conversation was one-sided. Boone's end of it was limited to an occasional "Okay, uh-huh," and a final "Fuck you." When he replaced the receiver in its cradle he turned to me with a puzzled expression on his face. "Well, I'll be dipped in shit," he exclaimed.

"Was it Olgemyier?" I asked.

" 'Course it was Olgemyier," he said distantly. "And the crazy little sumbitch wouldn't tell me nothin' except where he'd have the limo meet us at La Guardia. He said the other deal, what they want to talk to us about, was 'Top Secret.' Now can you figger that?"

. . .

Olgemyier paced back and forth in front of a movie screen that covered one entire wall of a sumptuous executive suite at G.O.D. As he paced, he rattled. It was all that shit hangin' around his neck.

"Slides," he was saying to me, Boone, Otis, and Tyrone. "Slides. We're going to be looking at slides if that simp ever gets here." He paused to frown at his wristwatch. "God," he gushed, "where *is* that man? Why can't anybody be on *time?"* His voice bounced lightly off walls covered with huge color-photograph blowups, all just enough out of focus so's you couldn't tell what the hell they were photographs of.

"Art, sweetie," Olgemyier had said. "You're looking at art. Don't try to judge it, okay? Just look, look and let it seep in."

There were drifts of pillows tossed casually around the floor next to some low, slate-topped tables. "And," groused Boone, "not a goddamned place for a man to sit down."

"Relax," soothed Olgemyier, "Jesus. Look at you, you're rigid." As he spoke he paced and nervously wound his watch. "God, *I'm* rigid."

Boone lowered himself awkwardly into one of the pillow piles, grunting with the effort. He pulled an ashtray over to him and, lookin' around, concluded, "Lord, if this ain't a goddamned whorehouse!"

Just then the double doors at the back of the room pushed open and a short, plump, balding man huffed in, blotting his forehead with a handkerchief. Olgemyier spotted him and stopped in his tracks. "Christ, where have *you* been?" Olgemyier shouted at him as he made his way to the platform in front of the screen.

"Science has its own pace," the stranger said. "Science has its own pace."

Introductions were made all around. The fellow's name was Habluetzel, Professor Phillip Habluetzel. As we were introduced, he acknowledged each of us in flat, even tones with little or no expression. His eyes darted around the room behind glasses thick as Mason-jar lids, and they never settled on anything for more than a second. His blue suit was rumpled, maroon tie slightly askew, and the case he carried was scuffed and worn. Olgemyier spoke to him in hushed tones for a minute or so and when he was through, the Professor nodded vigorously.

"Okay," shouted Olgemyier, pressing a button on an intercom, "are you set, projection?" A muffled acknowledgment came back. "All right, then," said Olgemyier, speaking to us, "prepare to be utterly overcome. Are we all ready?" he asked, scanning our faces.

"Goddamnit," Boone said, shifting around trying to get comfortable, "just get on with it, Olgemyier, and tell us what the hell you've got . . . and can the dramatics!"

"Tense, we're tense!" Olgemyier said, and he clucked his tongue at Boone. Professor Habluetzel stood motionless, a trace of impatience on his face.

Olgemyier continued. "Okay, Mister Boone, let's review: We've been talking visual, right? We're all in agreement that we need to do something splashy" (and here he giggled) "that will really jack up Billy's visibility, right?"

There was a murmur of agreement from the floor as Olgemyier began to pace in front of us.

"Okay so far?" asked Olgemyier. "Everybody with me?"

"Yes," Boone replied, irritated. "But not for long if you don't get goddamn on with it."

"Fine, just fine. Okay. Anyway, what do you suppose would be an evangelist's fondest dream, hmm? I mean, forget the healing and the laying on of hands and all of that for a moment. Why, don't you just suppose," he continued, jabbin' a finger at us as he walked, "that a preacher like Billy, an evangelist, would just be a cut above all the other evangelists if he could actually do some of the things that Jesus Christ did? Well?" He stood now facin' us, feet apart, hands planted on his hips. *"Well?"*

My God, Olgemyier was *preachin'!*

"Yes!" we all shouted back at him, almost without realizing what we were doin'. "Yes, Lord! You're right, Olg'!"

'And what was the *one* thing, the single stunt Jesus pulled off," Olgemyier continued, "that brought Him more notoriety than anything else?" But before we could answer him, Olgemyier hurled the answer at us. "WATER!" he shouted. "TH' BOY WALKED ON WATER!

"GENTLEMEN! DEAR FRIENDS!" he said, snapping out a telescoping pointer to its full, three-foot length, "BEHOLD!"

He swept the pointer toward the screen which suddenly was filled by a color photograph of a man . . . by God, it was Professor Habluetzel, and he appeared to be in . . . no, hell! He was *on,* yes, walking *on* a swimming pool!

For a moment, nobody spoke. Then there was a snicker, then a giggle, then an outright guffaw, and Boone hollered at Olgemyier, "WHAT TH' VERY FUCK IS THAT? HAVE YOU LOST YOUR GODDAMNED MARBLES?"

Olgemyier obviously had expected a slightly different reaction. The pointer dropped limply at his side and he looked crestfallen. "Jesus," he said, "can't you see it?"

"OF COURSE I CAN SEE IT!" Boone roared back. "WHAT THE HELL IS IT?"

Now Olgemyier was hurt, and getting defensive. "Christ, Boone," he said, "will you just relax? What do you think you're lookin' at here, huh? Just tell me what you think you see on the screen. Answer that and save the hysterics, okay?"

Boone shook his head in disgust. "Horseshit is what I see. Horseshit and nothin' less."

"No, you numbskull!" Olgemyier cried, and listenin' to him made my face hurt rememberin' what had happened when I'd once crossed Boone with harsh words. But Olgemyier got away with it. "NO, DAMNIT!" he hollered. "What you see is a man, Professor Habluetzel here!" He jabbed his pointer into Habluetzel's arm, causin' him to jump. "Habluetzel, honest-to-God walkin' *on* water! Now, DO YOU SEE THAT? JUST ANSWER THAT SINGLE QUESTION!"

"Well," Boone began slowly, "it sure as hell does *look*

that way, but . . . Jesus Christ, Olgemyier, what're you tryin' to tell me here? That this, this Habluetzel whatever-he-is is a miracle-worker? Naw, I'm sorry. There's only been one miracle-worker I ever knew about. An' the boy lived two thousand years ago. So this is, as I said, a loada horse-shit."

"Mr. Moses," interjected Habluetzel evenly, "perhaps if you understood the scope of what we are proposing here, before you judge too hastily . . ."

"Well, yes," Boone smiled drily, "that might make it easier to fire that little bastard over there." He nodded at Olgemyier, who was standin' with one hand on his forehead, elbow cradled in the other hand, shakin' his head.

"You see," Professor Habluetzel began, but Olgemyier jumped in on top of him. "Jesus, Boone, didn't you tell me you wanted somethin' visual? You did. You told me that! Jesus, every week since February of God knows what, you've been tellin' me that. And I heard. And, God, I've tried. I drove Creative. There is blood on those little pussies' desks, do you hear me? Gore! Jesus, how they gave!" He slumped into a folding chair at the platform's right side and threw his hands up in despair. "Where have I failed?" he appealed to the heavens. "Where? I mean, we're talkin' location. . . ."

Silence. Then Boone. "Well, son," he said more gently, "sellin' sacred chickens and pushin' pictures of Jesus is a hell of a long way from what I gather you're gettin' at here. I mean, are you suggestin' that Billy here . . ." He left the thought dangling.

"IS IT?" Olgemyier shouted back at him. "IS IT SO FAR? Aren't we givin' the people what they want? Huh? Haven't we just done three and a half million in four months? Give me a break! Let's get serious here, okay?"

Boone turned to no one in particular and muttered, "Walkin' on water? We're gonna . . . walk on water?"

Professor Habluetzel tried again. "Allow me to attempt to explain."

Olgemyier's enthusiasm went right back up against the red line. "Just wait till you hear this," he chortled. "Trust me. Give the man two minutes, okay?"

"Well, perhaps a bit longer than that," Habluetzel corrected, indulgently. "Now, gentlemen, it is my understanding that the Reverend Hargus has already achieved a degree of fame rarely attained during the career of a cleric. Since coming on board here with Project W.W. 2, or 'Water-Walk Two,' I've immersed myself in what I call 'Hargusabilia.' I've read of the wild adulation when he appears, the blind faith in his powers . . . uh, perhaps that's an unfortunate choice of words, but anyway, the—"

"Sweetheart," interrupted Olgemyier, "let's not do the boy's bio, hmm? Just get to the point. We're playing to a pack of carnivores, if you get my drift." He jerked his head toward me and the others.

"Yes," said Professor Habluetzel, "certainly. Well, just imagine, if you will, gentlemen, that our Reverend Hargus might actually be able to . . . walk . . . on . . . water." He drew out each word for dramatic effect.

"IMAGINE IF HE COULD DO WHAT?" hollered Boone, risin'.

"Wait, Boone," I said, pulling him back down. "Let 'im finish."

"We are not suggesting," the professor went on, "illusion, sleight of hand, or any other deceit. We will not employ flotation devices, hidden wires, or anything similar. Dr. Hargus will . . . walk . . . on . . . water."

"Just tell 'em," groaned Olgemyier.

Habluetzel ignored him. "You see, gentlemen, my particular scientific discipline is entomology."

"Huh? Wha'?"

"Bugs, gentlemen. I pick apart bugs."

"See?" Boone whispered to me. "Wha'd I tell you? A fuckin' mental case."

Habluetzel forged ahead. "In studies in which I was involved investigating the characteristics of harmonic beat frequencies it was my extraordinary good fortune to make a startling discovery."

Olgemyier couldn't contain himself. "Slide!" he hollered, and the photograph of a water-walking Habluetzel was replaced by one of a mosquito, magnified until it filled the whole screen, frame to frame.

"The bugs!" marveled Olgemyier. "Just look at that cutie, would you?"

Professor Habluetzel smiled tolerantly. "Yes," he said, "the bugs."

He pulled off his thick glasses, revealing little squinty eyes, and dug in his hip pocket for his handkerchief. Holding the glasses up to the light, he proceeded to polish them briskly as he began his explanation:

"At the University, the University of Virginia at Charlottesville, my colleagues and I were recently involved in a project intended to demonstrate a practical method for initiating procedures of birth control in the common Culex mosquito, this fellow here," he said, tapping the screen, "or actually, this *lady,* here," he corrected.

"Yes, we learned, gentlemen, that the female Culex in an aroused state of sexual anticipation emits a very specific audio tone from the area right . . . here, immediately adjacent to and following the middorsal labia of the pudendum."

"Can't you just say 'ass'?" asked Olgemyier. "Christ, you're pointing to its ass. Just simply say 'ass'!"

Each time Olgemyier interrupted Habluetzel, the Professor would wait for him to finish, holding the pointer in both hands across his thighs, a portrait of patience. Then he would continue.

"The mating period of the female Culex lasts anywhere from a matter of minutes up to four months, depending on local environmental factors and the male population present. The larger number of males in a given area, the shorter the resultant mating period, and vice-versa."

Otis stifled a yawn and Olgemyier muttered, "God, is this exhausting?"

"Goddamnit," Boone hollered at 'im. "Would you let the man talk?" Somethin' in this had begun to pique Boone's interest, which meant he could smell a dollar or two startin' to waft outta the Professor's speech.

"Thank you, Mr. Moses," the Professor said.

"Boone, son . . . just call me Boone." Yessir. It looked like Boone definitely was on the scent.

"Now then," Habluetzel continued, "those constant and invariable frequencies emitted by the female Culex serve but one purpose . . . that is, one purpose until now," he smiled drily, "and that is to drive the much smaller male Culex into a state of mating frenzy.

"This slide," Habluetzel explained, again pointing to the screen, "is of the male Culex as seen under the microvideoscope. Observe how the insect salivates profusely from the mandibles, indicating sexual frenzy."

Olgemyier gave a little cry and bit his knuckle.

"The salivating resulted in this case from artificial stimulation when we introduced a tone of 452,178 hertz into his sensory mechanisms through the use of a special audio oscillator."

"Tease," chided Olgemyier.

"We decided," the Professor went on, "to see what might happen if this precise tone was generated through a massive, electrically charged grid immersed just below the surface of a body of water in which mosquitoes were breeding—a farm pond, for example." A projection of a farm pond, a truck with a generator on its bed, and a group of men shone on the screen.

"We anticipated that the male Culex, lured by the tone's siren song, would fly into the grid and be electrocuted." Again he smiled faintly. "That, gentlemen, is precisely what occurred."

"Killjoy!" snapped Olgemyier.

Habluetzel pushed on. "Male Culexes are able to pick up the female's tone from a distance exceeding forty miles. We did indeed prove that a drop in Culex reproductive activity developed in precise relationship to the decrease in the male population terminated in our tone-emitting grid.

"Now then, gentlemen, it is what we did *not* anticipate that brings us to our discovery."

"Thank God," Olgemyier moaned.

"We found that the female Culex, deprived of her, uh, pleasure, shall we say . . ."

"PUH-LEEEEZE!"

". . . would emit this 452,178-hertz tone from her microscopic ovipositors in ever-increasing intensity over shorter lengths of time." Again, he indicated the bug's rump.

"Honest to God," Olgemyier said, exasperated. "You have an anal fixation!"

"Goddamnit, Olgemyier!"

"Aw, Boone . . ."

"May I continue, gentlemen? Thank you. So, therefore, as we generated the mating tone artificially with the oscillator, while the female Culex emitted the same tone in the augmented manner I described, the two intertwined to create what we call a Harmonic Beat Frequency. That, in turn, triggered sympathetic vibrations that oscillated out of phase with the original beat frequency. Now, gentlemen, the intriguing part."

"God," groaned Olgemyier, "not yet, please; we need the rest."

Habluetzel shot him a glance that said you fucking imbecile, and then continued:

"We learned that the human body—yours, mine, anybody's—absorbs these vibrations, and does so at a startling rate. Once charged with these frequencies, our bodies are able to perform a feat routinely done by the Culex, and that is, gentlemen . . . support itself on the surface of the water."

He paused as Boone and I simultaneously, slowly, sat forward.

"Yes, it's true," he emphasized, "absolutely irrefutable scientific fact: Properly infused with the necessary audio frequency and its sympathetic oscillations, a man can be made to . . . walk . . . on . . . water."

Professor Habluetzel stood before us, silent. The room was absolutely hushed. Then, Boone let out a low whistle and said, "Well, kiss my ass."

"No," I said, "the way this thing's soundin' I think we better kiss that mosquito's ass!"

Boone puzzled for a moment, then asked, "Habluetzel, now just how in the hell could you fix this deal up into somethin' somebody could take out on the road?"

The Professor nodded, looked down at his feet, and smiled. "Well," he said, "there are some, shall we say, complications."

Uh-oh, I thought.

"You see," he went on smoothly, "until I was approached by Mr. Olgemyier's staff the thought had not occurred to anyone that there might be any possible application of our discovery other than the obvious one of mosquito control. Of course, once Mr. Olgemyier indicated interest, having read of our experiments in one of the scientific journals, we, ah, awaited the opportunity to present it to you after doing a little further research to gauge its practicability."

"It's startin' to sound," said Boone, "a little . . ."

"Expensive?" Habluetzel finished the thought for him and, for the first time, grinned . . . widely.

"What the Professor's tryin' to say," Olgemyier interjected, "is that there's gonna be some bucks involved, okay? We're talkin'—"

"Twenty percent of the gross, gentlemen," Habluetzel interrupted. "Twenty percent of the gross."

Boone groaned, then smiled, and then laughed out loud. "Son of a bitch," he said. "They got us." He paused a moment, still smilin'. "Well, all right, goddamnit," he said finally, "the deal's just too good if she'll really work."

"Oh," Habluetzel interrupted, " 'she,' as you say, will most assuredly, 'really work.' "

"Well, then," Boone asked, "just what the hell are we lookin' at here, ballpark figure?"

Habluetzel avoided a direct answer. "Aside from the financial considerations," he sidestepped, "there are still tests to be conducted, and the equipment and high degree of technical skill demanded rule out anything other than performances that would be carried out under the strictest control with great care and preparation."

"Now, just what the hell does all that mean, Professor?"

"Well, Mr. Moses, how this thing would work appears to break down like this:

"First, we must consider that a climate conducive to mosquito infestation obviously is required."

"Obviously . . ."

"Christ!" Olgemyier broke in. "Are you tellin' me we go to Panama and he walks th' canal? Gimme a break."

"If I may continue, Mr. Olgemyier? . . ."

"Yeah, ya little maggot," added Boone, "shut th' fuck up for five minutes, will ya?"

"Actually," Habluetzel smiled, "summer conditions would seem to be our only requirement. The Culex is indigenous to all of North America, and, therefore, locale is really just a matter of taste. Secondly, and perhaps most importantly, Reverend Hargus must be exposed to the Harmonic Beat Frequency and resultant sympathetic vibrations for a sufficient length of time prior to each performance to avert . . . well . . . embarrassment at the least, disaster at worst. That is absolutely crucial.

"Now then, a cautionary note, and just possibly, a big one. You see, unfortunately we are unable at this point to assess the effects of prolonged exposure to the Culex frequencies on the human body. While we have no real reason to suspect detrimental impact, we can't rule it out. And indeed, some scientists engaged in this research do believe a degree of risk is involved."

"So what are we talking—tummyache?" Olgemyier broke in. "Honest to God, Habluetzel, stop trying to scare everybody."

"As for your original question, Mr. Moses," the Professor went on, "about, uh, 'taking it on the road,' I believe you phrased it? Well, I'm afraid that prospect seems quite impractical."

"Here we go again." It was Olgemyier, jumping back in. "Jesus, we're not talking about doing this thing like Saturday-night bingo, Habluetzel! I mean, we're thinking maybe doing this just once a year, an annual shot. God, if we can pull this off, once a year'll be enough! We're talking World Series, New Year's Eve, Rosh Hashanah, and Christmas, all rolled into one. Annual extravaganza, okay? Hell, make the pussies wait! Let 'em BLEEEEEEED for this one!"

"Well, then," the Professor reconsidered, "on that sort of schedule I suppose this would fall into the range of possibility . . . though, uh, *expensive* possibility, hmmm?"

"Well," muttered Boone, "I guess pullin' this big of a deal even once a year rules out comin' up with somethin' for our revivals, doesn't it? Shit. What about our revivals, huh?"

"Booney, darling," Olgemyier said, annoyed. "I love you, you know that, don't you? Look at me! Look up here. See this face? Does this face love you? But, God! Let's look at the facts: Are you gonna spend the rest of your life schleppin' through two-bit civic centers and hick-town football stadiums?"

"There's five million dollars a year out there in those two-bit civic centers and football stadiums, I'd remind you. Five million dollars," Boone said sternly.

Olgemyier sighed the sigh of the defeated. "Booney, dahhhling." God, he could be condescending when he put his mind to it. "I *spill* more than five mil' a year in the back seats of taxicabs. I mean, *really!*"

"Oh, yeah?" Boone shot back. "Oh, yeah? Ha! How about the ten million plus we've done offa that radio program for the past four years runnin', huh? How about that? I suppose that's just pocket change?"

"God, you are dreary at times, Booney. Dreary! By the time you pay all those tacky stations to carry the program, and by the time you pay those Japs to put the thing together, and after you've thrown in all the production costs, paid salaries, greased the necessary palms here and there, *and* paid *our* fee, well, Jesus! Couldn't buy you a cheeseburger and a Coke, now, could I, Booney boy? Hmmm?"

"Now, you see here, Olgemyier." Boone was losin' control. "Why, you goddamn pimple. I oughta squeeze your head until your brains splatter against the wall, boy, that's what I oughta do to you!"

"Honestly, Booney, settle. Just settle. Look, the point is this: Everything we've done to this stage of the game, everything, has been like pissin' in the wind compared to what we *can* do, startin' right now! Trust me. We're not talking road show goin' from this hog wallow to that one, we're talking a shimmering, annual extravaganza that'll shake this entire country! Incandescent! We're not talkin' a radio program, we're talkin' television *mega*-specials! And, Jesus! We're most certainly no longer talkin' an annual gross of fifteen lousy million dollars. Hell, we're talkin' *nettin'* maybe . . . God, I just don't know. I tried out some figures on my calculator this morning and the thing went into overload. Booney, you got your head stuck in the sands of the past, boy, and you've got to get it out! Everything that's happened until now is history, understand? You're in New York now. My turf, and we play hardball. All that other stuff is . . . well, back there, somewhere."

He waved a hand behind him and then his expression changed, softening as he continued to look at Boone, who somehow appeared smaller, shrunken a little.

"It's over, Booney. Phase one, gone. Billy's outgrown it. We got superstar material now, a stallion. And you gotta give him his head, capeesh? And this man," he laid his hand on Professor Habluetzel's forearm and smiled at him warmly, "this man is the answer, right, Professor?"

Habluetzel nodded and smiled wanly.

Boone looked down at his hands for a moment. Then, clearin' his throat, he shifted his weight on the pillow pile he was sittin' on. "Well," he harrumphed, "I know all that stuff. Did you think that I didn't have that all figured? Shoot. I knew *all* that stuff, didn't I, Billy?" He turned to me as he spoke and gave me a hearty slap on the back. Too hearty.

I studied my shoes.

"Well?" Boone pressed after a minute, his voice growin' a little anxious. "What about it, Billy? Tell em, okay?"

"Yeah, Boone, sure," I said. "You had it all figured."

"See there?" Boone asked, lookin' all around him. "See? I told you, didn't I? Yessir. Okay, then," he laughed as he grunted to his feet, "I guess that about settles 'er, don't it? By God, they'd better watch out for you and me now, huh, Billy? What about it there, Professor? We'll smoke 'em now, won't we? Right, Olg'? Otis? Ha! This is gonna be somethin'!" He grinned at us too broadly, and we forced little strained smiles onto our faces and nodded back at 'im.

"Right, Boone."

"Sure . . ."

"You got it."

"Okay, everybody!" shouted Olgemyier, suddenly back to his much more familiar self. "That does it. I'll get Legal working on the papers this afternoon. SLIDE!"

A graphic displaying a series of dates and cities flashed up on the screen. "Look at this, everyone," said Olgemyier. "Here it is. Tentative schedule for The Event that will cause a country to tremble. Oh God! I just can't stand it! Looky, we're talking Dallas next summer. Can we make that, pussycat?" He smiled at Habluetzel, who nodded self-assuredly.

"You are just *sooo* academic," gushed Olgemyier, reachin' over and squeezin' a pinch of Habluetzel's cheek.

The Professor winced and, usin' both hands, brushed 'im away.

But Olgemyier had begun to build up a head of steam: "God! Dallas, numero uno next year; then, in '64, we're talkin' L.A.; '65, Chicago; '66, oh Jesus, *New York! New York!* . . . and . . ."

"Whoa, there, little feller," Boone interrupted. "Now, what the hell is all this, exactly?"

"Dates, sweetie. Ap-pear-an-ces! Walk on the water with the water-walking *wizard!* We're talking advances paid. Dates booked, set! And set, I might add, for ten goddamn *years!* Oh, God, is this serious? No more rolling into town and throwin' up a tent anymore, okay? Now, where was I? Oh yeah: '67, New Orleans; '68, K.C.; '69, Cleveland. I ask you, is that serious? Huh? *Booked!*"

"Precisely," chimed in Professor Habluetzel. "And after Dallas, we just allow for the initial shock to dull a little, and then—"

"Knock it off, Hab', okay? Shock, schlock. After the boy here walks on *water* in Dallas—why, Jesus Christ! They'll *kill* to see him in L.A. And," he giggled as he relished the picture, "can you just imagine what'll happen here in New York? Ohmigod! Am I getting excited? Here, somebody. Feel me . . ."

"But isn't the whole deal just a little bit dishonest?" I asked.

My God. You would've thought I'd just farted in church. The whole room seemed to lock up for a moment, frozen, mouths stuck in midword.

"Wha . . . what? Who said that?" asked Olgemyier. "Billy? . . ."

I glanced left and right, embarrassed. "Well, uh . . . no; I mean, I just wondered, I mean, you know . . . oh, God! I just thought that . . ."

"Billy," Olgemyier said, cocking his head at me curiously. "My good friend, Billy—fuck 'em if they can't take a hoax."

THE NEW YORK
DAILY NEWS

GOV'S VOW TO SHEA TERRORISTS: "IT'S YOU OR ME!"

NEW YORK—A visibly shaken Governor Nelson Rockefeller today pledged a "do-or-die" investigation into Sunday's Hargus Crusade horror.

Sixteen of the thirty-eight people shot and wounded during the Shea Stadium assault remain in extremely grave condition today. At Queens General Hospital, night nursing supervisor Rebecca Harris said . . .

REEL 13

◆

August 14,1966.

A Sunday morning.

"Jesus Christ! Is that goddamned phone ever gonna stop? Boone!" I shouted, "Will you answer that fuckin' thing and then leave it off the hook? GodDAMN!"

Ameline came over and knelt down by the couch where I was stretched out, arm crooked over my eyes, tryin' to shut out the light, if not the racket. "Billy, honey," she said, troubled, "you just look awful, darlin'. What can I get you, baby, hmm?"

"I'll tell you what you can get," I snapped back at her as th' noise and commotion just became too much. "You can get *fucked!* That's what you can get. And you can also get away from *me!*"

"Billy!" hollered Boone, "it's Lyndon . . ."

"Lyndon? Lyndon who, an' what th' fuck do they want?"

"Lyndon, as in White House Lyndon, an' I don't know *what* he wants 'cause he ain't on the line yet."

"Inform him just what I informed Ameline, here . . ."

"Huh?"

"TELL HIM TO GO FUCK HIMSELF! JESUS CHRIST, DO I HAVE TO PAINT EVERYBODY GODDAMNED PICTURES? TELL HIM WE'LL SEE 'IM AT THE RANCH WHEN THIS FUCKIN' CIRCUS IS OVER, AND TELL HIM NOT TO CALL HERE AGAIN! SHIT!"

"Okay, Billy," Boone said, "okay. Just settle down, for God's sake. Please!"

"GRAPEFRUIT JUICE!" I screamed. "GRAPEFRUIT JUICE . . . *NOW!*"

My order sent fifteen people flyin' off in seventeen directions at once, two of 'em havin' doubled back and crashed into one another. From where we all were, the penthouse suite atop New York City's Warwick Hotel, the noise from the street below was a constant low roar. Nothing shut it out. We had a collection of Red Foley's gospel tunes on the hi-fi in the background, but that didn't help. And Boone, Olgemyier, Otis, Tyrone, and Ameline weavin' in and out of a dozen other people I didn't even know, 'cept for Nubby and Stubby, didn't help a fuckin' thing either. The penthouse suite was big, but not *that* big. There was an unending murmurin' of voices concentrated around a big easel where charts and blueprints were bein' pored over as Olgemyier and his "geniuses" planned, and revised, and planned again. Because this was it: "The Big One," as they say. We'd been pullin' off the water-walk now for three years and had played to multitudes, but never such as this one promised to be. Shea Stadium, New York City. The logistics were incredibly complicated. But, by now, all the big-ticket items had been completed and we were goin' over the little details, fine tunin'. Little or not, these were just as important because they were the kinda things that would snap the whole event into focus. So I lay there, with a headache that felt like someone was rollin' a safe across my forehead, and suffered . . . if not exactly in silence. "WHERE'S THAT GODDAMNED GRAPEFRUIT JUICE? DON'T MAKE ME GET OFF THIS COUCH AND KILL ABOUT FOUR OR FIVE PEOPLE! Owww, shit! My *head!*"

"It's comin', Billy," Ameline said. "There was none in the fridge. They just ordered it. It takes a minute to get it here, honey, that's all."

I lay listening to the rumble reachin' us from outside. The police estimates put the crowd down there at ten thousand and climbing, and I silently cursed Olgemyier, who'd insisted we stay at the Warwick.

"Simply *everybody* does," he'd purred.

Boone walked over and stood, lookin' down at me.

"Billy?" He said it like I was an eggshell that'd crack if he spoke any louder. He wasn't far wrong, either.

I lifted my arm off my eyes an inch an' squinted up at him.

"What, Boone? What is it? Can't you see I'm about to die?"

"That's what I wanted to know, son. I just wondered if you might be feelin' any better, that's all."

"I'd feel a damn sight better," I said, "if I knew what the hell was goin' on down there, and why all these damned people are runnin' in and outta here. Do we have to have that?"

Boone stared at me for a moment sympathetically. "Billy," he reminded me. "There's nothin' we can *do* about it no more. They're there because they're there. That's just like askin' if we have to have the sun and the moon. Ain't able to do much about them either, are we?"

I dropped my arm back across my eyes an' Boone reached down and gave my shoulder a little squeeze before he walked over to the knot of men gathered at the charts.

"Y'all need any help?" I heard him ask.

"Huh? Uh, no. Thanks, Boone, but I think we about got it, here."

"Oh. Okay," the old man said, "but if you run into anything . . ."

"Sure, Boone, sure . . . and thanks. Really."

"Daddy," called Ameline, "you c'n help me. I need a drink. Bloody Mary, Daddy, okay? And heavy on the Mary, hmm?"

"Can you sit up a minute, Billy?" It was Otis, lookin' down at me, concerned. He had a goblet of grapefruit juice on a little silver tray.

"Yeah, okay" I said, gruntin' as I pushed myself up. "Owww! Jesus, my head's about to split! I don't think I'm gonna be able to do it, I swear I don't. We're gonna have to cancel out. I can't go through with it."

Olgemyier started over toward me, breakin' away from the plannin' group. "Billy," he said, "tell me I didn't hear what I thought I just heard. Not go through with what?"

"With this Shea deal," I said, holding my head in my hands. "I'm sick, Olgemyier. Sick! Jesus, have some sympathy!"

"Billy," he replied, "I got sympathy just oozing out of me. And I also got a contract here that says we'll be there. Come hell or high water or headaches. And judging from the street out there, and that lake we got installed at the stadium, and now you—well, we got all three. And they're all covered in the contract."

"My PILLS!" I shouted. "Where are my goddamned PILLS?"

"NUBBY! STUBBY! 'MAN WANTS HIS PILLS!"

"*Fuck* th' man," two little voices squeaked from the bedroom.

"GET 'EM, YOU LITTLE BUTTHOLES!" screamed Boone.

"All right, all right, already," they hollered back.

In a minute, Stubby came bobbin' in, his piano leg undercarriage seesawin' back and forth. "What's th' matter with him?" he asked, holdin' the bottle of pills up to Boone with a short, fat arm.

"Shhhh," Boone said. "His head. Splittin'."

"Oh," whispered Stubby. Then he walked over to me, lay one squat little hand on my shoulder, and screamed in my ear, "HERE Y'UR GODDAMNED PILLS ARE, YA FUCK!"

I lashed out at him with both arms and both feet, but he sidestepped, almost gracefully, and laughed like a banshee.

"I'LL KILL YOU, YOU FREAK!" I screamed, immediately regretting it as th' movin' company inside my head rolled the safe back across to the other side.

Boone held me back and pressed me down into the couch again. "Don't, son, don't. Just lay back down. Here, take your pills with a little of your juice. There y'go. Atta boy."

I closed my eyes and sighed as Boone sat down beside me

on the edge of the sofa and patted my shoulder. Stubby watched for a moment, then, with a disgusted grunt, he turned to go.

But Boone's foot shot out and caught him amidships. He squeaked and a look of shock seized his face as he sprawled headlong toward the glass coffee table. There was a tremendous crash as he hit. Shards of glass tinkled to the floor and blood splattered out in great gouts.

Stubby had gone clear through the tabletop and lay face down in a soup of smashed fragments and pink froth. He slowly pushed himself up to his hands and knees. His head swiveled like a dog's and he fixed Boone with a stare that was a mixture of hatred and horror. When he'd fallen, everybody in the room had turned toward the crash, and then had frozen like statues.

Finally, Otis broke the stillness. "Good aim, Boone," he said. "Now somebody call th' ambulance."

After they'd come to take Stubby away and the Warwick's housecleanin' people had been in, sweepin' out and soppin' up, the routine set earlier in the day resumed.

My pills, two Valiums and a Percodan, were startin' to take hold and I felt better. I even sat up.

"Where are we?" I asked.

"New York City," somebody answered from somewhere.

"Oh yeah, yeah. Where's Habluetzel?"

"Outside," somebody shouted.

"Well, send th' son of a bitch in here, and Boone?"

"What, son?"

"Can't you get *some* of these fucksticks outta here?"

"I'll see what I can do, son."

"How do you feel, Reverend?" It was Habluetzel.

"How does he feel? Christ! Just look at 'im," Ameline said, crossin' the room toward us. "He's nothin' but skin and bone. The only things he can keep down are dope and baby food, and his hair's fallin' out in clumps. How does he feel? Shit."

Habluetzel nodded. I hardly recognized him in his wig

and dark glasses. Each year, he wore a different disguise when we got ready to pull a water-walk. "My colleagues would disapprove of my involvement," he explained, as he stacked the packets of cash in his briefcase. He took his Coke-bottle-bottom glasses off and squinted down at me.

"Take a loada shit off your feet," I said to him, unpleasantly. "Pull up a chair."

"When did your hair turn white?" he said.

"About a month after the Chicago walk," I told him. "I see," he replied, giving Ameline a nervous, apologetic little smile. "And that's when it also began coming out?"

I nodded, turnin' back to holler again at Boone. "Boone! Now goddamnit! Get about seventy-five of these people outta here! I'm not kiddin', now! I want 'em OUT!"

Habluetzel reached over and patted me on the knee. "Judging from your appearance, Reverend," he said, "I don't believe you should allow yourself to become overwrought!"

Outside, Sixth Avenue, that broad thoroughfare that bisects Manhattan lengthwise from Greenwich Village to Central Park, had been sealed off for two days between the cross streets of 48th and 57th. Police manned the barricades, shunting vehicular traffic east to Fifth Avenue and west over to Seventh, while allowing the thousands of th' faithful to walk into the zone on foot. And now, the radio said, there were between ten and fifteen thousand of 'em down there jammin' Sixth in front of the Warwick, spillin' around the corner onto 54th Street. They were hollerin', wavin' banners, kneelin' in prayer in the middle of the avenue, and mostly cranin' their necks upward toward the penthouse windows, jostlin' each other, tryin' to get a look. Police bullhorns barked, sirens wailed, and the strains of about two thousand people singing "Shall We Gather at Shea Stadium" lay like a foundation underneath it all. The sound rolled forward into the base of the hotel, then washed up the side of the building and spilled into our suite like surf.

"I CAN'T STAND IT!" I screamed suddenly, jumping to my feet and clappin' my hands over my ears.

"Jesus Christ, boy," said Boone, rushin' over to soothe me. "Stop the screamin'. You're making it worse. Here," he said, pushin' me toward the balcony. "Just go over there and wave at the bastards for a minute. Maybe that'll shut 'em up."

"Anything," I said. "Anything. Which window, goddamnit? Which one?"

"Hey, you! Yank up that window for the Reverend!" Boone hollered at some nondescript lackey, who jumped to comply. "Now, son, come on over here and stand there for a few minutes. Please?"

"I'm comin'," I said, "I'm comin'."

I walked over to the raised window, bent over, put my hands on the sill and leaned out. My God! There were rivers and currents of people! Pooling here, eddying over there. Suddenly, somebody looked up and saw me.

"Look! It's HIM! There he IS!" A roar built as their faces turned upward. It swept up the side of the building like an avalanche run in reverse and pinned my ears back! And suddenly, I felt it. Just like in Reverend Beamer's office so many years before. As I leaned outside, bathed by their adulation, the glory of the Lord started wellin' up in me. It began as a little hot spot in the pit of my stomach, and then radiated out, all over me, to the ends of my fingers, tingling the tips of my toes. I stood there, eyes closed, smiling as the sound beat upon me! Lifting, pushing, tugging, kneading me with unseen hands . . . and then—OHMIGOD!

SATAN!

As sure as I was standin' there, I opened my eyes and saw, just across the street, floatin' at my level in front of a big building, the hideous face of Lucifer Himself, red eyes burning, leering at me, mouth twisted into a drooling, terrible grin. Horrified, I clamped my eyes shut and shook my head . . . and it was gone! Gone where? Ohmigod! I knew immediately. My *crotch!* It had invaded my heathen region!

Something was stirring there. I opened my eyes and stared down at the throng, fascinated, as the warmth I'd been feeling all over me started contracting, pulling in until it had focused in my Satan Center. And sure enough, my rod, my demon rod started to lift and swell in my pants, pulsing higher and harder with each thundering cheer sweeping up the side of the building. "HARGUS! HARGUS!" Higher and harder as though the sound itself was caressing me!

BETRAYED! I thought. BETRAYED AGAIN BY THE FOUL SHAFT! ONLY HOURS TO GO UNTIL I WALK THE WATERS AGAIN, AND I'VE BEEN BETRAYED BY MY OWN DISGUSTING, WEAK FLESH!

Instantly, I knew what I must do! As the roar from below filled my ears and penetrated deep inside my head, consuming me . . . I knew.

Carefully, I reached down and unzipped my pants. The loathsome thing shot out through the opening like a mad bull, possessed! Slowly, so no one would notice, I pulled my head back inside the window and carefully straightened up. With my left hand, I laid my member across the windowsill. With my right, I reached up and gripped the raised sash.

Then, clenching my teeth and tensing every muscle in my body, I counted silently to myself, one . . . two . . . THREE! And with all my might, I SLAMMED THE WINDOW SHUT!!!

"Doctor Stanley, Doctor Stanley, line one . . .

Dimly, I remember becoming fuzzily aware of sounds around me. Very low, subdued sounds. The squeak of rubber-soled shoes walking somewhere. What sounded like a cart rolling quietly down a corridor. A soft whirring off to my left.

And the voices:

"Doctor Cammarata, report to O.R., please . . ."

It was a woman's voice. Nice, unhurried, soothing. Soft sounds. Sounds like you might hear in . . . *a hospital!*

Suddenly, I became aware of the sheets, cool and crisp. I opened my eyes as I also became conscious of an unpleasant, dull ache somewhere . . . "there." I turned my head a little and made out Ameline, lookin' down at me, eyes red and puffy, twistin' her fingers. And Boone was over in the corner, sitting in a chair. Head in his hands. I looked back toward Ameline as the door opened a crack and Otis peered in.

"Is he out from under yet?" he whispered.

Ameline turned to him. "I . . . think he may be comin' around right now. I . . . I can't quite tell yet. Billy? Billy, honey? D'you hear me?"

Ameline's image kept comin' into focus and drifting out again. I tried to answer, but my tongue felt all thick and dry.

"Water," I mumbled.

"Daddy! He's comin' out! He . . . he wants some water!"

Boone looked over at us. "He can't have none, honey. Not for, lessee, another four hours yet, remember? He c'n only have that there cracked ice."

"Where?"

"Right there. To your left on that little stand. Yeah. Try to feed him a piece of that with a spoon."

Ameline slipped a little sliver between my lips as Otis walked into the room. It melted on my tongue and felt good. The cold sensation also helped to pull me out of the anaesthesia a little bit more. My God! I *was* in a hospital! As the room came into sharp focus I saw i.v. bottles hangin' by my bed, and the tubes snakin' down into the back of my hand and crook of my elbow. My eyes must've shown the quick panic I felt because Ameline reached over and took my free hand, sayin', "There, there, Billy. Just stay quiet. Relax. You been through a lot."

"Shea?" I managed to kinda croak.

Boone spoke. "Don't worry none about Shea, boy. We took care of it. We're still a-goin'. It's just pushed back a week or so, that's all. They've made the announcements on the radio and the TV, and it's been in all the papers, front page. 'Exhaustion,' and you've been ordered to have 'total bed rest.' The whole damned city's bleedin' for you, they're so concerned. Everything's gonna be just fine. This is nothin' more than a . . . a temporary little setback, that's all."

Suddenly, the door banged back, givin' me a start and Olgemyier came steamin' through. "Well?" he practically shouted. "How's his dick?"

"Shhh! Shhh, you fuckin' idiot, SHHHHH!"

"Huh?" I sat up, and a searin' pain shot through my pelvic area. I clenched my teeth against it. "What'd he say? What about my dick?"

"You mean he doesn't *know?*" Olgemyier asked. "No one's told him? God! What's the matter with you people?"

"He just now woke up, ya fuckin' imbecile," Boone hissed.

"What?" I shouted, *"What about my dick? What is it?"*

Pain. Pain. Otis hurried over to me, held my shoulders, and gently eased my back down. I reached up and grabbed the front of his shirt.

"Otis, TELL ME! WHAT'S HAPPENED TO ME?"

"Boy, it c'n wait. You're in no condition—"

"WHAT, GODDAMNIT? WHAT?!"

"Billy! Now STOP!" It was Ameline. "You just *stop* that, you hear? Otis? Daddy? Do it. Tell 'im. It ain't fair. . . ." She turned away, stifling a sob.

Boone stood up and walked over to me. He looked old and tired, very tired.

"Billy," he began, and then stopped.

"Go on," urged Ameline.

"Son, I'm sorry, powerful sorry. They tried. God knows they tried, but . . . well, some things even the miracle of modern medicine can't make just right again, son."

It hit me then like a load of bricks: the *window!*

"Boone, d'you mean . . . it . . . is it . . ."

"No, son. Not entirely gone. They . . . they saved a little more than half of it. When you slammed the window down, the other half fired clean across the street, most likely . . . and . . ."

"BOONE!"

"I . . . I'm sorry. I'm doin' a poor job of this, but I just don't know what to say." He sounded pitiful.

"Well, go on; tell him the rest of it . . ."

"Well, Billy, they done what they call 'reconstructive surgery' . . . and they sorta rebuilt you down there using sorta spare parts. . . ."

"Tell 'im all of it. . . ."

"Okay, okay. Just lemme do it best I can, will you?"

"What kind of spare parts, Boone?" I asked. "What do you mean?"

"Well, son, doctors for years now have been using . . . oh, all sorts of things to fix up people with . . . oh, bad hearts an' stuff, fouled-up innards an' things. Often times, if some ol' boy comes in with a bad heart valve, well, doctors have found out that the heart valve of a . . . a pig, you see, is just so darned close to a human's that it fits in there and just works slick as you please."

"A *what?*"

"An' they also found that they can take a section of an ol' hog's intestines and if they have to remove a piece of some person's intestine or somethin', well, they can sew that ol' pig's gut in there an' no one's ever the wiser; works like a charm. So—"

"Boone, stop. Just stop . . . are you telling me that I now have . . . a *pig's* dick?"

A tear crept down Boone's cheek.

"Yes, son. And I saw 'im. He was a fine-lookin' boar. Promise."

No one spoke. Nothin'. Not for several minutes.

Finally, Otis looked at me sheepishly, grinnin'. He spoke, tryin' to ease the tension, "Ah bet ever' time you walk past the bacon in the market, she'll get hard on ya. Ya reckon?"

I'll bet.

. . .

August 28,1966.

A Sunday morning.

"Billy, the motorcade's scrubbed, ya hear me? We gotta go out in a helicopter. Cops say we couldn't get within five miles of the stadium on the ground. The governor's sendin' in a chopper and they're gonna pick us up off the roof. They've called out the National Guard and some of 'em have panicked. They're *beatin'* people. Jesus!"

Two weeks had passed since the episode we all referred to as "the guillotine," a code word to keep the press guessin'. We were right back where we'd started—the Warwick penthouse—and nothin' had changed. There were reports that several hundred people had camped out on the sidewalk on Sixth Avenue the whole time I was in Bellevue Hospital, awaiting my return.

"WHO TH' FUCK ARE YOU?" I shouted at three total strangers who walked into the suite. That's all we needed. More fuckin' PEOPLE!

"Shhh, son. Take it easy," said Boone. "Remember, you're still a little shaky now."

"I KNOW, BUT WHO—"

"They re security, Billy, that's all. Now just settle down."

"I need a drink," Ameline said. A Jack Daniels and Coke materialized magically and she took a big slug. She always seemed to get just what she wanted. Christ, they'd had *her* picture on a couple of magazine covers! Called her "gorgeous," and the "stabilizing force" in my life. Atheist bastards.

A huddle of five people breezed by, jostlin' Ameline and sloppin' her drink on the floor. "Watch it, ya shit heel!" she hollered. They never even heard, as they melted into a larger group of about twenty people gathered around a long table that had been nearly filled with telephones.

Half were dialin' and the other half were already talkin', or fieldin' phones as they rang, which was incessantly. Olgemyier was holdin' court at the other end of the room, standin' on a chair shouting last-minute instructions to coordinators who'd be handlin' logistics from this end. A force of a hundred and fifty under Otis's direction had already been out at Shea Stadium since the night before, fine tunin', making the necessary last-minute adjustments on the audio equipment and the huge pool that nearly covered the baseball infield.

The five who'd damned near run over Ameline broke free of the bigger group and steamed back across the room toward Olgemyier's people, and they damn near creamed Ameline again.

"GODDAMN YOU!" she screamed, and slung her drink at 'em in frustration. It splattered across their backs. They never even broke stride.

"Billy," she said, appealing to me for some relief, "honest to God, I can't stand any more of this. I just can't! Not another second!"

"Well, go th' fuck home then, goddamnit!" I barked at her.

"You go to hell, Reverend Hargus," she snapped back. "You . . . you *puke!*"

"ALL RIGHT! ENOUGH! BOTH OF YOU!" Boone strode over and grabbed Ameline by the wrist. That was the last straw. The dam burst and she slumped to her knees, sobbing.

"Oh, Daddy," she wailed. "Just look at us. Look at us all! Look what's *become* of us. I ain't hardly got a mind left anymore . . . and . . . an' Billy here ain't got a dick *or* a mind. And he's near dead. Just look what's happened to him. . . ."

"Ten minutes!" somebody shouted in through the door.

I threw him th' finger.

"Where's that fuckin' Habluetzel gotten off to again?" I hollered. The voice behind me made me jump: "I'm right here, Reverend Hargus."

"Oh, uh, yeah. Well," I said, "what are we lookin' at now, when we get out there?"

"You mean in terms of charge-up time?"

"Yeah. How long's it gonna take to get me ready?"

Habluetzel looked at me close. "May I?" he asked, gingerly reachin' a hand toward my face.

"Yeah," I said. "If you gotta, then go ahead."

"Okay, turn this way, toward the light a little bit. Fine. Hold it right there," he said. He produced a physician's eye-examining light, raised up my eyelid, and peered inside.

"Uh-huh. Hmmm. Okay, Billy, other side. Yeah. Uh-hmmm. All right." He took a step back and thought for a moment.

"Well?" I asked. "How long a charge this time?"

"Frankly, gentlemen," said Habluetzel, "I don't know what the Reverend's tolerance is at this point. Or even whether he has any left. Just like we unfortunately were unable to anticipate the side effects, the hair loss, the apparent metabolic acceleration, the muscle atrophy, well, we are now unable to tell how much more he can take, if any."

Boone walked over to the window and looked out at the Manhattan skyline, hands thrust in his front pockets. "Well," he said to us, without turnin' around, "you'd just better goddamn figure it out, hadn't you? We don't wanna kill the boy, do we?" He laughed bitterly. "Killin' the goose that laid the golden egg. Shit."

"Boy?" Ameline scoffed. "Jesus Christ, your 'boy' there is a hundred years old."

"Just shut up!" I growled.

"I truly am sorry about how everything's turned out for you," said Habluetzel, "but . . ."

"Look," I said, "I feel fine. Somebody get my goddamn pills, okay?"

"Uh, you just took some, son," said Boone, forcin' a smile.

"I KNOW WHAT I JUST DID, GODDAMNIT! AND I WANT SOME MORE! IS THAT SO DIFFICULT?"

"Son," Boone said, his voice quakin', "you've gotta try to get this thing under control. He handed me my bottles, Valium and Percodan. I shook out my two-and-one combo and chugged 'em, just swallowed 'em. I no longer needed anything to drink to get pills down.

"Billy," Boone pressed, "after these, no more, please."

"DON'T RIDE ME, DAMNIT!" I screamed. "WHY DOES EVERYBODY HAVE TO RIDE ME? WHAT'D I EVER DO TO YOU EXCEPT MAKE YOU A BUNCHA GODDAMNED MULTIMILLIONAIRES? HUH? HOW COME YOU GOTTA RIDE ME? JESUS!"

"All right, Billy, all right . . . my God, what're we goin' to do?"

"Ever'body just let me be a couple of minutes, while these things kick in, okay? Just let me be. Two minutes, that's all I want, okay?"

"Okay, Billy . . ."

"Right, son . . ."

"Whatever, ya meathead. . . ."

It was almost two minutes on the nose, I'd learned from experience, before my particular combination of "narcs," as I called 'em, would take hold. And in two minutes, I started feelin' good again.

"Hey, Boone," I hollered across the room to where he was standin' with about fifteen of 'em. "How long till we leave?"

"You better go in and wash your face, son," he answered. "We just got maybe twenty minutes till the chopper'll be here, and the Governor's gonna be ridin' out with us."

"Boone, fuck the Governor, and come on over here a minute an' let's talk. Grab me a brew outta the refrigerator, will you?"

Boone came over carryin' a pair of 'em.

"Ahhh, bless you, Boone, bless you," I said, startin' now t'feel reeeal good.

"Boone," I said, "y'remember Dallas? 'Member that first time we walked? How they laughed at us?"

"Yes, son," he replied. "I sure do."

"You remember the newspaper? How they crucified me? The goddamn sons-a-bitches. And the po*lice!* 'Member that shit? Them takin' my clothes off, looking for some gadget or somethin'? Bastards testin' the water, all that shit, an' laughin' an' laughin'?"

Boone nodded.

"Boy, I guess we've done fuckin' showed 'em, ain't we, Boone? Huh? Just like you always said we could! Right? They ain't laughin' now, are they Boone? No, sir! You better believe it! And just look at us! Rich! All of us. Remember how you used to say we was goin' to get filthy? Well, we did it, didn't we? An' just exactly like you said. Tell you what, though, I got a real strong feelin' right down here," I pointed to my gut, "that says we're gonna be in for something *really* big, directly. Yep. *Big!* You believe that, Boone?"

Boone looked at me and nodded. There were tears in his eyes. He pulled his handkerchief from his pocket, dipped it in an ice bucket on the table in front of us, and began to wipe my face with it.

"God, God," he muttered to himself, "why's he sweatin' so? What's wrong?"

"Daddy," said Ameline, stealin' up on us from behind, "cryin' over that son of a bitch don't work. I know."

Habluetzel joined our happy little party. "I'm not a physician," he said, peering at me intently, "but perhaps we should call—"

"Th' fuckin' morgue," interrupted Ameline.

"Honey," Boone scolded, "now that's just about enough."

"Yeah, Boone," I continued, "they sure as hell ain't laughin' now."

"No, son," he answered, "but we damn near killed you to make them stop."

"Naw, Boone. Shit! You ol' worry wart! I'm fine, I swear . . . fine! The Lord loves me. You know that, don't you?"

Boone smiled. "God knows He must, boy," he said, shakin' his head. "He must."

"Boone!" Tyrone hollered from across the room. "It's the po-lice. They wanna talk to you."

Ameline sat across from me, lightin' one cigarette off of another. "Butt-fuckin'," as she inelegantly referred to it. Someone handed her a double Chivas and she killed it like it'd been skim milk. She took a long drag on her cigarette, leaned back, and sighed, the empty glass rollin' out of her hand onto the couch.

She fixed me with a half-lidded stare. My God, but she had her daddy's eyes! Even fogged by the liquor she'd been drinking, they still pierced right into you. Well, I never once said she wasn't pretty.

Directly, she looked away and began to speak, almost as though she was talking to herself, and yet her voice reached me through the clamor all around us.

"Remember the day Daddy first came haulin' you back outta Texas, Billy? You all rawboned and raggedy, stumblin' offa that old bus, gawkin' at them Tulsa buildings, lookin' for all the world like you'd landed on Mars."

She shook her head, chuckled, and picked at a little frayed spot on the back of the couch. I smiled, too, because the reminiscence was sweet. The Lord knew I couldn't forget how she'd looked that day, standin' there waitin' to meet us.

"I loved you right then and there, you know," she said, turnin' back to me.

"I know, Ameline," I acknowledged. "But you never loved Jesus. And that's your biggest damn fault. He comes before all. You gotta love—"

"Billy, please. Let me say this." Tears welled up in her eyes. "Just let me get this out. Please do me that favor."

"Yeah, but you never *did* love Jesus. You jus' . . ."

She stared at me hard.

"Oh, well," I said, "go on. I'm sorry. Say your piece."

"Billy, it . . . it's just not that easy. I . . . No. Let me start again. You see, you may not believe this . . . but . . . I'm goin', Billy."

"What do you mean, 'goin' '?"

"Away. I'm goin' back to Tulsa. I have to. But I want you to know before I leave that someday, if you ever get to lookin' back on all that's happened to you—what you've become—it . . . it was never, ever any of your doing, Billy. I know what I'm talkin' about."

"Then why don't you clue me in, woman? You aren't makin' *no* damned sense at all. You just go shootin' off—"

"Billy! You *promised. . . .*"

"Aw, shit. Okay, go on."

"Thank you. You never had a chance in the world of winding up a real person." She retrieved her glass from the couch and idly ran a finger around the rim as she talked. "From the day that goddamned Edna did what she did . . . to the day Daddy let you get to believing you were Jesus Christ, or whatever the hell it is you think you are, you . . . you just never had a prayer." She paused and bit her lip as, once again, tears crept slowly down both of her cheeks. "And, honey," she went on, "you'll never know how I ache inside because I saw it happenin' and didn't understand enough to try to stop it when I still could."

"Christ, Ameline!" I said. "Honest to God, all I ever did was the will of the Lord. And what are you talking about, anyway? Why, hell. Your problem was you never could keep your hands off the lump in my shorts. Shit."

"Billy, don't," she said, pleadingly. "Please, don't. Just let me finish."

I sighed, waiting, as she hugged her arms to herself like the room had suddenly gone cold, and looked away.

"I loved you," she said, almost apologetically, "with all my heart. And . . . I still do. Too much to stay. And Billy, I don't think the Lord ever 'willed' anybody into killin' themselves."

I didn't say it out loud, but I thought it: Ameline might a-been a heathen, she might not a-loved Jesus, but somewhere underneath all her torment was a good and pure heart . . . and the hurt I felt inside me as I watched her weep was the kind no drug could take away.

"That it?" I asked, softly.

"Yeah," she said, "that's it."

• • •

They had begun to chant in the street below: "BILLY SOL, BILLY SOL, BILLY SOL," runnin' it together until it sounded like one word.

"Jesus!" Ameline said, "can't we go" That racket out there's drivin' me nuts!" She looked at me. "But you love it, don't you, Billy?"

I listened to it for a moment or two.

"It's the Lord's will, Ameline," I said reverently. "You're listenin' to the will of God."

"Christ!" Ameline snapped, "I need another drink."

Boone walked back over to us. He was frownin'. "Son," he said, "we've got a little problem here. Most likely nothin', but somethin' we gotta think about. I was just speakin' to a Lieutenant Walden down at police headquarters. Seems some son of a bitch has called th' papers sayin' you won't get outta Shea Stadium alive."

"Death threat," I muttered. "Boy, they're really out there, ain't they, Boone?"

"Yes, son. That goddamn risk is always there, never does go away."

"Daddy," sobbed Ameline. "Honest to God. I've had it. I just can't handle this anymore. . . ."

"Put a lid on it, Ameline," I barked. "This has happened before. L.A. was hardly no goddamn picnic, y'know."

But Boone appeared genuinely worried. I noticed, as he poured himself a few fingers of Chivas, that his hands were shakin', and I'd never remembered seein' that before, ever.

"Things are out of hand, son," he said. "I don't know. It . . . it's just like the whole damned thing's goin' haywire here. Your sickness, th' goddamn pills, Ameline, Olgemyier, *me!* And now this here loony who says he's gonna put a stop to you, permanent. I . . . I just don't know no more. . . ." He thought for a moment, and I saw a decision bein' made.

"Ameline," he ordered. "Go in the other room and get Olgemyier out here, and right now! Somethin's gotta be done.

. . .

"ARE YOU INSANE? HAVE YOU GONE AROUND THE BEND?" Olgemyier had burst into the room, right on Ameline's heels, screamin'. "Booney, look: We call this thing off and you're GUARANTEEING they'll put an end to you. You stop this now and it's a GODDAMN WAR!"

"Sit down, simmer down, and let me straighten your young ass out," Boone said. "If these cops, an' the Guard, an' all those other see-curity people can't get a handle on this . . . this little 'problem' here, then Billy ain't only not gonna walk on water, he ain't even gonna walk across this goddamn room, cuh-fucking-peesh? OLGEEE-boy?"

"Lemme warn you, Moses," Olgemyier said, his voice suddenly turnin' cold, cold like I'd never heard it before. "You don't know what you're dealing with, mister. Certain, uh, 'things' are beyond your control now. If *I* say there is no danger, then there is no danger. Period. Final. We are going to go walk on water. End of conversation."

"Why, you little piece of shi—"

"HOLD IT! BOTH OF YOU!" I shouted. "*I* make the decisions about what *I* do! Understand? Neither one of you makes 'em for me! Get th' picture? Now, Boone, please don't argue with me. I'm goin'."

"DADDY!" screamed Ameline. "WE'RE GONNA KILL 'IM! ALL OF US! WE'LL ALL HAVE HAD A HAND IN IT!!"

"Shut up, Ameline!" I snapped. "Just shut up!"

"Okay, Olgemyier," Boone surrendered. "Okay. You win, but by God I'm tellin' you right now, and you better hear this and hear it good: THIS IS IT! NO MORE! NEVER AGAIN! GOT IT?"

"Fine with me," said Olgemyier. "Terrif, but you sure as hell are gonna do it today!" He took me by the elbow and guided me away. "Jesus, Billy, you look just . . . *fab!* You been doin' something to your hair? Listen. You simply *have* to tell me.

"Okay!" someone hollered. "Let's hit it. Chopper's on the roof!"

Suddenly, the room swarmed with people, every one of them shoutin'.

"How we gonna get 'im to the roof?"

"Boone, cops are here. . . ."

"Where's Tyrone?"

"He left hours ago, haulin' the choir out. . . ."

"Christ, I bet they never make it. . . ."

"Anybody seen that fuckin' Nubby and Stubby?"

"Naw, but if you do, stomp on 'em, will ya?"

"Kill em, sweetie. Just positively butcher 'em, hey?"

"AMELINE! Call Otis an' tell him we're on our way. . . ."

"BILLY . . ."

". . . PHONE . . ."

"FUCK THE PHONE!"

"We're goin' . . ."

"ALL RIGHT! CLEAR THE HALL! GODDAMNIT, GET OUT OF THE WAY THERE, WILL YOU?"

"BILLY!"

"Honey, I . . . I love you. . . ."

"JESUS CHRIST, GIRL, GET TH' FUCK OUTTA THE WAY AN' LET HIM GO!"

Sunday afternoon.

Shea Stadium.

The bullets whined over my outstretched arms.

"GODDAMNIT!" screamed Boone. "GET DOWN, YOU CRAZY GODDAMNED SON OF A BITCH!! DOWN!"

"I DID IT!" I exulted. "I ACTUALLY DID IT! BOONE! BOONE! DID YOU SEE ME?" He didn't hear me.

The shots seemed to come from somewhere high above the third-base side of the field, though others would say later they'd been fired from the first-base side, and still others insisted it was a crossfire. I'd just been ready to take my first step onto the water when the gun, or guns, had opened up. And I'd tried to claw my way into the water; I'd beat on it and stomped on it tryin' to get in so I could get out of the line of fire, but I had been unable to. I had *remained on the surface.* An' . . . an' no signal! I'd walked on water without ever havin' had the signal flashed to me by

Otis that I was sufficiently charged to pull off the stunt! Hell, I wasn't even sure Habluetzel's goddamned gadgetry had worked on me this time. Maybe it had, maybe it hadn't. What I do know is that I walked on that goddamned water, I did. And without *no* signal to take th' step!

A bullet tore through my robes and hit a woman in front of me square between the eyes. She slid under the water, which had turned a vivid pinkish red with the wounds of dozens of people runnin' into it. I remember thinkin', ironically, Good thing there ain't no sharks.

As always, with such moments of madness, it took a minute or so for what was happenin' to sink in with the tens of thousands of people lookin' on. But when it did, the stadium rumbled, it shook, and then all but exploded. Suddenly, thousands of people were shoving, screaming, and sobbing. People were pushed out of the upper deck to fall on people fifty feet below. Police were clubbin' anybody within range of a night-stick. National Guardsmen were slammin' rifle butts into people around the pool, tryin' to shove 'em back as they threatened to collapse the sides of the thing. Others lay stacked two and three deep in puddles of blood. All of a sudden, hands grabbed me and started draggin' me off toward the helicopter. People tore at my garments as I went by. They screamed and screeched, "OH, MY GAWD!" "HELP MEEE!" "HELP ME, THY REVEREND!"

Somebody pushed me roughly into the helicopter where the Governor cowered, rolled into a ball in a rear seat. "HIT IT!" somebody shouted. "GET THIS DAMN THING AIRBORNE!" The rotor blades started their soft lop-lop sound, picked up speed, and we began to lift. Tyrone and Boone were in each door, kickin' and clubbin' people off the landin' skids. Fires had broken out all around the infield, and we rose slowly through smoke and tear gas, burnin' our eyes and makin' us choke. A couple of desperate souls managed to hang on to the skids, and dangled there until we got about seventy-five feet off the ground, and then they fell away.

"SON OF A BITCH!" somebody yelled, as a shot slammed through the canopy and embedded in the instrument panel. "THEY'RE STILL SHOOTIN' AT US! GET THIS FUCKIN' THING MOVING!"

"I did it," I said to no one in particular. "I did it."

They ignored me.

I tugged at Boone's sleeve. "Boone," I said, "I did it. . . ."

He was watchin' outside, grimacing as though he expected a bullet to slam into his eyes at any second.

"Boone, goddamnit!" I hollered at him. *"Are you deaf? I said I did it!"*

"SHUT HIM UP!" screamed the pilot. "SOMEBODY SHUT THAT SON OF A BITCH UP!"

I smiled.

Sunday evening.

Warwick Hotel.

Boone hung up the phone. He shook his head and slumped down on the sofa beside me. "Not a goddamn trace of 'em," he said. "Those bastards!"

Olgemyier staggered into the room. One sleeve was ripped off his coat and a trickle of blood had dried from his forehead down beside his nose and onto his chin.

"Thank God we made it," he said. "Jesus! What a scene! I can't believe it really happened. My God!"

"It happened," said Boone. "It happened."

"God," Olgemyier added, "the *press!* They're gonna *kill* us on this one. You just wait. They'll have a fucking field day!"

"Well, you fuckin' idiot," said Boone. "Everything that's happened this day, the tragedy, the horror . . . and all you can think of is if you're gonna get a couple of negative headlines? You're a true piece of shit, Olgemyier. Grade A."

"Hey, sweetie, I *live* in this town, remember? You an' your bunch of crackers can go hide in the goddamn boondocks, but I gotta *face* these jackals!"

"Where's Ameline?" I asked.

"Son, she's gone," said Boone. "She'd already had it before this thing this afternoon." He hauled his watch out of his vest pocket. "She oughta be damn near on the ground in Tulsa, I reckon."

"Tyrone?"

"He was on the chopper with us. 'Spect him any time now, son."

". . . Otis?"

Boone looked at me hard. "Billy," he said, "Otis was shot. He's dead, son."

"Yes, I know," I sighed. "Otis is fine. He's with . . . th' Lord."

"Boy," Boone said to me earnestly, "I want you to lie down now and get some rest. This . . . this t'day has left us all in a state of shock, an' . . . and I want us all to get some rest, now."

"Honestly," said Olgemyier, "I did like Otis. Jesus, I'm sorry. I mean, can't you see it? Look. Am I sorry?"

I closed my eyes and sank back into the couch. "I did it, you know," I said, rubbin' my eyes. "You know that, uh, I no-kiddin' did do it, don't you?"

"Yes, son," Boone said. "Sure we do. Sure . . ."

"Don't patronize me, goddamnit! I mean I did it! ME! *I did it!* Myself! I WALKED on that shit!"

"Oh, Jesus," said Olgemyier, slappin' his thighs and rollin' his eyes at the ceiling.

"Look," Boone reasoned, "we can talk about it in the mornin'. Most important thing for all of us now is to try an' get some rest, okay?"

"TALK ABOUT IT IN THE MORNING!" I hollered. "TALK ABOUT IT IN TH' MORNIN'??!? IS THAT WHAT PETER SAID TO JESUS—'LET'S TALK ABOUT IT IN TH' MORNIN', JEEZE'?!?! DO YOU FUCKIN' BLOCKHEADS UNDERSTAND WHAT I'M SAYIN'? I DID IT, GODDAMNIT! I DID IT!"

"Now, look here, son. That goddamned Habluetzel and

his fuckin' music machine done cooked your head, boy. Now, I'll be a son of a bitch if you ain't gonna lay down!"

"Well, Boone, I guess you're a son of a bitch, then, 'cause I sure as hell ain't layin' nowhere nohow! You musta seen it. I never got no signal outta Otis. Hell, Habluetzel said he wasn't sure I was charged up. I went ahead an' did it anyway! Olgemyier, you musta seen me. I DID IT!"

Olgemyier closed his eyes and wrinkled his nose at me. "You *slayed* 'em, sweets. You were *gold!* Was he gold, I ask you?"

"Naw, you fuckin' idiot!" I pushed myself off the couch and stood in front of 'em. "What the hell is the MATTER with you people? I WALKED ON WATER! NO CHARGE! NO NOTHING! I, BILLY SOL HARGUS, WALKED ON . . . WATER! DON'T YOU KNOW WHAT THAT MEANS? CAN'T YOU SEE IT?" I held out my hands, appealing to each one of 'em.

"WELL?" I roared. "FUCK YOU, THEN. FUCK TH' BUNCH OF YOU!" I headed for the table with the phone array. "I'm gonna tell 'em," I muttered.

"You're gonna WHAT?" shouted Boone.

"Everything!" I said. "The whole son of a bitch!"

"He's sick," said Olgemyier. "Sick! Now, this second, we put him away, right? And he talks to NO-BODY! GRAB 'IM!"

I picked up a phone and started dialing the Police Department emergency number.

Just then, the door opened and Tyrone dragged himself inside.

"GET 'IM!" screamed Olgemyier.

"Huh?" whimpered Tyrone. "What'd I do? God, I ain't done nothin' 'cept damned near *die!*"

"NO," Olgemyier hollered, pointin' at me, "HIM! HIM!"

". . . Billy? What'd he do?"

"JUST GET 'IM. . . ."

"Hello, Police Department? . . . *The sons-a-bitches tried to kill me. . . .*"

"ARGGGGGGH!"

Boone, Olgemyier, and Tyrone gangtackled me.

"NOOO!" I screeched. "JUST STAY OUTTA THIS! LEMME HAVE THAT PHONE!"

"HANG IT UP! HANG IT UP, GODDAMNIT!"

Boone and Tyrone sat on me as Olgemyier dived for the receiver and slammed it back in its cradle. "Jesus," he said, "just pray that they didn't have time to put a tracer on that. Shit!"

"GET OFFA ME! MY OPERATION, DAMNIT! YOU'RE GONNA—"

"Son," said Boone, soothingly, "just settle down. You hear me? Settle! If what you've gotta say is that important to you, then we'll talk. Right now. Okay?"

"Okay, but you gotta let me up."

"I will, if you promise you won't try for that phone again."

"All right . . ."

"Promise?"

"Yes. Cross my heart and hope to die."

"Okay, then." Boone eased himself off of me and nodded to Tyrone to do the same. The second I could, I leaped to my feet and started screamin' at 'em: "I DID IT, I DID IT, YOU FUCKIN' OAFS!! YA HEAR ME? DID IT, DID IT, *DID IT!*"

Boone was shocked, I could tell. Good. Maybe it would get him to sit down and listen, then.

"All right, son," he said, tryin' to smile. "Let's discuss it, okay? Now, just what is it you did here?"

"NOT HERE—THERE! AT THE STADIUM!"

"Okay, okay. Easy, son. Whoa, there. Easy."

"Go ahead," piped up Olgemyier. "We're listening."

"Boone," I nearly begged. "Olgemyier, Tyrone, I honest-to-God did it! I . . . I walked on water! You know, when I stood up there in the pool, or, I mean, *on* the pool?"

"Yes, son, I saw you but I thought you were just standin' on top of somebody or somethin'."

"No, I was standin' ON THE WATER!"

"Jesus," said Olgemyier, "I thought you were crazy. I'm sorry—*brave!* That's the word I was looking for, *brave!* Okay?"

"Well, that's when it happened," I said. "That's when th' Lord told me."

"I see, son," soothed Boone. "Now, what was it th' Lord told you?"

"DON'T BE HUMORIN' ME, GODDAMNIT!"

"Sorry, son, I didn't mean it that way. . . ."

Olgemyier had gotten up and drawn all the drapes. "Don't be so tense, Billy," he said. "Jesus, you wanted to talk and we're talking." He turned to Tyrone. "Are we talking?"

"You guys all think I'm crazy, don't you? Well? Don't you?"

"No, son," said Boone, "you're just a little shook up. Hell, all of us are."

"Tense," said Olgemyier. "Tense is the word. Look, wake up tomorrow and everything'll be jussst fine, okay?"

"Horseshit! I can tell. You think I'm crazy," I insisted. "I did it, damnit! And I don't need Habluetzel. I DON'T NEED ANY OF YOU!" Now I was tellin' 'em, by God. "Open up them damn drapes!" I hollered. "I want to wave to my subjects!"

Boone leaned back on the couch, laced his fingers behind his head, looked up at the ceiling, and smiled. But it was flippant. It sure as hell wasn't happy.

In a moment he bit off the end of a cigar, spit, and then fired it up, and watched the smoke drifting into the air. Olgemyier was up pacing now, hands behind his back. Tyrone went over and pulled the drapes back a crack, and stood silently, lookin' down at the street. Finally, Boone spoke.

"Well, now, ain't we hot shit?"

"What're you sayin', Boone?" I asked.

"I said," he repeated louder, "ain't we just hot shit?"

Well, all right now. Maybe ol' Boone was a-startin' to

come around here. "Yeah," I agreed, "you're damn right we are, Boone. Hot shit on a sizzlin' stick!" I liked that, for just comin' offa the top of my head. I walked over to Boone and clapped him on the shoulder.

"Get your hands off," he said curtly. "I think you're missin' the point here, boy. Because, you see, I can't stand shit —lookin' at it, smellin' it, and most of all, bein' around it. So I want to thank you for openin' up ol' Boone's eyes here, boy. You don't need anybody? Well, by God, you just keep a-going down the road you've headed out on and you're gonna get your chance to prove it . . . because you won't *have* nobody! Startin' with *me!* I have had it! You understand me? Had it! You have finally got one notch too big for your britches, boy. I have tried for my very last time to guide you. You have demonstrated for *your* very last time that you no longer care to listen one whet. You don't need anybody, huh? Ha! You just wait, boy, and I'm predictin' you won't have to wait very long." He clamped his cigar in his teeth, grunted, and pushed himself up off the couch.

"What the fuck are you talkin' about, Boone?" I asked. "You ain't makin' one bit of fuckin' sense, as usual."

"Oh yeah, Billy," he said with contempt. "Oh yeah, I think I'm makin' *perfect* sense. You see, I agree with you, boy, that you don't need anybody. No sir, I think you're entirely capable of goin' it alone . . . REVEREND Hargus. Right into the fuckin' toilet. And when they come along and flush it, and you come squirtin' out the other end soggy and beat to a pulp—and it's gonna happen, mark my words— well, my address is still Boone Moses, Tulsa, Oklahoma." He turned toward the door at the back of the room. "You can look me up there. I'd like to see you again sometime if it's only to kick your teeth in."

"Wha'? What are you sayin', Boone? What are you doin'?"

"I'm leavin', Billy boy. This is where ol' Boone Moses gets off."

Olgemyier piped up at this point. "Jesus!" he said. "What

are you talking about! You say this looney doesn't need help? God, Boone, he needs help by the carload! We let him outta this room, and I'm in Cleveland! Jesus!"

"No, Olgemyier," Boone argued, "your rotten ass'll be perfectly safe. Billy will be seein' to that, now."

"Oh, yeah?" I screamed at him as he started for the door. "Sellin' me out, huh? Just like Judas done to Jesus, is that the idea, huh? Well, you just go, you old fuck!" I saw him cringe, but he kept right on walking. "Get out, ya goddamn lowlife, ya washed-up guttersnipe! I don't need you, you're sure fuckin-A straight about that!" His hand reached for the doorknob. "I DON'T NEED YOU, I'M TOO BIG! NOTHIN' CAN HAPPEN TO ME! I DON'T NEED ANYBODY . . . HELL, I DON'T EVEN NEED JESUS!"

Boone froze like he'd had a stroke. With the door half open, he turned slowly and looked back at me. "Don't need Jesus, huh?" he said quietly. "Billy, of all the people I've ever met, I never knowed one who needed Jesus more."

He stepped into the hall, pulled the door shut behind him, and was gone.

Olgemyier and I stared at the closed door for a moment, then Olgemyier spoke. "Jesus," he said, "is he brutal!"

"Well," I answered, sighin', "he's old, old and tired. We got on a fast track here and he couldn't keep up, that's all. Face facts, Olgemyier. The man was slowing us down."

Olgemyier looked up at me in disbelief, and I thought right then that I saw something else in his eyes, too. Fear.

"Hey," I said, "now let's get on with it. Let's go call 'em."

Yep, fear.

Olgemyier jumped up. "Call who, Billy? What do you mean, 'call'?"

"The press, the goddamn police, Lyndon, EVERYBODY!"

"Sweetie," he said, "look. Listen to me, okay? You're upset. All right? Let's wait. See? We hold off a year, then we kill 'em again, okay? How's that sound?"

"Like what it is," I replied. "A loada shit. We don't wait. We call 'em RIGHT NOW! And we tell 'em, 'BILLY SOL HARGUS WALKS ON WATER! BILLY SOL HARGUS IS . . . A SON OF GOD!!' "

"Oh, Jesus," Olgemyier sobbed. "Billy, please don't do this to me. Think, for God's sake, *think!*" His whole body twitched. "Trust me on this one, okay? You've *got* to. Nothing! We say nothing! Understand? You rest, we lay low, and we say *nada!*"

"Huh-uh, Olg'," I said quietly. "That ain't the way it's gonna be. Because I can do it, see? I *want* to do it!"

"Hey, fine, sweetie, terrific! Just terriff!" He was approaching the point of panic.

"GODDAMNIT!" I wailed at 'im. "LISTEN TO ME!"

"Jesus, Billy," he sobbed again. "Please, just settle down, *please!* God, I'm begging you!"

"I will if you'll *listen* to what I got to say. . . ."

"Okay, okay, I'm ears. I'm nothin' but ears, promise."

"I can *do* it, and I can do it exactly like my Brother *Jesus* did it!"

". . . Your, uh . . . *Brother?*"

"Yes," I told him excitedly. By God, *finally,* I thought, I was beginning to get through to him.

"Yeah," I went on. "Don't you see it? I walked on water without Habluetzel's goddamn tin-can gadgetry. You know what that makes me, don't you?"

"You really think Jesus is . . . your Brother?"

"Sure," I said. I *was* gettin' through! "Of course! Me and Him are water-walkers! Why, hell, He didn't know until He was halfway through His life that He was gonna be such a big deal! See? Just exactly like me. Our Father didn't mean for Him to find out everything for quite a while, either. . . ."

". . . Our, uh . . . Father?"

"There y'go, Olg'! Now you got it! And may I just add here: Blessings on you, my son."

". . . Blessings?"

"Yeah! No need to thank me. Hell, I hand 'em out like that all the time. You want another one?"

"Uh . . . no, no thanks. I appreciate it, but uh . . ."

"So anyway," I rushed on, knowin' I had finally gotten him to see the light, "let's go over to the phones and—let's see—maybe a press conference! Yeah, that's it! A big press conference to announce that a Son of God once again walks among men! Whaddaya say, Olg'?"

Lookin' down at him, I saw that the fear had been replaced by terror.

"Olg', what's the matter, boy? Come unto me," I said, taking a step toward him. "Allowest me to touch you. . . ."

He shrank away. "Hey, Billy," he said, "I . . . I got an idea how to go with this thing. Gosh, I don't know why I didn't think of this before!"

"Call me 'Lord' . . ."

"Hey, okay! Fine, just fine, uh . . . Lord."

Suddenly, there was something in his expression that I couldn't quite put my finger on, but something was there, almost devious, and the fear was retreating.

"Yeah," he said, almost to himself, "I believe I really *do* have it!"

He got up from the couch and smacked his fist into his palm. His confidence was comin' back and he was gettin' excited. And I knew at that moment that he had joined the team, the team of . . . the Lord!

"All right, Olg'," I said, grinnin' at 'im. "What is it? What you got, boy?"

"Just a minute," he said. "You'll see."

He ran to the desk, grabbin' some paper and a pen, then sat down beside me again.

"Okay," he said, "now listen to me; pay attention, here." He started scribblin' some notes. "Okay, now. We go with your idea. We *do* call the press and we tell 'em . . . Jesus! What do we tell 'em?"

"How about the goddamn truth?" I asked, gettin' annoyed again.

"Easy," Olgemyier said. "Easy, Billy. Let's not rush this." He spoke soothingly. "Look, uh . . . Lord, we can't take chances with the single biggest, uh . . . announcement in the history of mankind, can we? Huh?"

"Why, no," I agreed, "of course not . . ."

"Right," he went on. I could see the wheels turnin'. "We gotta handle this just right. Now, first thing is we gotta explain away what happened out there today."

"I WALKED ON WATER, YA IDIOT!"

"No, no. Easy, babe, easy . . . that's not what I mean. I mean all those people gettin' shot."

"Oh yeah . . . that."

"Trust me on this," said Olgemyier. "You're big, okay? You understand? Big!

"Biggest ever," I reminded him, "with one exception, a couple thousand years ago."

"Uh . . . yeah, yeah. Anyway, we blame the government for what happened! That's it. Any questions, it was involvement—no, make that meddling—on the part of Washington, D.C. Leave it right there, ambiguous, hazy. Something about—this is what you get when the State tries to impose itself on the Church. Yeah, perfect! Shit, it's true, y'know. They're up to their ass in this anyway."

"Huh?"

"Forget it. You don't know. Just forget it. Anyway, uh . . . call the President. Christ, he loves you."

"Worships—"

"Yeah. That, too. Tell him to put a lid on this like he did in Dallas, okay? Then, let's see, let's see . . . the water-walk . . . hmmm." He thought for a moment, then slapped his hand on his thigh.

"GOT IT!" he chirped. "We tell 'em you're gonna do it without the bugs. . . . No! Jesus, we don't tell 'em *shit* about how it worked. Christ, we just say—"

"Just tell 'em the goddamned truth, Olgemyier, the *truth!* That I'm gonna walk just like Jesus did! That's all!"

"OH, GOD!" screamed Olgemyier, reaching over and grabbing my face in his hands. "THAT'S IT! YOU ARE A GENIUS!"

"Certainly," I said. "What'd you expect me to be?"

He ignored me.

"God," he said, excitement building further, "this is perfect! *Perfect!* Now, Billy . . . uh, sorry, Lord. . . ."

"Thank you."

"Where'd He do it? Huh? Where?"

"Where'd who do what?"

"Jes—your Brother. Where'd He walk on water that made such a big splash? Oh, God!" he giggled.

"The Sea of Galilee," I said.

"Perfect! See, Billy, not only are we gonna do it the *way* Jesus did it, but we're gonna do it *where* Jesus did it! Is that gold?"

"Like the streets of heaven," I said. "Bless you."

"Uh . . . sure. Thanks. Gotta use the phone, start layin' this out. . . ."

"Olgemyier?"

"Yes?"

"Find my pills, please."

"Here, try these," he said, fishin' a bottle out of his pocket. "You'll love them. Put you right up there in the clouds."

He headed for the phones, jotting down notes: "Worldwide TV. We're talking . . . oh, I suppose, sixty, maybe seventy-five million for the rights . . . oh, Billy? Damnit, I mean Lord?" he called back.

"Yes, my child?"

"I'll do the talking, I mean if it's okay with you, of course. You shouldn't have to do any talkin' anyway, see? I mean, a Son of God oughta have a mouthpiece, right? The press is gonna go nuts over this, see, an' you just lay back and be cool. You walk—I talk!

"God!" he said under his breath, but I caught it. "Am I gonna be a hee-RO! Jesus!" He started to dial.

Well, fine, I thought to myself, the individual who releases news of a Son of God should be a hero. Fine.

"Hello? Walter Cronkite's office, please. Tell 'im it's Murray. Thanks.

"Walter? Wally? Mur'! I know, I know, it *has* been too long.

"... Just fine, how 'bout yourself?"

"... Good, good. Listen, Wally. I got something big. Our boy—"

"LORD!" I hollered at him.

Olgemyier clamped his hand over the mouthpiece and called back to me. "Uh, yeah. Sorry, Lord, sorry. . . .

"Now, Wally . . . uh, the . . . Lord here—

"... Huh?

"... Hargus, Reverend Hargus! Who'd you think I meant? Anyway, you'll soon see what I mean because—now trust me on this one—he's gonna walk . . . on the Sea of Galilee!

"... Honest! No, I wouldn't shit you . . . we're gonna actually retrace the footsteps of Jesus, dry and wet!

"... How's that? Special apparatus? Walllllly! That's cold! Cold, d'you hear me? I'm hurt! We're using nothing, trust me, not even a Mae West!

"... When? Jesus! Soon, okay? We're talkin' immediate future. Now, look. Can I count on your guys to cover?

"... Walter, baby, *of course! Front row center*—trust me!

"... Would I lie?"

Right then is when I heard it, quiet, off to my left, over by the window. God! I'd even forgotten that he was there! It was Tyrone, still lookin' out the window, and he was cryin'.

Suffer him to come unto me that he might find comfort, I thought, and got up and walked across the room.

The Chicago Sun-Times

HARGUS MISSING! WORLD SEES TV DUNK!!

Followers Adrift in Sea of Concern

NEW YORK—Twenty-four hours after his devastating humiliation in the Sea of Galilee, the world-famous evangelist Dr. Billy Sol Hargus is missing.

The Federal Bureau of Investigation and Interpol, the international police agency, are cooperating in a global search. . . .

REEL 14

◆

February 5, 1967.

A Sunday morning.

"Psssst! Tyrone!" I hissed. "This way! Shhh! Damn! Will you watch where you're walkin'? Come on, let's go in through the back—and watch that trashcan over there. . . ."

"Where? I can't see shit, Rev. . . ."

"Right th—"

Remember the old *Fibber Magee and Molly* show? That's exactly what it sounded like: Fibber's closet. It was enough to wake the dead, or worse, the state police.

"JESUS CHRI—" I started to yell, but caught myself. "I mean, Jesus Christ, Tyrone, do you *want* to get our ass caught?"

"Gawd, I'm sorry, Rev," he said, "but I'm jus' so nervous an' ever'thing. 'Sides, there ain't a light on in there nowhere. Shit, Billy, they gone, an' here we are stuck an' the sun goin' be up directly. What we goin' to do? Lord, Billy, we might as well give up and surrender. It's goin' to be daylight an' . . ."

"Father," I prayed, "would You strike this nigger dead, please, if he don't shut th' fuck up!" I glared at Tyrone through the gloom but he couldn't see me. Hell, you couldn't hardly see your hand in front of your face. The night was cloudy. No moon at all.

"Hold it a minute, Tyrone!" I said. "Look, a flashlight! See?

". . . Hey! Step-Edna? Elroy? It's me, Billy!"

At the sound of my voice the light poked outside and shone directly in my face, causin' me to scrunch up my eyes and turn away.

"Who's out there?"

"It's me, Step-Edna, Billy. Shut out th' light!"

"Wha—? My God, boy, IT'S YOU!" She shouted. "OHMIGOD! QUICK, GET INSIDE HERE. HURRY!" She clutched her nightgown together and held the screen door open for us, shinin' the light down at our feet so we could get up the low steps.

"Hurry up!" she whispered. "There's people swarmin' all over this neck of the woods lookin' for you. Lord! What's happened to you?"

"He's pretty shook up," said Tyrone. "He ain't hardly making no sense no more at all."

"Don't listen to him, Step-Edna," I said. "The Lord loves me."

"See what I mean?" Tyrone asked. "He won't talk 'bout nothin' else."

"Who's down there, Edna?" It was Elroy, hollerin' from upstairs.

"You better get on down here, Elroy," she answered. "It's Billy."

"Who?"

"Billy! Our boy, Billy!"

Feet pounded through the hallway and down the stairs, and ol' Elroy came skiddin' to a stop, still tyin' his robe in front of him. He looked at me like he was seein' a ghost.

"Billy? Is . . . is that really *you?*"

"Yes, Elroy," I said. "Jesus loves me, and I see He loves you, too. He fixed your mouth."

"Naw, son," he said. "Edna here just lightened up on me, that's all." He put his arm around Step-Edna's shoulders and gave her a little squeeze. "Where in th' hell'd you come from, boy? And . . . how?"

"We can't stand here," Step-Edna said, bendin' down to

glance out the window. "Somebody might see and then we'd have it, sure!"

"What're we gonna do?" asked Elroy.

"Upstairs," Step-Edna replied. "Come on, boy—you, too, Tyrone—upstairs, and make it quick!"

Elroy looked at his watch as he led the way through the kitchen to the stairway. "Three A.M.," he said. "Damn!"

" 'Tweren't safe no other time," moaned Tyrone. "And it ain't safe now!"

"He's right," Step-Edna agreed. "We can't even turn on a light at night, Billy. Christ! They just won't leave us alone."

We groped our way up the stairs to the second floor hallway, tiptoein' and whisperin'. "Like breakin' into your own damned house," Elroy complained.

At the top of the stairs, Step-Edna stopped us, causin' Tyrone to bang into me.

"Look, honey," she said, takin' my hand. "Remember? This used to be your room. This'll do fine. See? We moved in that old couch from downstairs."

We all pushed inside, me and Tyrone sittin' down on the edge of the bed, Elroy and Step-Edna easing quietly onto the couch.

"See, Billy?" Step-Edna went on. "Everything's just the way you left it, nearly. Remember?"

I didn't answer her but bent down so I could pull up the shade a crack and look out into the parkin' lot. Nothing. At least, so far.

"No, maybe you don't remember," Step-Edna mused, sadly. She dabbed at her eyes with her gown. "God, son," she said. "It's no wonder, I guess. I . . . I'm fifty-seven years old now."

"You're still pretty, Step-Edna," I said.

"Yeah," Elroy chuckled, "and she's settled down some, too."

"An' just listen at you, Elroy," Tyrone exclaimed. "You talk jus' like a reg'lar white man now!"

Elroy managed a smile as he pulled over a night table and lit a small candle.

"Goddamn ya, Tyrone," he laughed. "Never will be no different, will ya? But I love you, boy," he added, givin' Tyrone a pat on his knee. "You brought m'son home." He smiled at me, but it turned into a frown as I announced:

"I'll be with the Lord soon, you know."

Tyrone pointed his finger at my head and gave Elroy and Step-Edna a knowing wink. "He needs some rest," he said. "A looong rest."

Tyrone's head shone in the candle's glow. He'd shaved his hair off one morning 'bout a month earlier, frettin' about bein' recognized as the search for us went worldwide. "Lord," he'd sobbed, as he scraped the razor over the top of his head, "they got my goddamned pitchur up, *everywhere!"*

"Son," said Step-Edna, "what're you boys goin' to do? You know you're welcome to stay here, but it won't last. Can't. They's sure to find you in two or three days. Where you gonna go?"

"God my Father guides these feet," I told her, as she and Tyrone exchanged glances.

"Well, son," she went on worriedly, hurrying to keep up her end of the conversation, "we saw it, you know, everything on th' TV. It was awful, Billy. Oh, honey, we just sat here and *died* for you." She reached over and took Elroy's hand for support; he nodded, agreeing with her account of how they'd witnessed The Event.

"God, Billy," she continued. "There you were out there bobbin' around in that awful Galilee like an apple in a washtub! In that tiny little rowboat! Lord! And those news commentators! Honestly, son, shootin' 'em would be too good for 'em!"

"Yeah," said Elroy. "Goddamn, why you liked to of *drowned!"* He giggled, and quickly apologized. "I'm sorry, boy, honest. It wasn't funny." But he snickered again.

"The Lord," I explained quietly, "felt I would better serve His purposes through failing. I go to join Him, shortly."

"See?" Tyrone said. "See that? He ain't got all his oars in th' water! It 'fected him, 'fected him *bad!* Lord, I knew he couldn't swim a lick. But would he wear a life jacket? Just in case? NNNNoooooOOOOoooo! The mo-fuckin'-ron just said, 'Jesus didn't wear no life preserver,' and over the side he went! What the hell was I supposed to do? Lord, Lord."

"Well," said Elroy, "the way the television people handled it was a sin. Yessir, if anything was a sin on that day, it was them TV bastards and their snide remarks. Why, just as soon as you sank outa sight, Billy, you know what they had the gall to do? Huh? They run in a douche commercial on ya! Can you believe it! A *douche commercial!*"

"Elroy!" said Step-Edna. "Shhh! Lower your voice." She peeked out the window, fretfully.

"All right," he said, "I'm sorry, it's just that . . . every time I think about that, well, GODDAMNIT, I—"

"ELROY!"

"Sorry . . ."

"Oh, it was terrible, Billy," Step-Edna whispered. "Son, I gotta know something, though. How come, after it didn't work, you had to go back and keep tryin' it? Over and over again! Oh, honey, I cried for you. Honest to God, both of us. Cried! The humiliation of it all! You, steppin' outta that little tiny boat, arms raised to heaven. You know what? That was the last part we saw go under—your arms there, slidin' beneath the water. Lord, son, you . . . you just went down like a . . . a pair of lead shorts! Why, oh, why did you have to keep doin' it? Every time you climbed back in the boat and then stepped over the side again, those . . . those television bastards said, 'THEEEEEEEERE . . . HE GOOOEEESSS AGAIN!' and then they'd *laugh!* Honest, Billy, you near dead, and them *laughin'!* Afterward, we couldn't face anybody for weeks!"

She buried her head in Elroy's shoulder and sobbed.

"It was the will of the Lord," I said quietly.

Step-Edna didn't hear. "And . . . and it was horrible," she rambled on, "just horrible, the way that Mr. Olgemyier jumped offa that buildin' up there in New York. Awful!"

"Yeah," Elroy said, "and don't you just know they had to

go an' show all that, too? Camera got right in real close." He shook his head. "Wasn't nothing left of 'im but a handful of metal."

No one spoke for a minute, each of us, I guess, goin' over those tryin', painful events in our minds. Then, Step-Edna raised her head a little off Elroy's shoulder and looked at me. When she spoke, the cutting edge of panic had crept into her voice, and she stared at me like she was seein' me for the first time that night.

"Billy," she said. "What *are* you gonna *do?* It's still on the radio and the TV every day, all about how they're lookin' for you and closin' in. And . . . and they've been *right here!* Elroy had to go and talk to 'em. They called him your daddy. And they interviewed that Boone Moses, too. . . ."

Elroy laughed contemptuously. "Do you know, Billy," he said, "that that son of a bitch laughed at you, too?"

"And him a-owin' the government fourteen million dollars," said Step-Edna, spittin' the words out. "Why, *shit!*"

"It's the will of the Lord," I said quietly.

"And I guess you know about that Professor Has'n'tootle, or whatever his name was, don't you?"

"Habluetzel," Tyrone corrected.

"Yeah, him," said Elroy. "Well, ain't it just a little bit peculiar how *he* died? Drowned, all hung up in that wire, some kinda grid, I think they called it. They're saying that one was murder!"

I smiled.

"Honey?" Step-Edna said, dabbin' at her eyes again with her nightgown. "Didn't you marry that girl? That Moses feller's daughter? The pretty one?"

The candle sputtered and flickered and Elroy bent forward, cuppin' his hands around it till it steadied.

"What about the girl?" I asked, quietly.

Elroy and Step-Edna looked at each other. "Well, son," Elroy began, "they got her in one of them special hospitals. Seems they found 'er sittin' crosslegged out in the middle of a highway there in Tulsa one night here not too far back, with a pistol in her mouth. Some ol' boy saw her and ran over and kicked it out of her hand before she could pull the trigger."

"Jesus loves her," I said, quietly.

"Why, you know what?" said Step-Edna. "That's the same thing *she* said on TV, screamin' it out while they strapped that coat affair on her!"

"It's the will of the Lord," I said again, quietly.

"Aw, good goddamn!" Tyrone suddenly exploded. "When you gonna stop that 'Lord's will, Lord's will' shit and talk some damned sense, Billy? God!"

I put my hand on Tyrone's shoulder. "It's the Lord's will that you're upset," I told him, softly.

Tyrone looked at Step-Edna and then at Elroy. "We got to do somethin' here," he said. "I'm afraid the boy's gone over the edge."

"HORSESHIT, I HAVE! HORSESHIT," I screamed, trying to make 'em see my point.

"Jesus!" said Elroy, flinching. "Hold your voice down, son, *please!*" He flipped up the shade an inch and took a quick peek outside.

"Yes," Step-Edna whispered hoarsely, twistin' her fingers in her gown. "You . . . you don't understand how it is now, Billy. They're all around here all the time." She peered over Elroy's head, and they both looked out at the parkin' lot.

Elroy dropped the shade back in place.

"Look, boys," he said. "You can stay here long as you want and we'll cover for you as long as we can. But they're here every day and they're sure to find you."

"I'm goin' with the Lord," I whispered.

Step-Edna touched Elroy's hand. "Looks like we taught him pretty good, maybe," she said.

"Naw," Elroy replied. "He's a fuckin' loon!"

"Oh, shit! Now we're in for it!" said Tyrone. "Look, they's lights out in front. Blow out the candle!"

Elroy took a fast look. "Relax," he said. "Just some damn tourists. It'll be dawn directly and they're already startin' to line up, that's all. Ain't no police out there."

He turned back to me and Tyrone. "Jesus, Billy, goddamn tourists like to run us nuts! Y'see, son, we got pictures of you, books, coffee cups, T-shirts, calendars, and I don't know what all. We sell th' crap so fast we can't keep it all in stock. It's impossible."

Step-Edna shook her head. "Elroy here charges 'em a dollar and a half just to look inside the pickup where you was born! And the stupid bastards don't even know it ain't the same truck. Wait'll you see it, Billy—it's brand spankin' new and it's got your picture painted on the doors!"

"And, son," said Elroy, "you remember them little plastic Jesus dolls you used to sell? Well, we found a company in California that makes 'em up to look just like you. Best item we got," he said, matter-of-factly. "They go for eight-ninety-five and only cost us thirty-six cents. The damned tourists *fight* over 'em, don't they, Edna?"

She nodded, holding the shade back again to watch outside.

"I mean, *fight* over 'em," Elroy said, amazed. "Why, we've seen 'em down in the dirt right outside there, beatin' on one another over one of them damned dolls. Crazy, I'll tell you. Absolutely crazy." He shook his head.

"The Lord's will be done," I said, reverently.

Tyrone remained silent, lookin' down at his big hands.

"Billy," Step-Edna asked, "the way they're huntin' you, what does it mean?"

"Nothing," I answered. "Not a damned thing. The sons-a-bitches just wanna laugh some more, that's all. It's the will of the Lord."

"Shit, Rev," said Tyrone, "what the hell are you talkin' about? *Don't mean nothing?* They liked to *kill* your ass a couple of times. I s'pose that's *nothing?* Shit!"

Tyrone lified the shade about a foot and peered out as dawn started slippin' up on us from the east.

"Stay down, son," whispered Elroy. "Drop the curtain back."

The light was becomin' enough to bring a gray illumination to my little room, and Step-Edna looked at me close.

"God, Billy," she said, "just look at what you been through, honey. Oh, baby, you . . . you look older than I do!"

"By about fifty years," agreed Tyrone.

"And," Step-Edna pointed, "that awful *wig* thing! I . . . I don't mean to be talkin' bad, Billy, but it looks like somethin' crawled up on your head and *died!*"

"He got to wear it, Edna," Tyrone explained. "All his damned hair fell out."

"Jesus H. Christ, everybody!" I said. "I'm fine, goddamnit, *fine!* Honest to God, *fine!*"

Step-Edna stared at me and reached over to clutch Elroy's arm, fightin' down the panic again.

Elroy, not takin' his eyes off me, patted her hand.

"Let's all try an' get some rest," he suggested. "All of this'll look better after we've slept on it, don't ya think, son?" He smiled at me weakly.

"Yes, honey," Step-Edna urged. "Please?"

"You two go back to bed," I said. "The Lord's gonna watch out for me."

They looked at each other gravely and then back at me. "Yes, I believe He will," Step-Edna said, "because I don't think you could have gotten this far without Him. Come on, honey."

They rose, Step-Edna brushin' my cheek with a kiss and Elroy pattin' my shoulder, and then they tiptoed from the room.

"It's a shame, Rev," Tyrone frowned, closin' the door. "Them poor folks ain't got no damned notion of what th' hell you're thinkin'."

"Ain't nobody's damned business, neither," I said, " 'cept between me and the Lord. Now, let's go over that list I gave you and get to work."

Tyrone dropped down on my bed, shoulders bowed. "Rev," he said, "I want you to listen to me now. I ain't never since I first set eyes on you told you I wasn't goin' t'do what you wanted me to do. Never, ever. But, Billy," he said, peerin' at me intently, "I *ain't* gonna do this! I can't!"

I sat silent, just lookin' at him.

"Rev?" Tyrone repeated, raisin' his voice. "You hear what the hell I'm sayin' to you? I ain't gonna DO IT! I hate t'be the one to have to tell you this, but there's somethin' wrong in your damned head, boy. You're CRAZY!"

"Anything wrong in there?" It was Step-Edna, callin' through the door.

"Damn you, Tyrone. . . ." I hissed.

"Uh, no, ma'am," I said. "We're fine, just fine."

"Well, settle down then, you two," she replied. "And get some rest, hear?"

"Yes, ma'am."

"Tyrone," I growled, turnin' back to the matter at hand, this man's obstinacy in the face of the Lord, "now you listen to me. The Lord Himself directed that I do this. I've told you that a million goddamn times. I got no say in it at all! It's *His* orders."

"Well, yeah," argued Tyrone, "but He ain't said *shit* to me!"

"LISTEN, goddamnit!" Jesus, what the hell was it gonna take? I wondered. "The Lord wants me. He told me so. He wants to take me exactly like He took my Brother Jesus. Now, don't you *dare* start that whimperin' again! You are *gonna* do what th' hell I tell you to do, when I tell you to do it, and that's it! I will *not* stand by and see you go to hell for defyin' the WORD OF GOD!"

"Oh, Rev," said Tyrone. "You poor son of a bitch. If I'd ever thought it was gonna wind up like this, well, I . . . I don't know, I think I would've done something to stop it a long time ago. Rev, you're out of your goddamned mind, boy. Now, *you* hear *me!* I love you, you crazy son of a bitch; you understand that, don't you? Well, you know what you're askin' me to do?"

He reached out and took me by the shoulders. "You are askin' me, your own *Tyrone* . . . t'*kill* you! Do you realize that, son?" His eyes searched mine, pleadingly, and he shook his head and looked away. "No, by God, I can see it in your face, Billy. You *don't* understand."

"I understand the will of the *Lord!"* I said. "And I thought *you* did, too! I ain't askin' you to do one single solitary thing but the Lord's *will!"*

Now it was my turn to appeal to him, and I picked up my Bible off the nightstand and held it up between us.

"Help me. Please, Tyrone, help me?"

"Help you, boy?" He answered, softly. "Help you? Son, you don't know what the fuck you're sayin'. Hell, you probably don't even know what day of the week it is, Billy. And you want me to go off with you somewhere and . . . and . . . an' NAIL YOU TO A CROSS??!?! Oh, God, Billy. God almighty!"

Elroy peeked in the door and we both jumped. "Boys?" he said. "What th' hell's wrong in here?"

Tyrone leaped at the openin'. "Lord, Elroy," he said. "We got to get some help for 'im, *fast!"*

"Why, horseshit, Tyrone," I said, slappin' him on the back and grinnin' real big, "now just what th' hell you talkin' about, mister? Help? Why?" I waved a hand at Elroy. "Pay 'im no mind, Elroy. We're just a-talkin', that's all. Was we a-gettin' too loud? Gosh, I'm sorry. Tyrone? Let's you an' me hold it down some, 'kay? So ol' Elroy here and Step-Edna can get 'em some sleep. Whaddaya say?"

"I say you're needin' a straitjacket, Billy." He was dead earnest.

"Well," Elroy said, frownin', "you boys just be quiet." He closed the door softly, with me smilin' and loopin' an arm around ol' Tyrone's shoulders.

The second the latch clicked, I slipped my arm up six inches and put a headlock on 'im. Squeezin' hard, I hissed at 'im, "Now, *look,* ya *son of a bitch,* I'm only going to say this one more time. This here deal is the *Lord's Will!* And it's the Lord's Will *that you help me!* If the Lord wants to take me like He took Jesus, then don't I obviously have to have a *cross?* And don't I obviously have to be up there on it? Would anything else make any sense? *Of course not! And you're gonna do what's gotta be done!"*

I relaxed my grip on 'im and he began to cry.

"Aw, Jesus!" I said, exasperated. "Stop it! Stop that crap!"

But he started the same ol' song and dance all over again.

"I'm scared, Rev," he blubbered. "Honest to God, I'm scared. You jus' ain't makin' no damn sense at all!"

Suddenly, there was a racket downstairs at the diner's front door. I clamped a hand over Tyrone's mouth.

"Shhh! Somebody's down there in front! Listen!"

Tyrone sucked in his breath. There was laughin' out front, and somebody started poundin' on the door. Then voices:

"Is this where he lives?"

"Naw, but the dude was borned here, or somethin' or other. . . ."

"HEY HARGUS! . . ."

". . . CAN YA HEAR ME IN THERE? HEY! . . ."

". . . Hell, he ain't in there—fuck 'im, let's go."

"Yeah, he probably run off to Roosha or some damn place. Probably a goddamn Communist. . . ."

"Yeah, that's what they say. . . ."

Car doors slammed as one of 'em said, "Well, one thing's sure. Wherever the son of a bitch went, he sure didn't *swim!"*

Laughter trailed out of the parking lot, minglin' with the sound of the departing motor. In a moment, everything was still again.

"Oh, Gawd," whined Tyrone, "what in the hell *are* we gonna do?"

"Now, look," I said. "Listen to me, now. There ain't much time. I don't have nobody but you. Now, Tyrone, I've never lied to you about nothin', have I?" I lied.

Tyrone shook his head, tears startin' to trickle down his cheeks again.

"Now, I swear to you, the Lord's comin'. He's told me so.

I know how I gotta be set up to be able to be ready for Him to come get me, and there ain't nobody to help me but you." I smiled at him. "You, Tyrone Jefferson, my most trusted, faithful disciple."

"Rev," he said, obstinately, "I don't care what you say to me or what you do to me. I can not, repeat, can not *nail* you to no cross! Please, I'm beggin' you on my kneeeees, *please* don't ask me to do that!"

"Stand up, for Chrissakes," I said. "You're gettin' my shoes wet. Now, look, Tyrone, I don't care *how* you stick me up there. If you don't wanna nail me, then don't! *Tie* me up there! *Glue* me! I DON'T CARE! Just . . . GET ME UP THERE SOME-GODDAMN-HOW!!"

"Lordy! Don't scream, boy! God almighty, don't be havin' no more of them fits on me! Jesus!"

I grabbed the lapels of his raggedy ol' jacket.

"THEN HELP MEEEE!!"

Tyrone picked up a pillow and stuffed a corner of it into my mouth. "You *got* to shut *up,* Rev!" he said. "Shit, they gonna find us before anybody can do anything at all, just by homin' in on your *mouth!*"

Suddenly, more car doors slammed. More voices. The sun was just liftin' a finger above the eastern horizon. Somebody tried the front door, then stood shakin' and rattlin' it when it wouldn't open.

"HEY, IN THERE!" they shouted. "OPEN UP THIS HERE PLACE!"

"You'll have to wait till six," Elroy hollered back at 'em. "Forty-five minutes! . . ."

"COME ON, MISTER, WE DROVE THREE HUNDRED MILES TO SEE THIS DUMP!"

"Sorry . . ."

"SORRY AIN'T GONNA CUT IT, GODDAMN YA!"

A rock crashed through a window downstairs as a car drove away.

"Lord, Rev," whispered Tyrone. He was shakin'.

"Don't tell me," I said. "Let me guess. You're scared."

"Gawd sakes! I sure am. I think we've had it, Billy."

"No, we haven't," I told him. "Not if you'll help me."

I stood up and started slippin' off my pants.

"What in the fuck you doin' now, Rev?" asked Tyrone, eyes big as saucers.

"Takin' off my clothes."

"I know, but . . . *why?*"

"I wanna wear my old bathrobe, Tyrone. That's what I wanna be wearin'. My old bathrobe."

Tyrone looked at me and tried to push a smile on his face. It came out lopsided and panicky. "Lord, Rev," he said, tryin' vainly to sound lighthearted, "we ever get outta here, you can't wear that ol' robe. Ha! Why, that'd be crazy!"

"I know," I said. "I know. Now. For the last time, help me, d'you hear me? Help. The Lord, see . . . THE LORD is comin'! I have *got* to be in the wilderness *on* a cross waitin' for Him. You only get one shot at this, Tyrone. It ain't like catchin' a cab, y'know. So HELP ME! HELLLLLLLLLLLLPPPPPPP ME!"

"I swear I'll do *anything,* just *promise* me you won't *holler* like that no more!"

"Then help me, Tyrone. Stop making me beg."

We held each other's gaze for a moment, then Tyrone looked down, sheepishly.

"What we goin' t'use, Billy?" he asked.

"Elmer's."

"Okay," I said. "Check list: You got the recorder?"

"Check."

"Extra batteries?"

"Check."

"Tapes?"

"Uh, check."

"Elmer's?"

"Uh-huh. Full bottle outta Elroy's cabinet downstairs. I did it all, Rev, just like I always done."

"You're good people, Tyrone," I told 'im. "Good people. It was the Lord's Will that you be good people."

"I still don't like this," he said.

"Shut up, you fuckin' maggot," I said.

"We about ready to go, Rev?"

"Close," I said, "close. Boy, I'm really gonna tell 'em . . ."

"What you talkin' about now?"

"The truth," I said, "I'm talkin' about the GODDAMNED TRUTH!"

Tyrone smiled, "Rev, you don't have to get up on no cross to do that. A soapbox'll do!"

"No, sir, Tyrone, when they hear the kinda truth I'm gonna put on 'em, they're gonna realize that A SON OF GOD SPEAKS!!! Now, look," I said, drawin' him aside confidentially, "the Lord's comin' for me, oh, maybe in two, three hours or so. I swear to God He is." I glanced back over my shoulder to make sure no one was eavesdroppin'. With a matter like this at hand, you couldn't be too cautious.

"Yessir," I went on, "He's gonna reach right down with His terrible swift sword, and . . . *cut* me down! And then He's gonna take His gourd of life and draw me UP! UP!" I shouted, throwing my head back. "UP INTO HEAVEN WHERE I WILL SIT AT HIS KNEE, AND REMAIN THERE, FOREVER AND EVER AND EVER . . . AMEN!"

Tyrone began to cry again. The fear was back. "Rev, you worry me so when you go on like that . . . that crazy talk. I can't stand seein' it in you. I . . . I . . . oh, I don't know. Jesus!"

I heard Elroy's bare feet slappin' down the stairs. "I'm comin', goddamnit!" he hollered. "Jesus Christ! Knock off the hammerin'. Keep your pants on!"

Tourists. Either the first ones had returned or this was a new crop. And they sounded like they were ready to tear down the door.

I could hear Elroy down there, arguing with 'em. They wanted plastic Billys. Elroy was tryin to explain to 'em, more patiently than I would have, that he was out of 'em.

"Goddamnit," someone shouted, "we'll take anything, then. Anything!"

"All right," Elroy hollered back at 'em, "calendars! That's the best I can do. Calendars, four-fifty a copy."

"We'll take, uh . . . lessee . . . five! Five of 'em!"

And so it went.

"Now!" I whispered to Tyrone. "This is it. We make a break!"

"Oh, Jesus, Rev," Tyrone wailed. "I don't know if I can do it—leave, I mean."

"GODDAMNYOUSONOFABITCHINBASTARDYOU MOVEYOURBLACKASSORILLKILLIT!!"

He actually squeaked. Like a mouse. "Ohhh, Gawd, Rev! Anything! I'm goin' . . . look at me. I'm goin'. Just, PLEASE, don't do that again. I beg you, Rev, please, please," he bawled.

"Okay, then," I said, firmly in control. "Out the back. Just like we planned. Up off the highway, on th' bluff there just above the dam. We ditch th' pickup in the lake, right?" I looked at him sternly.

"Ri-right," he said, voice quaverin'.

"Hey!" called a voice from the stairs. "HEY, LOOK! IT . . . IT'S HIM!!"

"OUT!! GET THE HELL OUTTA MY PLACE!!" screamed Elroy. "YA SONS–A–BITCHES GOT NO RIGHT!! OUT, GODDAMNIT . . . OUT!!!"

"Jesus Christ!" moaned Tyrone. "Let's GO!"

"No . . . wait a second . . . all right—NOW!"

"Put some damned clothes on, Rev. Please? Lord, Lord!"

"I'm wearin' THIS! Come on! And, for Chrissake, stop that insufferable WHIMPERIN'!!!"

Well, that's how it was—straight, unvarnished fact. Some of it nice, some of it not so nice. But this Messiah business is tough and it's meant to be tough. "If thou faint in the day of adversity thy strength is small." Proverbs: 24, 10. You gotta suffer before you prosper, and now that this here historical account is wrapped up, I'm ready for the prospering part.

Everything's set here. I'm wore out after lugging these four-by-fours up that damn bluff, but it makes no nevermind because it's all over now. I'm on that mountaintop lookin' into that valley waitin' for that chariot to come by. Just wished I coulda got a couple of thieves up here somehow but, shit, there weren't no way.

Tyrone dug the cross in about three feet, and she seems solid enough even in this rain. GOD, BUT AIN'T IT A-COMIN' DOWN! 'Course, I know what *that* means—somethin' more than a storm happenin' here. Yessir, somethin' more than a storm. . . .

Jesus! Would you look at that lightning!

EDITOR'S NOTE—*At this point, the Hargus narrative ended. However, the tape recording identified as reel number 14 bore one final conversation between Dr. Hargus and the person experts determined was Tyrone Jefferson, the Doctor's close associate. As were the previous Hargus/Jefferson conversations, the final exchange between the two is transcribed here in its entirety.* (ED.)

Rev, where's your sense? This damn storm ain't lettin' up, it's gettin' worse! Let's *please* go before we both catch our *death!*

I'm comin' loose, Tyrone. Now stop your complainin' and *do* somethin'. The rain's dissolvin' th' damned glue! Th' Lord ain't gonna have a thing to do with me if I fall offa here. . . .

God almighty, Rev. We been out here the whole damn day and I'm tellin' you again there ain't *nobody* comin' to get you except them guys in th' white coats—an' the sooner, the better!

TYRONE, DAMNIT! DO SOMETHIN'!

All right, all right. . . . WHOA! JESUS, REV, did you SEE THAT?! That lightnin' like to *hit* yo' ass! It's th' CROSS! It's stickin' up there like a damn lightnin' rod ATTRACTIN' IT! GET DOWN, BOY! GodDAMN! You're jus' TRYIN' to get us *kilt!*

You got the range, Lord! Praise Jesus!

Rev, stop that! I'm SCARED, I tell you. You stay out here in the middle of this an' you're gonna get your ass blowed a . . .

Tyrone?

OHMIGOD! TYRONE?!?

OH, NO! NO! LORD, YOU *MISSED!* ME, LORD, TAKE *ME!* NOT HIM, MEEE! WHAT'S WRONG, LORD? I DID IT! EVERYTHING! JUST LIKE YOU SAID! JESUS CHRIST, TAKE MEEEE!

God??

. . . *Lord??*

. . . ANYBOOOODYY???

. . . HELLLLLLLLLPPP MEEEEEEEEEE!!!

EDITOR'S NOTE—*This concludes the authorized transcription of the Hargus Tapes, Library of Congress Document 498-13-DICM. However, in the interest of setting forth a complete record and in order to adhere to conditions set forth for the tapes' transcription, the Editors have added a brief entry recorded on a fifteenth reel of tape. The fifteenth reel, separate and distinct from the authorized Hargus Tapes transcription, bore only the remarks of the individuals who discovered the still-classified site at which the Hargus narration took place. Those remarks are transcribed here in their entirety.* (ED.)

What do you make of it, Paul? Klan?

I don't know. Mebbe. This here smoulderin' cross, and all. . . .

Klan, or some of them Devil-worshippers, I'll bet. They's a bunch of 'em been slinkin' around these hills, you know.

Yeah.

Hey, sergeant.

What you got, Cunningham?

Look at this. Tape recorder. Found it right over there under that piece of canvas.

Let's see.

Here. See? Damn thing's runnin'. What do we do with it?

Shut it off.

THE NATIONAL ENQUIRER

PSYCHIC "SEES" HARGUS

LOS ANGELES—Renowned psychic Marylayna Urini claims to have been visited by a spiritlike representation of the Reverend Dr. Billy Sol Hargus last week, as she sat in the parlor of her Palmdale, California, home reading a transcript of the Hargus Tapes.

"The encounter was only a flash," said Ms. Urini, "but it convinced me that Dr. Hargus, somehow, will one day walk among us again. . . ."

Epilogue

◆

He never wrote a book.
He never appeared on television.
He never was on the radio.
He walked among men an epoch ago
 but speaks to the multitudes still.
For His Message is as modern as the
 hills of Galilee are ancient.
False prophets rise, to inevitably fall.
But His Truth shall endure forever.

Don Imus/Charles McCord

Acknowledgments

◆

Billy Sol Hargus has appeared on the *Imus in the Morning* radio program since the late 1960s. What you've read is his life story.

I wrote the original manuscript. Charles McCord and I then rewrote it and, thanks to Charles, turned it into at least the Second Greatest Story Ever Told.

Charles and I have completed the book, and Kinky Friedman has written the music and lyrics for "God's Other Son—the Musical," which our friend Jerry Zaks, the noted Broadway director, among others, has refused to have anything to do with.

The book is dedicated to Michael Lynne, who is now the president of the movie studio New Line Cinema. Mr. Lynne has been my attorney and friend for the past twenty-three years and now finds himself in the uncomfortable position of having to talk "option," or risk destroying what has been a wonderful professional and personal relationship.

I'd like to thank the following people for their help—not all that much, by the way: Fred Imus, Kinky Friedman, Esther "Lobster" Newberg, Jonathan Coleman, Judy Lee, Fred Hills, Dick Snyder, Robert and Vincent Andrews, Jack Romanos, Carolyn Reidy, Michael Jacobs, Jackie Seow (for the cover), Jeffrey Katzenberg (for the mouse ears), Dr. Peter Guida (for saving my life), deirdre Coleman (for being the love of my life), Richard Blumenthal (for not fucking up the deal Lobster made), and special congratulations to one of America's corporate geniuses, Sumner Redstone, for kicking the shit out of that pansy Barry Diller.

Acknowledgments